GAY CLUB!

Pronouns matter!

Published in the UK by Scholastic, 2022
Euston House, 24 Eversholt Street, London, NW1 1DB
Scholastic Ireland, 89E Lagan Road, Dublin Industrial Estate,
Glasnevin, Dublin, D11 HP5F

ISBN 978 0702 31367 7

A CIP catalogue record for this book
is available from the British Library.

Printed by CPI Group (UK) Ltd, Croydon, CR0 4YY

Paper made from wood grown in sustainable forests
and other controlled sources.

1 3 5 7 9 10 8 6 4 2

www.scholastic.co.uk

"*Gay Club!* wears its activism with pride, and is packed with drama, plot twists and politics" – **Dean Atta** (author of *The Black Flamingo*)

"*Gay Club!* holds up a mirror to the experiences of being LGBTQ+; to the messiness, the humour, the hardships, and most of all, to the love and celebration" – **Adiba Jaigirdar** (author of *Hani and Ishu's Guide to Fake Dating*)

"*Gay Club!* is bold, funny, brilliant, and bright... Green's witty, insightful prose and pin sharp humour is a joy... This book reminds you that we are all allowed to have a love life, whatever our leanings. And that we are all allowed to love life, full stop. Everyone should read this book" – **Rebecca Root** (actor in *The Queen's Gambit*, *The Danish Girl*)

"Funny, heartfelt, and angry in all the right ways, *Gay Club!* is a love letter to the messiness of our big gay family, and a manifesto for creating the change that the youngest members of that family need so badly today. A triumphant call to action" – **LC Rosen** (author of *Camp* and *Jack of Hearts (and other parts)*)

"One of the most hilarious, romantic writers in the game right now" – **Becky Albertalli** (author of *Love, Simon*)

"Quite possibly his best work yet. It left me crying with laughter late into the night because I literally could not put it down. Brilliantly controversial, so very witty, and full of enough queer joy to make any heart burst. Truly outstanding from start to finish – now I want to join the gay club too" – **Calum McSwiggan** (author of *Eat, Gay, Love*)

"Simon James Green has an impeccable ear for authentically funny dialogue. This book will make you laugh the way your best friend makes you laugh" – **Ciara Smyth** (author of *The Falling in Love Montage* and *Not My Problem*)

"As wonderful and inspiring as ever! Simon's books are lifesaving for m⋯ ⋯ew **Todd**

"Once again, Simon James Green has knocked it out of the park. *Gay Club!* is Simon at his very very best. Hilarious and heart-warming with a gorgeous cast of characters and a beautiful message at its heart. I defy you to find a queerer book in 2022. Sign me up to Gay Club immediately. Shut up and take my money!" – **George Lester** (author of *Boy Queen*)

"Gay Club! is so smart and so funny, and full of characters who are also smart and funny. It's everything I want from a book and from life. Everyone will love it! May I suggest you all join Gay Club with utmost urgency" – **Wibke Brueggemann** (author of *Love is for Losers*)

"*Gay Club!* cements Simon James Green's position as the master of LGBTQ young adult fiction. No one today writes with such heart and lightness of touch – an author whose skill both intimidates and inspires his peers" – **William Hussey** (author of *The Outrage*)

"Sharp, witty, and strikingly thoughtful, *Gay Club!* is an absorbing celebration of identity and the power of community. Simon James Green has penned a timely love letter to young readers that's guaranteed to change lives" – **Julian Winters** (author of *Running With Lions*)

"Set in a world full of drama, scandal and intrigue – a.k.a. high school – *Gay Club!* is a heartfelt, joyful tribute to messy LGBTQ+ friendships. Simon James Green had me rooting for Barney and his friends from the very first page" – **Phil Stamper** (author of *The Gravity of Us*)

"A fun and fabulous story which builds towards a powerful and important message for us all" – **Rob Gillett** (Queerly Radio and Queerly Books)

"Smart, sharp and blisteringly funny, *Gay Club!* is a celebration of the LGBTQ+ community, a clarion call for unity, and a truly sensational book" – **Matt Cain** (author of *The Secret Life of Albert Entwistle*)

GAY CLUB!

Pronouns matter!

SIMON JAMES GREEN

SCHOLASTIC

For everyone in our big, messy, LGBTQ+ family.
Out, in, really not sure – if your heart is in the right
place, this is for you. Welcome to Gay Club.

1

I'm walking towards my destiny and I'm on top of the world. There's a definite bounce in my step as I stride down the corridor. It's *not* a sashay (dear god, I wish I could sashay, but I tried it in secret once and I looked like I needed urgent attention from the orthopaedic trauma team), and it's not a *strut* (that would be way too arrogant), but it's *confident*. The sort of confident that only top-of-the-food-chain sporty guys can get away with without attracting comments, because why would a boy like me be happy and self-assured? Why would a "massive gay dork" (big thanks to Nico Murphy for that generous quote; I'll be sure to use it on my CV) be feeling just a little bit good about himself?

I surreptitiously check (for the fifth time) that the flies of my chinos are done up, that my light blue Oxford shirt (unbuttoned at the collar, so as to be smart but not formal) is tucked in, and clutch my leather (OK, *faux* leather, *you wouldn't know!*) folder tightly, like it contains sensitive government business. I mean, it kind of does, I guess. Along with the agenda for today's meeting, I've got the blueprints I've been working on since the middle of last term: the strategy for how I'm going to turn the LGBTQ+ Society around, when, in approximately twenty-five minutes, I'm elected president. That isn't meant to sound arrogant. I usually have zero confidence that things will go in my favour. But I've studied the club, I've seen what it needs, and I've done the work to impress. It's like playing chess: you plan forward in order to win.

Of course, you can't always account for the other players' moves, no matter how much you play out the options, and this one was a surprise: former president "Big Mandy" (an ironic name, since she is actually relatively small, both in stature and in ambition for the club) immediately resigned the minute she got her uni offers in (*"Don't need to waste my time doing extracurricular now – woo-hoo!"*), and now it's only the four of us left in the whole club. Bronte is running for president too, because she runs for everything (lacrosse captain, drama club artistic director, debate team leader: you know, fully keen but somehow still cool). That leaves George and Maya, but they are my best mates, so they'll vote for me. Also, Maya used to date Bronte and can't even look at her since they split up, a couple of weeks ago. Since then, George and I have spent a lot of time sitting with Maya, eating tubs of Ben and Jerry's and slagging off Bronte's cruelty and heartlessness, so, you know, we're all pretty invested in her demise.

In any case, it's me the club needs, because I'm actually going to turn things around. The LGBTQ+ Society has four members. In a school of a thousand. Where there are definitely more LGBTQ+ kids, some of them out, a few of them dating, but none of them wanting to join the club because it's seen as "tragic".

But I've never seen it like that.

It was midway through year ten when I first walked through the door of Room 120. There was an A4 sign Blu-Tacked to the door – the club's motto:

**You don't have
to come out
to come in**

I'd done low-level surveillance on the club for quite a few weeks. It's important to scope out the state of play before making your move. I would stroll past the door multiple times during Thursday lunch, waiting at the end of the corridor, pretending to be rearranging the contents of my rucksack, while checking to see which students were going in. *Were they like me? Was I one of them?* The gay guys I'd seen presenting TV shows were loud, and camp, and ostentatiously dressed . . . but I was quiet, and nervous, and disastrously dressed. I'd seen gay teenagers in movies . . . but

3

they were American, and beautiful, seemed to be in their twenties, and liked boys in the most poetic and eloquent of ways. I was a British fourteen-year-old, traumatized by random boners on a daily basis, who whacked off to high-school wrestling videos on Instagram. Was I gay? Or just a hormone-addled mess?

Maybe I was both.

I didn't know anyone like me.

...Until I walked through the door of Room 120, with the prepared excuse that I was looking for "Bake Club" if I got cold feet, which was stupid because Room 120 is a history classroom, not home economics, but I clearly wasn't thinking straight. Didn't matter, I didn't need any excuses, because that afternoon I finally found my people. George and Maya were both in year ten too, but I'd never spoken to them before. I knew from my surveillance that they came to the club, but I think I'd convinced myself *so hard* that I was the only one that I was still kind of surprised to see them there – like, maybe they were just confused, and were only accidentally attending, mistaking it for D & D club, or something. No sooner had I walked in on that first day than they were both straight over.

"Finally!" Maya grinned.

"Were you expecting me?" I replied.

"We saw you spying," George said.

That was it. We've been best friends ever since. Bronte was in my year too (I *was* expecting to see her: she's been out – very visible and taking no one's shit – since year eight), Mandy was in year eleven (when she could be bothered: she was constantly in trouble for her low attendance), and presiding over us all was sixth former Ed Lester, who was fantastically handsome, super-smart, and dating a lad called Xander from Branscombe Boys – a private school about twenty minutes away. With their "European mini-breaks" and tales of wild LGBT parties, Ed was my idol – a shining beacon of what life might one day be like. So, sure, Mandy and Bronte were frustrating and irritating, respectively, and Ed was untouchable and basically from another planet compared to me, but they were still somehow part of my tribe, and they faced a lot of the same stuff as me and Maya and George. On some weird, deep level, we fought and bitched about each other (and in the case of me and Ed, some of us hero-worshipped each other), but we all got each other, too.

I want the other queer kids in the school to find their people, too, with us. I've seen the way some students roll their eyes whenever anything LGBT is mentioned – like they're sick of us. "That's so gay" is still a phrase that rings around almost every classroom, even though the teachers are meant to challenge homophobic language. And sure, a straight couple getting with each other in school would cause a *ripple* (everyone loves a bit of goss), but two boys, or two girls, would be an *earthquake*. So, *sorry, Mandy*, pinning some rainbow flags on our club noticeboard and raising money to give out pin badges during Pride (which is all the club has really achieved in the last year, other than everyone sitting around eating Haribo) won't change anything. We need to unite and fight. Campaign. Be visible.

I think we can make things better.

We at least have to try.

And I have a *plan*. (Of course I do. I always have).

I feel a hand squeeze my shoulder.

"You've got this, Barney!" George says, striding up behind me. He's gives me a little wink. George is pure sophistication and class. Tall (well, taller than me) and slim, his dark brown hair is styled in a side-parting and smart quiff. As sixth formers, we're meant to dress "business casual" – a definition that is interpreted very loosely by many, but taken to the next level by George, who today is sporting an impeccably tailored dark-blue suit with waistcoat, starched white shirt, hand-crafted brown brogues, and a burgundy bow tie. A cane would complete his dapper, man-about-town look. I might get him one for his seventeenth. "You've got this," he repeats.

"You think? No, yes, I *have*. Haven't I?"

"There's no one who'd be better." He sweeps his hands in front of him as we walk along. "Barney Brown – *President*, LGBTQ+ Society."

"It's got a ring to it," I agree.

"You'll need business cards."

"Oh my god, stop."

Then I suddenly *do* stop and turn to him. "OK, but what if—"

"Barney."

"No, hear me out!" I glance up and down the corridor to check the coast is clear, and lower my voice anyway. "What if Maya buckles at the last moment? Like, I know she *said* she'll vote for me, but she was with Bronte for a few months... *They did things.* Things that might... inexorably forge a bond of loyalty with another person!"

George frowns. "What part of Maya throwing darts at a picture of Bronte when we were last round at yours and screaming a list of obscenities, before burning the photo while chanting some kind of curse she found online, makes you think there's a special bond between them?"

"People do and say things when they're hurt – they don't always mean them." I sigh. "When my folks split up, Mum told Dad he doesn't know how to satisfy a woman, and that's in direct contradiction to some of the stuff I've had to hear through the bedroom wall over the years."

"Well, that's a gross thing that neither of us wanted to think about."

"Sorry," I mutter.

George puts his hands on both my shoulders. "You'll get one hundred per cent of the Black lesbian vote – Maya will come through. And you've got one hundred per cent of the white trans guy vote." He grins at me. "And assuming you also vote for yourself..."

"The white, gay boy vote."

"*Right*, that's seventy-five per cent of the total queer vote, which makes you president of the LGBTQ+ Society, so let's just go and do this."

"You're right."

George shrugs. "Always."

We walk on, round the corner, and find Maya hovering outside the door of Room 120. She's done her hair in two puffs, with big hoop earrings, and, if I'm not mistaken, a bit of smokey eye. She's also wearing yellow dungarees and Converse with rainbow laces. It's a bold mix that straddles a line between playful and . . . children's party entertainer.

"Bronte's in there already, so thought I'd wait for you," Maya says, as we approach.

Her whole energy is "on edge". This is partly Maya's standard energy – she identifies as a "disaster lesbian", and while I'm not sure that's an official identity on the LGBTQ+ spectrum, I do get what she means, since I feel like a disaster gay most of the time. It's a feeling of not quite fitting it, not quite getting it right, *them* never liking you back, general awkwardness, almost total messiness, and low-to-mid-level anxiety about . . . well, most things.

"You look nice," I tell her. I more or less mean it, but the time to question people's sartorial choices isn't right before you want them to cast a vote for you.

"It's not for Bronte's benefit." She gives me eye contact for too long. "OK, it is," she relents. "But this is me saying,

'I'm fine, I'm over you, I'm happy enough to wear yellow dungarees and I've got some earrings in and a bit of eye make-up because I'm free and single and you and me are over and I've moved on—'"

"Maya, *breathe*," George tells her.

She takes a breath, then exhales. "I hate her goddamn guts."

"So I can count on your vote?" I ask.

Maya's eyes widen. "Omigod, *yes*! Like you even need to ask, Barney! I'm not going to vote for *her*."

George smiles, a satisfied look on his face, and gestures to the door. "After you, then, *Mr President*."

2

Bronte has brought Maya a cupcake.

"I saw this, and remembered you love red velvet," she says, all nonchalant, as we walk in and sit down, pushing the cupcake across the table towards Maya, like it's nothing.

It's not nothing.

And she didn't just "see it".

It's in a Hummingbird Bakery box. We don't have a Hummingbird Bakery in town. That thing's been same-day couriered from London – probably costing more than the cupcake itself. It's a *planned* cupcake, a cupcake that's required logistics, and it's sheer *treachery*.

The way Maya's looking at the box with disdain gives me confidence that she isn't fooled and won't be swayed.

"Actually, I'm cutting down on sugar," Maya says.

A strong opening.

"Really? I could have sworn I saw you downing a full-fat Coke at break," Bronte replies.

Check. . .

"Which is why I really can't have any more."

. . .Checkmate.

Maya pushes the little box back towards Bronte, who just smiles to herself, sweeps back her shoulder-length, expensively glossy, dark-brown hair, and busies herself picking lint off her fluffy white sweater which will definitely turn out to be designer.

The treachery quelled, I pull the agendas (typed and copied by me, as usual) out of my folder. It's short. After apologies for absence (none), and a minuted vote of thanks to our absent, outgoing and utterly ineffectual president, it's time for the main event: the vote.

"So, I've made some ballot slips, and I've got some pencils for us all," I begin. "Now, obviously voting needs to be conducted in secret, so—"

"Actually, Barney," Bronte interrupts, finally looking up from her sweater, "before we get to this, would you mind if we skipped to 'any other business'?"

I give her a tight smile. "I mean, we've got an order on the agenda, so. . ."

"We can tweak it, though, right?" Bronte gives me a tight smile back.

"Kind of ruins the point of an agenda," I say.

"OK, Barney, I get that you like lists and order, but I'm more free-wheeling, so how about you free-wheel with me, yeah?"

"No," I say.

Bronte smirks, probably amused at how "uncool" and "uptight" I am.

And then she rips the agenda in half.

Honestly, I'm not a dork, but I'm stunned.

Maya gasps.

"Oops!" Bronte says, eyeballing me.

"That's a tree."

"It's not a tree, Barney, it's barely a twig."

I glance at George, who's watching all this with a completely neutral face, then at Maya, who looks like she's about to bubble over with fury, and then back at Bronte. She looks determined. I mean, OK, fine, *whatever*. I can be spontaneous . . . although, when I'm president, agendas *will* be respected. "Fine, go on," I say, indicating for her to take the floor.

Bronte picks up her pen and sits back in her chair. "This club is unsuccessful," she begins, waving the pen around, and jabbing it accusingly in my direction on every syllable of "unsuccessful". "Four members. It's pitiful. One of the key things we need to address is how we expand that."

"Totally agree," I say. If this is some desperate, last-minute pitch from her about her "great" presidential ideas, she's too late. I already have all this mapped out in my campaign statement that I'm prepared to read any minute.

"So, like, *what*, Barney? How would you do that exactly? Run off a few posters? I seem to recall you trying to

12

do something similar when you tried to establish that board games club – I'm . . . not sure it worked?"

I ignore her. I will not stoop to her level. No, it didn't work. It seems my love of analogue pastimes isn't shared by a single other student at the school – I couldn't even get George or Maya to come. (Apparently, they've both had really bad experiences with very long games of Monopoly). But so what? That was year ten, when I was flying high, feeling inspired by having found friends at the LGBTQ+ Society. I've learned to keep my hobbies to myself now, and, slightly ironically, found plenty of like-minded people online.

Bronte shakes her head in contempt. "See, I think we need to go right back to basics. People just aren't *invested* in the club; I'm talking at a fundamental level."

I nod. "Uh-huh? So how would *you* solve that? Shall we start with your campaign statement, since you raised the issue?" I sit back. Bronte is the sort of person who is great at flagging problems, but never seems to have solutions. It's easy to hate on things.

Bronte's got a twinkle in her eye though – and she's looking right at me. "No, no statements yet. Just one, simple solution," she says. "We open the vote for president up to the whole school."

There's complete silence.

Shock. That's what it is. That Bronte would suggest something so absurd, and that she would be so brazenly obvious in her motivation for it. She knows George and

Maya will vote for me (especially now Maya has refused the cupcake), but a whole-school vote would be a very different story. She's much more popular than me. Yes, she's here in this club (which admittedly looks like a club for losers right now), but she's respected. She's A-list. She's also rich, and rich kids have power – school's just a microcosm of adult life in that regard, right? Rich kids have the right clothes, and have fabulous house parties, and glamorous holidays, and swagger around with that confidence that seems so attractive to lesser mortals. Plus, Bronte's got fingers in all the school societies – the theatre kids will vote for her, the debating team, all the sports clubs. . .

I literally only have this. LGBTQ+ Society is the only thing I've got. No one else knows who I am. I'm shaking in anger: there's no way she'll get this through, but it's the *audacity* of it.

"Ugh!" Maya says, getting right in there. "What a RIDICULOUS idea."

"It isn't ridiculous, it's *progressive*," Bronte retorts.

"It's self-serving," Maya replies.

Bronte takes a deep breath then fixes Maya with an amused stare. "I like your dungarees. Yellow suits you. Very carnivalesque."

"Carnivalesque?!" Maya nearly screams. "Is that a dig?"

"Why would it be a dig? It's a compliment – everyone loves a carnival!"

14

"Ha!" Maya says, shaking her head. There's a pause. "*Interesting* sweater," she mumbles.

Bronte nods.

"That's the one from Milan, isn't it?"

A small smile plays on Bronte's lips.

Maya looks down at her Converse, leg bouncing, chewing her lip.

George clears his throat, then makes his power move, sighing, slowly getting his large, black-framed glasses out of his bag, cleaning them, putting them on, leaning forwards, and peering at Bronte like she's some weird curiosity in a museum. "I'm struggling to find a single reason why we would open the vote up to everyone, Bronte?"

Bronte leans forward too, apparently not cowed by him. "There are more LGBTQ+ students in this school than there are sitting around this table. Don't you think they deserve a say in the running of a club that purports to represent them?"

They're staring each other down.

"If they want a say, all they have to do is walk through that door and join us," I say, trying to break the tension.

"And yet many of them won't be out," Bronte replies, still staring at George. "Just because you're not out doesn't make you any less LGBTQ+. I'd be shocked if you're suggesting otherwise, Barney?" She carefully adjusts her gaze back to me and smiles.

"Of course I'm not," I tell her. "But the sign on the

door is very clear: *You don't have to come out to come in.* You literally *do not have* to come out. You can still come in, join the club, but you don't have to actually come out."

George nods. "It's pretty clear."

"Super clear," Maya adds.

Bronte doesn't even register either of them has spoken. "I just wonder if a better, less aggressive slogan would be more along the lines of, *You don't have to come out, and you don't have to come in.*"

I throw my hands in the air. "Genius! Please, Bronte, please tell me you're hoping to go into marketing! With slogans like that, businesses will be biting your hand off for some more advertising gems. I can see it now – major supermarket: *Don't buy our food, it's rancid!* Mobile phone network: *No one has worse reception than us!*" I look at her in disbelief. *"Aggressive*? What are you talking about? It's *literally* saying you don't have to do anything – how is that aggressive?"

"You're angry because you know I'm right," Bronte says. "Coming in *implies* you're questioning, at the very least. Whether you like it or not, whether you have a sign on the door, or not, that's the implication. And for some" – she actually clutches her chest – *"poor students*, that's too much of a risk. They won't come in. Yet, *do they not deserve a voice?*"

"Hang on," George says, "there are a thousand kids in this school, and at the most optimistic end of the statistics,

16

that would be around a hundred LGBTQ+ students. Are you saying we give the other nine hundred cishet ones a vote on who gets to be president of the society on the off-chance the other queer ones no one knows about are concerned whether it's you or Barney buying the rainbow bunting for the Pride display in the library?"

I mean, there is more to being president than just that, but I get George's point.

Bronte smiles again. She's doing way too much smiling. It's making me nervous. "If the aim is to make students at this school genuinely invested in the club – and I think that *should* be the aim – then yes. Yes, I do think we should do that. When people have a voice, when they feel they can influence things, it means more to them."

George nods, thoughtfully. "OK. Let me be absolutely clear: *NO.*"

"Same," I say.

"And it's no from me," Maya adds. "Much as I'd love the predominantly white, cishet kids to have opinions on my life as a queer Black woman *and in case you couldn't tell that was sarcasm, Bronte!*"

Bronte blows out a long breath and shakes her head. "Honestly, I have no idea why you're being so hostile and intolerant!"

"Let's move on," I suggest.

"It's really quite upsetting to be met with such a barrage of *hate* from people I thought were open-minded. . ."

17

"Item two on the agenda. . ." I continue.

"Like, I just *assumed* you would all be on board with such an inclusive policy, which is why I mentioned it in passing to the headmaster, and he agreed it was a really great idea, and exactly 'the shot in the arm' the club probably needed, and he's really excited that we're doing it."

I think I'm about to explode.

"The wheels are already in motion," Bronte adds.

"Then un-motion them!" I say.

"You un-motion those wheels *right now*, Bronte O'Halloran!" Maya hisses.

Bronte sucks in a breath. "I don't think the Senior Leadership Team would like that. We can't operate the club like our own private cabal. What we're currently doing is deeply undemocratic."

George must see my bottom lip starting to wobble, because he grasps my forearm by way of support. "You can't make decisions about the club without everyone agreeing. And we're not agreed. You need to tell him you made a mistake."

Bronte rolls her eyes. "Oh, don't be so dramatic! Honestly, your faces! Chill out! I'm sure you'll still win, Barney, impressing everyone with your charts and graphs and little agendas. And just think: the win will be even greater because it won't just be your best mates voting you in, it'll be actual people who don't even like you. What could be more meaningful?"

3

"We need a meeting with Mr Hubbard." I swallow and give Mrs Buchanan my best attempt at a smile. "*Please.*"

The problem with Mrs Buchanan is that she hates me. She hates most of the students. As far as she's concerned, we're the flies in what would otherwise be the very smooth and perfect ointment of her day. She's in her sixties and has worked at the school for ever, so she's seen it all. Every excuse. Every trick in the book. Honestly, she's impossible. Unfortunately, she is the dragon in twinset and pearls who must be slayed before we can reach Mr Hubbard – and she guards him fiercely.

She considers me with weary eyes, looking me up and down, in a way that makes me want to check if my flies have now somehow become undone, despite my relentless checking.

"All of you?" she says, eventually, glancing at George and Maya, who are flanking me.

"Yes, please," I say.

Her face gives nothing away. "And what is it regarding?"

"A constitutional crisis," I say.

This elicits no response whatsoever, which makes me wonder if there's anything I could have said that *would* receive at least a flicker of concern on her hard face? Asbestos in the gym? Anthrax in the cafeteria? A zombie apocalypse in the boys' toilets?

She sniffs, turns to a large A4 diary on her desk, and lazily flips through a few pages. "Two weeks tomorrow, at four p.m."

I blink at her. "No, it's urgent."

"No, it isn't," she says.

"It's a *constitutional crisis*," I tell her again.

"Why aren't you in class?" she replies.

"I've got a free."

She turns to her computer, taps a few buttons, and squints at the screen. "Barney Brown . . . 12R . . . no, you've got English lit." She looks back up at me and gives me a passive-aggressive smile.

A little squeak escapes from my mouth, because I can *see* Mr Hubbard through the windows of the partition, but I can't *get* to him, and this needs to be sorted out, like, *now*, because otherwise it'll be too late, Bronte will get her way, and will almost certainly get voted in as president, regardless of whatever nonsense she spouted in the meeting about people being impressed with me. No one's bothered if your ideas are good, or you've got experience, or that you genuinely care and want to make a difference. It's all about personality. Bronte's a super-rich mega-bitch with high-waisted jeans, and that's a concept (and look) people can get behind and latch on to. What am I?

Luckily, before I am sucked too far down into my existential crisis, George steps forward, like George always does, because George is calm and collected and speaks with real gravity in his voice that makes people do whatever he says. "Mrs Buchanan, this is regarding the LGBTQ+ Society. And like the inspectors put in their last report, the school's willingness to engage with its LGBTQ+ students has a positive effect on our wellbeing." He gives her a small smile . . . then sticks the knife in: "Of course, the inspectors have a web portal that allows students and parents to upload any concerns they may have – like their voices *not* being heard, for example."

Mrs Buchanan is back tapping away on her keyboard. "Thank you for threatening us, George Piper of 12S" – she squints at her screen – "who should be in chemistry." She smiles, victoriously, at George. "Your voices *will* be heard. Two weeks on Friday at four p.m."

Maya steps forwards. "As a queer Black woman, I will *not* be silenced, and—"

"OK, that's enough," Mrs Buchanan says.

"Oh my god, you're literally silencing me!" Maya replies.

"My apologies," Mrs Buchanan says. "Please, you were saying, Maya Phillips, who should be in geography?"

"Yes, *thank you*, I was saying that I *will* not be silenced, and our voices *shall*, nay, *must* be heard!"

Mrs Buchanan nods. "I completely ... *nay*, wholeheartedly, agree. And they shall be!"

"Thank you," Maya says.

"Two weeks on Friday at four p.m."

It's at this point – honestly, I'm *not* a dork – I start crying. OK, yes, it was a plan of last-resort, but crying wasn't hard to do, with the stress of it all. And the frustration. I should have been president by now, and I'm not. *Of course* Bronte managed to bump into Mr Hubbard and he just happened to be free when *she* wanted to speak to him, because that's the sort of lucky chance that happens to people like Bronte. Lucky chances can't be planned for and I can't stand them. Luck is such an unfair concept – always about being in the right place at the right time, rather than working hard or being good at something. Why is she doing this? She's already basically president of the *whole world*, or certainly half the clubs and societies in school, which is *our* whole world; could she not leave this one thing for me? I actually do want to help queer kids in this school, and I honestly question if Bronte really has the *time* to do that (what with all her other commitments), or the *inclination* (since she's never been one for rocking the boat, either with teachers or other students).

"Oh, Jesus Christ!" Mrs Buchanan mutters, clocking my tears and throwing me a look of utter contempt. She heaves herself out of her ergonomic office chair, muttering something about "Generation Z snowflakes", "trigger warnings" and "oat milk lattes", shuffles over and opens the door to Mr Hubbard's office, and says, "Phil? Have you got a minute to see three sixth-formers?"

George hands me a tissue from a little pack he produces from his leather satchel as we're ushered in.

"I'm sorry, I don't know what's wrong with me," I sniff.

"You care, that's all," he replies. "There's no shame in that."

Mr Hubbard raises a quizzical eyebrow when he sees me. "Are you OK, Barney?"

"Hayfever," I reply, not missing a beat. "I forgot to take my Benadryl this morning." Honestly, my ability to lie so smoothly surely means a career in politics awaits?

Mr Hubbard indicates for us all to sit down on the sofas that surround a really shit wooden coffee table that some past student made in design and technology, and that now sits in his office, I imagine as an example of how "proud" he is of the students here, rather than because he thinks the coffee table is stylish. He's a well-groomed guy, in his forties, always in a nice suit. He knows good furniture when he sees it, and he knows the coffee table's not it. It's purely performative.

23

"So!" He smiles, leans back on the sofa, and crosses his legs. "What can I do for you all?" His eyes sweep across us, and I think I see him smile. I once overheard a teacher talking about how it was "so interesting" to see all the sixth formers not wearing school uniform because they get to see our real personalities. And here we are: George, kitted out like he's off to a wedding, Maya, on her way to enthusiastically audition for a theatre-in-education company, and me, a travelling sales rep for a vacuum cleaner company.

"OK, so, this is about the LGBTQ+ Society," I begin. "And it seems discussions may have been had that have now plunged us into a full-on constitutional crisis."

And I explain the full extent of the crisis.

After which, Mr Hubbard (who has been doing a lot of thoughtful nodding over steepled fingers), says, "Mm, but I think letting the whole school vote is actually quite an exciting and progressive idea, do you not agree?"

Do I not agree? *Do I not agree*?! Would I be here if I agreed?!

Maya sits forwards. "Bronte's only doing this because she knows we won't vote her in as president. It's very calculated. Which is her all over."

"I don't think we should cast aspersions on Bronte when she's not here to defend herself," Mr Hubbard says.

"She's emotionally *cold*," Maya continues, ignoring him. "Take it from me. *Ruthless*, even."

24

Mr Hubbard raises his eyebrows. "OK, well, in many ways I think it's *great* that there's real passion from you all about who leads the club this year. That's what we want, isn't it? We want people to care?"

"Yes," I say. "That's the point. We *do* care who gets to be in charge of *our* club. Other people don't – else they would have joined."

"I don't get to vote who's football captain," George says.

I click my fingers. "Bingo. Exactly!"

"Maybe you should?" Mr Hubbard suggests.

George shakes his head. "Why? I don't know the first thing about football, and I've no idea what qualities are needed in a captain. I can *like* football – hypothetically, I mean, I can't stand it: it's a hotbed of the worst kind of toxic masculinity in this school. And I can *support* the football team, but why would I vote on who leads them? Isn't that decision best left to people who actually appreciate all the nuance?"

I'm just nodding along to all this good stuff.

"Everyone votes for Head Prefect," Mr Hubbard replies.

"But that's a *general* position," George counters, his tone low, keeping his eyes fixed, unblinking, on Mr Hubbard. "That's like voting for your MP – it's someone who's meant to represent us all. The public at large don't vote for who wins BAFTAs: you've got to be on the committee.

Same with any trade organization. It's the *members* who vote, because it's representative and specialist."

My god, *George*. I honestly never, ever want to be without him.

"I wholeheartedly concur," I bleat, which is such a pathetic addition to George's excellent argument.

Mr Hubbard nods over steepled fingers some more. "It's a persuasive argument," he says.

Finally!

"Maybe you should be running for president, George?" He grins.

"No, thanks," George replies. "Barney's your guy. It's a job that requires optimism and patience and diplomacy, and I honestly have such a low tolerance level for bullshit."

Mr Hubbard opens his mouth, looking as though he's about to pull George up for inappropriate language, but then seems to think better of it, possibly because George is still just staring at him with an expressionless face, and just chuckles ... slightly nervously. "Look, I might normally agree with you," Mr Hubbard says, "but this is a big and important year for the society, as you know."

What is he talking about? I look at George, who is ever so slightly squinting at Mr Hubbard, and then at Maya, who shrugs. I turn back to Mr Hubbard. "What do you mean?"

Mr Hubbard frowns. "Bronte mentioned it, yes?"

My blood runs cold as I sense deeper treachery ahead. *"No."*

"Oh." Mr Hubbard shrugs it off and gives us all a big smile. "Well, exciting news, then! Rainbow Youth, which is a national LGBTQ+ organization, is going to select one lucky school LGBTQ+ club to be their global ambassadors for the year. It's a chance for us to really stand out as a school, and a chance to make a real difference, not just here, but, well ... *globally*. That's why I agree with Bronte: it's the sort of thing we should get everyone involved with, especially because we'd be able to show that the whole school community is behind it and invested in it." He stands up, grabs a sheet of A4 from his desk, and hands it to me. "All the details are here. I told Bronte about it two weeks ago – it's an amazing opportunity for the school, the club, and whoever ends up being president. Think how good *that* would look on your uni applications! I can't believe she forgot to tell you!"

4

The fury bubbles away in me all through my afternoon English Lit class, leg bouncing, fists clenched, practically grinding my teeth, and I'm about to have a full-on meltdown just as Miss Francis tells us to put away our copies of *Wuthering Heights* and lets us go. I bolt out the door, through the corridors and out of the main entrance, the automatic sliding doors (one of the new additions since our school got a huge injection of cash for a refurb) barely opening in time as I charge through.

George and Maya are waiting for me by the giant (two-metre high!) shiny letters spelling *Greenacre Academy* that have been constructed as part of the new landscaping (honestly, there's no money for proper lockers or library books, but there is for anything that makes the school look more glossy to potential new students). I don't stop, they just pick up my pace alongside me, as we head up the pristine path (Italian porcelain tiles I'm told!) and out of the main gates.

"One minute, get it *all* out," George instructs me, Maya hitting the stopwatch on her phone as we charge along.

I take a deep breath. "OK, right, *fine!* Let's start with some facts: *Rainbow Youth* are offering schools everywhere the chance to be global ambassadors – a role that, according to the leaflet, involves not only championing and advocating for the needs of LGBTQ+ young people all over the UK, which is something I genuinely feel passionate about, but also attending events with a 'number of LGBTQ+ celebrity patrons', which can only mean either Elton John, Elliot Page, Stephen Fry, Cynthia Nixon, Lena Waithe or Tom Daley, possibly all of them, and, frankly, in any combination *I would be beside myself* but also really able to hold an intelligent conversation with them, despite my excitement; literally, I would even put my fear of deep water aside and learn about diving so I could talk to Tom about that; and *not only that*, the role also necessitates 'liaising with other *international* LGBTQ+ youth groups' which, since one of Rainbow Youth's sponsors is *Virgin Atlantic* basically means Upper Class flights to New York to go and chat with some American gays our age. And I say all this not because those are the things that are most important to me, although I openly admit they're appealing, but because *Bronte*, a girl who already is up to her neck in extracurricular, and whom I'm pretty sure wouldn't normally be so enthusiastic about becoming president of the LGBTQ+ club, now suddenly *is;* and not only that, has (a) actively, or at least allegedly actively, kept all this information from us, (b) used underhanded methods to change the constitution, which I admit doesn't exist in paper form, which *is* a mistake, so that (c) the voting methods swing to be hugely in her favour so that she ends up being the one to congratulate Tom on his medals and tell Elton how much she loves 'Candle in the Wind', before being pampered on a flight to the USA and probably getting to meet Michelle Obama. She is cunning, she is devious – I'm talking about Bronte, not Michelle – she is *despicable* in the way she has manipulated not only us, but also Mr Hubbard, and under no circumstances can we let that ENTITLED LOWLIFE win this election to be president. I will do whatever it takes, but as god's my witness – that's just a saying, I'm still an atheist, as I don't believe an all-powerful being would put people *like Bronte* on this earth – we have to WIN THIS THING, wipe the smug smile from her *frankly very average* face, and prove that having wealth and influence does not mean you always get your own way!"

I'm power-walking down the pavement, hot, shaking, fuelled by fury, George doing big strides and not breaking a sweat, Maya puffing and working hard to keep up.

"Ten more seconds," Maya tells me.

"I hate her. I know that's a strong word, but it's true."

"Eight seconds."

"She cannot be trusted."

Maya nods. "Seven seconds."

"Is she the Devil incarnate? I think it should be investigated."

"Five seconds."

"She looks a bit like a horse."

"Harsh but fair," Maya adds.

"She certainly *brays* like one."

"One second."

"OK, I feel better now, who wants tea and biscuits?" I pull my keys from my pocket as we arrive at my house – a small, Victorian terrace on a street that's infuriatingly close to school, which means I never feel like I can get away from the place. Since my folks got divorced, and Dad moved near York (I haven't seen him in three months) and Mum's working all the extra hours she can to pay the mortgage alone, I pretty much have the place to myself these days.

Maya swipes her phone off, slides it back into her dungarees' front pocket and smiles. "Have you got any of those Viennese Fingers?"

We're sitting around my kitchen table and, *my god*, do we have plans?

We do. We have plans.

Bronte wants a fight? We'll give her one.

"OK," I say. "So, in summary: Maya, you'll design posters and flyers, and then mount a charm offensive to convince Mrs Buchanan to let you have access to the photocopier?"

"Uh-huh," Maya says, taking another of my home-made Viennese Fingers and clearly savouring the crumbly, buttery texture (it's true they *are* good). "And if she won't play ball, I'll use my charms on Mr Hubbard directly. It's literally our democratic right. They can't refuse."

I nod. "Great. And we're agreed using 'Vote Barney' is the best slogan?"

"It's direct, it does what it says on the tin, and it's a straightforward call to action," George says. "That's what people need: an easy-to-understand concept that cuts through the constant noise of modern life." He too takes another biscuit. "These are sensational."

"*Thank you.* Made with organic Welsh butter. OK, love it," I say. "What else?"

"I think the core team – by which I mean, us three – should all have 'Vote Barney' branded clothing," George continues. "There's a place that does them in town; you can literally turn up with a plain T-shirt or a hoodie and they'll iron on the design of your choice for, like, a tenner."

"You think?" I say.

"Yeah, yeah, *totally*," George replies. "It's a show of unity and strength, it subliminally tells people there's organized support behind you, that you've got back-up – I think that's appealing. Success attracts success, and a team seems successful, you know?" He sniffs. "I think we should go with white text on black."

I lock eyes with George. I love the idea, but is he really

going to sacrifice his elegant look and wear a branded hoodie . . . for me?

"Yes, I will," George confirms, reading my mind. "Only because I like you. And only for a defined, short period that clearly connects my clothes with the campaign." He visibly shudders. "Ugh. The thought of all that polyester is already bringing me out in hives. God, I'm a good friend."

"OK! A 'Vote Barney' fashion range it is!" I smile. This is all sounding really good. Has Bronte even got a team? Not to my knowledge. She's so arrogant she probably thinks she doesn't need one.

"Ooh, what about other branded stuff?" Maya pipes up. "Like, um . . . sweets! Cupcakes, maybe? Or, *or* . . . *pens!* Everyone always needs a pen, right? Every time someone needs one – bam! *Vote Barney!* Staring them in the face the whole time!" She triumphantly takes another Viennese Finger, with a flourish.

"Sounds great," I say, "but where's the money for all this coming from?"

Silence.

"OK, so I guess I have some savings," I continue. "I could do some chores, which Mum'll find highly amusing and try to exploit fully. Honestly, her rates are well below minimum wage, but I could just suck it up?"

"I'll throw in some birthday money," Maya shrugs.

"You really don't have to do that."

"Nah, I'd like to. *Love* to, actually. You can't put a

price on how much joy it will bring me to see Bronte's face when she realizes the full extent of our operation, and how she's going to be totally humiliated and lose." Maya sighs, contentedly. "Mmm, that will be a *gooood* day."

"Well, I'll pay you back."

"Shut up, you won't."

"So, Maya," George says, "you'll spearhead the marketing campaign, yeah? Nobody knows their way around Photoshop better than you."

Maya grins, because she knows he's right. She's been creating her own comic books since year eight. She does it all herself – artwork, page layouts – and she publishes them both online and as physical copies you can actually buy. They're loosely based on her own life (I can't wait to see the edition where she splits up with Bronte!) and she's actually got a nice little business going. Anyway, that's all to say she knows what she's doing, and then some.

"We need to hit the ground running, and fast," George continues, "since Bronte's given herself a two-week start in planning her campaign. Meanwhile, I'll set us up with a basic website where we can outline your key policies, and I'll manage your official social feeds. After that, I'm going to focus on our strategy, and adapting our campaign depending on how the opinion polls are looking. Someone's got to have oversight of the whole picture, and I think that person should be me."

"Agreed," I say. "And, this opinion polls thing? How

does that work?" I grin at him. "Is it going to be like in those high school TV shows where's there's an election? There'll be some sort of app on our phones, with some kind of algorithm that can extrapolate the data in real time?"

"No," George says, "because those things don't exist. I'll be paying some year sevens to ask questions in the lunch queue."

"A snapshot of voting intentions from a cross-section of the student body, perfect." I nod. "Make sure they don't spend too much time asking the ones queuing at the salad bar – they'll all be Bronte voters, being all conspicuous about their healthy eating like the tedious little virtue-signallers they are."

"Quite." George nods.

"And what about me? What should I be doing?"

"Happily," George replies, "Ally Bridges, who edits the online student newspaper, is in my chemistry class. So instead of focussing on Born-Haber cycles earlier today, I was buttering her up, and, *voila*! You have a one-thousand-word article, with the promise of landing page placement, complete with photo and link to our campaign website and social feeds."

"Brilliant! You're brilliant."

"ASAP though, so, can you get it done tonight?"

"Yeah, what kind of thing, do you think?"

"Barney, you can do this standing on your head," George tells me. "Something about the struggles of being LGBTQ+ at school – show them you get it, you understand – and some thoughts on what could be done to improve things."

"A mentoring scheme, maybe? Visiting role models to inspire people? Gender-neutral toilets? A proactive policy challenging homophobic language?"

"All of that, Barney." George smiles. "I want everyone else to see what we see."

"And . . . what's that?"

George reaches across the table and squeezes my hand. "That you're a good man, Barney Brown."

I drop my eyes, and chuckle, a bit embarrassed. "I think you have me confused with *Charlie* Brown there, but I'll take it." I glance back up at him. I don't know what I ever did to end up with such good friends. George is already swamped since he added further maths to his list of A levels, yet he's managing to find a whole load of time to help me out and run my campaign. Maya's family really aren't rich, far from it, but she still offered me some of her birthday money. "Thank you. Both of you. I really mean it, sometimes I—"

"You can save the big emotional speech for after we've won," George says. He picks his phone up and starts scrolling through. "Rainbow Youth have tweeted that applications open in three weeks' time. They'll be announcing what competing schools have to do for the shortlisting stage soon, and then the selected schools get invited to the big conference in London – 'a celebration of the power of queer youth everywhere', apparently."

"Cool," I say. "I'll start planning."

George rolls his eyes. "You can't, you don't know what they want yet."

"I can still plan. I can guess."

"Barney, let's focus on winning president first, yeah?"

I nod at George. "Yeah."

But I'll still plan. I just won't tell him.

"Ugh," George says, scrolling further. "And, of course, the first tweet in reply is from some troll account. Who the hell are 'Family Alliance'?"

I shrug.

"Are they a homophobic hate group masquerading as concerned parents, perchance?" Maya says, sweetly.

"'*Live your lives but stop indoctrinating children.*' That old chestnut. Deep joy." He scrolls some more. "Aaaand, another one! '*You've got equal rights now, so stop shoving it down people's throats, we're all tired of it.*' That corker from someone called Julie Gammons." George blows out a breath, and screws his face up. "Is that really her name? You couldn't make this up! Apparently, her pronouns are 'Up / Yours'."

He swipes the app away and puts his phone face down on the table. "Yuck."

"We should tweet back," I say. "Not to the trolls, to Rainbow Youth. Say we're looking forward to entering and it sounds amazing, get on their radar. . ."

"Good thinking," George replies.

"Planning ahead," I say. George ignores this, but I know he's clocked it, and I'm glad, because planning *is* important, and you can't do too much of it.

We all send supportive tweets, and Rainbow Youth like them within seconds, which feels like a win. But the tweets from Family Alliance nag at me. I know it's best to ignore trolls, to not give them the oxygen of a response, so I don't reply to them, but their hate does give me the idea I need for my article. So after George and Maya head back home, and since Mum texts to say she's stuck in a meeting until late, I go up to my room, sit down at my desk, flip open my MacBook Air, and make a start.

Homosexuality was decriminalized in England and Wales in 1967. In 2009 the age of consent was equalized for everyone. 2013 saw Parliament introduce civil marriage for same-sex couples in England and Wales. So, we've done it, right? We've got what we always wanted – LGBTQ+ people are equal. We're free. We don't need to keep fighting because everything is rainbows and glitter unicorns for us now.

Except, it isn't...

5

The next day, news about the election is read out during form time. Two weeks of campaigning, followed by official hustings speeches, and then voting day. No one seems to react – like they don't for any of the announcements, ever: it's just noise in the background – so I start to feel hopeful. Maybe no one will vote in the election anyway?

Then at the start of our lunch period, Maya storms past me in the corridor, looking even more harassed than usual. "ARGH!"

"Maya?"

"I'm on my way to kick something."

"What's happened?"

She walks back up to me, breathing heavily. *"Mrs Buchanan* has happened." She glares in the direction of the office. "Won't let me use the photocopier for the flyers and posters. Apparently I need to apply for an account and get budget approval for quantities over twenty, or some *utter drivel*."

"Shall I try?"

"What are you going to do? Start blubbing again? Sorry. I shouldn't snipe at you." She takes a breath. "Out with anger, in with love. Except where Bronte's concerned. Do you think it'd be wrong to portray her with a forked tail, horns and hooves in the new edition of my comic?"

"Park that, funny as it is," I say. I've hit upon an idea. "If we need approval for more than twenty copies, then I'll just go and get twenty copies. And then you can. And then we'll send George. Recruit a couple more people, and we'll have enough. Or, she'll just get bored of all the interruptions, and let us run off a few hundred in one go."

Maya smiles. "I like your thinking."

"*I* like my thinking!"

"I like playing her at her own petty game," Maya says.

"So satisfying," I agree. I hold my hand out for the originals. "These look good, by the way!"

We've gone simple on the flyers and posters too. The "Vote Barney" message is front and centre, a bold logo in block letters that we've replicated on the T-shirt (me), hoodie (George), and strappy vest top (Maya) that we're all now wearing, since George went and got them done during his free first period. The flyers have a list of policies as bullet points, and the posters have my face on them. I wasn't keen on that idea, but George told me it was important people knew who I was, and apparently, quite a few people don't. The photo's OK. It was taken last summer, after GCSEs, so I actually look quite happy, and I'm giving a thumbs up. Plus, I think Maya has Photoshopped out the spot on my chin, and possibly removed the bags under my eyes, given my skin a smooth finish in general and made my eyebrows look better, although I don't want to ask, I just want to believe I look this good in real life.

Maya heads off to finish the designs for our badges, and I stroll ("stroll" no less!) into the office, so confident about this, I'm smiling, full of the joys of spring. "Hello, Mrs Bu—"

Mrs Buchanan doesn't look up from her computer, she just puts her hand up to stop me.

So, I do stop. I stop, and I wait, since she's clearly busy and will momentarily be with me.

But several moments pass, and she's still just typing away, like I'm not there.

She seems very focussed.

Has she forgotten about me?

I test the water by clearing my throat . . . which elicits no reaction whatsoever.

I wait a bit longer, shifting from foot to foot, hoping the movement will jog her memory.

It doesn't. "Um. . ."

She immediately puts her hand back up again, but doesn't look at me.

I wait another three minutes, getting increasingly frustrated and anxious, before simply blurting out, "Please,

Mrs Buchanan, I need to use the photocopier!" in the style of a five-year-old child who is desperate for the toilet.

She does however, look up. "You can't."

"Why?"

"Because of Brexit."

I blink at her, confused.

"Toner shortage," she says. "It comes from Germany."

I breathe heavily through my nose. There is blatantly toner available – we've had multiple photocopied things given to us in class all day. Plus that wasn't the excuse she gave Maya just moments ago.

I storm out of the office, determined, like Maya was, to go and find something to kick . . . possibly the rest of my pride and self-esteem, right into the dustbin.

"Give it to me!"

The voice behind me, clearly addressing me, has such confidence and authority it stops me in my tracks.

But I know it's not a teacher. It's not quite deep enough, and there's something too jokey and upbeat in the tone.

Which means . . . bad news, probably.

I turn around.

And there he is. Tall, broad, his messy blond hair tumbling down over his forehead, stopping short of his deep, blue eyes. Of course Danny Orlando is perfect, because when you're called Danny Orlando life is never going to be any other way, is it? He arrived in town last year, showing up on the first day of Autumn term on a motorbike – and was quickly informed it was forbidden on school premises. But the image of it prevails. Like some all-American high-school hero, Danny Orlando roared on to the scene and shook every *one*, and every *thing* up, leaving a trail of shattered hearts in his wake, because, let's be real, "Danny Orlando" is a name that gets you laid, without having to try too hard. Well, that and the fact he turned seventeen back in September, passed his driving test, and has an Audi. He drives a better car than any of the teachers and "going for a ride in Danny's Audi" has become both a rite of passage for the popular and successful kids, and a euphemism. Contrast with me: "Barney Brown" is not a name that gets you laid, it gets you an "I was brave" tiger sticker when you go to the GP. I'm also still sixteen, and I certainly can't drive. And even if I could, my parents wouldn't be able to afford a car, having spent any money they did have on divorce lawyers.

"Give. It. To. Me!" Danny repeats, holding his hands out, palms up.

"Huh?"

"The hard sell!"

"What?"

He gestures to my T-shirt. "'Vote Barney'. So why should I vote for you? *Barney*?" He flicks his eyes to mine. "You *are* Barney, right?"

"Yeah. I'm Barney."

We've never actually spoken before. Danny's into sport – which I'm not – and he's into girls – which I'm

43

also not, at least, not in the same way Danny is. All that aside, his group of mates includes Nico Murphy, who very much *does* know who I am, unfortunately. All of which makes me worried that's the reason Danny Orlando also knows exactly who I am, and that this whole-school-voting-for-LGBTQ+-Society-president thing will become, for people like Danny and his mates, a gift that keeps on giving, because why else is he interested, if not to wind me up?

"Pitch yourself to me!" Danny demands. "Quick, though, I've got footie practice."

"Well—"

"Are you gay, then?" he interrupts.

"Um, yeah."

He nods, thoughtfully.

"OK," I continue. "So, in terms of my pol—"

"You don't *seem* gay."

"I don't seem it?"

"You don't *look* it."

"Oh, right?"

"Clothes, I mean."

It's unclear to me whether he thinks he's giving me a compliment or complaining that I'm not stereotypical enough for him. "There's more to being gay than muscles and tight T-shirts," I say, glancing at his muscles and tight T-shirt.

"Do you know Aaron?" he replies.

"Aaron?"

"Aaron. Aaron Sawyer. He's in our year."

"Sure," I say. "I don't really know him, no."

"He's gay."

"Uh-huh?"

Danny nods. "I think he's single right now. Maybe you two could—"

"Nah, I'm good."

"He's a nice guy."

"I'm pretty focussed on the election," I say.

"Oh, sure," Danny says. "I get it. Like me and football. Gotta keep your eye on the prize. Distractions help no one."

"Right."

Danny smiles. "He gives good head, though. *I am reliably informed.* He got with my mate Matt who's in his first year at Manchester over Easter break."

I try to play it cool, but I can feel my cheeks burning and I can't think of anything to say back to him. I can't have a conversation about sex with Danny. He's an expert. A *sex*pert. I'll just say something foolish that'll make it obvious I've no idea.

Danny frowns at me. "Are you OK?"

"Hm-mm!" I squeak.

He nods. "Good chatting. Gotta run."

"Oh, but my policies!" I bleat, realizing I couldn't sound any more dorkish if I tried. "Um – I've literally just had my article go live on the online newspaper, so you can pretty much check them all out there."

He frowns. "What online newspaper?"

"The *Tittle*."

"The *what*'ll?"

"The *Tittle*. That's the name of the online student newspaper?" Has he really not heard of it? He's been here since Autumn term last year.

"Tittle? As in . . . *tit*?"

"As in tittle-tattle."

He looks blank.

"It's another name for 'gossip'," I explain.

"Is it?"

"Uh-huh."

"Tittle-tattle," he repeats.

"That's right."

He blows out a breath. "OK, so you've got an article in the *Tittle-tattle*?"

"Just '*Tittle*'."

"*What*?" He looks exasperated, borderline annoyed with me.

"Never mind, I can . . . tell you the policies."

"Do you know who you look like?"

I shake my head.

"*Noah Schnapp*. From *Stranger Things*? Not when he was little, I mean the sixteen-year-old version."

"Oh, right?" I'm trying to picture those kids, trying to

work out which one he means. Is it a compliment?

"You have this kinda permanently enthusiastic face."

"Thanks?"

He grins at me. "So welcome!" And starts to walk off.

"Wait! I was just telling you about—"

He turns around, shaking his head. "Another time, I'm gonna be late." He squints at me. "'Vote Barney'. Maybe I will, maybe I won't! Everything to play for, huh? Exciting!"

He winks at me and heads into the office. "OK if I just run off some posters for footie try-outs?" he asks Mrs Buchanan.

"No problem, Danny," she replies, waving him through to the photocopier.

George joins me and Maya at our usual table in the cafeteria, sliding into the seat opposite with his bowl of chilli. "How's wearing that hoodie working out for you?" Maya grins.

George grimaces. "I wear hoodies at home. They're not completely alien to me."

"But. . ." Maya smiles.

"They're essentially loungewear. Post work-out-wear at best. I find them slovenly. Symptomatic of a society that has lost its self-respect and dignity."

I stare at him. I wear hoodies *a lot*.

"You *did* ask." He sniffs. "So, we're polling the lunch queue as we speak, and I'm waiting on an update from Ally about how many hits your article has got. Where are we at with posters and flyers?"

"Don't ask," I mutter.

"And yet, I *am* asking, because as campaign manager, I kind of need to know." He glances between me and Maya. "Mrs Buchanan strikes again?"

We both nod.

George rolls his eyes. "I'll just ask Dad to do them at work – we do not have time for her shit." He puts a forkful of food in his mouth, chews, and frowns. "Do they even put any chilli in this chilli?"

"See, I've got a theory," Maya says. "This is actually the bolognese from yesterday, and they've just bulked it out with some kidney beans and a sprinkle of cumin and rebranded it."

George nods and takes another forkful.

"So, Danny Orlando spoke to me," I say, getting back to my chilli. "He asked about my policies."

George stops eating. "Oh! OK. And?"

"Well, he said he *might* vote for me . . . or he might not."

I look at George and Maya's disappointed faces. "At least it wasn't an outright refusal to vote for me! It could have been! Point is, there's a chance."

"Getting him on side would be a result," George says. "He's influential. Get him, others will follow."

I nod. "He sounded kind of surprised I was gay." I poke my fork around my bowl.

"But he knew your name at least?" George says.

"Yeah. I mean, he was ninety per cent confident of it . . . although it *is* on my T-shirt, so. . ."

George nods thoughtfully and goes back to eating.

"He said he would read the article in the *Tittle*," I add.

"It's a *great* article, Barney," Maya says. "I read it, and it was fully, like, a *great* article. Clear, concise, intelligent. . . I mean, this election, it's in the bag, right?"

It's at this point, with absolutely no warning, that the opening bars of the karaoke version of "I Kissed a Girl" by Katy Perry start blaring out of a portable Bluetooth speaker system on a nearby table.

Maya rolls her eyes. "Ugh."

"Not a fan?" I ask.

"I hate this song, but I also know all the words and will sing it if I've had a few drinks, which makes me think I love it, which I also hate. But I'll listen to it. It's catchy. In a hateful way."

I squint at her.

But Maya's initially neutral face soon becomes a scowl. "Big Mandy" – our outgoing president – bursts through the doors of the cafeteria with a microphone and starts belting the song out, somewhat tunelessly, but certainly with enthusiasm and a surprising amount of gusto for one so small. Meanwhile, several groups of what I now realize are theatre kids stand up from random tables, and start doing some kind of prearranged backing choreography, three of them producing giant cherry chapsticks that they'd hidden under the tables, and waving them around. It's mayhem. Everyone's shocked, but some start clapping along, some are singing along, and loads of people are filming this on their phones. Then Big Mandy swaggers over to where Bronte is eating her lunch and starts performing the song to her, and her alone.

Maya's gone stone-cold frozen at this point.

Bronte's acting all embarrassed, but kind of making out like it's fun and she's enjoying it, like when musicians come and play an accordion around your dinner table at a Spanish restaurant.

On the button of the number, the theatre kid backing dancers fire party poppers, while Big Mandy goes down on one knee and booms down the mic. "Bronte O'Halloran, will you be my date for prom?"

The crowd in the cafeteria goes wild.

Bronte makes a little squealing noise.

Maya just stares.

And then there's this kind of silence, like everyone's holding their breath, while Bronte stands ... extends her hand to Big Mandy, who takes it, and stands too. Then Bronte takes the mic and says, "Mandy Presley ... I'd be honoured!"

Everyone cheers. People whoop. Phones everywhere are filming and probably live-streaming this.

Bronte and Mandy kiss. And I mean *kiss*.

People *applaud*. More whoops. Various "Awwww's!" Quite a few of the year ten boys look like they've forgotten how to swallow.

And then a new backing track starts up, someone throws Bronte an additional mic, and she and Big Mandy start to perform "Take Me or Leave Me" from *Rent*. It feels like the whole school, most of whom have now crammed into the cafeteria to see what's happening, are clapping along and generally cheering, like eighty per cent of them aren't homophobic arseholes given half a chance.

I turn to George, who is massaging his temples. "This kind of feels . . . planned?"

"Oh? You think?"

We sit through the rest of the number (it's too loud to talk), after which Bronte says, "Love wins, everyone! I want every single person in this school to have the courage to be their true selves, and live boldly and proudly!" and she walks out of the cafeteria, hand-in-hand with Big Mandy, to rapturous applause, while the theatre kids wave rainbow flags.

Maya closes her eyes for five seconds, then opens them, her face otherwise completely unmoving.

I suddenly feel like me getting some photocopied flyers made isn't really going to cut it any more, and that my "Vote Barney" T-shirt is kind of stupid and pointless . . . embarrassing, even.

I know George will have a balanced view on this: he'll have some sort of wisdom to impart. I turn to him.

And he takes a deep breath. "*Fuck.*"

6

I keep a low profile for the rest of the day because the only thing anyone is talking about is Bronte and the epic promposal. She's certainly got everyone's attention, I'll give her that.

I decide to take the back entrance out of school, because I'm sick of people looking at my T-shirt and asking who Barney is and what he's asking to be voted in as. Yes, thanks to Bronte and Big Mandy, this has now become a one-horse race, apparently.

But we'll sort it out. I just need to lick my wounds, regroup, and then we'll come back with something even better. I mean, I can't think what that's going to be right now, *Bronte's move was one I hadn't anticipated*, but I know George will have been thinking of nothing else all afternoon.

As it turns out, Maya has other ideas, and presumably anticipating my mood and how I'll quietly slope out of school, I find her waiting for me by the rear doors. "Nice try," she says.

"I'm feeling low," I reply.

She puts her arm around my waist and pulls me close. "I know. That's why I'm waiting for you."

"How are *you* feeling?" I ask, as we push through the door and into the warm summer air.

Maya chuckles. "How am I feeling about Bronte's big, fake promposal, you mean? Ha! I'm just fine."

"You think it was fake?"

"Oh my god, Barns, *yes*. Bronte doesn't do big displays of emotion like that. It's laughable – tragic, really."

Unfortunately, taking the back entrance means walking out through the car park, which means walking past Danny Orlando and Nico Murphy, who are leaning against the bonnet of Danny's Audi, drinking Cokes and chatting and bantering like a couple of bros in a TV commercial.

If I was hoping for a low-key exit, I was going to be disappointed. Nico Murphy hasn't missed an opportunity to wind me up in six years.

"Eyes front, walk with purpose," Maya says, reading the threat perfectly.

"Yo! Barnaby!"

Too late. I sigh and turn to them because I'm weak and maybe I can nip this in the bud. Nico Murphy is grinning at me.

Danny flicks Nico's chest with the back of his hand. "It's *Barney*." He points to my T-shirt and tuts.

I acknowledge them both with a nod, and make to carry on.

"Aren't you gonna come and chat?" Danny calls out.

"We're kinda in a rush." I gesture towards the gate.

Danny sucks in breath. "*Bronte* was able to give me a moment of her time. It's kinda nice to get to know the real her. Helps make a truly informed decision."

I need him on my side.

"Don't do it, Barney," Maya whispers, through barely-moving lips. And then she sighs as I start to walk towards them. "OK, great, you're doing it." She hurries up alongside me.

Danny smiles. "Wasn't so hard, huh?"

"Like your cock," Nico adds, grinning at me.

Maya guffaws wildly, then suddenly stops, her face falling into an unimpressed frown. "*Twat*," she says.

I ignore Nico and smile as nicely as I can at Danny. "What can I do for you?"

"So, *wow*, *Bronte*, huh?" he says.

I nod, tight-lipped.

"She knocked it out the park!" he continues. "Everyone's talking about her!"

"Inspirational," Nico adds.

"Indeed," I say.

"Like, I'd never seen two girls kiss before," Nico

54

continues, wistfully. "Not with all their clothes on, anyway." He gives me a wicked grin.

"OK, well, great chatting," Maya says, starting to pull me away.

"Whoa!" Danny says. "We're not done."

"No, we're done." I glance at Nico. "We're not doing this to be fetishized."

Maya crosses her arms and nods.

Nico laughs, and Danny flicks his chest again.

"Hey, no, sure, I get that," Danny says. "*Although. . .*"

"There's no 'although'," Maya says.

Danny squints slightly at us. "Well, there kinda is, because, like it or not, lots of straight lads are quite, um . . . how can I put it nicely? *Excited?* By the prospect of Bronte? After today's little performance? You know? And you can say that's wrong, and hell, I agree with you, it *is* wrong, but at the end of the day, in the voting booth, you know? They'll be holding their pencils – and that's not a euphemism – but they'll be hovering, ready to put their cross by your name, or Bronte's, and who are they gonna remember? They're gonna remember Bronte. 'Cause that kiss, man, it'll be etched on their brains."

"Firmly deposited in the wank bank!" Nico adds.

Maya steps forward. "OK, enough! I'm no fan of Bronte, but that expression of . . . whatever it was, was definitely not for the sexual gratification of the boys."

Nico snorts. "She literally sang a song about kissing another girl. C'mon, we can all agree that's hot."

"And there we have it!" Maya says. "The song as seen through the male gaze! *Straight girl tries on bisexuality to impress the boys.*" She shakes her head. "No, thanks." She nods, chewing her lip a bit. "None of this should be about anyone being hot. It should be who the best candidate is."

Nico glances at me. "Well, you're certainly not hot, Barnaby, we can all agree on that."

Danny slaps him on the chest again. "Point is, people respond *emotionally* a lot of the time."

I shake my head. "Right, well, if that's the criteria people are going on, then it's exactly why this shouldn't be a whole school vote. You know? This is more important than . . . boners."

"Nothing's more important than boners," Nico says.

"*Except,*" Danny says, smiling slightly, "that's just the straight boys. Now, I happen to know *for a fact* that a substantial number of year ten girls are super into manga and anime, specifically *yaoi,* and maybe that could play in your favour?"

"OK, *again,* this election isn't about sex."

"Have you even had sex, though?" Nico asks.

"That's . . . not important!"

"Have you ever done anything with another boy, though?" he persists.

"Absolutely *not any* of your business!" I retort.

He nods. "So, no, then."

"Leave him," Danny says. "We're all at different stages, man."

My eyes widen. I don't know what that's supposed to mean, but I think he's suggesting I'm somehow ... immature.

"OK," Nico says, "but, serious question, like, not being funny or anything, but how do you know you're gay, then? Or is it just that you think about boys when you whack off?" His eyes widen slightly. "Do you think about me and Danny?"

"Right," Maya says, "this chat is over, we're going, good-bye, and also, *fuck off.*"

We hurry away, with Nico's laughs echoing around my head.

"I still haven't decided on my vote, Barney!" Danny calls out after us. "There's still everything to play for!"

I don't turn back, I just flip him the finger.

George lives at the bottom of a nice cul-de-sac of six new houses, all detached, quite big, with pristine front gardens complete with white picket fences that George says makes him feel like he's living in some hellish version of the 1950s American Dream.

"What do you mean 'you flipped him the finger'?" George says, as he ushers me and Maya through his front door and down the hall towards his kitchen. "What kind of campaigning policy is that? Insulting the voters! And Danny Orlando, of all people!"

"He insulted me!" I protest. "Maya told him to fuck off too."

"I did!" Maya chirps. "Also, I really feel like I want a shower after talking to him and Nico."

George stops and turns to us. "Look, I totally get it: some people need to educate themselves. People like my older sister, who totally thinks a gender reveal party is a great idea, because there's nothing weird about announcing to the world what genitals your child will be born with! But you are an optimist, and as such you surely believe most people are redeemable. And what are we doing, if not trying to change hearts and minds?"

"We shouldn't have to be nice to people who don't show us acceptance or respect," Maya says. "There's no point trying to win them over."

George raises his eyebrows. "Look, while I probably agree with you *in general*, let's at least not do anything to make our chance of winning this thing *worse*. Remember, we'll be in a better position to deal with the ignorant ones if we win."

"Maybe," I say. I get what's he's saying. But I feel the same as Maya does.

"So get Danny Orlando on side; that's an order. Come on," George says, leading us through to the kitchen. We sit around the large wooden table, where George has already laid out some of our favourite after-school snacks: an antipasti platter, with some cured meat, cheese, olives, anchovies and sun-dried tomatoes, along with fresh crusty bread. Yes, we *are* a bit extra when it comes to food.

"OK, let's start with some good news," George says. "Your article in the *Tittle* has garnered a total of fifteen views."

I frown at him. "*That's* the good news? George, at least a dozen of those views were me!"

"Well, I was one of the other ones, but the journey of a thousand miles starts with a single step, and if just one of the other people—"

Maya raises her hand, mid-chew on some bread dipped in balsamic. "Me."

George nods. ". . . Was Maya, then we've reached the grand total of no one having seen the article and it won't have moved the polls." He swallows. "*Yet*. That's what you have to remember. It's up there now; we just need to lead people to it." He smiles, weakly, at me, then picks up an olive. "Mmm!"

"What's the bad news, George?" I say.

"Have you tried the olives?" he replies.

"No, I haven't, and you don't even like olives, so just hit me with it. I can take it."

George blows out a breath. "OK, OK, so, the results of the lunch queue opinion poll came back, and actually, some *good news*—"

"OK, but you said it was *bad* news. . ."

"Yes, I did, but actually, here is some *good* news, and that is that the vote is pretty evenly split between you and

Bronte. Quite a lot of 'undecideds', a few of no opinion whatsoever..." He checks through some papers the pollsters made notes on. "But, otherwise, a pretty even split." He smiles and nods at me.

"OK," I say. "*Good.*"

"Yes," George agrees.

There's silence.

George clears his throat.

"Here it comes," Maya mutters, popping a cube of feta in her mouth.

"Or, at least, it *was* an even split until after Bronte received her promposal. It seems that got everyone talking, and not only that, the view on the street was that it was a very positive message for LGBT students in the school – very *visible* – and that visibility was a good thing, seeing a girl with another girl, happy, being open, just ... 'living their lives with joy in their hearts' – I'm paraphrasing from the feedback, but you get the picture."

Maya slumps down on the table. "Ugh! Why are people so gullible?"

"So, after the promposal, the polls switched to being more in Bronte's favour?"

George nods. "Ninety-five to five percentage points, yes," he says, quickly, "but let's move swiftly on to how we're going to—"

"Fuck. Me." I mutter.

"It's fine!" George trills, which is super alarming

because George is *not* a person who ever "trills" anything – he's always calm, always collected – but it's like he can't stop the panic just bubbling up out of him.

"Ninety-five to five?! How am I even meant to come back from that?" I say, my heart plummeting. I can't. . . It's like the race is over before it's even started. I'm not usually a quitter, but I can't see a way to fix this. I swallow and look at Maya and George. They know how much I want this. But I wonder if their loyalty to me is actually just clouding their judgement here? "Look, I'm gonna put this out there. Maybe . . . maybe I'm not the best person for the job. If the ratings are that bad, maybe this is something we just can't make better?"

"So, you're just gonna let Bronte get what she wants?" Maya says, a super-unimpressed look on her face.

"Maybe you should run?" I suggest.

Maya laughs.

"I'm serious. You're likeable. You're kinda happy-go-lucky. . ."

"You mean I'm a disaster."

"No. . ."

"I'm more of a disaster than you, Barns; it is what it is. Remember when I asked out Chloe Deakins after catastrophically mishearing when she described herself to her mates as a 'thespian'? It's not the sort of thing people forget. Trust me, even if I wanted to do it – *which I definitely do not* – I'm not presidential material."

I sigh. "George, then! It's obvious you should run, George. People actually respect you."

George looks at me with emotionless eyes. "It's not respect; it's fear. People are scared of me."

I open my mouth, but I'm not sure what to say – he's kind of right. He's so sharp and acerbic, some people are a bit scared of him, even if that's really not the full picture (he's an absolute sucker for Christmas rom-coms, for example), just his school persona.

George laughs. "It's OK, honestly, I'm fine with that, but you can't rule through fear. Not an LGBTQ+ society, anyway. . ." He looks into the middle distance, eyes glazed, possibly contemplating if there was anything else he could rule through fear, before snapping out of it. "Look, shut up, two can play at Bronte's game." He shrugs. "Actually, she's done us a favour, because she's reminded me that this election isn't just about policies. It's so much more. It's about being a leader, and being *seen* to have leadership qualities."

I blow out a breath. "Right. . ."

"A good leader creates a spectacle," George continues. "They light up the room. Everyone wants to watch them!"

My mind flits back to Danny and Nico in the car park, and what they were saying about Bronte doing just that, even if it was for all the wrong reasons.

"And a good leader isn't just someone with experience or authority, although that's part of it. A good leader also needs to be relatable. People need to look at them and think, *sure, they're a lot like me, they understand me, they're going through a lot of the same things, I will put my trust in this person, I will follow them, because they get it."*

"Spit it out," I tell him.

"Well, I'm coming to my point, but first—"

"Oh my god, you're trying to manage my reaction to whatever this is!"

"Kinda my job, just trust me; so *first*, I want us to look at some of the feedback our team collected from the lunch queue."

"Feedback on what?" I ask.

"*You*," Maya says.

"Me? So you already know about this, Maya?"

"He ran it by me in the common room this afternoon to see whether I thought you'd be upset."

I let out an unsteady breath. "Oh, well that sounds lovely! So what devastating thoughts about me did the opinion poll team discover? That I'm a knob, I suppose?"

"No! No, not at all!" George says.

"Well, that's something."

"'A bit of a dick,' was said, certainly, but not 'knob'." George smiles at me, like this is positive.

"People talk out of their arse," Maya says, shrugging, like this is all nothing.

"Anything else?" I ask.

"Quite a few people didn't really know who you were. . ."

"Brilliant."

George rifles through his notes again. "'Nerd' comes up a few times . . . and also 'uptight virgin'."

I swallow. "I'm guessing that last one was Nico Murphy?"

"No, it was a year seven."

"A twelve-year-old called me an 'uptight virgin'?!"

George nods. "No respect, the younger generation. But also, some of this will be grandstanding in front of their mates, so don't read too much into it."

"And yet, here we are, dissecting it!"

"Well, maybe we can take something from some of the feedback?"

"You can sometimes be a *bit* uptight," Maya offers.

"And I'm also a virgin, so you're saying that it's true?" I stare at her. I mean, sure, it's true – but the nerve of actually saying it!

"It's about perception," George says, "and, it seems, you are not *perceived* entirely favourably. Now, *we* know that's unfair. We know the real you, but do the voters?"

I shake my head. "What should I do? Walk around wearing a 'Sex Me Now' T-shirt?"

Maya squints at me. "*What?*"

I shrug. How should I know what "the kids" will like?

"We kill multiple birds with one stone, Barney Brown!" George says, terrifyingly using my full name, which means he has a plan and is feeling pleased with himself. "*You* are going to start *dating* someone."

I laugh.

But it seems he's serious.

"You need to come across as a regular, relatable teen," he tells me. "And *we* need to raise your profile and get people talking about you, like they're talking about Bronte. People love a story. They love a *narrative*. So let's give them one."

My eyes widen. He does know this is me we're talking about? Other gay boys don't like boys like me. I'm skinny and untoned, and I don't have that polished, athletic look about me. I'm not a mess, most of the time, but I'm ... average. I'm very average. Danny Orlando saying I look like Noah Schnapp is just Danny either taking the piss, or tripping on mushrooms, because no way am I that hot. (Yes, I did look it up, and I'm choosing to take his comparison as a compliment.) Everyone says they go for "personality", not looks, but come on: personality is a bonus for most people, it's certainly not essential. And even so, I'm not convinced I've got much of one anyway. You're looking at someone whose life goals include achieving at least a 2000 (expert) rating in chess and getting one of those hostess trollies that keeps food warm during a dinner party. That isn't a personality – I'm just a geek channelling the spirit of a social-climbing, suburban woman called Joyce from the 1970s.

"Picture the scene!" George continues, presumably taking my silence as tacit agreement. "Barney is seen with a boy. Are they on a date? Oh, my! Did they kiss? Are they seeing each other? Is this a romance brewing? Bronte played her cards all at once, so there's nowhere for her narrative to go. But *we* can spin your story out, keep it going longer, get people really talking about what's going on. Not only does that keep you in the front of voter's minds, it reminds them you're just like them, at the end of the day: a kid who's just trying to work it all out, get on with school, get some OK grades—"

"*Excellent* grades," I interrupt.

"Sure, get some *excellent* grades, and maybe, just maybe, find a little bit of human connection along the way. A little bit of love."

"Maybe lose their virginity, who knows?" Maya adds helpfully, trying to elbow me with a nudge-nudge motion, but accidentally knocking over a tumbler of water instead. "*Shit!*"

"Sure, sounds amazing," I say, flatly, as I help Maya soak up the water with some napkins. "Just one problem: no one's gonna date me. Trust me on that."

"Well—"

"George, believe me, they won't."

"Yeah, but, OK, leaving aside this weird self-esteem issue which we'll have to deal with at some point, *not now*, do you really want a romance to play out publicly anyway? Under the glare of the media spotlight? No, thanks!" He chuckles.

"OK, but you literally just said—"

"Yeah, but I'm not talking about a real situation. We do what Bronte basically did. 'Cause that wasn't real, was it? Singing 'Take Me or Leave Me' in a perfect duet with a backing track? No, mate. Not a chance. That was fake. And *this* will be fake too. Fake dating, my friend. It's a well-trodden path, and one that never fails!"

He takes another olive, flicks it in the air, catches it in his mouth, and winks at me.

7

I lie on my bed, staring up at the ceiling, trying to work through George's plan and anticipate the various pitfalls along the way.

Paxton Lee is in the year below, is a fairly good friend of George's, and has apparently been hinting to George for some time about wanting to take a boy to his year eleven prom. Paxton is bi (another LGBTQ+ person who has never shown up at the club!), although he has pretty much kept that to himself. George assures me that Paxton isn't looking for an actual romance; he's just sick of hiding in the shadows, and wants to shake things up at prom, and show people who he really is. Plus, there's apparently a "dearth" of suitable candidates in year eleven, with the other obvious choices all dating each other. He'd be more than happy for this to be a transaction: he gets a "date" to take to prom, and I get everyone talking about me having a "romance", apparently making me "relatable" to the voting public.

And yet ... this whole scheme has set alarm bells ringing. First off, it's dishonest. I know everyone expects politicians to lie, but lies have a habit of coming back to haunt you, and it doesn't sit well with me. Second, you have to have been hiding in a bunker for the last ten years, completely cut off from society, to not know how fake dating inevitably goes (and surely George knows this, since he's incredibly familiar with every Netflix Christmas rom-com is existence), and Paxton's cute but there's no boyfriend in the plan. At least, not yet. I've got to keep my eyes on the presidency first.

I'm paralyzed with indecision, so I do the only sensible thing: I scroll through social media.

And on every platform, there she is: *Bronte*. Pictures of her and Big Mandy all over Insta. Videos of them both on TikTok. And on Twitter, an actual *thread* where Bronte, despite claiming to be "on hiatus", waxes lyrical about how happy and lucky she is, while various obsequious individuals tell her how much she "deserves" it and how pleased they are to see "two such gorgeous people together".

Everything is getting a lot of likes. One comment even calls Big Mandy the "First Lady", and that's what finally breaks me: I hammer out a message to George agreeing to the fake dating scheme.

Obviously that's not how I refer to it in the message. You should never leave evidence that can come back and bite you. I just tell him I'd be interested in meeting Paxton.

There's nothing incriminating in that.

George replies with a thumbs up, and my stomach churns at the thought: the wheels are in motion.

But I've never even been on a date, fake or otherwise. What do you actually do?

I turn my phone upside down, like that will somehow make it all go away, tap my MacBook awake, and log on to ChessNation.co.uk. This is my sanctuary. My safe space. There's something calming about the relative anonymity; it's just a load of other British chess geeks like me, geeking out about the thing we love.

I check out a post I left a couple of days ago, discussing the relative merits of different classic openings – the Italian Game, the Sicilian Defence, and so on. No one's responded, except for a profile called KingKyle who I can see is a newbie on the site. *Looks good, gonna try some of these next time I play.*

I respond: *Good luck. French defence is my personal favourite.*

He's online, as it happens, so a minute later and he pings me back:

KingKyle: Hey. Thanks for replying. Full
disclosure: I only just started playing, so I'm
kinda out of my depth here.

BarneyBoy: Welcome! And no worries,

everyone's got to start somewhere. Nice
username.

KingKyle: King's the most important piece, right?

KingKyle: Oh, not saying I'm important.

KingKyle: Just a joke.

KingKyle: Oh god, I should just NOT speak, ever.

I chuckle to myself. I like that he's as paranoid as I am about always saying the wrong thing, and then beating myself up about it publicly.

BarneyBoy: Technically, I suppose. Queen is
more valuable, though, really.

KingKyle: Not gonna call myself QueenKyle – get
enough of that at school, FML.

Ohh. He's at school. And he's gay.

BarneyBoy: LOL, snap! What school? What year?

KingKyle: Year 12. Sixth form, whatever.

Branscombe Boys. You won't know it.

I chew my lip. Branscombe Boys, huh? The private school, about half an hour away from here. My mind starts racing. I immediately think of Ed Lester, the LGBT club president when I was in year ten, and his glamorous relationship with Xander from Branscombe Boys. I don't believe in fate and destiny (only in plans and hard work) but could this be some sort of sign? Is this the universe telling me I could have my very own glamorous relationship with a lad from Branscombe Boys – and the presidential role that goes with it, in my dream scenario? No. I'm being ridiculous. I don't even know Kyle. I don't even have time for such a thing. Still, this'll be highly amusing when I tell him. . .

BarneyBoy: NO WAY I DO KNOW IT! I'm at Greenacre Academy! Year 12 too. Small world!

KingKyle: Shut. The. Front. Door! Hahahaha!

BarneyBoy: You have a GREAT chess club at Branscombe – I know because I tried to set one up at Greenacre and looked at yours on your school website with ENVY.

KingKyle: Do not be envious. I went to it. Once.

It's . . . not being rude, but it's VERY dorky. Like, beyond dorky. Like, they were not big on actually speaking, human to human, just playing in the worst competitive way. Was disappointed because I wanted to play after watching *Queen's Gambit* as it looked really cool. Reality is not as cool.

BarneyBoy: HAHAHAHA! Sorry about that.

KingKyle: Oh god, not you. I don't mean you.

BarneyBoy: Well, you barely know me tbf. But I'm definitely not cool.

KingKyle: That you in your profile pic?

BarneyBoy: Yeah.

KingKyle: Seem cool.

BarneyBoy: I'm not.

KingKyle: It's cute.

KingKyle: Oh god, SORRY.

And he logs off.

I can almost feel his panic from here, radiating through the ether.

Did he just say. . .

And why is my heart beating so fast, anyway?

He only said the pic was cute, not that I was. . .

And why would I care what he thought, anyway?

This is definitely not me already fantasizing about a European mini-break with my rich boyfriend from Branscombe. No. Nope. No way.

The speed at which he disappeared amuses me, though. I can picture him now, thumping his head repeatedly on his desk. I read back through the exchange, then click on his full profile with the bigger picture.

He's pretty cute himself.

Cheeky sort of face, but cherubic rather than devilish. His blond hair has taper-faded sides, drawing your eye to the longer curls on top. Bright, sparkling eyes.

I stare at him and imagine. . .

But I'm not looking for *that*. Eyes on the prize. No distractions. But, god, I wish I didn't feel so horny all the time.

And then I'm brought back to reality, and very much the prize, when my phone pings with a message featuring the most romantic three words that anyone my age living in the UK is ever likely to hear:

Paxton: Fancy a Nando's?

8

"How spicy do you go with your chicken?" Paxton asks me.

"Oh, I'm more of a lemon and herb boy," I tell him.

Paxton looks at me like I've just shat on the table, sniffs, then goes back to studying the menu.

It's twenty-four hours after I agreed to this thing, and we're sitting at our table-for-two, by the large window, just like George instructed, and indeed, specifically booked for us, because he "didn't want any screw-ups".

Paxton is tall and lanky, folded up in his chair in a way that looks really uncomfortable, and I'm not saying he isn't fully invested in this, but he's wearing battered trainers, black jeans and a black hoodie, and he's just occasionally moodily glancing up at me from behind his floppy black fringe, like even that's a real effort. I'm in my chinos, I ironed my best shirt, and I'm wearing a spritz or two of some Hugo Boss eau de toilette I got for Christmas. I even have the condom we got given during our year ten PSHE class in my wallet – not that I'm expecting to use it, and not that I *would* use it, since it's expired now; it's purely so I'm in the right frame of mind. Method acting, I suppose. This might be *fake,* but I need to believe it's an actual *date* so other people can believe it. What's the point, if we just look like two mates out for a bite to eat?

I put the menu down and reach into my bag, pulling out the wrapped gift I bought him. I push it across the table. Paxton stares at it, then at me.

"For you," I explain.

Paxton looks back at the present, then back at me again. "*Fake.*"

"What?"

"George said you knew this was fake."

"Yes, I do know it's fake," I hiss, "but the point is to try and make it seem real. Right? If you make counterfeit money, you don't just run off some Monopoly notes; you try to make it look like the real thing."

"You don't have to buy me stuff."

"Well, don't get too excited."

Paxton shrugs and glances back at the present. "What is it?"

"A good way to find out would be to open it."

Paxton rolls his eyes, then turns his attention to the gift, carefully peeling away the brown paper (classy – I'd date me!) and pulling out the book. "*Romeo and Juliet?*" he says, reading the title.

"Greatest love story ever told, right?"

"Where everyone dies."

"Well, *yes*, they do, but before all the death, there is love."

"And quite a lot of conflict."

"And conflict. But despite all that, there is still—"

"A potentially icky age gap between the main protagonists." He looks at me. "A bit like us."

"No . . . *no*, because you're sixteen, right?"

Paxton nods.

"Exactly. And so am I. I'm not seventeen until the end of July."

"You're the year above me, though."

"Only because of the random cut-off dates of the academic year system!"

"Still. People might talk."

I swallow. I think there's a twinkle in his eye, but I can't quite tell if he's winding me up. "We're both sixteen. We're legal. . . We can fully consent, not that there's anything to consent to, because nothing's happening anyway . . . so it's fine."

"I'm gonna call you 'Daddy'." Paxton smirks at me from under his fringe.

This is so not going to work out, not even in a fake way.

"Thank you for the play," he says.

"Sure. Enjoy all the . . . death and problematic underage sex."

He pushes his chair back and stands up. "Toilet."

I nod. As soon as he's disappeared to the bathrooms towards the back of the restaurant, I pull out my phone and hammer out a message to George:

> Me: George! Age gap between me and Paxton. Potential issue? Don't want to be caught up in Lolita-type controversy – optics for that would not be good. Back to the drawing board. . .

> George: What the hell are you talking about? You're not a middle-aged professor and he's not a 12 yo girl. Get a grip!

> Me: Different years, though! Sixth form going out with younger always frowned upon.

> George: Shut up. He'll be sixth form by September anyway. Get on with it. You need to be on dessert by 9pm – I don't want to hang around, mountain of physics homework to do.

I slide my phone back into my pocket just as Paxton returns.

"I washed my hands," he tells me, still rubbing them dry on his jeans. *"Pops."*

"Please don't call me that. I'll go and order – what do you want?"

"Bottomless Coke and half a peri-peri chicken," Paxton says. "Extra hot, please."

I nod and stand up.

"Can we have fries, Dad?"

"Sure." It takes me a moment. "I'm not your dad." I glance at the waitress bringing food to a nearby table and give an apologetic smile.

Paxton looks aghast. "You're NOT MY DAD?!" he practically screams. "Then who the hell are you?!"

I give him a warning glare, glance at the waitress again, who appears to be stifling a smile, then head off to the bar area to place our order.

"So," I say, placing our two drinks down on the table and sitting down again upon my return. "Should we get to know each other a bit? I guess that's how these things work?"

Paxton shrugs. "Paxton Lee. You can call me Pax, if you like. Or not. Whatever. Sixteen.

I wait for more, but apparently that's it. "Anything else?" I venture.

Pax shrugs.

"Literally," I say. 'Is there anything else ... about you?"

"My mum's from Scotland. That's where 'Paxton' comes from."

"OK, so that's a thing."

"Dad's from South Korea originally."

"OK."

"They don't know I'm bi."

"How would they be about it?"

"I dunno." Pax takes a slurp of his drink through the straw. "Guess I'll find out soon enough – when I turn up with you as my prom date." He must clock the look of worry on my face, because he adds, "Don't panic, I'll break it to them before you arrive at my front door with your bunch of roses."

"I was thinking more of his-and-his boutonnieres?"

"Huh?" Pax frowns.

"They're the little floral accessories, you know? Worn in the lapel?" I've lost him.

"OK, whatevs." He looks down, drawing little circles on the table with his finger.

"How do you know George?" I ask.

"Met him at archery."

"Oh, you do archery?"

"Not any more."

"But you kept in touch?"

"Obviously."

After more silence, broken only by the sound of clinking ice and slurping of Coke, the food arrives, and I think we're both grateful for having something to do, other than me fire questions at him, and him ask me absolutely nothing in return. If this *was* a real date, I'd be disappointed. On the plus side, there is literally no spark between us, so there's no chance of this ending the way a rom-com would end.

"Have you come out to anyone else?" I ask, slicing into my chicken.

He shakes his head. "Just George. And now you, I guess." He studies me for a moment. "You know who you remind me of?"

"Noah Schnapp?" I almost gasp, hope swelling in my chest that, maybe, I'm undergoing some kind of glow up.

Paxton squints at me. "*Who?*"

"He's one of the kids in *Stranger Things*. I dunno, a few people have said it, that's all."

"My *gran* on my dad's side."

Now it's my turn to squint back at him. "Your gran? Your *gran*? I remind you of an elderly woman, presumably of South Korean heritage?"

Pax laughs. "You don't *look* like her. Particularly. I just mean, she's always firing questions at me too. *'How's school, Paxton? How are your grades, Paxton? Are you seeing a nice young lady, Paxton?'*"

I blow out a breath. "Wow, OK, sorry. I'm only trying to be nice."

"I know." He smiles. "Hey, how's this election thing going, then?"

"It could be going better."

Pax nods and bends to put his mouth to his straw. "I'll vote for you," he continues, not looking up from his drink.

I mean, I kind of assumed you would, since we're fake

dating, but clearly I should not have taken that for granted!

"Thanks," I reply.

"I mean, I guess Bronte would be good too. That promposal was pretty cool."

"There's more to being president than creating spectacle."

"Oh, sure, yeah. But you gotta admit, she's a good role model. For the younger kids, I mean. Being so comfortable in her sexuality and everything."

I don't reply, and that's it, we don't talk any more while we eat, something which clearly doesn't bother Paxton in the least (it's like he's wrapped up in his own little world, just him and the peri-peri chicken), but which I find absolutely terrible and really awkward. By 8:50 p.m. George has messaged that he's hovering outside, ready to take the pictures, and that we need to order dessert "NOW MOFOS!" because he's in the middle of some horrific equations, or something, and needs to get back home.

The plan is that we will share a dessert and be snapped romantically feeding spoonfuls of it to one another.

"I'd kind of like my own dessert," Pax complains.

"We really need to get this photo," I tell him.

"What are you thinking of ordering, though?"

I glance at the menu. "The carrot cake?"

"*The carrot cake?!*" He looks appalled.

"Salted caramel brownie, then?"

"No, the caramel cheesecake's the one."

82

"OK, then, we'll get that—"

"No, but I can eat a whole one to myself."

In the end, I agree to his demands, if only because George is now firing more messages at me about what the hell the delay is. Five minutes later, one caramel cheesecake and one carrot cake arrive, courtesy of the waitress who clearly knows this is a date, and it's going terribly, and I instruct Pax that I'm going to spoon a bit of my cake into his mouth from across the table.

"I hate carrot cake, though," he tells me.

I take a deep breath. "Fine, swap plates, I'll feed you the cheesecake."

Pax doesn't like that one bit, and eyes me suspiciously as I switch the plates around, like I might be tempted to keep his cheesecake after the shot. Messaging George to "Stand by!" I slice off some cheesecake with the spoon, and offer it across the table towards Pax.

Who just looks at it.

"What now?" he says.

"*Eat it!*" I hiss.

"This is so icky. This whole thing."

"Try to look happy at least."

"If I do that, everyone will know this is fake. I don't do happy."

"*Eat the cheesecake, Paxton!*"

He eats it.

"Nice?" I ask.

He raises his eyebrows, as if to say, "It's OK."

A few moments later, my phone pings.

George: Touch him.

Me: Gross. No.

George: Just put your hand over his I mean. Wow.

Me: Ugh.

George: Your body language is all wrong. Both of you. Can you at least TRY, please?!

I turn back to Pax. "Would it be fine if I put my hand on yours across the table?"

"Is this real or fake?"

"It's fake, Paxton, all of this is fake! George just wants a nice shot, so look at me like you fancy me, and I'll look at you like I fancy you, and I'll gently stroke your hand, George will get the photo he wants, job done, we can all go home."

Pax turns to look out the window, sees George lurking by the lamppost with his phone (in black jeans, plain black sweatshirt and a black beanie, like some sort of burglar), and gives him a wave.

George holds his hands out in an expression of "WTF

are you doing, COME ON!"

Pax chuckles. "He makes me laugh when he's cross."
He sticks his tongue into his cheek and makes a gesture like
he's giving a blowjob, followed by nodding at George and
giving a thumbs up.

George's eyes widen, a murderous expression washing
over his face.

My phone pings.

George: Don't make me come in there!

George: No prom date unless we get this shot.
TELL HIM!

"Paxton, there's no prom date unless we get this shot. OK?
We need to get it."

Pax sighs. "Ugh, come on, then." He puts his hand on
the table. "I've never been touched by another boy before."
He lowers his voice. *"Be gentle."*

I give an exasperated sigh and place my hand on top
of his, gently squeezing.

"Mmmm," Pax purrs. *"Pappy."*

"Please don't make this any more weird than it already
is."

"You know, I've kind of enjoyed tonight. Been nice,
talking with someone who gets it."

Well, that's unexpected. I smile. "Yeah?"

"I don't exactly have any really close mates in my year anyway," Pax says, "but the ones I do have, I always feel like I'm hiding part of myself from them – which, is true, because I guess I am. And then, if I did tell them, well . . . some people can be funny about it, can't they? They say it's fine, they tell you it's cool, but actually, they're secretly wondering if you fancy them, or look at them in changing rooms. I know, 'cause I hear them say stuff like that about other people. I know that's how they think. I've even joined in with it sometimes, which makes it even more messed up, if I come out."

I squeeze his hand again. "Yeah, I know. And it doesn't, it's not messed up, I totally get it, but also, I know. I've been there too." And for a moment, I remember why I'm doing this, what these connections, the club, could mean to kids like me, like Pax.

He meets my eyes.

My phone pings. "That'll be George telling us he's got the shot," I say.

I slide my hand off his.

"Nice fake dating you," Pax says.

"Nice fake dating *you*," I reply.

9

George handles the details of how the photo gets out. He has people – I don't know, I don't even *want* to know how he does it, the less I know the better. But by lunchtime the next day, it's become the hot topic all over school. Meanwhile, we're going to "stoke the fires" a bit by staging what George has described as a "small, but cute, romantic gesture – nothing flashy or tacky like Bronte did" in the cafeteria in about twenty minutes. He hasn't said what it is, as apparently I'll be more convincing if I don't have a chance to overthink it. Paxton and I are under strict instructions from George not to confirm, or deny, anything at this stage. The plan is to put out a statement later, asking people to respect our privacy "at this time" – which, according to George, will set the rumour mill to overdrive, and ensure everyone is talking about *me* and not Bronte. Riding the crest of the gossip wave, and just when everyone's attention is on me, and only me, we'll drop our key policies, and watch the polls surge in my favour.

It's a fail-safe plan.

Until Mr Hubbard collars me in the corridor at the start of lunch.

"Bronte's filled me in about the photos, Barney," he says.

"She's . . . *what*?"

"And I agree with her, it's a gross invasion of your privacy."

I stare at him, trying to work out what to say and how to say it, just trying to work out what the endgame needs to be here, never mind how to get there.

"It's OK," Mr Hubbard continues. "It's understandable you're upset, so I don't expect you to say anything. There's no reason why you *should* say anything. I just want you to know that we'll be doing our utmost to track down the source and make sure they face appropriate consequences."

"What? No! No, that really won't be necessary." I try to give him my best totally-not-a-problem, everything-is-fine smile. "It's just some photos."

Mr Hubbard squeezes my shoulder. "Just know we've got your back. And if we need to escalate this to the authorities, then that's exactly what we'll do."

And off he goes.

Shit.

"The authorities"? Who are they? The police?

Shit.

"Barney!" It's Maya, running towards me, still

wearing her "Vote Barney" strappy top, with a look of utter panic on her face. "Shit!"

"You're telling *me* shit?!"

"It's Bronte," she continues, waving her phone about. "She's told Mr Hubbard about the photos, I know!"

"Yes, she has, but also – George just messaged – she's currently outside the library. She's persuaded her dad's company to donate five hundred pounds' worth of LGBT books to the school. She's about to give a speech, surrounded by piles of gay YA novels, and the local paper have come to cover it!"

I stifle a growl. "Whatever she's doing, we'll do it better!"

"George wants us over there, *now*."

Maya and I hurry through the corridors, me ignoring the stares and occasional comments of "Look, it's lover boy!", and Maya muttering about how much she hates Bronte's dad and how he's just as bad as she is, thinking he's "The Big I Am" because he owns a double-glazing firm.

She first met Bronte's parents at a five course dinner at their house and, after enduring her mum barking on about 'the woke agenda' (including endless repetition of the phrase, "It's political correctness gone mad!"), the starter was served with a lengthy spiel from Bronte's dad about how he always gave jobs in his company to "the most qualified person – I don't see race, sex or sexuality, only excellence!". Bronte then had a row with him, revealing he exclusively employs straight, white men, six of whom have failed to meet their sales targets for the last five months, "So how can they possibly be the best?" The awkward silence was only broken when Bronte's mum laughed scornfully at Maya when she used her butter knife for the fish course. ("I'd never even seen a fish knife before!")

Maya is still steaming as we round the corner and join the back of a group of students surrounding Bronte, who is standing on a chair outside the library doors.

George is immediately by my side. He's wearing grey checked suit trousers, burgundy braces with the burgundy bow tie, and a white shirt with rolled-up sleeves, like he means business. "Don't scowl," he tells me. "Look happy, and like this is fine. Remember to clap. You don't want to come across as bitter."

"She told Mr Hubbard about the photos!" I hiss. "He's ... trying to find out the source!"

George shrugs. "He'll have a job. Used a sock puppet account from a burner phone; I'm not worried."

"He mentioned getting the authorities involved."

George actually laughs at this. "OK, well, I'll look forward to government agents raiding my house at three a.m. because I know they'll see it as a matter of national security." He looks me up and down. "Where's your branded hoodie?"

"In the wash. I dropped ketchup down it. Where's yours?"

"So you opted for a 'Hug Life' Care Bears one?"

he replies, ignoring my question.

"Cute and relatable?"

There's silence for a moment. George turns his attention to the library doors, where Bronte is clambering up on a chair. "You know, if you need to borrow some shirts, you only have to ask," he mutters.

Ouch.

Bronte quietens down the crowd. "Friends! Fellow students! Members of the LGBTQ+ community and our allies! Thank you for joining me!"

George nudges me. *"Smile."*

"After securing this generous donation of LGBTQ+ titles from a local business, I had planned simply to deliver them to the library quietly. We've all seen those terrible videos where influencers give homeless people food and record it so everyone knows how kind they are, and we all know it's just fishing for likes. But actually, recent events have shown me that, in this case, I *do* need to make this very public. Just today, we have witnessed how a couple of simple photographs of two boys has gone viral around this school and made them the subject of petty gossip and rumour. Their crime? Being seen together in a mid-price chain restaurant, sharing a moment of intimacy."

George nudges me again. *"Stop* smiling, doofus, she's talking about you."

"And I ask you this," Bronte continues. "Would a cis-gender, heterosexual couple attract this level of interest? Or is this yet another example of students who may identify as LGBTQIAP being seen as a side show? Here for your entertainment and amusement?"

In spite of myself, I'm nodding along to this.

George nudges me again. "Stop agreeing, stay neutral."

"Today, I deliver five hundred pounds worth of young adult novels and works of non-fiction, covering the full gamut of the queer experience. Read. Think. *Learn.* Put yourselves in our shoes. Understand what it can feel like to be seen as different. Don't share and dissect and gossip about the private moments of other people. Let them be! Leave them to work things out in their own way, if indeed, that is what they are doing! Is life not hard enough? Who wants their every move to be analysed and reposted on social media? How horrible. How inconsiderate. I want every student in this school to promise not to share those intimate photographs of my opponent in this electoral race. I want every student to respect his privacy. I want every student *to forget about him.* But I do want every student in this school to realize that we're all in the same boat: we're all just trying to find our way through the nightmare that is secondary school, the nightmare that is growing up, and the nightmare that is love, romance and human connection in an increasingly disconnected world. And maybe, just maybe, if we all understand those *nightmares*, then the *dream* can finally come true: *the dream of a better, more tolerant world.*" She takes a moment to survey the enraptured crowd. "Thank you."

Everyone applauds. There are whoops of appreciation.

Bronte hops down from her chair, scoops up various books, and starts throwing them into the adoring crowd. "Love is love!" she shouts, as a copy of *Love, Simon* hits me in the face.

Some very loud clapping and whooping is coming from behind my left shoulder, and I turn to see Danny Orlando, all smiles and muscles, in his football kit as always, waving a peeled banana. "Man! What a speech!" he says to me. "Inspirational, right, Barney?"

"Uh-huh," I nod.

He edges a bit closer to me. "Look, maybe I owe you an apology, because I saw those pics of you and Paxton, and I've been one of the people Bronte was talking about. I talked about it with my mates. I even shared it, Barney. And, I'm sorry, man. I should not have done that. What you do is your business, no one else's." He blows out a breath and shakes his head. "Bronte's really made me think, and I'm gonna think more about what she said, and less about you and Paxton, and I guess we'll all be better people." He grins at me. "Did you screw, though?"

"Go away, Danny."

"Barney will not be commenting on the rumours at this time," George says, fishing his thick-rimmed black glasses from the back pocket of his suit trousers and putting them on.

"Is he even sixteen, though, you dirty dog?"

"*Danny!*" I hiss. "Yes, he is, so it's all – not that it matters, because we're not – so. Yes!"

Danny smirks and taps his nose with his finger.

I think I hear George groan.

"Dude, say no more. Love is love, like Bronte says!" Danny smiles, then puts his lips around the tip of his banana while maintaining eye contact with me.

I swallow and grit my teeth.

He gently presses his mouth into the banana flesh, still not taking his eyes off me.

"Look, can you not do that?" I say.

"Huh?" he mumbles, mouth full.

"You *know* what you're doing."

Danny swallows and holds his hands up, then glances over at Bronte, who is having her photo taken by the reporter from the local paper, smiling as she brandishes fistfuls of sapphic rom-coms. "Hey, Bronte!" he shouts. "I think you got my vote!"

Bronte gives him a thumbs up back.

Danny turns to me. "Buuuut, it's still early days, and a guy can change his mind, so ... everything to play for, huh, Barney? God, who knew this gay club thing could be so exciting?"

He winks at me, puts the banana in his mouth again,

but really deep, like, the whole thing is practically in his mouth, he could seriously choke, and ambles away. I don't know what's more annoying: Danny winding me up in such a crass and pathetic way, or the fact I now have a semi.

I'm just about to ask George and Maya what the hell we're meant to do now when Bronte herself pushes through the crowd of her adoring fans, making a beeline for me. Maya immediately assumes an air of officialdom, pulling a notepad and branded "Vote Barney!" pen from her bag, poised as if to make notes on this encounter.

"Barney," Bronte says, a kind of sad smile on her lips. "How are you holding up?"

"Yeah, good, thanks." I shrug. "Nice speech."

She breaks into a big smile. I think it's disingenuous, but I can't quite place it. "Oh, Barney, *thank you!* That's so sweet."

"No worries."

"I hope you didn't mind me wading into your little problem and advocating for you. I'll be honest, I'm disgusted. The *violation.* Some people in this school..." She shakes her head.

"You say violation, some might say visibility..." I squeak, but she doesn't even seem to hear me, which is probably for the best because even I'm not sure any more. Like, I want LGBT kids to be *seen*, I think it's important to be *seen*, but I also don't want us to be considered juicy, salacious gossip, just *because* we're LGBT.

"And, *my god*, what are the chances, huh?" Bronte continues.

"Chances of what?"

"Of someone from school who knows you just happening to pass by the window of Nando's, where you just happen to be sitting, and which just happens to be perfect for photos, and just at the exact time you happen to be engaged in what looks like an intimate moment with Paxton." She looks directly into my eyes. "Quite incredible."

I swallow. "I mean, I guess no different to the chances of you and Mandy both *just happening* to know the lyrics and harmonies to 'Take Me or Leave Me'." And now it's my turn to look directly into *her* eyes.

She laughs. "Oh, you cynic! Barney! I'm surprised at you!"

"Just saying," I shrug.

"Saying, or *accusing?*"

"No one's accusing anyone of anything," George chips in, putting his actual arm between me and Bronte. "Barney is merely making an observation."

"Which he's entitled to do!" Maya adds, brandishing her notepad. "And may I say, I share his *observations.*"

Bronte turns her attention to her. "What are you making notes on?"

"*Details*," Maya replies, finishing writing with a flourish.

Bronte nods. "There doesn't seem to be any ink in that pen."

Maya grits her teeth. Bronte is right, sadly. Maya accidentally ordered fountain pens and they didn't come with any ink in them. Maya blinks, fishes her pencil case from her bag, plucks out a little ink cartridge, attempts to insert it into the pen, and ends up squirting herself with ink.

"Would you like a tissue?" Bronte asks, after a pause.

"No, thank you," Maya replies. She clears her throat and turns to me. "Have you got a tissue, please?"

"Um, no," I say.

Bronte offers a tissue. "I'm *fine*," Maya tells her, ink dribbling down her face. "Back to the song. *I Kissed a Girl*? Really? Katy Perry as a lesbian icon when we have Janelle Monae, Hayley Kiyoko, and MUNA?"

Bronte smiles. "You'll need to take that up with Mandy, she chose to sing it." She sighs. "Can you please let me get that ink off your face?" She leans in with the tissue, and gently wipes below Maya's left eye.

"And like Barney said," Maya mutters, as Bronte dabs away, "singing *Take Me or Leave Me*? It sounded pretty rehearsed!"

Bronte screws up her face. "Really? You both think it's odd that two queer girls who both like drama happen to know the lyrics and harmonies to one of musical theatre's great lesbian anthems?" She rolls her eyes. "Get a grip." She finishes up with Maya and turns to me. "This thing with Paxton is so obviously fake. Whatever will be next for you two? No, let me guess: a borrowed jumper? A super-thoughtful gift?"

At which point, there's a cough behind me, and we all turn, and there's Paxton, in his dishevelled school uniform, shirt partly untucked, tie loose around his neck, holding up a little paper bag. "Salted caramel brownies? You mentioned that they're your favourite, right? I, um . . . made them myself?"

George locks the door of Room 120 and proceeds to pull down the blinds, so I guess this is an emergency. The room is plunged into darkness as he tugs the final cord with a flourish, at which point he turns to me, Maya and Paxton. "Sit," he tells us.

George goes to turn the lights on, runs a hand through his quiff, and then joins us at the table in the middle.

"I'm sorry," Pax says. "Clearly, I messed up. When you didn't show in the cafeteria, I assumed something had gone wrong, so I came to find you. I couldn't just wait there, it was getting weird, just watching other people eat."

"Sorry, home-made brownies?" I say. "That was the romantic surprise?"

Pax's eyes widen and he looks at George for reassurance.

"Yes," George says. "It's important for people to clock

99

these little moments between you both to keep the chatter going."

"Except Bronte's put a stop to that by making out it's wrong to gossip about us," I say. "Plus, she clearly knows our game, so the best thing is we just scrap it and campaign on some actual issues instead – which Bronte's already got a head start on."

I sit back. I am right.

"You're wrong," George tells me, taking off his glasses and waving them around as he speaks. "Bronte's actually done us a favour. The plan was always to put out a statement asking people to respect your privacy anyway, so she's just done it for us. Of course no one's going to take any notice of that. And she's actually drawn attention to you, in effect sharing the attention she had built up for herself. If you tell people not to look at something, it just makes them want to look more. Maybe they'll be less obvious about it, but you'll still be the hot topic."

I groan and hold my head in my hands.

Maya rubs my back. "Actually, I think he's right, Barns. Also, if you back out of this with Paxton now, it'll just confirm to Bronte what she already suspects. We've got to keep going with this."

"And what does 'keeping going' look like, exactly?" I look at Pax, who just stares back at me, sadly. He doesn't want this any more than I do.

"Pax, tomorrow morning, you'll receive a note during

registration about a delivery waiting for you at reception," George says. "It'll be a bunch of flowers from an admirer." He indicates me. "You'll pick them up and be happy."

Paxton frowns. "Flowers? I think it'd be better to leave them at reception until the end of the day. They'll get crushed if I—"

"I don't care if they get crushed, the point is you carry those fuckers around with you all day and everyone sees." He stares at Pax, who just nods, like he's scared.

George turns to me. "Meanwhile I've commissioned an artist from Poland that Maya's worked with before on some of her comics, to create some m/m fan art of you and Pax. At an appropriate moment, probably when we've gone public with you both, we'll share it on our social channels, as though it's come from a campaign supporter in the school. With any luck, a good portion of students will start 'shipping' you both. Emotional connection equals engagement equals votes. Finally, at the hustings next week, we'll end with a promposal to Pax – we'll knock them out with your ideas and then leave them with the warm, fuzzy mental image of two boys getting it on. It'll be like catnip for people."

"Ugh, we're still doing a promposal?" I say. "But after Bronte—"

"This will be classy, though," George replies. "*Simple.* You'll finish up by saying that you know everyone's been talking about it, and, thanks to everyone's support, blah

blah, you feel empowered and able to tell the world that you, Barney Brown, like Paxton Lee, and will you, Paxton Lee, give me the very great honour of letting me be your date to year eleven prom?" George lets the moment linger, but then comes back to reality. "Or words to that effect. You work out the actual phrasing."

I glance at Pax, who's staring at George, and then turns to me. "And what do I do?" he says.

"Cry, ideally," George replies. "Tears of joy, obviously."

"I can't do that," he replies.

"Just a single tear?" George asks. "Think of something sad – like your predicted GCSE grades."

Pax looks mortally wounded by that.

"Do you not just think," I say, "that all this promposal business is a bit repetitive and . . . unrealistic? The grand gesture? It's too Hollywood. It just doesn't feel like real life." I nod at everyone in turn. "I'm right."

"You're *wrong*!" George grins at me. "Are you telling me LGBT kids don't deserve a Hollywood ending? That it should always be doom and gloom, death and homophobic beatings?"

"No, of course not, but—"

"You, Barney Brown, are a figurehead. President – in waiting – of the LGBTQ+ Society. A beacon of hope! Let all those kids in the closet see you, and *believe*. Believe it could be them. That something big, and wonderful, and exciting, and over-the-top beautiful and romantic could happen to them just as much as it could anyone else." He leans across the table, towards me. "And by the time the rest of this plan has been actioned, everyone will be *so* invested in you and Pax, they'll be freakin' pissing themselves when it's made official."

"Well," I say, grimacing. "What a delightful image."

There is no point arguing. George is adamant. And I do trust George. He's so good at endgame, he should really be playing chess with me.

"Onwards!" George says. "And, good news, the latest polling suggests our strategy *is* working: your approval ratings have gone up, Barney! Not as high at Bronte's yet, but the trajectory is good. People are talking about you. They actually know who you are now!"

"Woop! Woop!" Maya shouts.

"But we need to set out some concrete policies and action," I say. "We're not gonna win this thing on me fake dating Paxton and people randomly thinking it's cute."

"It is quite cute, though," Maya says.

I give her a warning stare.

"She got her dad to donate some books to the library, big deal," George says.

"But it got attention. Even the local paper!"

George shrugs. "I've already told the local paper to hold fire on running the story ... because we're gonna go one better."

We all lean forward.

"You're going to donate some LGBT books too. *To the local primary school.* Gay books plus small kids equals better photo op. Also, even better, you're going to *read* one of them to the children, and, actually, *not* you, but a drag queen. Even better photo op!"

I sit back. "Okaaay. *I think.* How am I going to pay for this? No one in my family owns a double-glazing business. We're fully skint."

"Sell something," George says.

I blink at him. "Like what? A kidney?"

"We don't need *that* many books." George rolls this eyes. "Sell your PlayStation."

"No."

"*Sell it.* You never use it anyway, you know you don't. And that's a much better headline." George sweeps his hands in front of himself, spelling out the words. "'*Local Teen Sells PlayStation to Buy Queer Books for Small Children*'. That's so emotive."

Maya nods. "And so much better than '*Annoying Privileged Girl with Rich Dad Makes No Sacrifices Whatsoever to Buy Some Books for Library That Already Has Loads Thanks to LGBTQ+ Society.*'" She puts her hand to her throat and pulls a face like she's about to vomit. "I hate her so much."

"Do you?" I smile at her. "I saw the way you just stood there as she caringly removed that ink from your face."

"It was *ink*, Barney. It could have been toxic, how

should I know? It was an emergency."

"Barney?" George says. "You up for that?"

I sigh. "Sure."

"How much are you selling your PlayStation for?" Paxton asks, getting right in there.

I shrug. "I dunno. A hundred and sixty?"

"PS4, is it? Are you bundling some games in too?"

". . .OK?"

"I'll give you one twenty."

"One forty."

"One thirty-five, final offer."

"Um . . . OK?" I say.

Paxton grins. "Thanks, Pops."

"Well, that was easy," George says. He glances at me quizzically. *"Pops."*

"Just a little in-joke," I explain.

George squints, then shakes his head. "OK, so Pax will transfer the funds, Barney will buy a few picture books – *Mary Has Two Mums*, *Gary the Big Gay Giraffe*, that sort of thing. Maya, can you find us a drag queen?"

"I . . . guess?"

"Google is your friend. I'm sure lots of them advertise. We need a relatively kid-friendly one, so no one who's dressed too provocatively, and no names like. . ."

"Dixie Normous," Paxton says.

"Right," George replies, raising his eyebrow slightly at Paxton. "Make sure you say their drag name out loud several times before you decide to book them."

Maya nods, and jots it in her notebook . . . with a pen that still doesn't have ink in it.

"I'll sort out the logistics with the school," George continues. "Barney, you also need to start thinking about your speech for next week. This is our main chance at making a lasting impact, and it's got to be right. Let's get a list of key angles together, decide what things to focus on, and work out how you're going to say it. Yeah?"

"Yeah," I say.

"Come on, Barney," George says, obviously picking up on my despondent tone. "You were born for this. Politics in general. It's totally *you*. We just need to oil the wheels to make it happen."

"Am I, though? Born for it? That online careers quiz we did in year ten—"

Maya throws her hands in the air. "Barney! Why do you always come back to this whenever you're having a wobble?"

"Because it said I should be an arable farmer!"

"It told me I should be a dog groomer," Maya replies. "And I'm allergic."

"It's very specific, though, so it must have known something I don't," I hiss. I gesture to George. "And how did it land on *funeral director* for him?"

"I could totally see him driving a hearse in a top hat," Maya muses.

George seems genuinely pleased with that. "Thanks!" He turns to me. "Don't be so ridiculous. No offence to arable farmers, you're destined for other things."

"Leader of the Gays," Paxton says, meaningfully.

"Exactly," George agrees. His face softens, as does his voice. "You're going to do great things, Barney."

"Am I?"

George nods. "And remember, you're not alone. We're all right here, standing beside you."

I look at them all. They believe in me more than I believe in myself. And I realize that, actually, *yes*, it is OK, because I've got them, and even if things don't go the way I want, I'll still have them. I guess that's what real, genuine friendship is: that feeling that it could be the end of the world, but with them by your side, it doesn't matter, you'll face it together, come what may.

"Great things," George repeats. "Just not in a 'Hug Life' hoodie, yeah?"

"Yeah," I agree.

11

Despite feeling upbeat at the end of lunch, my mood quickly gets worse during the afternoon when I see that Bronte's campaign bunting has arrived, and is being hung all down the corridors. Alternate flags feature Bronte's face (would you even dare?) and the messages *Bronte for President* and *Come Out for LGBT* – which hardly feels like the most original slogan in the world, but it doesn't matter, because, once again, Bronte is one step ahead of me. Maya assured me that she's just ordered some pin badges ("The gays love a pin badge, Barney!") and that they're going to be miles better "than a few flags", but by then Bronte will probably have moved on to something even more fabulous anyway. I'm itching to make a splash and drive the story here, and I'm annoyed that I haven't managed to. It doesn't help that Bronte's acting all surprised about the bunting on her social media that she's still claiming to be "on hiatus" from: *Can't believe my team surprised me with this bunting – featuring*

MY FACE! OMG, you guys! I mean, first of all, she can piss off with her "my team" bullshit, since it's basically just her and Mandy, and also: of course she knew. I bet she spent hours cropping and filtering the jpeg before she emailed it over to the printers; but the lie aside, it's the whole tone that bothers me. It just sounds ... successful. Like she knows she's already won this thing.

When I get home, I grab an entire unopened packet of choc chip cookies, a giant bag of Cheesy Wotsits, a packet of poppadoms, some mango chutney, a KitKat, a slice of carrot cake and a sausage roll, and head up to my room and log on to ChessNation.co.uk. I just want to think about something else for a bit.

I've got a private message, and my heart skips a beat when I see it's from Kyle.

> Kyle: Hey. OK, so I just wanted to apologize about last time, when I said your pic was cute. I'm not a creeper, honest, and I'm sorry if I made you feel awkward.

I smile to myself, and tap a message back to him:

> Me: It didn't make me feel awkward and I don't think you're a creeper. Totally fine.

I think for a moment, then add:

Me: Also, your pic's not so bad either. ;)

I tell myself that's fine – *I'm not flirting* – I've merely paid him a compliment, since he paid me one. I delete the winky face before I hit send, then click out of private messages, and head to the discussion boards, but a few moments later there's a *ping* noise, and a new private message has arrived. Kyle's online, and he's replied.

Kyle: Oh, thank god. I thought you hated me. I sent that DM days ago and have been waiting for you to reply.

Me: Sorry! Busy few days at school. I'm running for president of LGBT Society = chaos!

Kyle: OMG, we're having an election too! We always do as soon as year 13 go on exam leave, but this year it's SOMETHING ELSE! Chaos? Yes!

Me: Are you running?

Kyle: Ugh, god no! No offence. Haven't got the stomach for all the BACKSTABBING and BITCHING – which is ten times worse in all-boys schools, I'm telling ya! How many candidates?

Me: Just me and a girl called Bronte.

Kyle: You gonna win?

Me: Not sure.

Kyle: We have FIVE candidates here! FIVE!
That is basically half of the LGBT Society, so
five people will all vote for themselves, and for
the other five, it will depend who has slept with
whom, who has cheated on whom, who someone
fancies, AND SO ON. And all because of that
Rainbow Youth thing because everyone wants
to win and go to London and be ambassadors or
whatever. You lot going for that too I assume?

Me: Oh, yes. Haha! So who will you vote for?

Kyle: Frankly, I hate them all. (And haven't
messed around with any of them, so feel no
allegiance/have no particular reason to see their
dreams shattered, other than general underlying
feelings of dislike).

Me: hahahaha! We have WHOLE SCHOOL
voting for our president!

Kyle: ???? WHAT? WHY?

Me: Don't get me started. It's a circus already.

Kyle: Gimme your email. I'll send you – I kid
you not – the 10-page manifesto from one of
our candidates, colloquially known as BJ Ben,
for reasons you can probably guess. Probably
shouldn't do this because if you get selected,
we'll technically be up against you, and if Ben
wins he might use some of this in our application,
but honestly, I do not care. (But please don't tell
anyone and if you do I will deny everything!)

Me: I kind of have the receipts, if I screenshot
this discussion?

Kyle: Huh. I should not apply for secret service.

Me: But I won't betray you. Can't wait to read the
manifesto. BarneyBoy16@icloud.com

Kyle: Cool. Keep me posted. I want ALL the
drama! (And thanks for saying you like my pic . . .
you absolute FLIRT) ;)

He logs off, while I check I definitely *did* delete my winky face on my reply, and him adding one just then wasn't in reference to that, but I did, so it couldn't have been, so I don't quite know what to think about that. Then, thirty seconds later, his email with the manifesto drops into my inbox, along with another attachment which turns out to be a gif of a rainbow teddy bear slapping his forehead repeatedly, which, when I open the manifesto, sums up things *completely*, because, really? I thought this whole thing was meant to be *serious*?

Gay Ben's Big Gay Manifesto

1. Lobby school to make every Friday "Fri-gay" – when we all get lunch queue priority, gay anthems play over tannoy system, and LGBT students can leave ten minutes early.
2. Queer up the food offering in the cafeteria. Rainbow cupcakes? Sushi (made by trained sushi chef) and more emphasis on gay food groups in general – pies out, cod in soy butter sauce in.
3. More money for the LGBT Society – funding for dedicated LGBT Society room, including giant beanbags, scatter cushions, hot tub and fairy lights.
4. Get hot gay celeb to come in and give talk as inspirational gay role model. LGBT Society get to have lunch with him too and maybe

aforementioned hot tub?
5. Investigate possibility of instigating coup
to overthrow headmaster. Ideal replacement:
Britney. (Or Troye Sivan).

It's half a page. And where's the stuff that could make a difference? Where's mention of tackling homophobic bullying, or training teachers about pronouns, or any of that? The other nine pages of the manifesto turn out to be assorted thirst trap photos of Ben, and that's it. I email Kyle back:

Me: Um. . . this is a joke candidate, right?

Kyle replies a minute later:

Kyle: Nope. He's serious. Worse thing is — he's
also in the lead and currently most likely to
win. Granted, that may be because of historical
blowjobs. Depressing, huh?

I sigh. It *is* depressing. Worse, it looks like it's true: people don't seem to care about real issues, it's all about the spectacle. Bronte's ratings went sky high after her promposal stunt, and that had nothing to do with whether she'd made a good president or not. Even I have gone up in the polls since the stuff with Pax. This guy Ben is clearly running on some joke policies which will help no one, and the fact he looks hot with his shirt off. There's even one of him in some pretty tight swimming shorts which doesn't leave much to the imagination.

I think I'm getting this all wrong. If I'm going to get the presidency and the chance to make real changes, maybe I'm going to have to play by this other set of rules a bit more?

I message George:

Me: Hey. Just thinking about this fan art thing you've commissioned. How about we aim for less cute and a bit more . . . sexy? What do you think?

George: We can do that.

Me: Classy still, obviously. NOT PORN. But a hint of sexy.

George: You got it.

12

This continued discourse about my relationship with Mandy is beyond upsetting. I won't mention the individual concerned, but we are NOT fake dating, it's real, and we are very much in love. I should not have to say this. I am so tired.

30 ♡   10 ⟲   0 ⬭

I slam my phone down. "Continued discourse"? I mentioned it *once* and only after *she* accused me of faking things with Paxton. And how does that one exchange make her "so tired" exactly? You know what? *I'm* "so tired" of her attention-seeking social media posts, and I'm pretty sure this particular one was prompted by everyone talking about the ridiculously large bunch of flowers Paxton's been lugging around all day. He's had people coming up to him constantly asking who they're from, and Paxton's been great, actually, playing it coy, and just telling people the little card says "From an admirer", which everyone has taken to mean me and which, the general consensus seems to be, that it's the most romantic gesture ever. My god, the electorate are easily manipulated. Meanwhile, some of Bronte's faces on the bunting have (predictably) been the victim of graffiti, and she now has (variously) a moustache, devil horns and, of course, a penis ejaculating on to her hair. I think Bronte's tweet actually stems from concern that's she's becoming irrelevant, and it's her desperately trying to move the discussion back to her – because *today*, it feels like it's all about us.

Two days later, when the plans are in place and news breaks about my book donation to the primary school, Bronte is clearly sent into a tailspin. It's nothing she does – she's as cool and collected as she always is on the exterior, but the Insta post from Mandy says it all, the caption underneath the photo of her and Bronte kissing reading:

> *Bronte O'Halloran is one of the kindest, most*
> *thoughtful, vulnerable, hard-working, beautiful*
> *souls there is. The world is a better place with*
> *her in it, and she's only just getting started.*
> *You're going to see so many great things from this*
> *brilliant woman. She's my girlfriend – but she's*
> *your president. I love you and adore you. Xxx*

Normally, this would piss me right off, but it's so OTT, so utterly desperate, that I just laugh.

"I certainly wouldn't call her 'vulnerable'," Maya tells me, as she unwraps the box of pin badges that arrived at reception just before morning break. "She's hard as nails."

"*Interesting*!" I say. "So, 'kind', 'thoughtful' and 'beautiful soul' are all accurate?"

Maya rolls her eyes at me. "She's not all bad."

"*Oh my god*! You're thawing! Was it the ink moment?"

"*No*," Maya says. "The problem with Bronte is I was always left with the impression I never really meant anything to her. Like, she could be with me, or not with me, she didn't really care either way." She rips a strip of tape off the badge box. "It's nice to feel wanted, you know? To feel like you mean something to someone, you're not just a shag, or whatever. But sometimes she can be . . . OK to be around." She clears her throat and I smile to myself.

The badges were a good move – a lot of kids now have them on their blazers, and while most are "Vote Barney" ones, we also have some fun LGBTQ+ slogans too, so there's something for everyone. I really feel like we've trumped Bronte with this – bunting is bunting, you see it, and move on. But the badges are personal – we're actually giving people something that they'll keep and remember.

While Maya continues handing out badges during lunch, George and I head to the primary school with my box of gay picture books. I'm back in my "Vote Barney" hoodie, with a white T-shirt, and chinos, while George sports a tan tweed number, complete with waistcoat and pocket watch. I don't know how he pulls it off, but he does.

"So, you say a few words," George tells me as we walk along, "hand over the books, pose for some pics, introduce the drag queen, she reads one of the stories to the group of kids the school has selected, more pics, lots of smiles, lovely article gets written, you're the best, we splash the links all over our socials, wham, bam, everyone loves Barney."

"Sounds good."

"Remember these kids are, like, five, or whatever, so keep your tone jolly and fun, right? Think kids TV presenter."

"Got it."

"Don't swear."

'Why would I swear? Of course I won't swear!"

"OK," George says. He nudges me, gesturing towards a pink van parked outside the primary schools with *Girlz on Tour!* painted on the side, and a tall, slender Black lady with long blonde hair, a silver-sequinned mini dress and high heels leaning up against it, smoking a cigarette.

"Where did Maya find her?" I whisper.

George shrugs. "Got her to come down from Lincolnshire – all the London ones were super expensive." He strides over, me bringing up the rear because drag queens always slightly scare me if I'm honest (they're so sassy and confident), and extends his hand. "Bambi Sugapops?"

Bambi flicks her cigarette to the ground, blows some smoke out of her mouth, and twists her foot over the butt. "Hiya, hun!"

"I'm George, nice to meet you, and thanks for agreeing to do this today. This is Barney, he's donating the books and will introduce you to the kids."

Bambi offers me her hand. "All right, babe?"

"Um, yes. Thanks."

"Ooh, you've got a good firm grip!"

"Have I?"

"Very *manly*!"

I laugh. Nervously.

"OK!" George says. "Shall we...?" He gestures towards the school gates.

"Let me just have a quick suck on a mint, hun," Bambi says. "Want anything to suck on, Barney?" She offers me a tube of mints.

I swallow. "I'm good, thanks." I glance at George, who just smiles at me and mouths, "It's fine," and I really hope it will be. The last thing my campaign needs is to be derailed by an innuendo-prone drag queen that I've brought along to entertain a bunch of five-year-olds.

Sunny Tree Primary School have set us up in the main hall (I mean, it's *tiny*, but I guess it's big if you're small too), and I'm standing in front of their little stage, which has random nativity scenery on it, next to Bambi, holding copies of the books, a group of little kids sitting cross-legged on

120

the floor in front of me, and, directly behind them, some teachers and a bunch of parents the school invited along too. I scan the crowd as the headteacher gives me an introduction and I do a double-take when I see Danny Orlando standing at the back, his football top plastered in the gay pin badges we've been giving out. He meets my eyes, gives me a massive grin, points at the badges in an exaggerated way, then gives me a thumbs up. *What the hell is he doing here?*

". . .So, over to you, Barney!" the headteacher says.

There's a ripple of applause and I unfold the piece of paper in my hands. "Hello, hi, I'm Barney Brown, and I'm running for president of the LGBTQ+ Society at my school." I point to the slogan on my hoodie. "Vote for me! Haha!" Awkward – no one cheers, or even laughs. I swallow and glance at Danny again. *Why is he here?* He'd better not be filming this or anything. How did he even get in? "I just want to say that it's . . . um . . . it's . . . it's. . ."

"Wednesday?" Bambi offers.

"Um, ha! No, it's. . ."

"Always sunny in Philadelphia?" (This gets laughter from the teachers and parents. I don't know why, but it puts me off even more than seeing Danny Orlando.)

"No, um, it's. . ."

"A wonderful life!" Bambi shouts, extending her arms like a showgirl. (More laughter).

I laugh too. "Shut up." I say it jokingly (although I'm also serious), but the children all gasp.

One small girl says, "He said a swear!"

"That's not swearing," I say.

"Actually, in this school, it *is*," the headteacher tells me, a stern and disapproving look on her face.

What?! "I'm so sorry." I clear my throat, feeling my cheeks burning.

"Are you a teacher?" a small boy asks.

"No. So! Where was I? Oh, yes! I think it's really . . . yes?" I say, looking at another small girl who now has her hand up.

"I've forgotten," she replies.

"OK," I say. "I wanted to donate these—"

"BOOKS!" a boy shouts.

"Yep! Books!" I smile. "That's right. And I wanted to donate them because—"

"WONKY DONKEY!"

"No, not that one—"

The kids all groan in dismay.

"But just as good, is—"

"I NEED A WEE!"

"Do you actually, or is that the title of another picture book you like?"

A teacher bends down to talk to the kid.

"OK, so, as I was saying, one thing I wish I had when I was at primary school—"

"ARE YOU A REAL LADY?" a boy asks, pointing at Bambi.

"We ask questions later," the teacher tells the kid, while helping the "needs a wee" kid to his feet.

"This is BORING!" another kid says.

"OK, so moving on then," I continue, "I want every kid in this school to be able to see themselves in the—"

"The wee came out," the boy on his feet mutters sadly, now standing in a small puddle on the floor.

"Ah, I see that," I say, "but, um, it's simply about knowing that lots of different people are out there—"

"You have weird shoes!"

"And we should all celebrate differences, and—"

"Have you got a cat?"

"Accept each other and—"

"How old are you?"

". . . Accept ourselves." I look at a kid with her hand up. "Yes?"

The girl swallows. "I . . . I . . . um . . . I like to go to the beach and when I do, I build sandcastles with Daddy and . . . and . . . and. . ."

I mean, this had better be worth it, but I suspect it won't be.

". . . and my favourite colour is pink."

"Absolutely. And now, I'd like to introduce Bambi Sugapops—"

"ARE YOU A REAL LADY?"

". . . Who has kindly agreed to read one of these great books to you!"

I start the applause off and step back a bit as Bambi steps forward.

"Hi-ya, kiddies! And in answer to the young man asking, I'm a drag queen, and in my case that means I'm a man who dresses up as a lady as part of a performance – a bit like an actor. So, no, I'm not a *real* lady, I'm pretending. But it's important to know that other people might be born as a boy, like me, but know that they're actually a girl. A *real* girl. And that's a different thing."

The kids are all silent and nodding at this. I mean, great, *finally*, but also: what did I get so wrong with my bit?

"We're all different," Bambi continues, "and that's what this book I'm going to read you is all about. It's called *Gary the Big Gay Giraffe*." She turns the page. "Gary was a lot like the other giraffes in many ways. He had a big, long neck..."

I glance at George, who is watching all this with his typically neutral face. Did I manage to get any point across? Why were these five-year-olds so annoying and hostile towards me? Maybe I can make up for it by saying something intelligent to the reporter from the local paper.

"...But Gary was different in one very big way. While the other giraffes were cream and brown, Gary was ... RAINBOW COLOURED!"

Well, no surprises there, but the kids seem to be enjoying it, and, to be fair, Bambi reads the book really well, and does lots of funny voices, and everyone's giggling and having a good time, even the parents and teachers. Bambi's a bigger hit than I am, but I guess that's fine. The reporter is taking photos throughout, so I make sure there's a big smile painted on my face, and pretty soon the story wraps up (Gary finds some other big, gay rainbow-coloured animals so feels less alone – yay! Like the LGBTQ+ Society!) and then there are more pics, some applause, and the kids get taken away as the crowd starts to dissipate.

"Gotta run, hun! Gigging tonight," Bambi tells me as she gives me air kisses. "Loved your speech!" She gives me a wink, blows me a kiss and totters out.

"Barney, this is Katherine Freeman from the local paper," George says, walking up to me with the reporter I saw at Bronte's speech outside the library. She has dark, shoulder-length hair, and, despite probably only being in her early twenties, has the aura about her of someone's unimpressed mum before they're about to give you a telling off.

"Time for a few questions?" she says.

"Sure, fire away!"

George's phone rings. "Ugh, excuse me," he says, edging backwards. "You'll be OK, yeah?"

I nod. "Of course."

Katherine Freeman gives George a tight smile, like she thinks he's taking his role as my campaign manager a bit *too* seriously.

George gives a thumbs up and heads to a quiet corner of the hall. "Yep? What's happened?"

Katherine watches George walk off, then turns on me. "What do you say to concerned parents who don't want their children being introduced to LGBT issues?" Katherine asks.

She catches me off guard with the question; I was expecting friendly local paper chat, not tabloid-style conflict. "Um . . . well, I would say being LGBT is *normal*, and it does no harm to show kids that there's lots of different people in the world. If you talk about these differences when people are young, they'll be better prepared for their futures, and of course it will mean the world to the kids who are LGBT to see themselves validated in this way."

"And what about bringing a drag queen here today? We heard one young man was confused about whether they were male or female. Do you think all this, and in a wider sense, the whole pronouns thing in general, is simply *confusing* for kids?"

I moisten my lips. *The whole pronouns thing?* Dear god, Katherine Freeman is angling for an opinion column in one of the nationals. But I need to keep her on side. "Look . . . some people might think pronouns are ridiculous," I say, hoping that acknowledging that fact will soften her stance towards me. "But actually, asking people what their pronouns are is just good manners, respectful, and literally costs you nothing. And it's practical. Some people have gender-neutral names, for example. If your name was Alex, I don't necessarily know if that means I should refer to you as she, he or they."

Katherine nods. "Why do you think this is such a hot topic?"

I blow out a breath. "Amongst our generation, I don't think it is."

"So, it's the older generation who have the issues?"

"Boomers, Gen X, to an extent, yes, I think it is. I mean, some millennials can be obtuse about it too – it's like, kids today, we just accept it, we can see love is love, and you can be who you want, and it doesn't matter. But the older you get, the more you get beaten down into this rigid, binary way of seeing the world. This idea that things have always been a certain way, even though *we* made them that way, and so now they can't ever change, you know?"

"Interesting," Katherine says. "Thanks, Barney. I'll try to get this in the next edition." She glances at my branded hoodie. "Good luck with the presidential campaign."

"Thanks," I say. I think my answers were good. I guess I need to expect difficult questions. It's part-and-parcel of any politician's job.

Katherine heads off, and I glance at George, who is still on his mobile in the corner, one finger in his ear to block out the noise.

"Very moving speech," Danny Orlando says, walking up to me. "And I overheard some of what you said to that reporter – nicely handled, man! She was fierce. But also weirdly hot."

"How come you're here?" I ask.

"Oh, my little sister goes here. School invited us, and I had a free, so thought I'd come and see you in action!" He grins at me.

I try to smile back.

"I'm wearing the badges!" He points at one that says, *All the cool girls are lesbians.* "So true, right?"

"Uh-huh."

"You know, all this you've done, selling your PlayStation, it's made me think . . . maybe I should vote for you? Like, listening to you . . . you're clearly so passionate. . . I mean, you could barely formulate a sentence, you were so passionate—"

"Yeah, OK, ha ha," I say.

Danny shakes his head. "No, no, don't get offended, man. Like, I get it, public speaking – whoa! Scary!" He steps a bit closer. "But what I like about you, Barney, apart from the fact you look like Noah Schnapp, is that you're not afraid to put yourself out there. You've come here, with a drag queen, and now . . . *that picture.*" He winks at me.

I swallow. "What picture?"

"The one that was shared on your social media accounts this afternoon. The fan art."

"Oh! The fan art." I haven't seen it, but I have to pretend that I have, of course.

Danny raises his eyebrows. "All in all, Barney, I've gotta say – *impressive package.*"

He smiles and saunters off.

Impressive package? As in . . . I'm the real deal? I'm solid on the issues, I do charity type things, I hang out with drag queens proving I'm cool. . .

"On reflection," George says, suddenly by my side, "I probably should have ignored you when you asked for the fan art of you and Pax to be more sexy, and I probably should have shown it to you and Maya for a second opinion before posting it, but we were in a rush to get here, and I wanted to get it out there, and I kind of wanted to surprise you with all the great feedback at the end of this, you know, icing-on-the-cake type of thing, lots of reasons, all of them stupid, and now . . . so. . ."

"What? What's wrong with it?"

"I messed up, OK! On this, I messed up. Took my eye off the ball. It's fine, because you should absolutely lay the blame for this on me and make it clear you're innocent."

"*George.*"

He winces slightly. "Mr Hubbard wants to see you in his office."

13

On the plus side, the artist has made me look really cute and handsome – Pax too – I mean, we've got amazing abs, great hair, we're *hot*. It's just, unfortunately, we're also depicted on a bed, basically dry-humping each other, in boxer shorts that are barely containing huge bulges.

I wish Mr Hubbard would click the photo off from his computer screen.

"See," Mr Hubbard says, "in my book, this is basically pornography."

"No one's naked," I reply. "And it's a cartoon, not real."

"It's very suggestive, Barney. And rather obscene. Would you be happy with your mother seeing this?"

I shrug.

"Do you think this imagery is appropriate for someone who hopes to represent the school at a global level?"

"It wasn't posted on a school account."

"Not officially, but the account is connected to a school club."

"But—"

"There's no 'buts'. We don't need to see it. It's not the image we want to portray." He looks at me. "Is it?"

I sigh. "In my defence, this went up without my approval. It was swiftly taken down when the mistake was realized."

"But not before it was widely shared," Mr Hubbard says. "And if Bronte hadn't drawn my attention to it as soon as she did, would it still be up there now?"

Of course Bronte told him about this.

Mr Hubbard leans back in his chair. "Society is becoming increasingly sexualized, I don't deny it. Everywhere we look, sex sells. Our screens are full of suggestive, sexual images, young people are practically raised on a diet of porn, and we're fighting a losing battle against that. The question is: do we stoop to that level? Or do we try and stay classy?"

"Stay classy, totally," I agree. "As I say, I didn't approve this picture."

Mr Hubbard frowns and shakes his head. "What also concerns me is that other students in the school would actually create this sort of thing. First covert pictures of you and Paxton, and now highly sexualized imagery. I'll be making it clear in assembly that it's unacceptable. *Go.*"

I swallow, feeling like I need to say more, but Mr Hubbard has turned to some papers on his desk and is reading through them, jotting notes as he goes. I sigh, get up, and walk out of his office. Why did I even suggest making the picture more sexy to George? I'm a hypocrite – hoping people fetishize us, for my own gain, when that's exactly what I despise happening to LGBT people. Mrs Buchanan glances up on my way out and gives me a *look* loaded with disapproval and possible disgust, and, as I walk along the corridor on my way out, every kid and teacher I pass seems to *look* at me too.

"What the hell?" Pax hisses as he scoots up behind me.

"I didn't know."

"I did not sign up for this! This was not in the deal. Everyone's staring at me!"

"I know. I'm sorry."

Pax shakes his head. "No. I'm not doing this. It's already gone too far. I'm out."

"Pax, don't. Please. We can fix it, everyone will have forgotten—"

"They *won't*! Pictures have a funny habit of sticking around. What's the betting it'll haunt us for *years*?"

"Look, it's a screw up," I say. "But let's talk to George, and—"

"GOODBYE, BARNEY, IT'S OVER!" Paxton shouts, storming off, other students stopping, staring, and watching.

I look down at the floor as the inevitable whispers and

chatter starts after the shocked silence. I didn't sign up for this either. I've got this all wrong. And now I've made myself a laughing stock, and everyone's talking about me for the wrong reasons. I've basically engineered leaking my own nudes . . . albeit, in cartoon form, with bits of me *I wish* were that big. I don't know, maybe Bronte *would* be the better president? I shuffle away, and keep a low profile for the rest of my lessons; but honestly, I think it's time to call it a day. I think it's over.

And then, on my way home, I *know* it's over, as I spot two year ten boys unpin a couple of the campaign badges from their blazers and drop them in the bin.

I stride up to the bin, and inside, there are loads of badges – a few with my name on, but mostly it's the ones with LGBT-positive slogans and symbols. Ten, twenty, thirty, I don't know, but they're all in there.

I look back up at the year ten boys, who are just standing there, watching me. "Wow," I say, deeply unimpressed.

"Ah, come on," the taller lad replies. "I can't go home with a rainbow badge on my blazer, my parents will kill me."

"Plus, they're not really for us, are they?" the shorter of the two adds, glancing at me. "Straight people, I mean. This is a gay thing."

And just as the last ember was about to die, the flames suddenly take hold again, setting me ablaze with determination.

I've been going about this all wrong.

None of this personality stuff matters.

It's not about people talking about me.

There are real issues at stake. Things that make it hard, or impossible to be an LGBTQ+ kid. Things that mean you can't be yourself. Things that make you feel less, or worthless, scared, angry, *alone*.

And there are other people who think it just isn't their problem, because they're OK, life isn't so bad for them, they'll never be abused or attacked for who they are or who they love.

Those are the important things that I need to try to change.

Those are the things I *will* change.

It's not about me at all.

It's about *everyone*.

I'm back in the race, and I know what I need to do now.

14

I bury myself in planning my hustings speech for the next few days. George and Maya must know I'm over the other election shenanigans because they pretty much leave me alone, as if they know this just needs to be about me and my speech now.

But by the following Wednesday I'm craving some company, and Maya has messaged me inviting me over to George's for one of our regular LGBTQ+ Society socials (Bronte has already sent her regrets in this instance, surely because she's busy planning more underhanded shenanigans) with the promise that it'll all be fun, just some food and maybe one of George's favourite Christmas rom-com films (even though it's May – but that really doesn't stop him, and believe me, we've all tried). The deal with our socials is that we all bring an item of food we've cooked, and this evening I'm turning up with this sensational mac and cheese dish. It's a Martha Stewart recipe, so I had to change all the weird American measurements into British ones I could actually understand, but the finished result is a triumph, featuring incredible quantities of unctuous, bubbling cheese, and topped with crispy chunks of bread. Honestly, I know I haven't had sex, but I instinctively feel this is going to be better. And I've also made a lemon drizzle cake, because it's become a bit of a joke that I go the extra mile and always turn up with two dishes, but it's more about my concern that if I don't make something sweet there's a real risk that everyone else will make savoury dishes, and what then? No dessert? Nightmare. This is just compounded by the fact everyone is now used to me providing the sweet treat, so no one else usually bothers, meaning if I suddenly don't bring it, there's a higher chance no one else *will*. I mean, this might all seem rather pathetic, but it's one of the things that keeps me awake at night.

Anyway, I'm looking forward to it. I'm ninety per cent there with my speech for tomorrow, so it'll be good to kick back with George and Maya for a bit, before it all gets serious again. Maya opens George's front door and gives me an awkward hug as I try not to drop my dish of mac 'n' cheese and cake box.

"You did bring dessert, I assume?" Maya asks as we walk through to the kitchen.

"Of course. Lemon drizzle, and I also made Martha Stewart's . . . Pax?" I stop dead just inside the kitchen door. Paxton's sitting with George at the table.

"Martha Stewart's *what*?" Pax asks.

"Mac and cheese," I say, still staring at him. What's he doing here? I thought he'd made his feelings clear and it would just be the three of us tonight?

"I did chicken pie," Pax says. "Hope it's going to be OK. Puff pastry top."

My eyes widen. "Sounds . . . nice."

Pax nods and smiles at me. "Hope so."

"Did you make the puff pastry yourself?"

"Of course I didn't."

I put my dishes down on the worktop and join them at the table. "OK, Pax, I'm glad you're here, it's nice to see you, and, again, I just wanted to apologize for everything that happened. It's my fault, no one else's. I need to take responsibility for the fact I'm the candidate here and ultimately the buck stops with me. Everything with you, the fake dating, and then the stupid, *stupid* fan art, it was a mistake. *My* mistake. I should have stopped it, I didn't, and I'm sorry."

Pax laughs. "Shut up. Nice speech, but please, shut up."

"OK," I say. "Well, welcome to the LGBTQ+ Society social. It's always nice to have new members."

"Yeah, I'm not really here for that."

I raise my eyebrows.

"I mean, George said about the food, and that always appeals, but I really just wanted to check about tomorrow?"

"What about tomorrow?"

137

"Your speech," Pax says.

"What about it?"

"Well, like, when are you going to do it?"

"The hustings are at the very start of lunch. I'm on after Bronte."

"No," Pax says. "I mean, when are you going to do the bit where you ask me to prom?"

I stare at him and he raises his eyebrows, expectantly.

I look at George, confused.

"At the end, I assume?" he continues.

I screw my face up. "What are you talking about? Obviously I'm not gonna do that now."

"What?" Pax says. "Why not?"

"Why not?! Because you broke up with me!" I say. "I mean, you *fake* broke up with me, whatever, since we weren't a thing anyway. You said it was over!"

"Exactly," Pax says. "I *fake* broke up with you."

"*What*?!"

Pax turns to George. "He doesn't know, does he?"

George takes a deep breath.

"Fuck's sake, George," Pax mutters.

I look manically between Pax, George and Maya. Maya just shrugs. I home in on George. "Tell me," I say.

"I told Pax to tell you it was over," George says, breezily, like this is all fine. "I told him to do it in public so people would overhear, and the gossip would keep going. We need you to be the person everyone's talking and

138

thinking about, Barney! We need to spin this story out. The ups and downs of romance! It's never a straight line from A to B, there's got to be detours and setbacks: that's all part of it. It's what the people want." He smiles.

"You fake ended our fake dating?" I say. "And now. . .?"

"Now," George says, "you will fake ask Pax to prom and it'll be fake back on again."

I bury my face in my hands. "Oh, bloody hell."

"Yum, yum! Who's for some of Paxton's chicken pie, then?" George says. "Or, I've made a moussaka!"

"You're a . . . Machiavellian . . . nightmare, George, I can't believe you. . ." I look up at him, annoyed and impressed in equal measure. "Why do you think manipulating me like this is a good idea? That stupid fan art was a disaster, got me in trouble with Mr Hubbard—"

"Oh, that doesn't matter!" George says. "Again, the point is, it got people talking. It got you in people's heads. That's why I did it. Anyone for a portion of Maya's chicken katsu curry?"

"Hold on one second and just you back-pedal a bit, mister!" I say. *"That's why I did it*?!"

George blinks at me. "Oh, Jesus, Barney, I wish you'd trust me. Yes, I asked for the fan art to be more sexy than you were thinking; yes, I knew how people would react to it; and yes, I absolutely posted it on purpose without showing you, knowing that you'd veto it, but also knowing, rightly, it would go viral around school."

"How dare you," I growl.

"Thank me later."

"For what?!" I howl.

"For the fact you have overtaken Bronte in the opinion polls. You're on sixty per cent. And the general consensus amongst the students is that the school, and Bronte, overreacted about the picture. They're both seen as prudish and out of touch by most of the students we polled." He glances at my incredulous face. "Come on, you know it's true. However much some people want to bury their heads in the sand about it, the fact is all teenagers are curious about this sort of stuff. And some teenagers find it, dare I say, *titillating*? My god, what a newsflash! So now no one is thinking about Barney the virgin any more, are they? Greek salad?"

"I actually cannot believe this!" I say. "I'm not some puppet. You can't just pull my strings, George, and have me do whatever you want!"

"You agreed I had one job: to get you elected. And that's exactly what I'm going to do," George says, spooning a generous portion of mac and cheese onto his plate. "This looks *nice*, Barns!"

"Yes, it's nice, it's *Martha Stewart*!" I hiss. "And your words are all very fine, except I'd like to know what's going on!"

"Not being rude though, Barns. . ." Maya begins.

"Go ahead, stick the knife in!"

"I'm not sticking the knife in!" she protests.

"Tell me I'm a nightmare!"

"No, because you're not—"

"Out of touch, misguided, stupidly thinking some people in this school might actually be concerned about real issues that genuinely affect LGBT kids!" I turn fully to her. "Did you know about all of this?"

Maya swallows.

"Amazing," I say.

"It's not like his plan hasn't worked," Maya tells me. "You want to win, don't you?"

"Yeah, I do, but there are real issues we need to address. You know, there are students who won't wear LGBT badges out of school because of how their parents would react. *That's* the sort of thing we need to be focussing on!"

"I agree," George says. "And now everyone is focussed on you, and how relatable and cool you are, you can focus on the real issues in what I'm very confident, will be an excellent speech at hustings – which you're going to tell us all about while we eat, and then we'll all watch *A Castle for Christmas* to relax!" He raises his glass of sparkling water. "Cheers to that!"

15

To be fair, the school is taking the LGBTQ+ Society seriously, and that isn't something you could have ever said before. Last year I was fobbed off when I asked for funding for our own Pride celebration day, but now they've arranged for hustings to happen in the main hall, to an audience of several hundred, and they're also live streaming it on the school YouTube channel so other students who can't fit in the hall can see it. They've set up a microphone on the stage, there's projection facilities if we want to use PowerPoint, and one of the school technicians is even sitting in the booth at the back, operating the stage lights, checking the mic levels, and cuing any music we might want. Even though it's lunchtime, the hall is rammed. And not just students: loads of the teachers have come along too.

I'd never have predicted this level of interest in a million years. It makes me more nervous . . . but I think the other thing I might be feeling is a little bit of pride. Bronte's actions were deeply annoying, and clearly motivated by self-interest, but actually, they have created a buzz around the club, and people do seem invested in the outcome of this election, and maybe that's not such a bad thing, and maybe just a *very* little bit of Bronte's idea to open this up to the whole school wasn't completely terrible.

I'm sitting on the front row between George and Maya, who are both power-dressed in black suits with white shirts and black ties. I look like I'm under mafia protection.

Bronte's up first, any moment now, and I'm sure she'll deliver a good speech. The question is: will she pull anything out of the bag I'm not expecting? I take a shaky sip from my little bottle of Evian.

"What the hell is that?" George hisses.

"Water."

"No, no, no," he mutters, plucking it from my sweaty hands. "You can't be seen with bottled *mineral* water! It's an environmental catastrophe – really bad optics – *here*." He rummages in his rucksack and hands me a reusable metal bottle thing, then adds, "It's still mineral water, obviously, but if anyone asks, it's tap." He sniffs and nudges my leg with his. "Hush up, she's on."

Bronte glides serenely on to the stage, acknowledging the applause from the crowd and waving at a few whooping people – well, Big Mandy and a couple of her mates. She takes position behind the lectern and confidently waits for the noise to die down. "Friends from the queer community and allies: welcome, and thank you for joining us today. *President of the LGBTQ+ Society*. It's got quite a ring to it, hasn't it? And this year, more than ever, it's important to pick the right candidate, since there is a unique opportunity which could mean representing our school not just locally, not just nationally, but *globally*. It falls on your shoulders to make that first decision, the one that will shape our ability to reach the ultimate prize. And I'm not going to stand here today and bore you rigid with all my ideas and proposals. Most of you know me. You know I'm hard-working, dedicated, and sensible – and yet I still enjoy a laugh, because, at the end of the day, I'm just like you. . ."

"Except your dad is a millionaire," Maya whispers. "So, not really like us."

"So, of course, I could talk to you today about gender-neutral toilets, or tackling homophobic language, or the benefits of training teaching staff on the use of pronouns, and I've no doubt you'll hear many of these issues raised by my opponent later. . ."

She glances down at us. George gives her the subtle finger.

"No. Rather than prattle on about issues that are important to *me*, I want all of you to know that I am here to *listen*. I want to listen and understand what's important to *you*. What issues affect your everyday lives? How can I work for *you* to make *your* life better?"

"AKA, I have no concrete policies of my own," George whispers.

"She's so winging this," Maya adds.

Bronte slides the radio mic out of the stand and swaggers around to the front of the lectern, like a preacher from an American mega church. "I want to *hear* you! Black, Muslim, working class, differently-abled, non-binary, pan, aro-ace. . . If you're queer, I am here for you, I am listening, and I am ready to lead all of us into a brighter, more inclusive, more tolerant future!"

People applaud at this. I wouldn't call it rapturous or anything, but they seem to like it.

"But there are obstacles along the way. Just last week, I delivered five hundred pounds' worth of LGBTQ+ YA novels to the school library, generously donated by a local businessman. . ."

"Seriously, everyone knows it was your dad, just say it!" George hisses.

"Today," Bronte continues, "it has been brought to my attention that the school has received an anonymous complaint about those novels via a public post on their Twitter account. A parent too cowardly to put their name to a post that questions the need for such books, the *appropriateness* of such books, and outlining their concerns that younger teenagers may read such material and be 'inspired' to make life choices potentially detrimental to their future well-being."

"Get the feed up," George tells Maya.

"On it!" she replies, tapping at her phone.

"I want to address a couple of points this anonymous commenter brings up," Bronte says. "The poster thinks that access to LGBTQ+ materials in schools must encourage previously cishet students to experiment, because how else do you explain the increased numbers of young people coming out as queer these days? To which I say, BULLSHIT!"

There are a few gasps and everyone looks over to Mr Hubbard, to see if he'll react to her swearing. He stands with arms folded and a grim expression, but isn't stopping her.

"Access to LGBTQ+ materials, and an atmosphere of inclusion, makes students who always *were* LGBTQ+ simply feel more comfortable and empowers them to be their true selves! We are leaving behind the days when people had to cower in the shadows, living a lie, afraid of who they really were because of what other people would say, think, or do in response. We are leaving those days behind precisely because we are now talking about it, recognizing it as a part of life, just as it should be!"

People applaud. I join in. She's right. She's absolutely right.

"And this notion of 'appropriateness', this idea that LGBTQ+ identities are not something that should be discussed until a person is in their mid-teens, or something,

I also say, BULLSHIT! Because unless you are also saying that no child should watch a Disney movie where a prince and princess kiss, or a TV show where a heterosexual couple fancy each other, flirt, fall in love, or whatever, then your comment is rooted in homophobia, plain and simple."

More applause. I watch as Mandy looks up at Bronte, who is lapping up the love. I expected to see admiration on Mandy's face, but for some reason, it looks more like unease.

"And if you *are* saying that young people shouldn't see that sort of content either, then I say to you . . . BULLSHIT! Get your head out of the sand and wake up to the reality of life in the twenty-first century! Sex is everywhere. The metaphorical stable door isn't just open, it's off its hinges, and the horse hasn't just bolted, it's fled to another continent! The horse ain't coming back in the stable! So either you accept that, and help young people deal with that reality, by giving them the tools they need to be safe and not to live in fear and shame, or you keep your little head in the sand, and think the only thing young people should read about is little harvest mice wearing aprons! It's BULLSHIT!"

The applause is wild at this point. Everyone's engaged with this now . . . everyone except Mandy, who looks super uncomfortable, which is weird because not so long ago, she was loving the attention of singing a promposal to Bronte.

"Fellow students, let me assure you, I have not taken this lying down."

Nico and a couple other football lads call out whoops, but enough death glares get them to settle down.

"I have already spoken to Mr Hubbard and the senior leadership team. I have made all these points – albeit with slightly less swearing – and, fellow students, they *agree* with me! The post won't be ignored, it'll be responded to using all the arguments I have raised! The precious LGBTQ+ YA books will still be available in the library for every single student in this school to enjoy!"

A chant of "Bronte! Bronte!" starts up, which she allows for about five seconds, and then quells down. Mandy swallows and stares down at the floor. *What is up with her?*

"This is always going to be my promise to you: if you elect me as LGBTQ+ Society president, I will always, *always*, put the lives of the LGBTQ+ students in this school first! I will always champion you! I'm not afraid, I'll stick my neck out, I'll always do what's right. And the fight of LGBTQ+ equality will *always* be right!"

Bronte soaks up all the applause and cheering, smiling – not smugly, but sort of humbly. Like she's really touched by this outpouring of approval. When the noise has died down again, she takes a moment, and it feels like she's looking every single person in the room in the eye. "At the end of the day, I'm just a girl, standing in front of an electorate, asking them to . . . vote for me."

I mean, really? I wouldn't have ended with a naff half-quote from *Notting Hill*, especially as I'm not sure it's a reference many of the students here would get anyway. Unless she's hoping they think she made it up herself? I only get it because even though I insist *Notting Hill* isn't a Christmas rom-com, George insists it is, so we've seen it multiple times.

Anyway, it gets more applause, and now the floor's open to questions.

Nico Murphy stands up first. "Yeah, just wanted to say that I really like lesbians. Like, you girls are *so hot*."

Bronte looks at him, pityingly, while one of the teaching staff goes over to Nico, says a few words to him, and then escorts him out of the hall, while Nico mutters, "Aw, come on, man! I was being nice!"

Bronte rolls her eyes and scans the crowd. "Um, yes? Danny Orlando?"

"Hi!" Danny Orlando says, standing up. "Great speech, may I say? Lots to think about, digest. . ."

"And shit out," George mutters.

"So, what I'm wondering is, how does a straight, white dude fit in to all this? Lots of people in this school fit into that category, and you talked about wanting to help everyone, so, like, how does that work, because I didn't hear you mention straight, white dudes *at all*."

There are murmurs of agreement within the audience, although predominantly from straight, white dudes.

Bronte smiles, patiently, doubtless aware this is Danny trying to wind her up. "Thank you for your question,

Danny. You'll notice I didn't specifically mention straight, Black dudes either. Or straight girls, of any colour. . ."

"Or bisexuals!" an angry-looking girl sitting behind me shouts.

Bronte grimaces slightly. "Everyone is valid, and I want to listen to everyone. But, as a straight, white dude, Danny, I think you might need to acknowledge that, for once in your existence, this isn't about you."

This gets more applause, including from Danny. "Nice answer!" he shouts. "You might have got my vote, Bronte!"

Nico Murphy is escorted back into the hall by the teacher, holding his hands up in a gesture of contrition. "Just want to apologize to lesbians everywhere," he says.

Bronte rolls her eyes again. "Thank you for listening, folks. I do hope I'll be able to celebrate my victory with you all tomorrow. In the meantime, please welcome the other candidate to the stage, Barney Brown."

George leans in to my ear. "Ignore the tweet about the books; we've bigger fish to fry. Oh, and Danny's last question gives you a good lead-in."

I nod, take a deep breath, Maya and George both squeeze my shoulders, I turn confident, fun, happy Barney *on*, and bounce up the set of steps that leads to the stage, taking the mic from Bronte with a jaunty "Thank you!", sliding it back into the stand, unfolding my notes and grasping hold of the side of the lectern for dear life. Yes, I'm bricking it. But I can't let anyone see that.

I do the thing that Bronte did: I scan the crowd, making eye contact, while I wait for the applause to die down. There's a group of year ten girls on the front row to my right, giggling and whispering to each other, and not-so-subtly pointing at me, which I suspect is about the fan art. Danny and Nico are whispering also, Danny breaking into laughter and slapping Nico on the leg several times, before meeting my eyes and giving me the most unsupportive thumbs up I've ever seen.

Can't wait to see his face when he hears me start this thing.

16

I want to start by picking up on something Danny Orlando just asked: *where do straight people fit in to all this?* Stay with me, because I have a suggestion. The LGBTQ+ Society is everything to me. I don't say that lightly. It's *everything*. I spent my first three-and-a-half years at this school scared of who I was, frightened, and lonely. In the LGBTQ+ Society, I found a community. I found people who didn't judge me. A place where I felt safe. Somewhere where I *could* be myself, and that was OK, no one would bully me or abuse me or make me feel like I was an outsider.

But why does it have to be like that? Why do I have to have a special club to have that acceptance and feel that way? Why can't my safe, happy community be with *all* of you, every day of the week, not just for half-an-hour on Wednesday lunchtimes? A lot of us go and support the football team in the big matches. We show up for the athletics, and the orchestra and the school musical. Can't we all support the

LGBTQ+ Society too? Even if, like me with the two hundred metre sprint, it's not entirely your thing and you think you've nothing in common with those of us in it?

Let me tell you a story I think we could learn a bit of a lesson from. In the 1970s a lot of feminists were accused of being lesbians, and some feminists thought this damaged their cause. Lesbians were described as the "lavender menace" and excluded from the Second Congress to Unite Women in New York. But a bunch of them turned up anyway, infiltrating the meeting and standing up, ripping open their shirts to reveal "lavender menace" T-shirts underneath. They made space for themselves, demanded to be heard, and, after talks and workshops which the Lavender Menace facilitated, most people realized they had more in common than that which divided them. In the process, the insult "lavender menace" was reclaimed, and meanwhile, members were told to confirm, never deny if people accused them of being lesbians. Think about that. What if we did that? When people say "That's so gay" or "You're so gay", what if the reaction at our school was always "But I am gay"? When that statement no longer has emotional power, we'll have succeeded in making change, making this a truly inclusive school. And folks, according to a recent survey of our generation, only 48% of thirteen-to twenty-year-olds identified as "exclusively heterosexual". That's right, 52% of us – that's *the majority* of us – are at least a little bit gay, and let's be real, those stats are probably on the conservative side because admitting it

153

still has so much stigma for some people, so the real figures will be higher. Seems to me it's absolutely right we should all be in the LGBTQ+ Society. But even if you're not even just a teeny tiny bit queer, I still want your support. I want you as a member. Because if we all belong, if we all see, just like the Lavender Menace lesbians, that there's more that unites us than separates us, then we've removed all the stigma and we can be one, big happy family. Here for one another. Looking out for one another. Supporting each other. Our LGBTQ+ Society shouldn't just be a club that meets once a week because being LGBT – and accepting LGBT people – shouldn't just happen once a week. We should be free to be ourselves and accepted for ourselves twenty-four-seven. The LGBTQ+ Society is all of us, every day, everywhere!

Here's my gay agenda: we're all voting for this, right? So let's make the whole school the gay club.

17

There's silence. I think people are processing what I've just said.

And then two year eight girls stand up, rip open their school shirts, and reveal "Lavender Menace" T-shirts underneath. "We're in Gay Club!" they shout.

There's another beat of shocked, "WTF?!" type of silence, including from me, because *what the hell is this?* before three year nine boys are on their feet, also opening their school shirts, revealing T-shirts branded with "Gay Club" on them.

After that, it's like dominoes. Kids standing up, shouting that they're in Gay Club, or the LGBTQ+ Society, or whatever they choose to call it. And people are applauding and cheering. I lock eyes with George and Maya. They're both smiling as much as I am. Maya gives me two thumbs up, while George blows me a kiss. Of course they were behind this. They will have been down at the

T-shirt shop first thing, printing these things up after our chat last night, George doubtless persuading a few key allies to be stooges in the audience. But it's worked. Everyone's saying it. Everyone wants to belong.

Danny Orlando gets to his feet, clapping and whooping.

And it's like that moment when an instant barbecue catches light, because *Woompf!* The whole place erupts, cheering, on their feet, a standing-freakin'-ovation!

I'm laughing now, I can't even believe it.

"Any questions?" I ask into the mic.

The audience settle back down again, but Danny Orlando stays on his feet. "Incredible speech," he says. "Very moving, so much to think about. But I just want to say two things. . ." He surveys the audience, grinning. "I'M IN THE GAY CLUB!"

Everyone cheers and whoops. Then locks eyes with me across the hall. "Aaaannnd . . . BARNEY BROWN FOR PRESIDENT!"

The whole room erupts again. I just stare back at him, mouth hanging open, because did Danny Orlando really just say that? About me?

I glance down towards Bronte, who looks *furious*. She's whispering, urgently, in Mandy's ear, doubtless reformulating plans, working out how their strategy needs to change now. She misjudged this. And now, for the first time, it really feels like we're in the lead here. We read the room, and we delivered ideas that actually resonated with the student body.

Well, let's knock it out of the park then.

"OK," I say. "Well, I do have one more thing I'd like to say, actually. I wasn't sure if I should do this, but standing up here today, seeing and hearing your reaction to everything I've had to say, well . . . it's made me less afraid. This is what it can be like, everyone. We can be there for each other. We can support. And when we do, amazing things happen. So, um . . . Paxton Lee? I was wondering . . . would you do me the great honour of allowing me to be your date to prom?"

There's a collective gasp that's part "Awww!" from the audience. Everyone turns to look at Pax, over at the far right of the hall. He's doing a good job of looking the right mix of slightly embarrassed and really chuffed. "I do!" he shouts, getting down on one knee.

That gets a really big laugh and cheer.

This is the perfect ending – just like George said it would be – and now, that's the cue for *Don't Stop Believin'* to kick in (George said it would be good for me to have an "anthem"), and I bounce down the stairs, into Pax's arms. We have a bit of a hug, the school's new (fake) golden couple, and then we leave the hall hand in hand, walking into the sunset (OK, the corridor) and election victory.

I'm in the cafeteria with the team, still lapping up all the attention ten minutes later. We're the only thing anyone's talking about, and students are still walking past, telling me they're in Gay Club, and, against all odds (because, about seventy per cent of me expected them all to tell me to shove it up my arse), I think the gamble might have paid off.

I'm still too hyped to eat anything, but George treated us all to celebratory millionaire's shortbread, and that's one thing the cafeteria do quite well, so I've managed to demolish a slice of that while we wait for the polling team to come back to us with the latest on voting intentions. To maintain the romance angle (very important, regardless of my speech, according to George), it was suggested that Paxton sit on my lap. That, it turned out, didn't work, because I'm too short, and Paxton is too long, and so now I'm sitting on *his* lap. That's where I am, probably looking like a ventriloquist's dummy, when I lock eyes with Mandy who is looking back at us from where's she's hovering at the far side of the room. And then, it's like she's made some sort of decision, and she starts coming over.

"Red alert, enemy incoming," I mutter.

Maya and George both adopt poses of indifference and borderline hostility. It's heartwarming to see. Paxton just carries on munching through his millionaire's shortbread, which is fair enough.

"Hi," Mandy says. "Can we talk?"

"That depends what we're talking about," George replies.

"OK, look." Mandy looks around quickly, apparently checking we're not being overheard. "You should know this:

it's fake. That anonymous complaint post on the school's account that Bronte based her speech on? It's not real. We posted it, from a fake account on a burner phone. Now, I'm guessing you have questions, and you want the receipts? So, how about we have that talk?"

18

We're back in Room 120 – blinds drawn, door locked.

"Phone," George tells Mandy.

"What?"

"Hand me your phone."

She screws her face up. "Why?"

"To check you're not recording this." He clicks his fingers. *"Phone."*

Mandy shakes her head and hands it over. "Wow, you guys are something else, aren't you?" She blows out a breath. "Six ones if you want the passcode."

George raises his eyebrows as he taps it in. "You should get a better passcode." He glances over the phone. "OK, fine." And hands it back to her. "Talk," George says, sitting down with me, Pax and Maya, as we face Mandy, like some horrific interview panel, across the table.

"Bronte was desperate after the mood swung in Barney's favour over the cartoon of him and Paxton,"

Mandy begins. "Our polling put Barney in his biggest lead over her yet – although, worth noting, our figures put them both down around thirty per cent, with a whopping forty per cent undecideds. . ."

"Probably more down to your poor methodology, ours have Barney much higher, but go on," George replies.

"Bronte knew she needed something big, something that would really demonstrate her passion for LGBT rights. People complain about queer books in school libraries all the time, it's just . . . no one had complained about any in ours. So . . . Bronte instructed me to buy a pay-as-you-go mobile, set up a fake Twitter account, and post the complaint you heard about in her speech. A complaint she could then be the first to "see", and speak out against."

I shake my head. *Unbelievable.* And yet, totally Bronte.

"How can you prove it?" George asks.

Mandy reaches into her pin-badge adorned rucksack and pulls out another phone, which she slides across the table to George. "It's all on there."

George takes the phone and nods. "And why would you tell us all this now?" He folds his arms. "Seems . . . *odd.*"

I sit back. It does seem odd. It feels like it could be a set-up.

"Well, first of all, it's morally wrong, it crosses a line, and I'm ashamed to have been part of it. There are plenty of folk out there who despise us, hate us even. There are people who would happily see every right we've gained be taken away again. But stoking those fires of division when no division actually exists, well, what's the point? It's the sort of trick Russian bots pull, isn't it? Culture wars! Except . . . is there, really?" Mandy sits back in her chair. "And, to be honest, Bronte's insistence we do this just made my other decision easier. I only wanted to date her for a bit of fun before uni – I didn't sign up for *this*. I mean, there's a reason I quit being president. I'm going to dump her."

"You mean, you and her were actually *real*?" Maya almost howls

"Um . . . yes?"

"Really?" I add. "But the whole promposal thing? The duet together? It seemed so fake!"

Mandy looks at me with very unimpressed eyes. "Barney, we wouldn't be the first girls who found themselves falling in love while rehearsing a song sung by two lesbian characters from a musical."

"That's basically what she said!"

"Because that's what happened!" Mandy sighs.

"Oh. My. *God!*" Maya says. "She really went and got together with someone else!" She throws her hands in the air. "Genuinely, like I meant nothing to her! Goodbye, five months means nothing, move on!"

Mandy studies her for a moment. "Sure. But . . . I don't know, it's funny, how you never really know someone until you actually make it official and start dating. I'd always fancied Bronte, but obviously. . ." She vaguely gestures towards Maya, whose eyes widen as she crosses her arms over her chest. "But then you two split up and. . ."

"I mean, if it was me, I wouldn't just get right in there the moment someone's had a break-up, you know?" Maya huffs. "Call me an old-fashioned romantic, but dead relationships deserve some respect, but OK, we're all different, go on."

Mandy blows out a breath. "Sorry, OK? Anyway, a summer fling was kind of appealing. . . So I did the grand gesture to help seal the deal—"

"Footnote to add that Katy Perry is *not* a great example of a lesbian icon," Maya interrupts.

Mandy purses her lips, but chooses to ignore Maya. "But then Bronte kept going on and on about her campaign, so we never really had much fun. Even when we were 'having fun'—"

Maya looks like she's about to be sick.

"—she'd start talking about how she was polling. Bit of a passion-killer, right? Plus . . . I've seen a side to Bronte I don't like. I get it, she's ambitious, and I love that, but if she's prepared to be dishonest about it? And she's started treating me like someone who works for her rich family, having me running around after her, which isn't the greatest feeling in the world."

Maya raises an eyebrow. "Hmm. It's almost like really *knowing* and *understanding* someone is a good idea, before embarking on a very public relationship."

Mandy blows out another breath. I must say, she's doing a good job of staying composed during Maya's passive-aggressive onslaught. "So, I'm out. But I also need to put right this wrong. So keep the phone, it's all the evidence you need. What you do with it is your choice. Go public, don't go public, whatever you like."

"If we do, you'll probably end up implicated too," Maya says, unable to conceal a smile.

Mandy shrugs. "I'm literally about to go on exam leave. I think I'll cope with the 'drama'." She pushes her chair back and stands up. "Good luck. You've got my vote, Barney."

"Sure. Thanks."

"I'll let you out," George says, following Mandy to the door.

When she's slipped through, he carefully locks it again behind her, then turns back to us. "Get screenshots and put a tweet thread together. After Barney's brilliant speech, this'll finish her. Let's drop the bomb and end this thing." He glances at Maya. "If you're . . . OK with that, Maya?"

"Why wouldn't I be?"

"Almost felt like you were defending Bronte a bit there," George says.

"You still have feelings for her, man," Paxton sniffs.

"I *wasn't* defending her, I was trying to call Mandy out on grabbing people on the rebound when they're emotionally wounded – not a good look – and I *don't* have feelings for her, other than ones of *hurt and fury* that she was able to move on so quickly, and was actually wooed by a frigging KATY PERRY song, of all things!" She looks at Paxton. *"Man."*

With that, Maya sets to work (with completely unconcealed glee, she's literally grinning), and within minutes she's collected all the relevant evidence and it's all been put together on our official channels. Headed *The Truth About That Anonymous Complaint,* we detail exactly what's happened and include my view on it all – basically paraphrasing what Mandy's thoughts were – but obviously twisting the knife further, by asking, *what sort of person do you want as president? A liar and manipulator? Or me, Barney Brown – who you can trust.*

We're moments from pressing the nuclear button (as it were) when Maya asks: "What if Mandy denies it all – can we even trace the phone to her?"

George smiles, demonically. "Mandy may not have recorded our little meeting, but I certainly did." He pulls his phone out from his lapel pocket and twirls it between his fingers. "If we need to, we release the audio."

"Press send," I say.

The post gets likes and retweets within seconds. Three minutes later, and the chatter is already reaching fever pitch. Five minutes later, there's a hammering at the door.

"I know you're in there!"

Bronte's voice.

"Let me in *now*."

I mean, honestly, I've no idea how this whole thing became quite so dramatic, but here we are. George shrugs, unlocks the door, and jumps back as Bronte smashes her way into the room. "Take it down," she demands.

"Sorry, Bronte," I say. "The truth's in the public interest."

"It's very easy to deny."

"Except we have a recording of Mandy confessing everything," I say.

Bronte glares at me. "Well, I have evidence too. Evidence that you and Paxton are faking it. That night of your supposed date in Nando's? Remember the waitress who served you?" She grins, triumphantly at me. "That was my *sister*. She's earning some money in her year off before uni. She overheard your conversation. You were literally talking about your fake relationship and how to make the supposedly 'leaked' photo look realistic."

"Does your sister have a recording of this alleged conversation?"

Bronte laughs. "What does it matter? She's no reason to lie to me, in fact, she barely tolerates me, and the allegation alone will sow enough seeds of doubt in people's minds. Who needs actual evidence for anything these days? True or false, mud sticks."

"Feels like that would be a massive violation of customer privacy, though," George says, doing a great job of staying calm throughout all this. "Or do Nando's employees regularly reveal the private conversations of their customers? Would that go down well on social media? I'm trying to think. . ."

"Oh, shut up. Take down the post about me in the next two minutes, or the truth gets out."

"We'll issue an immediate denial. It'll look exactly like what it is: petty retaliation," George says.

"Plus, it isn't true," Pax adds.

We all turn to look at him. He takes an unsteady breath. "Can I kiss you?" he asks.

"What?" I say.

"Can I kiss you?"

"Oh, um . . . yes! Of course! It would be a pleas—"

He lunges towards me, clamps his mouth over mine, and starts snogging me. I mean, I was expecting a chaste little peck, not really this: this is like a proper kiss and I kind of wanted my first real kiss to be, well . . . real, but also it's fine because this is just a fake kiss to prove to Bronte that we're not fake, so probably doesn't count as a legitimate first kiss anyway. I guess it's good practice, though. Pax holds me tighter, his hands working all over my back, as his tongue works its way around my mouth. He presses in to me, and to my surprise, I start getting hard. This wasn't in the plan, it's a bit *too* real, but I carry on, because, actually, this isn't at all bad. In fact, it's quite. . .

Pax extracts himself from me. "That was with

tongues, in case you couldn't tell."

Bronte rolls her eyes.

"Real enough for you?" Pax continues. "Or do you need me to go down on him in front of you too?"

It's a bold move, and one, I hope, we don't need to follow through on.

At least, not right now.

Or . . . ever?

Ugh. I don't need to be thinking about Paxton right now.

I never fancied him before.

Do I really now?

I push it to the back of my mind.

"You won't get away with this," Bronte says, glaring at Maya. "And where do you get off calling it 'Gay Club' in your speech and on those stupid T-shirts? It's the LGBTQ+ Society! God, gay guys think they're the centre of the universe!" She storms out of the room.

We all stand in silence for a moment.

George glances at me. "Hmm. Something's put a smile on your face."

"Huh?" Was I smiling? I immediately adjust my demeanour. "Sorry." I snatch a look at Pax. He's back to looking glum. Maybe I wasn't good at kissing? How did *he* get so good? "I take it we're not deleting the post?"

"Are we bollocks," Maya says. "This thing is *not* going to go Bronte's way. But I'll warn you now, after the anger and threats will come tears. That's the way people like Bronte operate. *Watch*."

"I'm not sure that's a problem?" George says.

Maya raises her eyebrows in a "you'll see" type of way.

And sure enough, just five minutes later (five minutes in which George messages our polling team for the latest figures, Maya and Pax keep tabs on social media, and in which I replay the kiss with Pax in my head and get hard again), Bronte has new posts on all her socials:

> *It has been brought to my attention that the anonymous post about the LGBTQ+ library books was in fact faked by a trusted member of my team. I apologize to everyone I have let down. The team member in question has been let go. I am devastated. I should have checked the source for myself, but am reeling following a recent bereavement. The truth is, I have barely been holding it together these last few days and don't know how much more heartbreak I can take. I am so sorry. B.*

Maya simply has an "I fucking told you so!" look on her face.

"What . . . bereavement? Is that . . . real?" I ask. "Who died?"

"No one's died," Maya snaps. "This is classic Bronte.

It's for sympathy. And to distract everyone from the real issue!" She leans in to me. "Do not fall for this crap!"

"Damn it!" George hisses. "See, this is the clever thing. She's blaming it on a member of her 'team'. She knows we have the audio confession, but if we leak that, we're gonna look like the assholes, since she's apparently grieving. There's a tiny chance someone really has died, but regardless, we can't question it, and it's not going to look good if we keep hammering on about Bronte's fake tweet. She's deflected all this and unless we can prove it isn't true. . ."

Paxton frowns. "Would she really try to deflect one lie with another lie?"

Maya laughs. "I wholeheartedly believe she would *kill* to get what she wants. What do a few lies matter?"

George is scrolling through her Twitter. "She's already getting replies. People sending their love, thinking about her, blah, blah. . ."

"Is *anyone* talking about her lies and duplicity?"

George shakes his head and I throw my hands up in the air. Literally, at this point in the game, I don't know what to think or do any more.

"*Who* is *Piggles*?" George asks.

"It's her stupid guinea pig," Maya says. She raises her eyebrows. "Is that who it is? That's the bereavement? Piggles . . . is dead?"

George nods. "Apparently. Someone just tweeted to

say that 'Piggles was such a sweet soul'."

I laugh. "Oh. My. *Actual*. This is ridiculous. We're not allowing a period of mourning for a guinea pig." I look between George, Maya and Pax, who all have concerned expressions on their faces. "We're not. We can't. Can we? We . . . are?"

"You need to tweet your condolences," George tells me.

"Really?"

"Do it. You're so sorry, thinking of her, sending love, thoughts and prayers, *et cetera*. Don't want to be seen as heartless," George explains.

"I'm not heartless!"

"Exactly. And this is the moment to temporarily bury the hatchet and offer a crumb of compassion to Bronte and her most likely fake-dead guinea pig."

"If it's not dead, it probably will be soon. . ." Maya mutters darkly.

I'm on my phone. "OK, so, I'm putting *so sorry for your tragic loss, thinking of you and beautiful Piggles* and then a broken heart emoji . . . and a crying face?"

"Too much," George says. "Might come across as sarcastic."

I look up from the screen. "Could the whole thing be interpreted that way? Maybe I should delete 'tragic' in that case?"

"*Sorry to hear this?*" Maya offers.

"*Sorry to hear this sad news?*" George adds. "Because, yeah, 'tragic' is a bit OTT, right? It's not a massacre, it's a dead rodent."

"Are they rodents?" I ask.

"What did you think they were?"

"I dunno, like a type of mini pig, I guess?"

"Don't be ridiculous, Barney," George says. "How about just a simple *Thinking of you?*"

"Mmm," I say. "Is that a bit . . . dismissive, almost?"

Maya nods. "Yeah, like that's the bare minimum response, right? 'Thinking of you' but not even 'sorry'? She won't like that, she's all about the drama, that girl."

George looks down at his phone screen again and sighs. "See, there's a lot of responses to this already, all pretty similar. We need to come up with something more unique for you; you can't just parrot off the same meaningless platitudes as everyone else. What about a quote?"

I screw up my face. "About dead guinea pigs?"

"Or about death in general," George says, patiently. "Something that's a bit more special and moving. You're her opponent in the election after all, and if this is actually getting her sympathy, we don't want her stealing any of your vote."

Maya looks up from Googling. "'*They may be small, but guinea pigs leave an enormous paw print on your heart.*' This is actually a graphic, you could attach it to the tweet."

"OK, OK," I say, hammering out a new tweet. "So

that, and then maybe, *Piggles was so beautiful, he'll be sorely missed?"*

"*He?*" Maya says.

"*She?*" I reply.

Maya shrugs. George groans. "Ugh! The last thing we need in this late stage of the campaign is you blundering around misgendering a guinea pig! *They!* Use *they! They'll* be sorely missed."

"Do you know what?" I say. "Screw it. We're in the right here. We shouldn't let this obvious tactic, this conveniently dead rodent, get in the way of the real story. Bronte lied about a homophobic hate campaign. Surely the electorate aren't so stupid that they won't be able to see that? Right?" I nod at everyone. "We leave it. Rise above it. Let it run its course. And tomorrow, we sweep to victory."

19

I dropped Kyle a message last night, updating him about my speech, and Piggles, and asking how things were going at his school. Kyle had sent his guinea-pig condolences, (which was kind of sweet, coming from him) said my speech sounded "so good" (which was also sweet of him), and told me it was a nightmare at Branscombe Boys: Ben was still in the lead, and a campaign to get more boys to join the LGBT Society (and hopefully swing the vote in the process) had backfired due to Ben (who has, to date, only approached the whole thing as a joke) digging out the society's constitution and pointing out voting rights are only granted after three months of membership.

Not for the first time, that made me think all of my problems could have been prevented if *we'd* had a constitution, and (perhaps prematurely since I haven't technically been elected yet) I may have started making a few notes which could form the basis for such a thing.

OK, it's actually a couple of pages of typed A4, but I want to hit the ground running when I'm president.

Which I will be, right?

Because it's so close now.

Danny Orlando is leaning up against the main gates as I arrive the next morning. "Big day, huh, Barney?" He grins.

"Big day," I agree.

"So sad about Bronte, though." He shakes his head like he can't believe it.

"Do you mean the guinea pig?"

Danny clutches his chest. "Cuts you up man, when a pet dies. I remember my dog, Chester. Wrecked me for *weeks*. I still tear up, just thinking about him."

I glance at Danny. He *does* seem a bit upset, which is surprising, since (a) I assumed he was taking the piss and (b) I didn't think boys like Danny Orlando had emotions – at least, not ones they exhibited publicly. I'm pretty sure public displays of emotion are in violation of the Bro Code.

"Jack Russell," Danny continues. "Yappy as hell, but I loved him, you know?"

"Sorry . . . for your loss, Danny."

"Thanks, man."

"Of course," I say, readjusting my rucksack on my shoulder, "you might say the *real* issue here is that Bronte disseminated false information that she failed to verify, causing needless drama and potentially creating further rifts between communities."

Danny furrows his brow. "*Disseminate*? Isn't that something to do with bulls making cows pregnant?"

"No, Danny, that's *inseminate*."

He still looks confused.

"Sperm," I clarify.

"What's Bronte been doing with sperm? I thought she wasn't into sperm?"

"Right, OK, this isn't to do with sperm. It's about honesty, truth and who you trust to be your next LGBTQ+ Society president. Also, I'm not sure anyone is massively *into* sperm, FYI."

He grins at me again. "It's funny, hearing you say 'sperm'."

"Is it? Great. Well, I hope I can count on your vote today, Danny."

He sucks in a breath. "Yeah, man, but don't you think you should at least have sent your condolences to Bronte?"

I blink at him.

"Like, she's sad, man. So sad she forgot to check if that thing she did the speech about was true or not. Just seems like a nice thing to do."

"Uh-huh? Well, I had some really important stuff to think about last night, and I don't have time for social media. I can feel sorry for her, I *do* feel sorry for her."

"Yeah, but, you didn't *say* that on social media, so,

like, how do we know?"

"Putting it on Twitter doesn't mean it's true, Danny."

"Yeah, but you gotta say it!"

"I have said it. I've said it to you, and I've said it to her."

Danny shrugs. "OK, dude, whatever you say. You're the politician guy!"

"I'm not a politician, I just want to make a difference for LGBT students at this school. So. Vote Barney."

"Vote Barney," Danny repeats. "We're all in the Gay Club! I'm gonna stand at these gates, and that's what I'm gonna tell every single kid who walks through."

I raise my eyebrows. "Oh. Thanks."

"Can't be too careful. Like, my money's totally on you to win, but it's not over 'til the lady who we shouldn't body-shame sings, right?"

George and Maya are suddenly behind me, both dressed in their black suits from yesterday still, but now with a pink tie (Maya) and pink bow tie (George) – a hint, perhaps, of the celebratory festivities to come. "Good," George says. "We need to talk."

Danny gives me a wink and shouts "BARNEY FOR PRESIDENT!" as George and Maya literally push me forwards, at speed, away from him.

"Problem," George says. "It made no sense, so I asked them to run the sums again, but it still came out the same. Your ratings are plummeting. As of last night, you're down to twenty per cent."

"So, I swallowed my pride and called Mandy," Maya says. "She's obviously off the team now, and probably busy swooping in like a vulture to pick over the remains of someone else's relationship, but the last set of polling figures they did for Bronte shows a similar pattern. She's plummeting too."

"So we're *both* losing popularity?"

George nods. "Current estimates are that as much as sixty per cent of the students aren't sure who to vote for. Now, this is far from ideal, but it's also an opportunity. It means any small thing we do today could swing it. People are looking for literally any reason to vote for you or vote for Bronte, or not, as the case may be."

I blow out a breath. "Jesus, it's like no one even *heard* my speech. What more do they want from me?"

George stops and turns to me. "*Compassion*, Barney. That's what they want. Well, it's one thing they want. *Compassion*."

I narrow my eyes. "Is this about that infernal guinea pig?"

"There is literally no other reason for you falling in the polls!" George hisses. "You gave the best speech, you outed Bronte as a fraud, the *only* thing that has happened since is Piggles has been carted off to the glue factory, or whatever they do with dead fluffy rats! I know it seems ridiculous, but these are the things that speak to voters. They want to see someone who cares. After all, at the end of the day, young as we are, *we are all of us being beckoned towards death's cold embrace.*"

"Jesus, what a lovely thought." I sigh. "OK! OK, fine. What do you want me to do?"

"Wicked," George says. "So, Maya's set up a GoFundMe page in your name, and you're raising funds for a homeless guinea pig charity. . ."

"*What?!*"

"'*Digs for Pigs*'" Maya adds. "I found them last night online, they basically rehome unwanted guinea pigs."

"To get the ball rolling, you'll donate thirty pounds left over from when you sold your PlayStation, we'll plaster your good deeds all over our socials throughout the day, do some updates on the grand total, maybe you'll do a sponsored run to help raise the rest—"

"Or maybe I won't."

"Doesn't matter, you'll be seen to be doing something nice. *For poor guinea pigs.*" George does a sad face, complete with indicating where tears should be.

"OK, great. I love how this was meant to be about LGBT stuff, but now it's guinea pigs. And by 'love' I mean, 'hate'."

"Well," George says, "compassion is an important part of that. Someone who *cares.* It's a good quality. Which brings me to. . ."

Maya holds up the large bag she's holding. "Meet Lesley."

I don't look in the bag. I don't need to. "Is Lesley a guinea pig?"

Maya nods. "It's funny when pets are given human names."

"Is it?"

Maya nods again. She seems very pleased about all this.

"Now you can present poor, grief-stricken Bronte with a new pet," George says. "This morning. In assembly. Everyone will cry, trust me. The one lasting sensation I want everyone to remember when they see your name on the ballot paper is something warm and fuzzy."

Unfortunately, George says this just as Nico Murphy passes by, on his way to meet Danny at the front gate. "I feel warm and fuzzy when I see your name," he says. "And then it kind of feels warm and . . . sticky." He gives me sex eyes and pouts. "I guess you have that effect on me, Bar . . . Bar . . . ah! Ah! AHHHHHHHHNEY!" He adjusts his dick. "Fuck, you're good."

I present Bronte with Lesley in sixth form assembly.

She bursts into tears and screams at me. Apparently I'm "monumentally insensitive" and "trying to capitalize on her grief for my own gain."

So, I'm not sure we can class that as a success, really.

Morning break, despite her grief and having declared a social media break (again), Bronte finds both the time and strength to post a link to a lengthy blog post (as well as recording extracts from it for TikTok) all about the death of Piggles, her mental health crisis, and the associated lack of support within the LGBTQ+ community (she means me). Apparently this whole election has "broken her" although not to the extent that she can't finish the blog with a reminder of all her key policies and why people should vote for her.

I actually want to scream.

And then I do scream.

Bronte has been blue tick verified on her social media accounts.

"*HOW*?!" I howl at George and Maya. "Literally, a blue tick means you're a 'notable person in the public eye' – how can that possibly apply to her?"

George informs me that money can buy anything, including a PR person capable of oiling wheels at social media companies, despite those companies' claims that such things aren't possible and the granting of blue ticks is a genuine meritocracy.

Honestly, it sends me into a tailspin.

Maya took Lesley back to the pet shop in the hope of getting her money back. Unfortunately, word got out about this and sparked some of the animal-rights minded students, plus a few vegans, to accuse our campaign of cruelty, and "using living creatures for our own ends, with a callous disregard as to their welfare or rights".

Lesley is now back, and it looks like one of us is going to have to take her in. George put out a message that it was a "communication breakdown" and Maya has offered her resignation, which I'm obviously not going to accept but I have to at least think about so it looks like we're taking it seriously . . . which is what George put on our social feeds:

> *Barney's presidential campaign takes animal rights extremely seriously. We are listening and we are learning, and please be assured we are looking into this matter with the utmost urgency.*

George says Lesley might have to come and live with me. Maya's family already have multiple hamsters, George has an unspecified allergy and we can't give Lesley to 'Digs for Pigs' because apparently it would be wrong to raise money for an unwanted guinea pig charity and top it off by giving them an unwanted guinea pig. Fuck's sake.

Meanwhile, nobody cares about, oh I don't know, homophobic bullying? This whole thing has become a circus. It's not even about anything any more, it feels like a reality TV show. How much outrage can there be for maximum entertainment value?

There's also a disconcerting buzz around the school. People whispering. Chatting. Sharing gossip. I can't fathom what's going on, but it's clear *something* is. Other students keep catching my eye in the corridor, then quickly looking away. Is it because they've voted for me? Or is it because they're switching to Bronte?

Morning break ends with the local paper tweeting a link to the article they've written about me donating LGBT books to the local primary school. Good. This is exactly what I need to move the conversation back to something that actually matters.

I click on the link. The article's headline is:

"Pronouns are ridiculous" Admits LGBT Society Candidate

As if that wasn't bad (and inaccurate) enough, the piece is accompanied by a photo of Bambi Sugapops smoking a cigarette outside the school, while George and I talk to her (must have been snapped incognito by the reporter). It goes on to say how I apparently went on a "vicious tirade" about "Boomers, Gen X and millennials" after introducing Bambi, "who is well known for sexually explicit shows in London's salacious Soho", to some innocent five-year-olds "to tell them that it's good to be gay".

It's already being shared around school within minutes of going live.

I'm a heartless liar who loves animal cruelty, and thinks pronouns are ridiculous.

I think there's a high chance I'm royally screwed.

Polls close at one-thirty p.m.

"Oh, did you see Katherine's article, Barney?" Bronte says to me at the start of lunch. "She's sorry it took so long to get published, and only came out on the day of voting." She grimaces. "You said some pretty wild things, but I guess you have the right to your opinions."

I stare at her, breathing through my nose. "How are you on first name terms with the reporter from the local paper?"

Bronte gives me a sweet smile. "Katherine? She's one of my sister's best mates from uni. She's doing an internship. She's terribly good. I bet she'll have a column with *The Times* within a year or two, you'll see!"

Voting is now closed. George informs me the exit polls are inconclusive. It seems it's been a tight race. Tighter than it would have been if Bronte hadn't played the victim card and shafted me with her family journalism connections.

By the end of lunch, votes have been counted, and we're all waiting in the main hall for the results. Bronte and I are on the stage, awaiting the arrival of Mr Hubbard and Mrs Buchanan, who are counting and verifying the results.

The hall is rammed. Some seats have been put at the front, but most people have piled in behind them, smashed up against each other, with more people straining to get in through the various doors. At least people care; that's something, I tell myself. And if nothing else comes of this (by which I mean, if it goes Bronte's way), at least more students know about the club now, and that can only be a good thing.

I think I'm going to be sick when I see Mr Hubbard battle and push his way through the crowd, towards the stage, Mrs Buchanan behind him.

So this is it. This is the moment. My mouth's dry, breaths sharp and tight, heart hammering.

As Mr Hubbard takes his position centre stage, I remind myself to keep my expression light and happy if he announces that Bronte has won. I have to be a good loser. I'll smile, tell Bronte well done, and shake her hand. I'll say a few words thanking my supporters and congratulating Bronte on a hard race that she deservedly won. This is what I do. Prepare for defeat, because that's usually the way things go for me.

Mr Hubbard quietens down the crowd. "It is *so good* to see how invested you've all become in the outcome of the election for president of our LGBTQ+ Society!" he says. "When the suggestion was made to open this out to the whole school, I admit, I was slightly sceptical at first, but now I've no doubt it was the right decision. As Barney Brown himself said in his speech—"

He's talking about me – is that a good sign? I think it's a good sign. . .

"Opening the LGBTQ+ Society out to the *whole* school, to each and every one of you, shows how inclusive we really are, and how supportive we are of one another. And what I hope you all take from this is that *you all have a voice* – and that voice matters! We, all of us, have the capacity to change the world. You've listened to arguments, you've made judgements, and today you've decided who you want to lead our school's LGBTQ+ Society not just for the next year, but, potentially, to national glory in Rainbow Youth's search for their ambassador school."

He surveys the crowd like a benevolent dictator, and smiles.

I wish he would hurry up.

I hope I don't faint.

I really want some water.

"Democracy isn't just important, it's *vital*. Our right, as citizens, to choose the individuals who represent us is the foundation on which any civilized society is based. But democracy has to be seen to be working. Voters have to know that their choices will be respected. . ."

OK, we get it, we let the whole school vote!

". . .And when regular systems fail, we have to consider new ones. At the end of the day, people must be allowed to speak, and in this case, *they have spoken*. The person voted as the next president of the LGBTQ+ Society has won not just by a narrow margin, but a landslide. . ."

I guess that's good. At least that will give me a clear mandate if I win, and if I lose, I won't feel like it's all because of Bronte's manipulating and dishonesty.

Mr Hubbard takes a deep breath, like this is a seismic moment in history, and he wants to savour every last bit of it. "It gives me enormous pleasure to announce, that the winner of this election, your next president of the LGBTQ+ Society, on a landslide ninety per cent of the vote, is. . ."

He waits, dramatically, because no matter what you think about the importance of democracy and no matter how much respect you think it deserves, everyone loves a TV talent show-style dramatic pause moment.

Mr Hubbard smiles. "Danny Orlando!"

20

It's like a dream.

A bad one.

I stare into the middle distance, not focussing on anything.

Around me, there's cheering, but it's muffled, as if I'm not in the room.

Movement.

Danny Orlando, being crowd-surfed towards the stage, bouncing along, supported by what is apparently his legion of adoring fans.

This can't even be. . .

His name wasn't even on the ballot.

It wasn't on the ballot!

No. No!

That realization snaps me out of it. I immediately lock eyes with Bronte, who looks as stunned as I feel.

I look down at George and Maya. George is having a

frantic call with someone on his mobile. Maya just looks . . .
utterly confused.

The cheering is. . .

It's like a rock concert.

Bronte's at my side. "What the hell is this?"

"It's a coup, that's what it is!" I stride over to Mr
Hubbard, who is very much joining in with the clapping
and cheering. "We need to talk. Urgently."

"I know you're surprised. I was too!" he says.

I stare at him. *Surprised?!* This is a full-on assault on
democracy! The same "democracy" he was just extolling
the virtues of only moments ago. It's not "surprise". This
is outrage.

"Almost every single ballot had Danny's name
scribbled under your two names. It's the rawest form
of democracy!" Mr Hubbard seems genuinely excited
about this, as if the student body have just overthrown a
dictatorship. "This is voters getting down and dirty and
really telling us what they want!"

"No, but—"

"Barney," Mr Hubbard says, putting his arm
patronizingly across my shoulders like I need reassurance,
"you said it yourself in your brilliant hustings speech –
why not open up the club to the whole school? Let's all be
together. *As one.* Anyone can be part of it, so anyone can
lead it too, right? Really beautiful words, Champ!"

I can't say anything back. My brain has short-circuited

with the fact yes, I *did* say that, but also, *no*, that isn't exactly what I meant . . . yes, united is good, but still led by one of us! Someone LGBT still needs to be in charge. He also called me "Champ". I can't process that either.

I look to Bronte, which is really saying something, but I really need her to back me up. This is an outrage.

"A choice has been made," Mr Hubbard says. He looks over at Danny, still held aloft by all his mates. "UP YOU COME, ORLANDO!" He turns back to me. "Elections don't always go the way you would like. But you have to respect what the people want. Make the best of it. Maybe Danny will be a breath of fresh air? A new angle, new ideas – mixing things up is never a bad thing."

"What about the constitutional aspects of this, sir?" Bronte asks. "I hear what you're saying, but Danny wasn't officially on the ballot."

Mr Hubbard shrugs, only partially listening to her, as Danny slowly ascends the stairs to the stage, waving at the crowd like royalty. "I know, right? Pure anarchy, Bronte. But I love it. Besides, how would everyone react if I overturned the decision? Important lesson: sometimes playing by the rules doesn't get you very far."

I mean, *excuse me*? We are literally in an establishment that is all about rules. From what we're allowed to wear, how we can have our hair, what colour socks we're allowed to have, to what we're allowed to do from the moment we walk in, to the moment we walk out. The whole goddam thing is governed by rules which we're told we *have* to play by, else there's a raft of punishments. What the hell is he even saying?

Danny Orlando reaches the stage, saunters over, and shakes both of our hands. Mr Hubbard slaps him on the back like Danny's his best mate, and hands Danny the mic.

"Ladies and Gentlemen! It's so—"

"What about everyone else?" Bronte says, from behind Danny's shoulder.

"Huh?" Danny replies, turning to her, eyebrows raised.

"We aren't all ladies or gentlemen," she explains.

Danny furrows his brow, confused. "Boys and girls?" he ventures.

"Maybe just go with 'everyone', it's probably more inclusive?" Bronte suggests.

Danny nods. "Cool. Everyone! So good to be here, so good to be voted president of this epic club, man, so cool, thank you to all of you who voted for me. Kind of weird, like, I know there was a lot of talk about people not wanting to vote for either of the official candidates." He glances at us both. "Sorry, dudes – *everyone*, whatever – and, like, some of you really wanted to mix things up a bit around here, and since we can all be part of Gay Club now, like Barney said, I guess that's what I'm here to do. So, this is nice. I like it. Thanks for putting your trust in me."

"I really want to put my *trust* in you, Danny!" Nico

Murphy shouts from the floor. "I want to *insert* my trust, gently, but firmly, into *you*, Danny Orlando."

Oh, yes, everyone finds that highly amusing. I shake my head and look down at the floor of the stage. And there I was, starting to wonder why my heart can't be bigger, why I can't be happy we've got a new president, and one that everyone is excited about, because that would be good for the club and sometimes, maybe, you've just got to take the hit, for the greater good. But, no. It's not about my heart being bigger. This whole thing was nothing more than a joke to most of the school. They may not all be outwardly homophobic, in the sense of name-calling in the corridors, or beating gay kids up, but their bigotry just works in a different way: it's subversive, aiming to ridicule us, make light of what we stand for, and treat us like a joke.

And now I have to stand here, listening to all this crap, and a bunch of kids who think it's the best thing in the world that Danny has been voted president, when I would have done so much good with the job.

"Everyone!" Danny continues, giving Bronte a little thumbs up when he says the word, like he deserves a medal. "I guess some of you may have questions. Like, 'Hey, Danny Orlando, why does a straight guy like you even *want* to be president of the society?"

I turn to Bronte, and shake my head.

"And, 'Hey, Danny Orlando, what does a straight guy like you hope to bring to the society anyway?'"

Jesus, what have I done?

"Sometimes," Danny continues, "It takes a true outsider to see what's needed and make a real difference. Take a look at Gautam Mukunda's article in the *Harvard Business Review* – the dude studied a range of leaders from all walks of life and organizations, and found the best leaders tend to be outsiders who don't have a great deal of experience. What can I say? It's been officially studied. So, here I am. I humbly accept this role as president of Gay Club and fully intend to be the best leader. . ."

I grit my teeth. Danny Orlando is not the sort of kid who can just quote people who've written articles in the *Harvard Business Review* – of all niche publications. He was *so* expecting this. He *knew* it was in the bag. This wasn't a coup. This was a deliberate stunt – planned and executed with glee at the fact they were all keeping it a secret from me and Bronte and our campaigns.

"Thank you very much, and yay for bum sex!" Danny shouts, to a huge cheer and yet more rapturous applause.

Bronte takes a step towards me. "OK, he's a dick and we need to bring him down."

"I'm so sorry, Barney, you were right all along, and if I hadn't tried to manipulate the vote in my favour, none of this would have happened . . . *is how that sentence needed to start!*" I snap.

She slowly closes and opens her eyes, like she's letting my words just wash over her, and gives me a small smile.

"Meet me by the bench at the far corner of the playing field in ten minutes."

"Why?"

"Because this isn't over and I have a plan." She turns to Danny. "It's *not* Gay Club. It's the LGBTQ+ Society!"

She strides off stage.

I remain, awkward and alone, as Danny leaps down from the stage and weaves his way through the crowd, receiving back slaps and more cheers, so many cheers – the whole thing is basically a football match at this point. A spectator sport. That's what Danny has made this into.

But maybe Bronte is right.

This isn't over.

Queer kids deserve their heroes too.

And Danny Orlando ain't it.

21

I obviously do a terrible job of trying to play it cool and not act like I'm surprised to see Bronte smoking when I arrive at the bench, because she looks at me with disdain and says, "I just occasionally have one when I'm stressed. I know it's, like, *so* terrible, and *so* bad for you, but know what? I give no shits." She blows smoke out of the corner of her mouth, staring me down, for a reaction.

I shrug and perch on the edge of the bench.

"What did you want to talk about?"

Bronte smirks, stubs out her cigarette on the back of the bench, and throws it in the bin. "They're laughing at us. It's completely obvious this was all a set-up. Some nasty little joke. I'm down with being inclusive. I'm not down with LGBTQ+ students being ridiculed. But I'm not going to let them win. If we really want to, we can still force Danny out and take control of the club back. But I need to know if you're capable of helping me do that, because it won't work if it's just me."

I look up at her, towering over me , dressed in the beige double-breasted jacket and matching trousers that I assume was meant to be her "victory" outfit. "Like . . . what did you have in mind?"

"Danny is so out of his depth. Addressing people as 'ladies and gentlemen'? He has no idea, even of the absolute fundamentals. I suggest we start by making it very obvious to him that he doesn't know what he's doing, making it clear that he's being insensitive, or even offensive, and that he doesn't possess even a basic understanding of the issues. Once he sees that's the case, and once the fun of this oh-so-hilarious coup has worn off, it'll all seem too much like hard work, and hopefully he'll do the right thing and resign."

"And if he doesn't?"

"We take further action. As required."

I meet her cold eyes and swallow, hard.

"God, you're already pissing your pants. Forget it."

"I'm not!"

"I can see it in your face, Barney. But playing by the rules got us precisely nowhere."

I snort in disbelief – I mean, really? She thinks she was playing by the rules? – but from the look on her face, she seems to think she was.

She sits down next to me on the bench, leaning back, long legs stretched out in front of her, while I remain perched, slightly hunched over, my right leg bouncing up and down. "So, um . . . we just pull him up on stuff? Call him out? I can do that. I'm up for that." I swallow. "You know, if . . . if that doesn't work, and we think we need to do something else. . . Well, I guess we can discuss that, and see, and . . . what I'm saying is . . . one step at a time, right? We don't need to. . . I'm not saying that. . . He is just a kid and we're talking about a school club here, I wouldn't want him to. . ."

"We'll cross that bridge when we get to it."

"Right."

"But sometimes you have to fight for something you love. And you love the club, don't you?"

I nod.

"Great."

"OK, can I go?"

Bronte laughs. "Christ, I'm not holding you hostage, Barney."

"I just meant, have we finished?"

"We're done. For now. But let's keep this between us, shall we? The more people who know, the more complicated things get."

"But if I'm honest, I'm not exactly sure what we're keeping secret here? The others will want Danny out as much as we do. And George and Maya are my team, they know everything," I say.

"The campaign is over. You don't have or need a team any more," Bronte replies. "The more people who know what we plan to do, the greater the risk something gets reported back to Mr Hubbard, and we'll be prime suspects if it goes down ugly."

Oh, god: what does she think I have just agreed to?!

She continues, "Tell who you want, but every person you do tell increases that risk, however much you trust them."

"George is completely discreet, and Maya—"

"Yeah, it's Maya I'm worried about."

"She's—"

"She hates me, Barney."

"Look—"

"How *is* she, by the way? We barely manage one-word exchanges these days."

I automatically click into the pre-rehearsed ~~lies~~ things that Maya wanted me and George to say, should this ever come up. "Really *good*, actually. Just . . . loving life."

"Well, isn't that nice?"

"Uh-huh! Haven't seen her so happy in a long, *long* time. Really great to see. She's got lots on. Lots happening. . ."

"Is she seeing anyone?"

"Let's just say . . . there are girls who. . . There are girls. A number of girls – interested parties, if you like – but Maya is very much taking things slowly. No rush. Because life is about the journey, not the destination." I nod at Bronte.

"OK, well, regardless of how amazingly happy she is, I still wouldn't put it past her to use what we've discussed to try to hurt me in some way, since I'm clearly such a repugnant individual as far as she's concerned, so I'd appreciate you not saying anything."

All I can think is: *this can only end with me in prison, right?*

I tell George and Maya everything.

We don't keep secrets. Not like this, anyway.

We're all walking home together, after school, me checking over my shoulder every thirty seconds to make sure Bronte isn't following us, or that a potential Bronte spy is listening.

When I'm done, George is silent, deep in thought.

"*Classic,*" Maya says, laughing. "You know you can't trust her, right?"

"We're just temporarily uniting to get Danny out of the club," I say. "At least, I hope."

"She ruthless," Maya replies. "She'll stop at nothing. This is just the start. She's sucking you in, slowly, slowly, just with small, easy things at first, and before you know it, you'll be up to your neck. *Like a drugs mule.*"

"OK, well, I'll be sure to stop before I'm going to airports with condoms filled with cocaine up my arse."

Maya shakes her head.

"Sometimes you have to *fight* for something you believe in," I say.

Maya laughs contemptuously. "Did *she* say that? Are those *her* words?"

I shrug.

"Oh my god. She's never fought for anything, *or anyone*, in her entire entitled life. You're in bed with the devil, Barns. You need to be very careful."

We trudge on for a bit, and I'm wondering if, actually, I just need to drop this idea, maybe drop LGBTQ+ Society altogether, and admit defeat. "What about forming a breakaway society then? Start afresh? Do it our way? Show the school we're not going to put up with it? It'd send a strong, clear—"

I stop short because George is shaking his head.

"Nah, I thought that too," he says. "So I sounded Mr Hubbard out about it this afternoon. I mean, we *can*, the school won't stop us—"

"Good!"

"But they also won't provide any funding or officially recognize us. Which means no listing on the website, we're not allowed to fundraise around the school, or get money from the PTA, and we certainly can't run for Rainbow Youth." George slaps my back. "But cheer up. I'm thinking."

"Have we, and by 'we' I mean *you*, established how Danny getting elected actually happened?" I ask.

"It began as a joke," George says. "Most likely from Nico Murphy, but the idea quickly took hold. People thought it was funny. You guys were taking it all so seriously, it seems some students – actually, quite a *lot* of students – thought you needed to be brought down to earth a bit. The campaign was run on word-of-mouth, with everyone sworn to secrecy so none of us would find out. It explains why you guys were both polling so low – there was a third party in the mix we knew nothing about."

"How could we not have known?" I ask.

"Don't underestimate the lengths teenagers will go for a prank."

"And our supposed research team, asking the dinner queue?"

"It seems they may have been bribed, and, in some cases, threatened," George says.

"I really wanted this," I mumble.

"I know."

"Just this one thing."

"I know. And, look, maybe Bronte's plan isn't terrible, and maybe Danny will lose interest and be gone soon. But you need to be on your guard. What's her endgame here? What does she really want? Because it's not just getting Danny out, right? It's her taking over as president. So where do you fit in to that?"

"She will use you, and abuse you," Maya says. "*Trust.*"

I blow out a breath. "Know what? Let's just leave them to it. Screw it. Screw them. Screw the whole thing." I meet George's eyes. He's smiling at me. "*What?*"

"And what would our brave forebears at the Stonewall Inn riots say about that? Giving up at the first hurdle? Just . . . walking away?"

"I'm tired of fighting."

"*Hey*," George says, sharply. "We've always fought. We shouldn't have to, but we do. So don't take this lying down, Barney. You need to walk back into that club meeting tomorrow, and you *fight*. OK? We can't let *our* club be taken over by a bunch of people who think it's all a joke. Fight with Bronte, by all means, but remember, you're not necessarily on the same side, and if Danny goes, only one of you will be in charge, and the face of the campaign to be Global Ambassadors. I bet that's what's in Danny's head now, the fact he might get that on his UCAS – it looks great, but he doesn't really care. Yeah? Like the companies that have a rainbow flag social media profile during Pride, but have no problem dealing with governments in countries where being gay is illegal. So, we fight, Barney. Because this is us, it's who we are, and we're not going to let them win because we never got anything by shutting up and being quiet."

"OK. Yes. You're right. Danny out. Me for president."

"Beware Bronte," Maya adds.

"Absolutely."

"Did she ask about me?" Maya continues, all nonchalant, after a brief pause.

"Uh-huh. I told her everything you said we should. You're happy, successful, your life is brimming with joy and non-specific hot girls."

"Good boy," Maya tells me, giving me a little pat on the back and smiling to herself.

22

One thing's for sure: the LGBTQ+ club is now probably the most popular club in the school. Kids from all year groups are sitting in Room 120 as me, George and Maya walk in the next day. There are quite a few younger kids here, which is really sweet and warms my heart, and loads from the sixth form and years ten and eleven. But there's also Nico Murphy, so I know exactly what this really is: an extension of their oh-so-brilliant "joke".

Bronte's already here, having positioned herself next to where Danny Orlando is sitting, wearing football shorts that show off his muscular legs. As soon as Danny clocks our arrival, he claps his hands.

"OK, everyone!" he begins. I mean, this is already killing me, him taking charge like this. "I guess we should get going! Welcome to Gay Club!"

"You can't call it that!" Bronte immediately pipes up.

Danny is thrown off his stride for a moment,

which pleases me. "Huh?"

"You can't call it 'Gay Club'," she repeats. "How many times do I need to say it? There are other identities represented here, other than gay. *It's erasure.*"

On the one hand, this is exactly what Bronte and I discussed: pulling Danny up on stuff. On the other, a lot of people, me included, *do* use "gay" in an umbrella kind of way, and it's pretty hard to get it right in a way that pleases everyone.

Danny looks utterly confused. "What?"

"It's LGBTQ plus. Otherwise you're erasing identities."

"What, like saying 'plus' instead of the other letters, you mean?" I say. It just slipped out: I couldn't help it!

Danny seemed genuinely forlorn that he'd fallen at the first hurdle, and quite a few of the new kids were looking uneasy at Bronte's quite aggressive intervention. Yeah, people should be corrected if they get stuff wrong, but I also think there's a gentler way of doing that, especially when there are people in the room who are new to all this, and might be terrified of messing up.

Danny nods, and gives me a cautious smile, like he's trying to work out if I'm on his side or not. Bronte, meanwhile, looks at me with wide eyes and a "what the hell?!" expression on her face.

"What even *are* the other letters?" Nico Murphy asks.

"Look it up, you've got a phone, haven't you?" Maya

snaps at him.

Nico puts his hands up in submission. "*Wow.* I'm sorry for having a legitimate question!"

Danny sees an opportunity: "Actually, with so many new faces here, maybe that's not a bad idea! Nico?"

Nico scowls at Maya, pulls out his phone and taps away. "Huh. OK. So, Lesbian, Gay, Bisexual, Trans, Queer. . ."

"Questioning!" Bronte interrupts.

"It says the q is for 'queer' here," Nico replies.

"What, and you just believe everything you read on the internet, do you?" Bronte barks.

Nico points at Maya. "*She* literally told me to Google it! That's what I've done!"

"Right! There you go!" Danny says. "So which is it? Questioning or Queer?"

"Queer!" Me, George and Maya say, at the same time as Bronte, Paxton, and three random year ten girls who I've never met before say, "Questioning!"

Maya sighs. "OK, so, in some iterations I've seen the acronym written with two *Q*s."

"Two *Q*s?" Danny screws his face up. "So, *L, G, B, T, Q,* and another *Q*?"

Maya nods.

"That's ridiculous," Bronte says.

"Lots of people identify as queer!" Maya tells her. "What the hell's the problem with that?"

"What the hell's the problem with *you*?" Bronte

snaps back. "You seem very angry, considering your life is supposedly all joy and light now."

"Oh my god," Maya mutters.

I narrow my eyes at Bronte. We agreed not to talk about the chat we'd had – yet here she is, already using the information I gave her against Maya ... even if that information is false.

Nico blows out a breath. "OK, so, Lesbian, Gay, Bi, Trans, Queer, Questioning, Intersex, Asexual..."

"And also ally!" Bronte adds.

"Huh?" Nico says.

"Ally?!" Maya howls. "It does *not*! Since when was 'ally' under the umbrella?! Oh my god, you were talking about 'erasure' just now, how about the fact people in the aro-ace community *constantly* face erasure – like right now!"

"Some people feel that our allies should be included too," Bronte shrugs. "I'm just saying. It's about being inclusive."

"To the point where *everyone* is included, so the whole point of the exercise is futile?" I say. Honestly, I can't put up with this. Pulling Danny up on stuff is one thing, but having this public slanging match? Creating this hostile environment, when we've got new members here? Sure, get Danny out, but the collateral damage can't be destroying the club in the process. *Or was that Bronte's plan all along?* "Are you sure the *B* doesn't also stand for Bigot as well as Bisexual? I'd hate to see the homophobes and trans-phobes excluded *from Gay Club.*"

Bronte gives me the finger, so I give one back. Does that mean our agreement is off?

"So is ally in, or not?" Nico asks.

"Well, you're here, aren't you?" I say.

"Oh my god, Barney!" Bronte says. "Some people are straight, get over it! You wanted a whole school LGBTQ+ society, didn't you? We need our allies, and I, for one, am extremely grateful so many of them are here today." She smiles at the group, and the sudden sweetness is so jarring, it only makes it worse.

"I agree," I mutter. "I love being outnumbered by cishets at Gay Club."

Bronte gives me a withering look. "In America, they actually have things called Straight-Gay Alliances, so."

"So what?" I reply. "They also have spray-on cheese in aerosol cans, it doesn't mean it's a good thing!"

"All right, everyone!" Danny says. "I'm going to call time on this discussion. Maybe we should start with getting to know who everyone is? Would that be . . . good?"

I shrug and vaguely nod.

"How about we go round, and do names and pronouns?" George suggests.

Danny raises his eyebrows. ". . .Yes! Sounds great. OK. Let's, um. . . How about we make some kind of circle of chairs?"

We all shift chairs about into a large circle. "What the

hell are you playing at?" Bronte hisses to me. "Are you in or out of this?"

"*In!* What are *you* playing at?"

"Start acting like it then!" she whispers. "Danny's the bad guy, not me."

I sigh and take my chair to the edge of the circle. Danny takes a seat next to me. "Pronouns?" he whispers, as everyone finishes shuffling about.

I give him some side-eye. "It's saying how you identify, gender-wise."

Danny nods, as he watches Maya angrily move seats when Bronte sits next to her. "Um ... so what are *your* pronouns?"

"He/him."

Danny nods again. "Can I be that too?"

"If that feels right to you, yes you can."

Danny nods again, pleased. "OK, cool." He glances around the circle. "OK, everyone! I'm Danny Orlando, and my pronouns are he/him." He smiles, like he's super happy with himself, and, in spite of my intense annoyance at this whole fiasco, and despite the plan, there's a tiny part of me which finds his reaction quite sweet.

It's all going fine until we get to Nico Murphy, who stands up with a huge grin on his face. "Nico Murphy, and I identify as a helicopter."

It's at this point, I lose it.

"No!" I tell him. "No, no, no, no, *no!* You don't get

to come here and take the piss. This club is the *one place* LGBT kids should be able to feel safe. Lots of us spend our whole lives having abuse hurled at us, or little muttered digs, and that's just the tip of the iceberg. In here, we're OK. In here, we're amongst friends and people who get it. Allies are welcome, but if you want to be part of this, then you need to be respectful. This isn't about you. This is for *us*."

I stare at him, and he just grins back at me, totally entertained, apparently. "You said it was a club for the whole school now," Nico says. "So, actually, it *is* about us too."

"You're such a dick," I spit. "Yes, you're welcome, like straight people can come to Pride, but you do it on our terms, not yours. You can't hijack this. Why don't you get out? And anyone else who's here because you think this is a fucking joke – get out too."

"Wow, you lot are sensitive!" Nico laughs, then he looks at me, his lip curling slightly. "Or are you just a sore loser, Barney?"

I stare back at him. He's much bigger and stronger than me, but I'm so pumped with anger again, I'm like one of those tiny dogs that bark at bigger dogs, with no sense of the size difference or danger involved. "You're right, I *am* sore about losing. I'm sore about losing to someone who stood on stage and told everyone he was straight. I'm sore about the kids who could really benefit from a club like this watching the whole school turn it into a farce. This matters to me; it matters to us. And if you don't get that, if you don't understand the importance of very simple things like role models and representation and community, then I suggest it's because you've never had to understand their value. That's called privilege, and it proves you have a lack of imagination, empathy and human goddam decency. So, well done, and yes, I'm sore about it, Nico."

An awkward silence follows, and I glance at Bronte, who gives me an approving look. Huh. Turns out I didn't need to try too hard to make Danny and friends look like idiots – I did it on autopilot.

Danny looks down at his trainers while Nico blows out a breath. "OK, well, I'm out." He stands up and walks to the door. "This whole thing is really fucking *gay*." He turns back to look at me. "Isn't this the part where everyone is meant to reply 'But we are gay!'? Take the power out of the word, you said?" He looks around. Everyone is silent. "Guess not then!" He laughs and walks out the door.

Five other people get up and follow him out.

I switch my attention back to Danny. *Go on, walk.*

"Maybe . . . this meeting was a mistake," Danny says, glancing up. "Maybe I should have met up with the core committee first, and then . . . opened things up?" He looks around the room. "So, um . . . let's do that. Meeting's over, except for anyone who was in the club before. So, you, you, you, you and you."

I sigh.

One of the year ten girls raises her hand. "Can I just

say, at no point during this meeting has anyone mentioned pansexuals?"

Five minutes later and me, George, Maya, Paxton, Bronte and Danny are sitting around a table.

"OK," Danny says. "I accept this hasn't been the best start. And I can see" – he glances at me – "some of you are upset." He sighs. "Barney?"

"*What?*"

"Can you please stop giving me the death stare, it's making me really uncomfortable."

"I have a suggestion," George says. "Feelings are understandably running high, and a lot has happened. I think we need to get back to basics. This is what it is, and we still have the Rainbow Youth competition to try and win—"

"Rainbow Youth are going to *love* for their LGBT ambassadors to be led by a straight boy," I mutter.

Danny frowns at me. "We can win this thing."

I laugh and his eyes widen.

"This is your speech in practice, man! 'Confirm, never deny', yeah?"

I roll my eyes. "Danny, you stood on stage and told everyone you were straight. Wrong thing to confirm!"

Danny nods. "Yeah. Yeah, I get that now. It was. But for the application, I'll do better." He nods again, trying to convince himself, or us, I'm not sure. "Ask me now. Ask me if I'm LGBTQQIAAP."

I sigh.

"Ask me!" he insists.

"No, it's stupid!" I say.

"Argh!" Maya squeals. "Danny? Are you gay?"

"You have to say *all* the letters," Danny tells her, seriously. "Else it's *erasure*."

Maya grits her teeth. "Danny, do you identify as LGBTQQIAAP *plus*?"

"*Thank you*. Maya, I *do* identify as LGBTQQIAAP plus." He blows out a breath. "Wow. Thought I'd feel different, but I still kinda feel like me."

"Straight, you mean?"

Danny frowns at me.

"Maybe we all need to take a step back, and maybe school isn't the best place to do that," George says. "Maybe we need a bit of team building?"

Danny's eyes light up. "Paintball?"

"Er, *no*," George says. "We actually do these regular 'meet' nights, taking it in turns round at each other's houses. We all bring food, and we just eat and talk, and sometimes watch a movie."

"Oh, OK," Danny nods. "Like, a movie, or a *movie*."

"A movie," George says. "Just a regular movie. Well, it'll be a Christmas rom-com."

"Really?" Danny says. "It's nearly summer!"

George looks like he's going to murder him.

"OK!" Danny submits. "Well, that sounds cool. I'm up for that." He smiles, like that's all sorted, then. "And I was thinking, maybe we should also clarify who's who on the committee – like, I'll need a VP and stuff."

I notice Bronte sit up slightly in her chair. Paxton groans. "Please god not more campaigns..."

"No, you're right, I'm just gonna pick," Danny says quickly.

I want to argue, but I catch George's eye and he does this thing to signal that I should shut up and let this happen.

"OK, I'm happy to host," George offers.

"Look," I say. "I'm not sure I really—"

"Shut up, you're coming," George tells me, doing that thing again with his eyes. OK, *fine*.

"I'm up for it," Pax says.

"See, your bf's coming!" Danny smiles. "You two are so cute, by the way."

I glance at Paxton, as dishevelled as ever, school tie short and chunky around his neck, hair falling over his eyes. He gives me a sweet smile and winks at me. Pretending to be his boyfriend seems irrelevant now, especially since I've lost the election, but I'm not about to make Bronte's day by admitting it was all a set-up. I guess we'll just have to engineer some kind of break-up, but a happy one, that doesn't implicate either of us as cheaters – the mirror opposite of my parents, basically.

After various logistics are discussed (Danny has football practice on Thursdays, Maya has to babysit on

Wednesdays, Bronte has to sacrifice a goat and drink its blood on Tuesdays), it's decided Friday is the one, we're all to bring food, and we'll have a chill evening (I mean, that's a joke, surely?) "getting to know each other" – which is code for trying to bury the hatchet and pull something semi-good out of this unholy mess.

The minute the meeting is adjourned, and George pulls me aside and whispers to me in no uncertain terms that getting appointed VP by Danny is the clearest path to the presidency and *not to fuck it up*. Then he stalks off towards Paxton, presumably to repeat the message.

"Turns out you've got balls after all," Bronte whispers as we make our way to afternoon registration. "You really showed Nico, and you've got Danny on the back foot too. Genuinely, I'm impressed."

I shrug. "Well, it's like we agreed. We make it hard for him. Show him up for what he is."

"Keep going," she says. "You're doing well. Really well, Barney."

She smiles at me, and an uneasy feeling bubbles in my stomach. How am I supposed to both get in Danny's favour and also drive him out of the club at the same time?

Kyle's not online when I get home and log on to ChessNation. He hasn't been online for ages now. I'm wondering if he's lost interest in the game, now he's realized chess isn't as sexy as it might appear on a TV drama.

That's fine, though; I have his details, so I send an actual email instead, like I'm my parents. It's enormously cathartic. I just let it all out: all the treachery and utter insanity of the last few days that's culminated in us all falling out and a straight boy being elected as our president. I ask him how things are going for him and that I hope we'll catch up soon. I do hope that too. Having someone to talk to about all this, who isn't at my school but is in the same boat, is exactly what I need right now. Plus, Kyle's funny and sweet and . . . well, I guess I like him.

I hit send and soon after I get a text on my phone:

Kyle: Hey, Barney. Got your email. I do not know what to say other than WHAT THE ACTUAL HELL?! Seriously, that all sounds horrific and I'm sending you the biggest virtual hug.

Me: Lol, thanks. So what's going on with you?

Kyle: Still hugging you right now.

Me: Oh. Sorry.

. . .

Me: Done yet?

Kyle: Nearly.

Kyle: There you go. Feel better?

Me: Lol, a bit.

Kyle: Yay! OK, so, no surprise, I'm sure: BJ Ben won. At least he's gay, but still, we're talking about a guy with ONE talent, and it's not one that's relevant to the role. But here we are. His campaign motto may as well have been "Will suck cock for votes!" as that is literally what he did.

Me: That's ... wild. So, you guys still going for the Rainbow Youth ambassadors thing?

Kyle: Yes. But, look, this is tricky territory because technically we're now rivals ... but also, I really want to keep chatting with you because it's the only thing keeping me sane through all this, so let's make a promise: no shop talk? Gossip and hilarity – cool. Actual nuts and bolts about the applications – conflict of interest. Not that I care, but best to keep it above board. OK with you? Sorry, don't mean to be all serious, but the boys will probs kill me if they know I'm chatting with our

competition. (All-boys school, remember – it's like
Lord of the Flies here, with proper violence only
ever a moment away – and we have to kill wild
pigs with makeshift spears for our lunch!)

Me: No, totally, I get it. And I'd like to keep
chatting too.

Kyle: :)

Me: :)

Kyle: I gotta go, but . . . you have mail. X

A little tingle dances up my spine. I don't know, I'm not
normally one for . . . well, whatever this is, I'm not normally
one for it. Although, it's never really happened to me before,
so maybe I am? But I like it. I smile and log back on to my
email.

Hey Barney, so I guess I'll just come out and say
this and I hope I'm not overstepping the mark
but . . . do you fancy meeting up in person? Kyle x

Underneath there's an attachment to click, and it turns out
to be another rainbow teddy bear, but this time animated
so he's repeatedly covering his eyes and blushing.

I sit back and swallow. I'm suddenly nervous as all hell, but I'm also grinning from ear to ear. *This does not happen to boys like me.*

> I'd love to. How about next Wednesday after
> school? Barney. Xx

A rush of adrenaline spikes through me as my Mac makes the *Whoosh!* sound telling me the email has gone. I've done it. I've said I'd like to meet him, and then ... well, I guess anything could happen, and perhaps I just need to enjoy whatever that might, or might not, be.

I do start thinking about what it might be, though. Imagining it. Because, as much as I try to deny it, there's part of me that wants that perfect relationship, like Ed Lester and Xander from Branscombe Boys had back when I was in year ten – the mini breaks, the glamour – oh god, I know that sounds pathetic of me, but they were my heroes, because they were gay and they had it all, at a time when I thought being gay meant you wouldn't have anything, and, I don't know, could all this be history repeating itself? Is it finally my turn?

And then a message pings through on my phone that stops my little daydream dead in its tracks:

> Paxton: Hey. Been thinking about when I kissed
> you. A lot. Really need to talk.

23

I manage to avoid Paxton all day Friday. I don't feel good about doing that, but I'm just not ready to talk to him.

Damn it, I should have known something was up when he put his tongue in my mouth! It's not like he needed to do that to fool Bronte.

Ostensibly, it's a straightforward (if awkward) conversation: he'll tell me that since the kiss he's been thinking about me a lot, and he's realized he really likes me, and do I feel the same? And I will have to tell him, look, you're a nice guy, we'll be brilliant mates, but I'm just not feeling anything more. I mean, we both could've predicted this would happen the moment "fake dating" was mentioned.

The delicate issue here, and I admit this is entirely selfish, but Pax and me being together is an accepted thing – a lie, yes, but no one knows that, other than George and Maya. And what I don't want, with the chance of the president position becoming free again soon, and the prospect of us pitching to be the Rainbow Youth ambassador school, is to be outed as a massive great fraud, Scooby-Doo style, at the crucial moment. I know that I can't string Paxton along, and I fully intend to be upfront with him and put a stop to all this ... but it needs to be stage managed in such a way that no one suspects anything untoward. I've no idea how Pax might react if I spurn his (now genuine) advances. Everyone knows spurned suitors don't always behave in predictable or logical ways. They can be erratic, emotionally all over the place (Maya). And they can also be vindictive (my parents). I don't know Pax well enough to be sure he wouldn't do something dramatic and devastating, like hire a billboard and plaster evidence of our deceit all over it.

"George, thank god," I say, when I finally manage to find him at lunch. *Why must he take maths and sciences and never be in my lessons any more?* "Crisis: Paxton is in love with me."

George's eyes widen, then his face softens into a smile. "Awww!"

"*No*, not 'awww!' I need to let him down gently, but how?"

"You don't feel the same?"

I stare at him for a moment. "What? No. Why would you think I would?"

George shrugs. "It would kind of be better if . . . you

stayed together? As it stands, our core team for Rainbow Youth includes a straight boy; me, a permanent single person; and two lesbians at loggerheads. It'd be great if you two could be the unofficial poster boys for a healthy gay relationship."

"A healthy gay relationship predicated on complete fabrication?"

"It's all about public image," George says. "You know that. You saw that for yourself in the presidential elections. I've been reading up on how this process works. We submit a video proposal to Rainbow Youth and their team decides the shortlisted schools. But those schools then get invited to a big conference in London, and their live presentations get streamed around the UK for *all* LGBT societies to vote on. The point is, there's going to be more at play here than just the contents of the presentation. Everything about us has to be just right – all our socials, how we interact online – and Rainbow Youth need to see that we're able to do that, that we're going to be good ambassadors. Long story short: you cannot break up with Pax. Not yet."

"Great, George, all very nice, but what about Pax's feelings?"

"Why can't your love grow?"

"What?!"

"You may not love him now, but (a) what *is* love anyway? It's *very* hard to define, and also (b) once you get to know him more, you might find yourself . . . yearning for the boy. Besides, he still wants a date to prom, so you both need to spin it out until after that anyway."

"OK, George, *no*. I'm not going to string him along like that."

"I'm not saying string him along, I'm saying you have an outcome that you both want, so it's in both your interests to keep it going – at least publicly. How you deal with that in private is up to you. And I agree, you mustn't hurt his feelings. He's . . . a precious bean." George flicks his eyes down for a moment, embarrassed he just said something so cloyingly cute, I think. "But keep your focus where it needs to be: getting Danny to make you VP. Because I think Bronte's right: he's totally not going to last. Now, what food are you bringing tomorrow?"

"Nigel Slater's honey mustard chicken. The thighs should still be warm by the time I get to yours, and it's served with an olive, preserved lemon and parsley garnish."

"*You*," George says, "are *so* gay. Did anyone ever tell you that?"

"It's been mentioned."

222

24

Despite my intention to arrive at George's early, speak to Paxton, and get everything sorted so we can have a relaxed evening, I miscalculate how long it'll take for the chicken thighs to get nice and sticky in the honey mustard sauce, and end up arriving late. There's also the small matter of the dessert I've also prepared, which also turned out to be more labour intensive than I'd bargained for. Oh well. It'll be an evening of loaded silences and awkward eye contact between me and Pax, but at least there will be food.

I'm just at George's gate when an Audi pulls up in the parking space on the road, some Coldplay song – "Hymn for the Weekend", I think – blaring out of the car's sound system with ludicrous amounts of bass, until the engine turns off and Danny Orlando hops out. He's wearing blue jeans with a white T-shirt – minimal effort, but, of course, he still looks fantastic anyway.

"Barney Brown!" he says, zapping the car alarm on with a *bleep* and reassuring *clunk* of central locking. "Fancy seeing you here! Nice outfit."

"Hey, Danny – thanks." We don't ever dress up or anything for these things, so I'm not quite sure why I'm wearing chinos and my nice, blue-checked shirt, but I am.

He walks round to the pavement and surveys the foil-wrapped tin and cake box I'm holding. "Whatcha got there, then?"

"My contribution to the food."

Danny's eyes widen.

"Sticky chicken with preserved lemon and parsley garnish, plus dessert – cherry clafoutis."

Danny seems stunned. And then I flick my eyes to what he's holding in his hands: a six-pack of supermarket Scotch eggs.

"Bring food, you guys said," he says.

"Yes."

He waves the Scotch eggs around in front of me. "So I brought food! No one said you meant *food*."

"Yeah, no, we each cook a proper dish. *Food*."

"No. You just said 'food'!" He runs his fingers through his hair haphazardly. "Argh, now I'm going to look like even more of a total dick. I thought this was casual, we all turn up with some picky bits or whatever – crisps, maybe someone shoves a pizza in the oven if they're feeling fancy. Not. . ."

He looks helplessly at everything I'm holding. "Garnishes and words I can't even say!"

"Look, it's fine, no one will mind. You'll know for next time."

"No!" Danny says. "I'll drive back to Tesco. I can get something. More things. Maybe I'll buy one of their lemon tarts, or some kind of cake?" He looks at me, desperate. "A roast chicken? Will they have any left?"

He's literally moving back round to the driver's side of his car. This is ridiculous. I should be pleased he's screwed up – it might be another push towards him resigning – but I just feel sorry for him.

"Danny, it's fine. Look, why don't you just take my dessert, and you can say you made it, and no one will know."

He stops, looks at me, then shakes his head. "No, man, they'll know!"

"They won't," I reassure him. "Just bring it in and present it along with my main course and it's all good."

He's staring at me, trying to work me out, I think. And his suspicions do remind me of George's instructions to get myself appointed VP, so, see, I'm doing this because of that. "Really? You'd . . . do that?"

I manage a tight smile. "Honestly, it's no big deal."

"I'll make it up to you," he says. He gets out his wallet. "I can pay you now for whatever it cost!"

"Seriously, it's fine, we can sort it out later. Let's just

go in, yeah? We're late as it is." I hand him the cake box.

"Thanks, Barney."

"No worries."

We walk up the path together and I ring the bell.

"What's the dessert called again?" he whispers, as the sound of footsteps comes from inside.

"Cherry clafoutis." The door opens. "Hey, George!"

"Gentlemen," George says, smiling. "Come on in."

We follow him through to the kitchen at the back of the house, where Maya and Paxton are already fussing about, getting plates, bowls and glasses ready, while Bronte flicks through a magazine at George's table.

"We've already heard *so much* about your sticky chicken!" Maya tells me. "And presumably you've also made a dessert?"

"Ah, actually, *no*. No time, sadly. But it's OK, because..." I indicate Danny, "our president has provided!"

Danny swallows and nods, proffering the cake box, like an offering to the gods.

Bronte frowns and looks up. "What is it?"

Danny nods again. "Yes. It's a ... cherry ... cherry-based ... um ... cherry ch ... Oh, I can never say it, um, cherry chaff ... chaff ... inch-ay."

"*Clafoutis*," I say. "I presume that's what you mean?"

Danny nods. "That's the one!" he puts it on the breakfast bar like it's dangerous and he wants nothing more to do with it.

"So, what is that?" Maya asks, peering at the cake box.

Danny's panicked eyes met mine. "It's . . . like a . . . cake," he says, prising the lid off the box. His face freezes. "Like a weird cake, that's more like a . . . quiche?"

"Kind of a flan," I add.

Danny clicks his fingers. "Bingo! That's a good description."

George crosses his arms, peering into the cake box. "So, what's in it, *Danny*?" George narrows his eyes. *He knows.*

"Well, I mean, *cherries*, obviously! And some other stuff." He surveys everyone's expectant faces. "Sugar?" he ventures. "Some . . . flour, I guess. . ."

I nod along. "Yeah, I think my gran made this once. There's butter, eggs, milk, kirsch, actually, which is a cherry liquor—"

"Those are exactly the ingredients!" Danny says, triumphantly.

"Almond essence—"

"And almond essence."

"And usually the grated zest of—"

"An orange."

"A *lemon*."

"Either or," Danny says. "Doesn't really matter."

"I mean, it kind of does, but OK," I say.

Everyone looks at the pair of us. George isn't buying this. I think everyone else is just . . . confused?

"But enough of my cherry chaff . . . Cherry

chaff-foo-loo-tay, what's everyone else cooked?" Danny claps his hands together and gives everyone a wide smile.

"Veggie chilli," Bronte says. "Served with plant-based sour cream, guac and some rice."

"Nice!" Danny says. "Maya? Can you beat that?"

Maya grimaces. "Well, I mean, veggie chilli is normally *my* speciality—"

"Oh, come on!" Bronte says. "You can't claim some kind of monopoly on—"

"It's *my* recipe! Mine! It's not in a book!"

"It's not *your* recipe."

"I can see you've roasted the butternut squash before adding it, and that's something I pioneered, as you know, because I literally cooked it for you when you first came to dinner at mine!"

"You know what they say? Imitation is the greatest form of flattery."

Bronte smiles; she seems to be genuine. Maya opens her mouth to speak, then closes it again, wrong-footed. She has another go, I'm pretty sure working up to some acid comeback, fails, and just turns to Danny. "I've made chicken tikka masala. There's rice. Poppadoms. Mango chutney." She glances at Bronte again. "I made a plant-based version for you."

Bronte's eyes light up.

"It's not to be nice!" Maya tells her. "Just . . . absolute bare-minimum considerate."

Bronte smiles while Maya scowls at her.

"Wow, you guys really go for it!" Danny replies, doing a good job of ignoring all this weirdness.

"Teriyaki salmon fillets," George says.

"Oh, yum!" Danny grins. "And Paxton?"

We all turn to him, and it's me he's looking back at. He looks at me with . . . romantic hope? *Oh god*. Is it? I swallow, and he doesn't take his eyes off me, as he says, "Chocolate strawberry cake. Two aphrodisiacs in one dessert, so be careful, everyone." He lowers his voice. "Served with . . . *cream*."

Oh my *god*. The boy's on heat.

"A feast!" Danny declares. "This is so cool. So, how does this work? We eat and talk?"

"Sure," George says. "Why don't you help carry the dishes over, Danny? Barney? Could you help me over at the cutlery drawer?"

OK, so, super-weird having my presence requested at the cutlery drawer, but I head over anyway.

"I know what you've done!" George hisses at me.

"Oh?"

"He didn't bring anything, did he? So you agreed to cover for him? You're like Iago from Othello – pretending to be an ally, while destroying him from the inside. I admire that."

I mean, that all sounds a little more extreme and serious than what I was thinking, and mainly, I was just being nice because I can't stand awkwardness, mine or anyone else's, but I just nod along anyway, to please George.

"Well played, Barney, well played," George continues. He turns his attention to the cutlery drawer. "I'm still going to give him the *bad* fork though."

"What's the bad fork?"

"It has a wonky prong. Horrible to eat with." George smiles, evilly, then heads over to the table. "Tuck in, folks!" I watch as he carefully hands out the cutlery like an assassin.

Maya and Bronte sit at opposite ends of the table, with Pax and Danny on one side, and me and George on the other. A good five minutes is spent with everyone helping themselves to various spoonfuls of different dishes, tapas-style. The food is, as always, an absolute triumph. Maya's cooked an excellent chicken tikka masala, Bronte's veggie chilli is as good, if not better, than Maya's (although I would never say that, obviously), and George's teriyaki salmon fillets are perfectly cooked, soft and tender, but beautifully caramelized in their sauce.

"Loving your sticky thighs, Barney!" Danny announces, taking another mouthful, and winking at me. Then he frowns, inspecting his fork, and I see George smile to himself. Danny looks back up again. "So, I wanted to say a few things, if everyone's cool with that?"

Everyone's too busy eating to argue anyway.

"First things first, and like I said at our first official meeting, I think it would be great to have some designated roles within the committee, to help bolster our offering."

He means, to make up for the fact our club is led by a

straight boy, but OK.

"I've given it a lot of thought," Danny continues, "and got a few second opinions. . ."

"Who from?" Maya asks abruptly.

Danny smiles, like we're all going to be pleased about this. "Well, Bronte, of course!" he chirps. "She pulled me up on a few things I got wrong at that first meeting, and I appreciate that." He looks at me. "And after your . . . well. . ."

"Outburst?" Bronte offers.

My eyes widen. *The traitor!* I stop eating and put down my fork.

"Sure," Danny says. "I knew I'd upset you, and I needed some cool, collected advice. Cue Bronte!" he laughs.

Bronte laughs too. "Always happy to help, Danny. We're all in this together."

I want to end her.

"So, um . . . Bronte?" Danny says. "I feel like you've got a good eye for detail, yeah? I think that's great. So . . . I would love to formally ask you if you'd accept the role of Executive Chair of the Gay Cl. . . I mean, LGBTQ+ Society?"

My heart sinks. I can't even look at Maya. She literally warned me about this. I just didn't think Bronte would screw me over quite so hard and quite so fast. Making me speak out, making my contempt for Danny so clear, and then swooping in and sealing the deal for herself by playing good cop. Plus, of course he'd choose Bronte anyway. She's more in Danny's league: popular and beautiful, with rich parents. Those types always stick together and look out for one another. Hot people hang out in groups. Not that I think Bronte's hot. Or Danny, obviously. Well . . . he is, a bit.

Bronte looks thrilled. "I'd be *delighted*, Danny." She glances at me, like *better luck next time*.

"Cool," Danny says. He chews some sticky chicken (I honestly hope I undercooked his piece and it poisons the fucker) and then makes eye contact with me. "So, um . . . Barney?"

"*What?*"

"I'd love you to be Vice President."

"What?!" I say.

"*What?!*" Bronte almost squeals.

"I've realized I'm a little bit out of my depth with a lot of this stuff, like even just knowing the LGBTQQIAAP thing. . ." He says the letters carefully, respectfully even, which is kind of sweet. "But I feel like you know your stuff, Barney, and, more to the point, you're really passionate about it. Like, the way you spoke to Nico at that meeting? You seriously *rocked*. And maybe, together, we'd be a strong proposition? Kinda like the ying to my yang?"

I study his face, trying to work this out. Is he serious? *His yang?* So is this just a part of the joke for him?

"Hang on," Bronte says. "You made me Executive Chair. So what's my role, if Barney's VP?"

"It's really important!" Danny says. "It must be, right,

because it has the word 'executive' in the title? You're an executive, Bronte!"

"What's the job description?" she asks, unamused.

"It's someone who helps chair the meetings, prepares agendas, minutes. . ."

"So, basically the club secretary, then?" Bronte fumes.

Danny nods. "Yeah."

Maya's stifling giggles and I can't help smirk. I try to hide it, but I think Bronte sees, because she gives me a deathly stare.

"Look, Bronte," Danny sighs. "It's tricky, yeah? I know you had your reasons, but that fake tweet about the library books? It could be used against us, you know?"

Bronte's jaw tightens into a scowl. "Sure. And what about Barney saying 'pronouns are ridiculous'?"

"I didn't, though. I was misquoted, completely out of context. I could sue," I say.

"He could sue," Maya agrees. "Sue your sister's friend's *ass.*"

"Barney?" Danny says, turning to me. "Are you gonna accept?"

"Uh-huh," I say. "Thanks."

I glance at Bronte. She hates me. But this time, *I* win.

A big smile spreads across Danny's face. "Awesome! And I was thinking we could create some other roles, if anyone fancies it? I dunno, maybe a social secretary? Treasurer? Head of Lesbians?"

I stare at him in disbelief, but I actually think he might be serious. I'll have to clear that up with him later.

"But also," Danny says, "before we finalize all this, we all know this is big deal, right? This Rainbow Youth thing? I even read their website last night, and it's major. Every Gay cl— LGBTQ+ society in the UK is gonna want this, so I think we can expect some stiff competition. And . . . maybe a bit of shit-stirring along the way, like we saw in the presidential election." He glances at me and Bronte. "So. Cards on the table. 'Cause I need to know. Has anyone got any skeletons in the closet? Anything that could bite us if it gets out?"

I look up from my plate and immediately lock eyes with Pax, who has an expression on his face of *are we skeletons in each other's closets*? But that's not . . . that just wouldn't count. "Skeletons in closets" is stuff like buying and taking drugs or some form of criminal activity, surely? It's not two boys who may, or may not, be fake dating.

Danny's looking around the table in full seriousness though.

Maya clears her throat. "I misappropriated a ream of A4 photocopying paper in year eleven. I needed it for making some copies of my comics, plus, I have a *thing* for bulk quantities of stationery and—"

"Everyone here's squeaky clean," George interrupts. "I'm absolutely confident." He sits back in his chair. "No skeletons in the LGBTQ+ Society."

For some reason (I'm sure nothing to do with worry or raking over past transgressions), everyone becomes very silent for several minutes, with just the sound cutlery on plates and the occasional comment of "Mmm, this is so good", even though everyone has already mentioned how tasty all the food is by now.

Eventually, Danny suggests we brainstorm ideas for the video we have to submit to Rainbow Youth, which is meant to showcase our society and can include segments on things we'd like to campaign for, achieve, or which are otherwise important to us. Since Bronte is point-blank refusing to do it, I make notes in my Moleskin notebook, and we've got everything from gender-neutral toilets (or at the very least, sanitary bins in both the girls' and boys' toilets we've already got), to teaching LGBT history, Pride celebrations, gender-neutral uniform options for the lower years, and better LGBT inclusive sex ed that is more than just a teacher shouting, "Always wear a condom, kids! And now ... back to straight people!" Pax suggests tackling how hard it is for queer kids to ask people out, because it's not always possible to tell who else is queer, and how they might react. I'm not sure what the solution to that is, but I jot it down anyway, and then realize that he hasn't taken his eyes off me the whole time we've been discussing this, and that, actually, this might just be Pax trying to tell me he still wants to talk, and that talk really needs to happen tonight.

As we clear up after dinner, and while George tries to

referee as Maya and Bronte argue about how to stack the dishwasher ("Heavily soiled items have to go on the lower rack, Maya!"; "Here we go! Get all the digs in, Bronte!"; "It's not a dig, they literally tell you to do that!" and so on), Danny pulls me to one side. "Meeting. President and his VP. That's you and me."

"OK," I say. "When?"

"You free Sunday? Come to mine, we can talk all this over and put the plan together, yeah?"

"OK."

He lowers his voice. "I'll make some food – as a thank you for the cherry ka-kafka."

I smile. "You don't have to, but thanks."

"Bring your swim shorts."

I squint at him. "Why?"

He leans in to me. "Big gay hot tub, baby! It's where I have all my best ideas!" He winks. "You really look like him tonight."

"Huh?"

"*Noah Schnapp.*" He reaches out and adjusts my shirt collar a bit. He smiles, satisfied, then picks up a stack of bowls and saunters off towards the sink.

I stare after him. I must have entered some parallel universe, because I don't live in a world where I get in a hot tub with Danny Orlando. I don't. And I won't. He's not getting to see my underdeveloped chest and puny arms, especially not next to his outstanding abs and pecs.

Also, I believe hot tubs are usually full of surprising and stimulating jets of water. I know what'll happen, and it ends with me doubled over, trying to drape a towel down over my crotch in a way that looks casual and accidental, and not like I'm trying to hide anything. Just *no*.

Bronte's by my side the moment Danny's wandered off. I hope the fact she's brandishing a knife is just because she's clearing up, and not a threat. "This isn't over. If you think you've somehow got everything you wanted, you haven't."

I glance at the knife. "I mean, you really tried to stab me in the back, Bronte. It just didn't quite work."

"*I didn't*. Change of tactics, that's all. I figured I'd have more success on the inside, if Danny thought I was an ally."

"Of course you did." I stare at her. "And why bother communicating that fact to me, when I can just make myself look like a hostile jerk instead?"

"God, you're pathetic. *Fine*. You cosy up with Danny. See how that works out for you!"

She slings the knife into the sink, eliciting cries of "Watch it, you MANIAC!" from Maya, then swans off, and I can't even tell what she means. Is she going to make sure Danny stays president to spite me? Or drive us both out somehow?

Maya comes over. "*I warned you*," she says. "More to the point, you now need to be doubly careful. She knows no bounds. She'll be in this for the long haul – whatever it takes,

Bronte always gets what she wants. Bronte is only about Bronte. No one else matters. We're all just trash to her. *She nearly killed me with that knife just then.*"

"So . . . what? Do I need to be checking my drinks for poison?"

"*Be warned.*"

I sigh, turn around, and there's Pax, staring at me, longingly.

Oh god. I have to bite the bullet sometime, and having one less thing to worry about would be good right now. I go over to him. "Hey."

"Hey!" His eyes light up.

"So, um . . . fancy walking home together in a bit, and maybe we can have . . . that chat you wanted?"

Pax releases a breath. "Ohh, thanks, Barney. I'd really appreciate that. I was beginning to think you were avoiding me."

"That's . . . not the case at all!"

He reaches out, takes my hand, and squeezes. "*Thank you.*"

25

Danny's all "Night, lovebirds!" and "Don't do anything I wouldn't do!" as Pax and I say our goodbyes and head off, in the opposite direction to the others, all of which does nothing to ease my nerves and make any of this easier.

There's a park about five minutes from George's, so we head there. It's a warm evening, and other than a few hardcore night joggers, and probably the odd dog walker, we should be fairly undisturbed.

"I'll just say it," Pax says, the moment we've sat down. "Ever since we kissed, well, ever since I kissed you really, I just . . . it's like I said, I've been thinking about it, and how I just know it's wrong."

I open my mouth, but I don't know what to say. That . . . wasn't what I was expecting.

"Kissing you was totally wrong," Pax repeats, shaking his head.

"Um. OK? Wrong as in. . .?"

"I'm not saying it was *gross*. . ."

My eyes widen. "Oh, OK!"

"Just, no chemistry, no connection, because. . ." He sighs. "Kissing you made me realize that I don't want to kiss you. . ."

I don't know why he keeps rubbing salt in the wound, but I just let all this wash over me.

"And I *know* we're fake dating anyway, so obviously that's the case, but the point is, it brought it all home to me." He turns to look at me. "I really fancy George."

"Oh. *Ohhhhh!*"

"Yep. So, when I first started mentioning to him about prom, and who would I take, and I'd like to take a boy, I thought he might get the hint? Turns out he didn't, because he fake set me up with you instead. So, is that because he's not interested? Or just because you guys needed something, and I needed something, so it all worked out that way?"

"Right, OK—"

"And like, I know he's trans, but is he also gay or bi? Or is he straight? He's never mentioned anything. And I'm not expecting you to tell me, it's his business if he wants it to be, but it just adds to the confusion."

I nod. *"Right."*

Pax blows out a breath. "He's kinda hard to work out. Not just this, I mean *a lot of things*. Like, what's his obsession with cheesy Netflix Christmas rom-coms all about? Even in May?"

"Ah, so, *yes*. Big thing. He's just always loved them. You know, the cosy feel, low peril, low stakes, poor children. . . That's to say, he doesn't love poor children, obviously, but he loves seeing how their lives get better."

Pax still looks confused. "But George is so . . . most of the time he seems really hard."

"Yeah, but he isn't. At least, he's only like that when he needs to be, I guess. Like at school, I get it, he's quick with a sharp put-down and he's pretty direct, and so a lot of people won't mess with him, which helps sometimes."

Pax nods. "We all put on a front when we need to."

"Right. But George is also quite soft-centred, when you really get to know him. Look at how he threw himself into helping me with the campaign. He didn't need to do that. It's because he cares and he likes seeing people happy and he's just . . . an all-round great guy, and if you think about it, of course that fits in perfectly with his love of Christmas cheese, and anything with Dolly Parton."

Pax smiles.

"Anyway, if you want me to I could—"

"You *can't*. He'll *know*. He doesn't miss anything. And I really like him as a friend too, and if I tell him I have feelings for him, that'll make everything weird, you know it will."

"Hmm," I say. "You're right. He doesn't miss a trick. He knew immediately that I'd given Danny the dessert tonight."

Pax laughs. "Barney, we *all* knew that. I think a three-year-old would have been up to speed on *that*."

"Oh."

We sit in silence for bit, enjoying the cool night air. It's true what Pax says: George doesn't really mention love interests, or even fancying anyone. I don't ask, because why should he? He might be asexual for example, or just want his privacy, and nothing's more annoying than other people asking you about dating and "if there's anyone you like" because you sound like your auntie, and if someone wants to talk about it, they will, you know? To be honest, that's one of the things I like about my friendship with George. I don't go out on dates. I'm not someone who asks boys out, or gets with them at house parties, however much I sometimes fantasize about how good doing that might be. I just do my own thing, and, as weird as some people find it, I focus on my studies and on stuff like the LGBT club. Eyes on the ultimate prize, you see? Get the grades, hopefully get into Oxford, and start my political career. It's mapped out. *Endgame.* I didn't factor in romance. So George and I work well together. We're both ambitious, and neither of us has time for the stuff that seems to occupy most other people.

"And there's something else," Pax says, breaking in on my thoughts. He looks at me, torn, for a moment, then sighs and stares down hard at the ground. "You probably think this is weird, like, I think I'm bi, or I thought I was, and maybe I am, but then . . . George is the only person I think about *like that*, do you know what I mean? The only person I actually. . ."

"Pax, that's not weird, it's really not."

"It's not normal, though, is it? Most people seem to have a really high sex drive, like, most of my year would get with almost anyone, but me?"

"OK, stop with this 'normal' thing. The biggest trick the devil ever pulled was convincing people there's only one way to love. There's loads of ways. Maybe you're demisexual. That's when you only feel sexually attracted to someone once you have a close emotional bond with them."

Paxton's eyes widen, like this is a revelation.

"So that's an option, right?" I continue. "And, like, I don't even know what 'normal' is, but I'll take a guess that it's boring as all hell and ends up washing the car on Sunday mornings and having a lawn made of astroturf. I mean, Pax, hello? By conventional standards, none of us in the LGBT Society pass as 'normal'. Statistically, we're all outsiders. But I love us. Maybe we are misfits, but we're family and we look out for each other, and we know how to have a good time."

"Bronte too?"

I laugh. "I mean . . . even she has her moments."

He takes an unsteady breath. "So, I'm not broken?"

"Oh my god, *no*! I mean, OK, I'm speaking as a virgin here, so I admit I'm not an authority on this, but sexual attraction only on a deeper emotional level makes sense to me. I think it's lovely. It's not about fleeting, physical lust.

It's connection. Shared beliefs. A way of looking at the world and living your life that just clicks. Surely you want to be with a person because they're funny, or kind, or a great person, or because they're all-round beautiful. Like George is beautiful. And like you're beautiful, Pax."

He swallows, blinks at me, and he's crying. I wrap him tight in a hug. "Even if kissing me was so atrocious it woke you up to how much you definitely *didn't* fancy me and how literally everything in the world is wrong."

"I didn't say that," he chuckles, sniffing, snottily.

"But that's the summary."

"Shut up. You're not a *bad* kisser, it's just—"

"Just leave it there, Pax. I'm not sure how much more my self-esteem can take, to be honest." I look over his shoulder and see a couple of people walking down the path, so release him from the hug before they see, just in case. "Let me have a think about George, yeah? I'd never do anything that might embarrass you, but there's a way to handle him."

"Sure," Pax says. "Thanks."

We sit in silence while the figures approach down the little path, and I relax a bit when I realize they're not guys, so will most likely leave us alone.

"I'm confused, are we still fake dating, or not?" Pax asks.

"I'm confused too. Technically, yes. Bronte and Danny definitely think we *are*. And you understand it's important they remain thinking that, right?"

Pax nods. "Yeah. Like, if we do fake split up, they've got to fake believe it's real."

"No, they have to *believe* it's real, not fake believe it. We just don't need any complicating factors."

Pax grins. "You mean, now you're VP? Scared Danny might change his mind?"

"No," I say. "*Maybe*." I laugh. "God, I was worried all this was about you telling me you'd fallen in love with me, and then I'd have to let you down, and then you might spill all our secrets, out of spite."

He stares at me. "Wow. That's what you thought?"

"I worry about stuff."

"This is important to you, isn't it? All this?"

I nod. "I really wanted to be president."

"You should have won."

"Thanks. I'm not sure many people agree with you, but thanks." I glance at him. "Sorry, I don't mean to keep sounding bitter about it."

"But you've every right to feel bitter. We all have. Because it's like you said, role models and community are important. I see that. I *know* that, god I do. Before I started hanging out with all of you, there's no way I'd have had the courage to even acknowledge who I was to myself, let alone anyone else. It felt like . . . well, like the end of the world, to be honest. Lonely. *So* goddam lonely. Did you ever cry yourself to sleep, when you thought you might like boys?"

"A few times."

Pax smiles, sadly. "Shouldn't be like that. But, even now. . ."

"Even now," I agree.

"But seeing you up there on stage, Barney. So . . . just being *you*. Unashamedly yourself. Telling everyone you're gay and being up there and shouting about it and standing up for everyone else and not caring?" He glances down the path to check we're alone, then puts his hand on mine and squeezes. "I may not have worked it all out yet, but you've changed my life, you've made it better, you've made me happier, and for that, you'll always be my hero. You'll always be my president, Barney Brown."

26

"Barney-Boy!" Danny Orlando beams, as he welcomes me into his huge, multimillion-pound house in the posh end of town. "My folks are away and little sis is having a sleepover with her mates, so we're home alone, come in, come in!"

I walk inside the massive hallway, a huge staircase facing me, with sweeping steps that come down on two sides, like something from the ballroom in *Cinderella*. I wonder about taking my trainers off, but see Danny has his on, so follow suit.

Danny closes his large front door and turns to face me, clapping his hands. He looks genuinely excited about my presence. "So! Suggestion: President and VP high-level hot-tub meeting? She's hot and bubbling, so let's grab a drink and jump in!"

"Ahhhh," I say. "My swimming shorts. I . . . totally forgot them!"

A lie. I did not. I deliberately didn't bring them for obvious reasons, previously stated.

"*Barney!*" He looks at me like I'm a total doofus. "No worries, it's fine—"

"Great! Sorry."

"I have spare shorts."

"What? You do?"

"'Course! I'll grab you a pair!"

"No, wait! I doubt they'll fit – I mean, you're bigger than me, you know, waist-wise."

Danny nods. "I'm pretty sure I've got some at the back of my wardrobe from when I was in year nine. Wait there."

Danny darts off up the massive staircase, leaving me standing in the vast hall, with the ignominious prospect looming of wearing swimming shorts for a thirteen-year-old because I'm so child-like and pathetic. *Great.*

A couple minutes later, and Danny returns wearing a white robe, having clearly put shorts on himself, and triumphantly brandishing another pair of shorts, in garish neon orange and green. "Change in my room," he tells me. "I've put a spare robe on my bed for you too. Round to the left, it's the first door on the right," he says, pointing up the stairs. He throws me the shorts. "I'll fix us drinks in the kitchen – vodka and Coke OK?"

"Um . . . sure. Thanks."

He smiles, then heads off down the far end of the

hallway. "Don't be long, dude! We have presidential *business* to attend to, haha!"

I hike up the stairs (this alone would account for why Danny is so fit and toned) and find his bedroom. It's huge. Two large sash windows are either side of a double bed, with checked duvet cover and pillowcases. There's a bedside table with nothing on it but an angle-poise lamp, a desk with a small pile of textbooks and folders, and his laptop. *But no mess.* There's no piles of clothes, or collection of ten random cans of Lynx body spray, nine of which are empty. It's almost like Danny barely exists. If it wasn't for the pungent whiff of *Deep Heat*, I wouldn't guess this was his room.

A door to the right leads to an en-suite bathroom complete with rainfall shower. Very nice. I have enormous house envy. I lock myself in (I get really nervous about changing and anyone accidentally seeing my . . . well, *you know*, god, look at me, I can't even say it, I don't know, maybe I need therapy?) and pull on thirteen-year-old Danny's swimming shorts. Huh. How do they fit so well?

I leave my clothes in a small, neat pile in the bathroom, pad back through to the bedroom, and put the fluffy white robe on. It's massive, and envelops me completely. He's also left a pair of those disposable spa slippers on top of the robe, so I put those on too, head back downstairs and wander in (what I hope is) the direction of the kitchen, although there are doors everywhere, and other small hallways leading off, so I've no idea if I'm right.

Eventually, a set of marble steps leads me down into a huge expanse of open space, a vaulted ceiling created with huge panes of glass, with bi-fold doors the entire length of the longest side. There's a massive dining table to the right, enough for fifteen or twenty people, and to the left, the main kitchen, complete with several ovens, an Aga, cupboards everywhere, loads of worktop space (but again, absolutely no sign that anyone really lives here – like, seriously, where are the piles of washing up, or all the Bags for Life?), and, in the middle, a massive marble-topped island, where Danny is standing, pouring Coke into two tall glasses.

"There he is!" Danny says, smiling at me. "Timed it perfectly!" He hands me a glass. "Bottom's up!" He makes eye contact with me.

"Thanks," I say.

I take a sip. It's strong. He hasn't been shy with the vodka.

"Bring it with you," Danny says, leading me out through the bi-fold doors. "There's towels out here already."

The floor of the kitchen seamlessly becomes the paving of the patio area we walk out on. Over to the right, there's an outside kitchen with barbecue area and another huge wooden table with chairs. Sun loungers are scattered around a pool (I'm trying not to be open-mouthed and too much in awe at this point; I don't want to come across like this is all amazing to me, although it totally is), and lots of rattan sofas and armchairs, with white cushions, like something you might see on TV in a swanky bar in Ibiza. We walk over to the left, though, where the hot tub sits, tucked in a corner next to walls of climbing plants with purple and pink flowers.

I bet Danny has the best parties in this place.

There are some pegs attached to one of the walls, so Danny hangs his robe up. His swimming shorts may as well just be Speedos, they're so short and tight. He turns around, his smooth abs and chest glistening in the sunlight, and my stomach flips. "You can put your drink on one of the ledges at the side," he explains. "Try not to drop your glass in the tub though, it's hell to clean out."

I nod as he walks up the two little steps at the side of the tub, swings a leg over and slides into the steaming, bubbling water with a sigh. I follow, trying to make the time between me being almost fully exposed and most of me being hidden under the foaming water as short as possible.

I haven't actually been in a hot tub before. The water is hotter than I was expecting, despite the heat aspect being fairly well sign-posted in the tub's name. The jets are on a gentle setting, with ripples of bubbles emerging from various vents beneath the water, one of which is under my bottom, and which . . . well, it kind of feels . . . um . . . nice.

But I shift across a bit, before it starts to feel *too* nice.

"Big gay hot tub!" Danny murmurs, lying back against one of the padded headrests, the bubbles swarming over his chest, his eyes closed.

I watch him for a moment. It's hard to believe we're

basically the same age. He can't have a body like that from sport alone. It must be some genetic/hormonal advantage. Or else, I'm genetically/hormonally deficient in some way. I feel like I should try to relax in here, but I feel so inferior, which is mad, since he's really the imposter here – head of a club he doesn't actually know anything about. I'm not here to be his mate. I'm here to claw back something which is ours – or, at the very least, if I can't be president in name, be the puppet master, pulling all the strings in the shadows. "So, why did you choose me?"

He opens one eye, squinting at me in the sunlight. "Huh?"

"As your VP? Why me?"

He smiles, opens the other eye and sits up a bit. "I like you."

I stare at him, not believing that for one moment, then roll my eyes.

He chuckles. "I mean, you saved my arse with the food situation the other night, which was kind, and you didn't have to do that. And you explained the pronoun stuff at the first meeting without making me feel like too much of an idiot, unlike Bronte, who kind of scares me, if I'm honest, and so I feel, out of everyone, you slightly have my back."

I take a sip of my drink.

"And I need a VP who knows what they're talking about, 'cause the more time I spend with you guys, the less I seem to know about anything."

He needs my help. Of course he does. It didn't take much for Bronte and me to prove that point. He's totally out of his depth, and he knows it. But why doesn't he just resign? Why doesn't he just admit he's the wrong guy for the job? That it was fun (and funny to some) while it lasted, but now it's over?

I put my glass back down carefully. "So, do you still think running as a joke candidate was a good idea? You think it's turning out well?"

Danny swallows and sits up a bit more. "What's your problem with me, exactly?"

I sigh and shake my head. "OK, look, a lot of LGBT people don't get a chance at things. We don't get to be ourselves always. Like in football – how many players are out? Hardly any. And, like, actors, in Hollywood. Lots of them don't come out because they're worried how it could affect their careers. So there's all this stuff we don't do, or can't do as ourselves. Something like this, president of an actual LGBT club? This we *can* do, and an openly queer person should be doing it."

"What is straight anyway?" he muses, staring into the middle-distance.

"Huh?"

He's back in the room. "OK, what if – go with me here – what if some kids see me as president, and they think, *if Danny Orlando*, sorry to talk about myself in the third person, *but if Danny Orlando, straight football-player guy,*

253

thinks it's OK to be gay, even if he's not gay himself, maybe it is OK. And maybe I can be gay. Or maybe, at the very least, I won't bully other people who are. Maybe that could be a thing? One thing Bronte mentioned which didn't make me want to scream at her was about the straight-gay alliance thing, in America? Maybe if we take the pressure of all the labels, and just let whoever wants to be part of this join, and that's the only criteria, maybe that will work better?" He holds my gaze for a moment. "Barney, you said all this yourself, dude. You stood on stage at hustings, and you said, 'let's be a whole-school gay club!' You said it! And I liked what you said." He shrugs. "I dunno, I guess it spoke to me, man."

"And I stand by that," I say. "But there's a difference between being a member, being part of the community, and actually running it!"

"Is there?" Danny replies.

I release a breath and look away. He's talked himself into this being a good idea. "And it looks good for your uni applications, right?"

He meets my eyes, but doesn't reply.

"Just saying," I mutter. I'm right. That's what this is about. He's got loads of sports stuff, but he's not-so-hot academically, and looking around at his place, I'm guessing his folks are super ambitious. They'll want him to get into a top uni. And for that, he'll need more on his application. Varied interests. Positions of power and importance. Showing himself to be a leader and a visionary.

And if he's mistaken for being part of a minority group that needs more representation and visibility at said top uni, all the better.

He's playing a long and clever game, and he's made me a pawn in it. And he's not quitting any time soon.

But, maybe, like Bronte says, it's better to be on the inside. Maybe that's my best chance of influencing things.

"Cheer up, dude!" he says, suddenly changing tone. "We're gonna make this fun. With me at the helm, this'll be a brave new era for the L-G-B-T-Q-Q-I-A-A-P society!" He laughs, splashing me with water on each of the letters. "Did I get that right?"

"I guess," I sigh, wiping water from my face. "You got me wet."

"Dude, you're in a *hot tub*."

"OHHHH!" I squeal, as high-pressure water suddenly jets up under my legs.

Danny laughs, moving away from the controls, and gives me a devilish grin. *"Big gay hot tub, baby!"*

27

I end up getting hard because of course I do.

Luckily, Danny gets out first, because he's doing a barbecue for us and needs to light the coals, so as soon as he's disappeared back inside the house, I haul myself out too, towel off while facing the wall and checking over my shoulder, then wrap myself back up in the huge dressing gown. *Job done.*

I shuffle back towards the house, just as Danny emerges with a bag of charcoal and some extra-long matches. "Oh, you're out. If you want a shower, you can use my bathroom. See you down here in a bit, yeah?"

"Thanks," I say.

By the time I emerge, all fresh and smelling of Danny's Molton Brown body wash, he's tending various sausages, burgers and chicken thighs over the hot coals. "Are other people coming?"

Danny looks surprised. "Nah, just us." He glances at

the mammoth amount of food on the barbecue. "Oh, I don't tend to eat it with bread, so I have more meat. But I've got some rolls if you want some? Otherwise, I have salad and I've some chips in the oven."

He's actually gone to some effort, and, in spite of myself, I find it quite sweet. "Sounds good. Thanks."

"See? I can cook too."

"Well, I haven't tried it yet." I smirk at him, and he threatens me with the barbecue tongs.

"Go and get us both another drink," he tells me.

Danny loads up a big platter with all the cooked meat. It's enough for a small army, even before you get to the bowl of chips he's made, liberally sprinkled with salt and oregano ("We had these in Greece, they're *a-mazing*!" he tells me), and the salad.

"All right," I concede, sampling the chicken thighs he's done. "This is good. You *can* cook."

He grins at me. "Hashtag boyfriend material, right?"

Ugh.

"What about this video we have to submit, then?" I say. "Any more thoughts?"

"I was thinking about a sport angle for part of it," he replies. "Like, homophobia in football – how that can be, um . . . like, stopped at a grass-roots level. Like, school football, I mean."

I nod. That's not a bad angle. "So, we show a kind

257

of . . . inclusive football match? And how everyone supports each other?"

"Isn't there a thing with rainbow laces?" he says.

"Yeah. We could get some of them. Would we be . . . asking the school team to help us with this?"

"Yeah. I'll ask them. I'm captain, so, not to pull rank, but they kind of need to go along with my ideas."

"And if they don't?"

I don't mean to be negative, but I know what some of the footie lads are like.

"They might find themselves benched for most of the season. Complete coincidence, of course." He picks up the tongs and drops another chicken thigh on my plate. "Have another."

"Thanks. OK, so, that's one bit of the video. But I feel like we have all these ideas, and what we need is structure. You know? What's the actual narrative here?"

I can hear myself, and I sound like a dork, (*what's the actual narrative here?*) but he'll just have to deal with it.

"Hmmm," he replies, chewing. "See, like I said, your speech at hustings really chimed with me, so couldn't we use that as the basis for this? Total inclusivity? That's our angle. 'Our LGBT Society isn't just a club that meets once a week; it's all of us, every day, everywhere!'" He smiles at me. "Your words, Barney Boy!"

I nod, trying not to show how thrilled I am that he's remembered (verbatim!) part of my speech. "So the football team is part of that, we can showcase other clubs. . ."

"Yup!" Danny says. "It's bold. I honestly don't think other schools will come up with that."

I cock my head. "Hm. True. Probably. They'll do the obvious. Still important! But obvious." And, I mean, if we're stuck with Danny as president, maybe we just have to make the best of it? Make it a feature. *Look at us! So inclusive our president isn't even LGBT!* We can still include our bit on the piss-poor sex-ed classes – every school needs areas for improvement, and it would be unrealistic if we didn't have *something*.

"Hey, I've got a question, Barney: what's the deal with Maya and Bronte?"

"Well, you know they used to date?"

"Yeah," he says. "But they split up, right? But now . . . is it anger or sexual tension between them?"

I smile at the fact he's noticed too. "Who knows?"

Danny's eyes light up. "Sexual tension, I reckon! The pair of them round at George's the other night!" He chuckles. "Do you think they'll get back together?"

"Why don't you play cupid, Danny. See if you can work your magic?"

He laughs and holds up his hands. "Staying well out of it, mate! She's tricky, Bronte, isn't she?"

I nod. "I find her quite prickly sometimes. Almost like . . . she doesn't need anyone else in her life."

"She's like that because she's had to be," Danny says.

"My folks know hers. They're never home, always away on business, and always have been since she was old enough to be left by herself. So, I guess she's only ever really had herself, you know?"

That's basically what's happened to me since my folks got divorced, and sure, it doesn't always feel great, but I guess at sixteen you can deal with it better than if it happens when you're younger. I think my personality is basically formed by now. Horrifying as that sometimes is to admit.

Danny must read my mind. "Same. I don't see my parents much either. They spend most of the week down in London, 'cause that's where the company is headquartered."

"What do they do?"

"Hotels," Danny says. "They're joint CEOs, but Dad focusses on the finance stuff and Mum designs the interiors. The Orlando Group – not exactly an original name. Orlando Hotels, Orlando Resorts, Orlando Lodges and the jewel in the crown – the Orlando Park Lane."

I whistle. "Seriously? All of them?"

He nods. "Dad inherited it from my granddad. Lucky break, huh? All I'm saying is, sure, it makes life easy because I guess we never have to worry about money, but then, I hardly ever see my parents, and sometimes. . ." He swallows. "Well, it might be nice. They literally hire a nanny to look after my little sister most of the time. Kinda why I turned up at the school to see your speech: no one ever goes to see her in stuff if I don't."

I nod, and despite everything he's got, and what a nice life he clearly leads, I feel sorry for him, and his little sister.

He meets my eyes. "Now! What about you and Paxton?"

I feel my defences go back up. I sniff, helping myself to a few more oregano chips. "What about us?"

"Don't be all coy!" he says. "How's it going? You're cute together, even I can see that!"

"You think?"

"Is he your first proper boyfriend?"

I nod, eating chips.

He's still looking at me, eyes sparkling with mischief, by the time I've swallowed. "Anyway, back to this storyboard thing. . ."

"Right, because maybe a nice thing for the video would be for us to feature you and Paxton, you know, just as a clear visual of a gay relationship, and it'll show the school in a good light?"

My mouth is dry. I take a sip of my drink. "I dunno, I kind of feel like playing things out in front of the camera, all public, isn't the best idea. It's hard enough, you know? I don't want to be a celebrity couple."

Danny scoffs. "You wouldn't be. I'm talking about a short section of our video. Maybe you could both just talk to camera about your experiences?"

"Maybe. I dunno."

"Great!"

"I'm saying I don't know."

"Do you want a burger?"

"I'm actually—"

He places one on my plate. "One hundred per cent organic grass-fed beef."

"OK, thank you, but just ... with Pax, you know, I would need to ask him first, see what he thinks. Me and him, we're ... it's still quite new, right? We're hanging out ... we *like* each other, I just, sometimes it's good not to push things too fast, yeah?"

Danny chews his lip, smirking at me. "So you haven't had sex yet?"

My cheeks start to burn.

"Do you want me to help you seal the deal?" he asks.

"No! Danny, no, I do not want that."

"Danny Orlando has a very high conversion rate."

"It's fine."

"I'm just saying, if you need some tips. Or advice."

"I'll keep that in mind."

He points at me, winks, and makes a clicking noise with his tongue. Then he turns his attention back to the barbecue. "It's still hot," he says, looking mournfully at the coals. "Such a waste."

"I mean, I couldn't eat another—"

"Idea!" He springs up and heads back inside the house. "Wait there!"

A couple of minutes of slamming drawers and cupboards, and some slicing later, Danny emerges carrying two foil-wrapped packages. He waggles his eyebrows at me and places them on the barbecue. "You'll love this!" he assures me.

Fifteen minutes later – during which I try to focus Danny's mind on the storyboard for the video, but Danny wants to try to explain the offside rule in football instead – Danny presents baked bananas with chocolate. Opening the foil package reveals a banana still in its skin, but stuffed with pieces of (now melted) chocolate, the banana's flesh is hot, sticky and soft. It's a mess to eat, but it's out of this world.

We eat in silence for a bit, and as the light starts to fade, festoon lights that surround the terrace area automatically come on, bathing everything in a warm glow. Danny lights a pillar candle inside a large lantern that sits in the centre of the table. "Are you having a nice time?" he asks, softly.

"Yeah, thanks," I reply, because, you know what? I've really tried hard not to, and I absolutely didn't want to . . . but I weirdly am?

28

"And what happened next?!" George scowls, as we walk down the corridor at school on Monday. He's already wearing his massive black glasses, and he's got an open-necked shirt, no bow-tie today: he means business. "Danny Orlando suggests your shoulders seem a little tight and, oh look! There's a nasty knot, *'Let me give you a massage, Barney!' 'Oh yes! Oh, Danny!'* He works his way down your back, and before you know it, you lose your virginity in this 'warm glow' of festoon lights that you speak of?"

"I actually just went home. He called me a cab."

"Of course he did."

"It wasn't a bad evening. He's . . . OK. I think."

George stops dead and turns to me. "Barney. He's a player."

"Well. . ."

"*He's a player.* That means he's not afraid of doing a bit of harmless flirting to get whatever he needs."

"I mean. . ."

"And one evening is all it took for him to get you wrapped around his little finger. Seriously, Barney, how could be so weak?"

"I'm not wrapped around . . . any part of Danny Orlando."

"*But you would like to* be! The entire way you've described this to me, everything you've said, '*Oh, the hot tub; oh, the wonderful cooking; oh, the candles!*' even down to the conversation you reported to me in a casual way, but which you knew damn well was loaded, '*Are you having a nice time?*' – all of it tells me you are already romanticizing this whole encounter, and have fallen for his charms hook, line and sinker! Haven't you?"

"No!"

"Ugh! Just admit it!" George shouts, striding off again.

I hurry up alongside him and try to keep up. "I think he was just trying to be nice."

"Of course he was! Being president will look great on his uni application, plus he might get to be a global ambassador for Rainbow Youth – *but he needs your help*! He's using you to keep afloat, but now that you're VP, you should want him to sink!" He stops and looks at me. "Plus, I don't want you to get hurt."

"He did have a good idea for the video," I offer.

"Did he? How lovely." We keep walking and reach the

265

door of Room 120. "In!" George says, pushing me through the door and closing it again behind us.

"Seriously, I'm not fooled by Danny," I tell him.

"Stop talking about him, then!" George hisses. "He's entirely irrelevant here. He may be president – *for now* – but we're the ones who need to steer this video and get us through to the finals, probably while making sure Bronte doesn't try to sabotage it all along the way. I'm following loads of the clubs at other schools on their socials. A lot of them are playing the long game already, putting stuff out there, highlighting what they're doing, even just LGBT stuff with a positive message, so they can show they've got form."

I take a deep breath. "OK. So what do we need to do?"

"We should make some mini-videos, just for Twitter and Instagram, where the main committee introduce themselves. And we make it cute. So, in your case, I'm thinking along the lines of, "Hey, I'm Barney, VP of the LGBTQ+ Society, and this is my boyfriend, Paxton.""

I look at George, and run my tongue over my lips.

"What?" he says. "It's nice. It's *human*. People will love it."

"About the Paxton thing, though," I say. "You know, with Danny asking about any skeletons in the closet on Friday..."

"Danny again?! Who cares what Danny thinks? Does he really think anything we might have is likely to play more badly than the fact our society is run by a straight boy?"

"What is *straight*, though?" I ask.

George narrows his eyes at me. "Oh, he's done a number on you, hasn't he?" He shakes his head. "OK, whatever. The 'Paxton thing' has happened now. If you just stop, it'll look sus. You can break up later, when it doesn't matter." He sighs. "What is it you wanted to discuss that requires us to be alone in this room?"

I take an unsteady breath. "OK, well, *idea*, and also, circle of trust?"

"What do you mean 'circle of trust'? Everything we discuss is within the 'circle of trust', why do you need to say it in here and not in the cafeteria?" He stares at me. "What? What is it? Tell me."

"Double circle of trust. This can't be mentioned outside of here."

George folds his arms.

I swallow. "Paxton . . . and you . . . would make a great couple!"

George's face stays entirely neutral. "And that stupid statement required a 'circle of trust', did it? Why? To ensure I didn't broadcast your stupidity for all to hear?"

I chew my lip. "Triple-locked circle of trust!"

"No, come on, we need to make these—"

"Pax likes you!"

George stops dead, hand frozen by the door handle.

"You can't tell him I told you because this is a triple-locked-circle-of-trust situation, but he does. He told me.

When he was mentioning about finding someone to take to prom, he was hoping you'd take the hint. But you suggested me instead. But it's not me he wants. It's you. But he doesn't know if you even like boys, let alone if you like him."

George doesn't move, he just stares at the door, breathing. "We'll round up the others. Best location will be the bench by the front entrance with the Greenacre Academy sign in the background." He exhales. "Let's just make these videos."

He pulls the door open, walks out, and lets it slam shut behind him.

"Hello. I'm Bronte O'Halloran, Executive Chair of Greenacre Academy's LGBTQ+ Society. One of the many—"

"OK, cut!" George says.

I lower my iPhone.

"You sound like a newsreader," George tells her. "Can you loosen up a bit?"

"Loosen up?" Bronte snaps. "Seriously?"

"Just a bit more casual," George suggests. "It needs to be relatable."

"I mean, shall I just rap it? Is that relatable enough?"

I really want her to actually try doing that, but we're already behind, and we've bagged barely any usable footage yet. "Time is money, people!" I shout.

"L to the G to the B to the T!

I'm executive chair,

And my name's Bron-tee!"

"*Wow*," George mutters, burying his head in his hands.

"Being queer isn't the only marginalization some of us are dealing with. I'm Maya Phillips, I'm Black, I'm queer, and I'm also vegan—"

"Stop!" Bronte shouts. "Why are you lying?"

Maya puts her hands on her hips. "I'm Black, queer and vegan. Where's the lie?"

"*Vegan*," Bronte replies. "You literally eat meat."

Maya holds out her hands. "I'm vegan now."

"Like, literally just this second?"

"We all have to start somewhere, Bronte."

"Fine, but being vegan isn't a marginalized identity."

"I know that," Maya says, patiently. "That's why I said, *if you had listened*, I'm Black, queer, *and also* vegan. Vegan is separate."

"OK, well it sounded like you were including it in the first bit."

"Shall we just go again?" I ask, brightly.

Maya takes a deep breath. "I'm not in the mood now."

"Oh, Maya!" Bronte says.

"No. You've ruined my flow. I can't get back in."

Maya strides away.

I turn to Bronte. "You should go after her."

"*Why*?"

I take a punt because these two need to sort this out.

"Because she's upset, you don't want that because you care about her, and Maya's blatently only gone vegan because *you're* vegan and she secretly wants your approval – but if you tell her I said that, I'll murder you."

Bronte sniffs, says *nothing,* and stalks away.

"I'm Barney."

"And I'm Paxton. Together, we're. . ."

"Barton!"

"CUT! What the fuck was that?" George asks.

Paxton points at me. "*He* made me do it."

"It's our cute ship name. It's casual and relatable?" I say.

"Yes, we want casual and relatable," George replies, with wild eyes. "Not awkward and dorky!"

"OK," I mutter. "We'll scrap that bit, then."

"You do that." George scowls and holds the phone back up. "Action."

"Hey, I'm Barney Brown, and I'm proud to be Vice President of Greenacre Academy's LGBTQ+ Society! Our vision for a more inclusive and—"

"CUT! Argh! You can't just leave Pax sitting beside you like a spare part, you have to tell the viewers who he is!" George says. "Introduce him, *then* do your spiel about your vision, OK?"

I nod.

"Action."

"Hey, I'm Barney Brown, and this . . . this is my . . . this is Paxton. Hello, Paxton."

"Hello!"

"Oh-my-fucking-Christ, NOW YOU SOUND LIKE PRE-SCHOOL CHILDREN'S TV PRESENTERS WHAT IS WRONG WITH YOU?!"

"OK, OK! Sorry!" I bleat. "Try again."

"The word you're looking for is *boyfriend!*" George tells me. He locks eyes with Pax, then quickly looks away again. "And try to look like you actually are!"

"Um . . . how?" I ask.

"Be a little bit affectionate. Nothing big. Just maybe a hand touching his, or gently placed on his knee as you chat, just casual, yeah?"

I nod. "OK. OK, Pax?"

"OK," Pax says.

"OK," George sighs. "And, action."

"Hey, I'm Barney Brown, VP of Greenacre's Academy's LGBTQ+ Society, and this is my boyfriend, Paxton Lee." I reach out, like I was told, and place my hand on his knee . . . except, because I'm looking at the camera, my aim is way off, and my hand actually ends up really high up his inner thigh.

We both freeze, fixed smiles on our faces.

"You are touching my penis," Pax whispers, through barely moving lips.

"I know, I'm sorry," I whisper back.

"Fuck me with a fucking barge pole," George says.

"I think I need to actually script this down," I say. "Let's film someone else instead."

"If you'd have told me, even as recently as last week, that I was going to be president of Greenacre Academy's Gay Club, I'd have said, 'No way, man! I'm not gay!' But now we're all gay because the whole school is gay. Or something like that. I guess life has a funny way of throwing you a curveball sometimes. ...Get it? Because curves aren't straight? No, but seriously, what do I hope to bring to my presidential role? And who am I to lead an LGBT society, and hopefully the group that's going to be Rainbow Youth's global ambassadors? Well, I'm enthusiastic. I'm passionate. I'm not afraid to speak my mind, and I'm a great believer that in order to get real change, sometimes you can't play by the rules; you gotta mix things up! I'm here, we're all queer, and I'm *your* president."

He puts his foot up on the bench and places his hands on his knee.

"I'm Danny Orlando."

He smiles and winks at the camera.

George releases a long breath. "And cut."

"That felt like we got it!" Danny says. "Did you like the bit at the end? *'I'm Danny Orlando.'* Cool, huh?"

"Mm," I say doubtfully.

"Anyway, look, good news: I spoke to the lads, and

272

they're cool with us filming a segment about homophobia on the sports field and how we've made school football a more inclusive place for gay kids." He nods. "And more good news, they're all happy to wear rainbow laces." He nods again. "As long as none of the filming implies they might actually be gay themselves."

"Right?" George says.

"Also, no one wants to actually speak," Danny adds.

"So they'll basically let us film them running around with rainbow laces on their boots?"

"Yes!" Danny says. "So that's cool!"

"No, it isn't," I say. "That won't tell anyone anything."

"OK, well, what I was thinking," Danny says, "is that, you know you mentioned 'narratives' when you came to mine, and that's like a story, right? So how about the story here is that two boys are playing football, but they happen to be gay, and maybe they hold hands or kiss just before running out onto the pitch, or hell, even during the match, and it's like, *so* not an issue. Like, no one even cares. And the voiceover will be saying, *'Our school football team is welcoming of everyone. There's no 'd' in team, even if there is in some of our players!'*"

"OK, that's *not* what the voiceover will say," George says, "but I quite like the idea."

"But you said none of the players will agree to it," I say. "So. . .?"

Danny looks at me and grins.

273

"*No.*"

"Barney, c'mon!" Danny says. "We'll get you and Pax in football kit, we've got spares, and all you have to do is role-play a little scene, kissy-kissy, or whatever, and kick the ball about a bit. Just until we've got enough filmed that we can use. It'll be, like, ten minutes of your time."

"No, but it's dishonest!" I say.

Danny shrugs. "Not really. You and Paxton *are* a thing. And you're just giving football a go. Trying out a new club. We're not saying you're on the team permanently." He gives me a smile. "Feels like the sort of thing a good VP would do."

"When?" George asks.

"Thursday, after school," Danny replies.

"Cool. I'll film." George looks at me and Pax. "OK?"

"Not rea—"

"Great!" George says.

Danny waggles his eyebrows at me as he extracts a KitKat from his back pocket. "Fun!" he says. "We are *so* gonna make the best video. Rainbow Youth are gonna love it! Virgin Upper Class flights to the USA, here we come!" He tears the KitKat open. "Anyone want a finger?" He winks at me.

"No thanks," I reply.

"Aww," Danny says. "'Course you do!"

And rather than split off a couple of whole, intact KitKat fingers and hand them to me, he snaps the entire four-finger KitKat width-ways, and hands me half, with me and George visibly flinching because it's so utterly barbaric.

I'd suspected it before, but this confirms it.

Danny Orlando is a monster.

29

By Wednesday we've made a bit more progress, but it hasn't been easy.

I filmed Maya doing this great piece to camera about LGBTQ-inclusive sex ed. It's only a minute long, but we had to shoot it fifteen times, because we wanted a moving shot of Maya walking down a corridor, with me walking backwards filming her, but some boys kept running past and screaming "YOU'RE SO GAY!" at us. We ended up filming it during a free period instead, when the corridor was empty, but the whole point was her speech references all the different types of students in a school – i.e., the ones walking by – so it's lost some of its impact. The plan was to intersperse her speech with quick shots of an actual PSHE lesson, but Mrs Cavendish vetoed the idea, saying she didn't want to be filmed showing year ten how to use condoms, or have it implied that her lessons were in any way lacking. I mean, they *are* lacking. Appallingly so. This is the woman who told us that "masturbation is OK, but you shouldn't do it with other people" and, another corker, "You can be who you want, but remember other people are entitled to their opinions and beliefs." She went on to say that she feels an "element of the left is intent on manufacturing conflict where none really exists, because it suits their agenda, gets column inches, and often, book deals." I mean, I wish I'd secretly recorded that class. The trouble is, when you're fourteen, and you're scared you might be gay, it's hard to be the one who stands up and calls bullshit. Not only is it a teacher you're saying it to (and a scary one at that), but you're basically outing yourself.

Meanwhile, our short intro videos on social media attracted some nasty comments from those Family Alliance bigots (George reported them, and the platform replied to say it's not a violation of their terms to call LGBT teenagers "disgusting perverts"); Maya and Bronte have had a falling out over the last piece of vegan lasagne in the cafeteria; George is being really weird, hasn't even mentioned Pax, and is just acting like I didn't say anything; and Danny has completely ignored my messages about needing to actually work out the format of this film. I mean, there's still no storyboard, and he just doesn't seem interested, which is driving me nuts, so I'm just editing it on the fly, hoping it will all come out OK in the end, which is a long way from the nice, *planned* video I wanted.

So, I'm kind of feeling like I just want to scream at

someone. Which is why I'm really looking forward to later this afternoon, when I'm meeting Kyle. I know he's going through similar things, and I honestly think it'll just be good for us both to let off steam for a bit, to someone who isn't directly involved; but yes, OK, he's technically from a rival school so there's only so much we can say.

We're meeting at Harrington Palace Park. It's about twenty minutes for each of us by bus. It's an old country house that became run-down and the council ended up buying and renovating to provide a cafe and some exhibition spaces, and it's set in acres of grounds, including some extensive woodland with lots of paths. It's highly unlikely we'll bump into anyone either of us knows there ... by which I mean, any other kids our age who are wandering around the woodland are likely to also be doing something they probably don't want anyone to know about, so honour among thieves and all that.

He's standing where he said he would be, just outside the entrance to the cafe. It's fairly warm; he's opted for shorts and a T-shirt, with a hoodie over it, and I wish I had too. He's shorter than me, slim, and he looks exactly like his photos: cute, with those gorgeous blond curls and a mischievous glint in his eyes.

"Barney?" he says, eyes lighting up as I walk towards him.

"Kyle!"

We stand awkwardly for a moment, neither of us quite

knowing whether to shake hands, hug, or do neither, before he says, "Aw, come here!" and he hugs me anyway.

"Um, so I got here early," he says as he releases me, "and there was a massive queue at the cafe, so I thought I'd get you a Coke – I hope you like Coke – and I got a sausage roll, in case you were hungry, 'cause I am, but then I didn't know if you were vegetarian, so I also bought a veggie one too – I think it's got spinach and some kind of cheese in it – but then I worried you could be gluten free, and this is like, *pastry*, so I also got a slice of flourless chocolate cake." He blinks at me. "Sorry, I'm talking too much."

I laugh. "All of that sounds perfect."

"Does it? Oh, good."

It's cute, how he seems anxious about this. We decide to get away from the crowd around the cafe and head towards the woods, with a vague plan to find a quiet patch of grass, somewhere we can sit and eat.

"OK, I can't wait," he says, as we clamber over a stile and onto a dirt track, "I know we agreed not to share stories of our competing entries, and I totally don't expect you to, but I've got to tell you about us!"

"Go on."

"So, one of our things in the video is about making sure problematic books and authors don't have space in the school library – you know, why dignify them by allowing them a presence? Well, we put this to the senior leadership team, and it was very much, *"Oh no, freedom of speech, everyone is allowed an opinion!'* and all that crap, you know, like opinions override everything, even if they're hateful and damaging to students, and forgetting that they already make choices about the collection, and that maybe someone can have an opinion, but that doesn't mean you have to amplify it, host it, or otherwise support it or them."

I nod my head. "Exactly."

"So we staged a full-on heist on the library. And we removed all the books by a certain well-known, massively overrated author, and we replaced them with all kinds of books by trans authors instead."

"That's epic," I say. (And also way better than anything we have planned – it's fun and anarchic – which irks me somewhat).

"Right?! But this is the thing, OK? The committee decided we're going to film this like it's a Hollywood heist movie, you know, *Ocean's Eleven* style. We got the full kit, proper camera, lighting, boom mic, the whole shebang, we'd even got a clapperboard, and honestly, quite apart from the fact it's quite hard to stage an actual heist when you're filming it like that, the whole committee just became *monsters*. Suddenly, everyone was a diva, people had tantrums, bitching. Honestly, Barney, I was at the stage where I just thought: you know what? Scrap it. Sure, I'd love for us to be the global ambassadors, and my uni application definitely would love it, but is it really worth all *this*?"

I nod sympathetically. "Our segment on inclusive

sex ed got ambushed by some year tens telling us we were gay—"

"Naturally." Kyle rolls his eyes.

"And then Mrs Cavendish bazooka'd the whole thing by refusing to let us film one of her PSHE classes."

"Inclusive sex ed is a good one," Kyle says. "Waaaa! Now we might copy you! Mwah, ha ha! You've fallen right into my trap, fool!"

"Might copy you!" I look at him, and grin. "Seriously, I love that heist idea. And it's clever to film it like that."

Kyle shrugs. "Like I said, for the amount of stress, and the fact everyone has fallen out, I now kind of disagree." He nudges me towards a path that forks to the left. "Let's head up there."

"Off the beaten track? I hope you're everything you claim to be."

"I'm a murderer."

"Exactly."

"Nah, you checked me out before you met me." Kyle glances at me, smiling.

"I did."

"So did I." He smirks. "Plus, my mum knows I'm here."

I laugh. "So does mine."

"She insisted on checking out your profiles," he tells me. "She says you're cute." He doesn't look at me, but I can see he's stifling a cheeky smile. "Up a bit further. If

I remember right, there's another track off to the left that you barely even notice, and if you follow it up, it opens up into a little grassed area. *Really secluded.* Great for doing murders."

The path in question is massively overgrown with nettles, and Kyle stings his leg as he beats a path through for us. He flops down on the ground in the grass clearing at the end, legs apart, rubbing his shin with a dock leaf, and then pulls his hoodie up over his head, his T-shirt riding up, revealing the waistband of his boxers above those of his shorts, as well as some of his smooth, flat stomach, and honestly, I have this overwhelming urge just to jump on him.

I don't. Of course I don't.

Spoiler: turns out I don't need to.

"How do nettle stings hurt so much?" he says.

"Need me to rub it better?" I laugh.

"Please."

I chuckle again, but then I lock eyes with him and my breath catches.

He reaches out, takes my hand, and places it on the sting. "Just there."

"Huh," I say, feeling super awkward, but it's only his shin, so it's not like this is intimate. I rub a few small circles over the spot with my fingers. "Better?"

He nods slightly, and smiles.

Then he reaches out again, and guides my hand up

higher, to his knee, and then . . . just above the knee. I watch my hand, almost like it's not mine, and then look back at him again. He's staring back, a gentleness in his eyes. I swallow, then focus back on my hand, and will it to move, because I want this, I like him. I start slowly stroking just below the hem of his shorts . . . and then . . . dancing just under the hem. . . I can tell he's already hard, and then he's leaning in to me, breathing suddenly heavy. "I'm glad we got to this part sooner rather than later."

I crack a smile. "Same."

"Can I kiss you, then?"

I can't speak. I just nod.

A wide smile spreads across his face. *"Freakin' awesome."*

And I'm about to laugh again, at that unbridled enthusiasm, which is *so* not anything I ever expected anyone to say about kissing *me*, only I'm stopped by his mouth on mine. At first, I'm tense, and the muscles in my mouth feel stiff and like they won't work, but gradually, I loosen up, start enjoying it more. It's slow and gentle, and as we get deeper into it, I lean back on the grass, him rolling over a bit, so he's half lying on top of me. I can feel his hard-on. I'm sure he can feel mine. I run my fingers under his T-shirt and up his back, then down again, to his boxers, slipping them under the elasticated waistband.

His body tenses. "Oh . . . um . . . *god*," he murmurs. "Oh no. *Oops.*"

283

I stop what I'm doing, my eyes searching his pained face. *Has he just...* "Um ... OK?"

"I've somehow ended up in the chocolate cake," he says, rolling off me, and scraping mushed up cake off his knee and leg. "Ahh, *man*."

He glances up and we both laugh.

"OK, well, it looks like I've knelt in dog poo now, but whatever," he says. He moves the other packets of sausage rolls further away from us, shaking his head at his clumsiness. "Try again?" A cheeky smile plays on his lips.

"God, yes," I say.

He glances over my shoulder, then back over his. "You know ... I don't think anyone ever comes up here..." He looks down at the ground, picking at blades of grass. "I think it's just you and me."

His eyes meet mine again.

I know what he's saying.

"Like, I know there's a risk, maybe a random dog walker, or something, but also, honestly, Barney, being totally honest, and this isn't normally me, it really isn't, I don't know what's happened, and I'm not saying we have to do *loads*, but maybe *something*, but also *nothing* is also OK, if you don't want to, like I totally respect that, and get that, but also..." He looks at me and sighs. "I just don't think I can keep my hands off you."

30

I wake up the next day thinking about Kyle. I walk to school thinking about Kyle. I couldn't even tell you what we were doing in English lit, history or economics because I'm thinking about Kyle. We didn't even do that much in the end. We kissed and cuddled, but, god, it was good. As well as being a really nice thing to think about, there's another huge bonus to all this: it stops me thinking about the horror that awaits me at the end of the day.

I find Paxton hovering nervously outside the changing rooms.

"They're all in there," he says. "*The team.*" He glances towards the closed door, the sounds of . . . well, *animals*, coming from inside: grunts, bellows, roars and weird squawking noises.

I swallow. I don't want to go in. It feels like we'll get eaten.

George joins us, with Maya and Bronte in tow. He's

roped them both in to help do the filming – more cameras means more angles means we can get it done quicker, and god knows, we're all nervous about this so the quicker the better. No one needs to say anything. We've all had bad experiences in the changing rooms, although no one more than George, for whom nowhere has been safe from accusations, dirty looks and malicious complaints when all he's trying to do is get his gym kit on and get the horror that is PE over and done with as quickly as possible. George nods his understanding. "Good luck, then."

I try to give a brave smile. I can't.

It's at this point two boys explode out of the door, one of them brandishing a towel which he's using to whip the other one, who is stark-bollock naked. He's stocky and muscular, with a surprisingly small dick. After a lot of howling, the naked boy clocks me and Pax, grins, and pushes the changing room door back open. "ALL RISE FOR THE BENDERS!" he shouts, to cheers from inside.

He turns back to us. "Get in, then."

Pax and I shuffle past him. The changing room is long and narrow, with sets of wooden benches down the lengths of each wall. It's claustrophobic in here at the best of times, but normally, in a PE lesson, there's a mix of kids, lots of them like me, and it kind of neutralizes the effect of the Alpha-male boys. This, however, is *all* Alpha-male boys. And it's hell. The whole place reeks of sweat, Lynx and toxic masculinity. Despite the aggressively heterosexual atmosphere, I've never seen so much ball scratching, penis readjusting and dry humping. Various boys clamber on each other, one gives another a piggyback, two lads appear to be simulating anal sex at the far end. No one is batting an eyelid.

Through the hormone-fuelled haze emerges Danny Orlando, already wearing his shorts and team shirt, and carrying two sets of kit for us. "All right, lads?!" he beams. "Fresh kits for you both. Get it on, then join us outside, yeah? I'm dishing out the rainbow laces too, gonna be epic." He turns to the rest of the changing room. "Greenacre Lions!" he booms. And then he roars, like a . . . well, lion, I suppose.

The boys all roar back.

This is nuts.

Danny disappears back into the haze, leaving me and Pax at the edge of this mayhem with no obvious place to change, since all of the boys are taking up acres of bench with their stuff. There's maybe half a metre of bench at the very end, so Pax puts his kit down on it, before the boy next along glowers at him and says, "Don't touch my stuff." Pax nods, and tries to pull off his trainers, but has to steady himself on the bench and accidentally touches a bit of the boy's bag. "DON'T TOUCH MY STUFF WITH YOUR GAY SHIT!" the boy shouts. "What you changing here for?" he points down the changing room. "There's space down there!"

Pax glances at me, I give him a small nod, we steel ourselves, and we walk further down, as the boy who doesn't want his stuff touched mutters, "Fucking pervs!"

The walls feel like they're closing in on us, and we're barely able to breathe in the fug. There's no obvious space for us to change, the benches are just a mess of huge sports bags, clothes, towels and kit. About halfway down, one lad steps in front of us, grinning, and says, "Welcome to temptation alley!" He steps aside, and about six or seven lads with their dicks out have formed two lines, leaving space for us to walk down the middle. "Fun game! Can you make it to the end without looking or getting hard?" the lad says, before starting up a chant that everyone joins in with: "Walk! Walk! Walk! WALK! WALK!"

I don't know what to do. My heart's pounding and my throat's tight. I want to get out of here, but there's a crowd of lads behind us, and a crowd in front, and everyone's watching, and a couple of them are filming, and all I want to do is get changed and shoot this stupid footage we need for this stupid film that clearly no one's gonna care about anyway because, despite everything, despite all my hopes about a whole school gay club, the concept is way better than the reality, because in reality, it's just the same old crap. Despite the school's words about inclusivity and making LGBT students feel safe and welcome, we're not, it doesn't matter, because people are still horrible anyway. People still hate us. And why? What have we ever done to any of them apart from having the audacity to be ourselves?

The chanting is louder. Echoing in my head. I feel like I need to be strong for Pax, but I'm powerless.

And I'm scared.

"LADS! COME ON!" The football coach is suddenly in the doorway. I watch him clock what's going on, but make a very obvious decision to ignore it – a "boys will be boys" kind of eye-roll. "LET'S WARM UP! WHAT ARE YOU DOING? COME ON! LAST ONES OUT GET BENCHED!"

The lad smiles and puts his hands on my shoulders. "Cheer up, it's just banter, mate. We do this every week, not just for you guys."

I barely dare breathe, but I try to nod.

"You're not special, it's like . . . an initiation. You're one of us now. It's what you want, isn't it?"

I try to nod again.

"Good man." He gently slaps my cheek, smirks, then joins the stream of boys pushing past, their chatter and banter gradually fading as, one by one, they walk out, and as they do, the tension in the room slowly dissipates, until it's just me and Pax.

I close my eyes and just stand there for a moment.

Finally, I release a slow, long breath.

I turn to Pax.

Silent tears run down his cheeks.

I put my arm across his shoulders and pull him close.

"It's OK. We don't have to do this. Let's sack it off."

Pax shakes his head. "I'm angry, that's all. And yes, we *do* have to do it. What just happened is exactly why we have to." He wipes his eyes with the palms of his hands and sniffs. "Let's go."

31

When Pax and I finally emerge onto the playing field in our kits, most of the boys are sitting about on the ground, fiddling with their boots.

"Turns out most of these evolutionary throwbacks can't re-lace their own boots," George says, coming up to us with a bunch of rainbow laces in his hand. "So Maya, Bronte and I have been doing it for them, like they're a bunch of four-year-olds." He looks at us both. "Are you two OK?"

"Yeah," I say.

"Let's get this done," says Pax.

Danny jogs up. "What was that shit in the changing room just now? I came in right behind the coach."

"Nothing," I say, my head still spinning. "Don't worry about it, Danny."

He nods, thoughtfully. "The boys can get a bit high-spirited sometimes. They don't mean anything by it."

"Danny?" I say. *"Fuck off."*

He raises his eyebrows. "Um . . . OK? OK, well, I was just coming over to say, once everyone's ready we'll just have a bit of a kick-about to get the shots we need. Maybe I could pass the ball to you, Barney, and then you can kick it to Pax? If you like? And then perhaps we can get some general shots of running about, calling for the ball, that type of thing? Teamwork, right? But, anyway." He looks at us all. "Right. Well, I'll fuck off then."

He fucks off.

Of course I've played football before. But this is something else. These boys from the school team charge around the pitch with such powerful force, and with such wild speed, that I'm actually frightened. They dart, they sweep, they shoot, they score, and it all seems to happen in the blink of an eye. I don't want to get close to any of the action. It's like when they made us cut acrylic with the big, scary electric saw thing in design technology: I just want to hang back at a safe distance because I'm genuinely worried I'm going to lose a limb.

But I'm also conscious that Maya, Bronte and George are filming this and the whole point of this segment is that me and Pax are looking like we're having a good old LGBT-inclusive time. So if I can't smile, I need to at least not look like I'm about to piss myself. And I need to do more than dally about on the edge of the pitch, because that's not inclusion. That's just what everyone expects the gay kids to do.

292

OK, just do it, Barney.

I brace myself and jog in the general direction of the ball. A couple of the lads are passing it between themselves, really fast, so when I get close, I kind of hang back a bit, terrified, but hopeful if it does come in my direction, I can quickly kick it back to one of them. And I mean quickly. I don't want it near me for any longer than absolutely necessary.

Danny gets the ball, sees me, shouts "Barney!" and passes it.

Shit! It's happening!

Amazingly, I manage to stop the thing and bring it under control. (Yes, he did pass it relatively slowly and gently, I did notice that, but let's gloss over the idea he might have been trying to help me out.) I decide to try to give Maya a good shot by running with the ball (dribbling, I think they call it?) a short distance, and then hopefully passing it back to—

SLAM!

I'm thrown forwards as what feels like a double-decker bus (but is actually Nico Murphy) collides with me, knocking me to the floor, his boot studs slicing into my calf, as my ankle twists and cracks, and I'm face down in the mud as he falls on top me, knocking the wind out of my lungs, and slamming my nose into the ground. There's a moment of nothing. And then I taste the blood, and notice that it's coming out of my nose, and then the white-hot, searing pain shooting from my ankle and my calf and—

He's lying on top of me. "Fucking disgusting little *poof*," he hisses in my ear.

He scrambles to his feet, kicking me in the stomach as he does so, making me both cry out, and cry. It's the pain. But it's also Nico's venom. His poison that's clearly been building up all this time and has just been looking for a chance to spill out.

Maya, Bronte and George are by my side. "He's hurt!" Maya calls out.

"Come on, you're fine, walk it off!" the coach shouts back, from across the pitch.

"I barely touched him!" Nico says. "It was just a tap, man!"

George tries to help me up.

Blood's trickling out of my nose.

I can't see for the tears.

Pax is here now too. He's trying to help me up, but I can't stand on the ankle.

I scream out, as another jolt of pain shoots through me.

I can't catch a breath.

And why . . . why is it *me* who feels shame? When Nico did this? Why is it *me* feeling embarrassed?

I just. . . I want to be as far away from all this, and all of them, as possible. I start crawling off the pitch, dragging myself, but I'm slow, and I'm sobbing, and I'm gasping through the pain every time I move.

Danny arrives.

I don't want him anywhere near me. This is his fault. Nico plays for the team he captains. I mean, they're best mates, for christ's sake.

Danny squats down next to me. "Let me help."

"Fuck off, Danny!" I manage to hiss, through tears, and blood. "Just. . ."

But it's no good. The tears get the better of me, and now I'm full-on bawling my eyes out on the edge of the pitch, while everyone looks on. I've never been in this much pain. My ankle, my calf, my nose. . . My ribs aching with every shallow breath I manage to suck in.

"He needs some first aid," I hear Danny say.

"OK, fine, can you quickly sort him out, Danny?" the coach shouts.

"No. . ." I mutter.

"Nico? Good spirit, but watch the aggression," the coach continues. "We don't want any red cards when we play against Broad Mill next week – OK? Play on!" He blows his whistle.

Then, before I know it, Danny's scooping me up in his arms, and carrying me off the pitch.

"I just want to go home!" I howl. Anywhere, away from here, where no one cares.

"Come on, mate—" Danny soothes.

"I WANT TO GO HOME!"

Maya, Bronte, George and Pax are walking alongside us, their faces occasionally coming into view as we bounce along.

"He can't walk," Danny tells them. "I can take him back in my car, but we need to stop his nose bleeding first."

"Does he need to go to A&E, though?" I hear Bronte ask.

"Maybe," mutters Danny.

We reach the changing rooms, and Danny puts me gently down on one of the benches. I slump against the back wall, Bronte (of all people) putting a comforting arm around me, as I sob into her shoulder.

"Fucking *dick*," Maya mutters, sitting the other side of me and holding my hand.

"That's the polite way of putting it," Bronte replies, sighing.

Maya nods and squeezes my hand.

Danny returns with a first aid kit and a bunch of tissues, which he hands me so I can sort my nose out. But the bleeding seems to have already stopped, my nose just feeling full and tender.

"Can you move your foot?" Danny asks.

I try to twist it left and then right. It really fucking hurts.

"OK," Danny says. "It's not broken. I think he needs to be patched up, but he'll be OK." He looks at me. "I could take you to A&E to make sure? Might be a long wait, though."

"Please, I just want to go home," I mutter.

"OK, I'll take you," Danny says.

Pax collects my stuff up, and Danny carries me out of the changing room, cradled in his arms again, my arms around his neck, and out to the car park where his infamous Audi awaits.

I do not want to do this. He is squarely to blame for most of this, but, also, I need to get home and there's no way I can walk it, even though it's really close. I'll just have to suck up his charity and deal with my feelings towards him later.

"Call us!" Maya says, as Danny installs me in the passenger seat and helps me on with my belt.

"Yeah," I croak. "I'm sorry."

"You don't need to be sorry, Barney," she replies. "We love you!"

Danny slams the door shut, and I hear him say a few words to Maya, George, Bronte and Pax, and then he comes round and slides into the driver's seat. "OK," he says, starting the engine. "Let's get you home, then."

We drive in silence. I'm furious. I don't want to talk to him anyway, and now he's behaving like some sort of saviour, and to make it worse, he drives really confidently and smoothly, way better than my parents, and like he's been doing it for years, and that pisses me off even more since I haven't even had a lesson yet.

He pulls up outside my house and I can't click the belt

and open the door fast enough. "Thanks," I mutter.

"Whoa! Hold up!" Danny says, leaping out the door and running around to my side. "Let me help you."

"I'm fi— ARGH!" My ankle gives away underneath me, but Danny catches me, and reluctantly I allow him to help me to my front door. He waits while I fumble around in my rucksack for my keys. "It's fine, you can go."

"Are your folks home?"

"No."

"Then I'll wait with you for a bit."

"Please just go."

"Need to make sure you're not concussed or anything."

"I'm not."

"Whatever you say, but I'm not leaving you."

I sigh. I'm too weak to argue, so I open the door and he helps me hobble inside. I hate that I'm so reliant on him right now. We make our way through to the kitchen, with me emitting little gasps of pain periodically, and he sits me down on one of the chairs. "Right! Ibuprofen?"

"Third drawer down," I say.

Danny sets about getting the tablets and fixing a glass of water. "Take two, it'll reduce the swelling and take the edge of the pain."

I do as I'm told, scowling at him as he goes back to the drawer and fishes out the first aid kit that's also in there. He unzips it, and picks out various items, including a really large bandage that I've never imagined ever needing ...

until now.

He fills a small bowl with warm water and adds a splash of antiseptic to it, then kneels down in front of the chair, inspecting my calf. "Ouch! He got you good there," Danny says. "OK, this'll sting a bit."

He wets some cotton wool in the warm, antiseptic water, and I wince as he presses it against my calf. *"Ah! Argh!"*

"Got to get it cleaned up, mate. You don't want it to get infected."

He continues to gently smooth the cotton wool over my calf, the stinging subsiding as he does so, or maybe I just get used to it? He gets through several balls of cotton wool before patting the area dry and applying some Savlon cream with his index finger.

He sighs. "OK. Let's sort your ankle out." He presses it gently, and I flinch, but the pain has eased off compared to when it first happened. "You got any frozen peas?"

"Huh?"

"A bag of frozen peas works wonders on a sprain. It'll take the swelling right down, and then we can strap it up."

"Um . . . in the freezer, maybe?"

I nod towards it, suddenly aware of how small my house is compared to his. The tiny kitchen, with one oven, the washing up piled in the sink, the peeling paint where the damp is coming up from god knows where. Danny pulls various drawers in the freezer open, juggles a half-empty packet of Cornettos and some oven chips, and finally pulls out a bag of frozen peas, which he wraps in a tea towel and presses against my ankle.

He's clearly done all this before. He seems to know what he's doing, and, in spite of myself and all my irritation, there's something a little bit comforting about that.

Danny rinses the bowl out at the sink, then refills it, and pulls up a chair next to me. He dabs some more cotton wool in the warm water, then begins gently wiping the blood off my face.

"I can do this," I say.

"I know. I just want to make sure there aren't any more injuries."

"Honestly—"

"Just let me do it, Barney."

He says it quite firmly, and I'm a sucker for authority, so I shut up.

He dabs around my nose, and softly wipes down my cheeks, forehead, and around my mouth and neck.

"Jeez, you are a *mess*," he mutters.

"Yeah, Nico made sure of that."

Danny gets a little closer to my face, concentrating below my eye. "Accident, though, right? It happens."

I take an unsteady breath. "Like him saying 'fucking disgusting poof' when he was lying on top of me? It happens, right?"

Danny slowly withdraws his hand and sits back.

"But that can't be news to you, what sort of person he is," I add.

Danny sighs, and seems lost in his thoughts for a moment. "No," he says, finally. "I'm sorry."

I shrug. "Whatever, Danny."

He gets up and takes the bowl back to the sink, packing up the other first aid supplies. "How's the pain?"

"I'll live."

"Let me strap up your ankle."

"It'll be fine, I can manage."

"I know how to do it, though. Do you?"

I shrug.

"Thought not."

He kneels down again, removes the frozen-pea tea-towel wrap, and winds the large bandage around my ankle and lower calf, securing it with some tape. "Come on, I'll help you through to the lounge and get you a cup of tea. Do you want tea?"

"Danny, thank you, but—"

"I'm not leaving until I've sat with you long enough to know you're not dizzy and you've not got a headache, and you're otherwise fine, so stop complaining, OK?"

"OK."

He helps me hobble through to the lounge, but as I ease myself on to the sofa, I wince again – something on my back, that I hadn't been aware of before. Danny's right on it, like some sort of A&E doctor. "Where's it hurt?"

"My back, but—"

"Top off."

"No."

He clicks his fingers. "Come on. Let me see."

I guess he's already seen me mostly naked in the hot tub, so there's no reason to be overly mortified by this. I pull my top off, and shuffle around so he can examine my back.

I hear him suck in a breath, then jump as I feel his fingers on my back. "Sorry," he murmurs. "You're bruised, but it's also grazed. Hang on."

He heads out and returns moments later with the antiseptic cream from the kitchen. He squirts some on to my back and I gasp.

"Does it hurt?"

"Just cold," I say.

"OK," he murmurs, gently starting to smooth and work the cream into my back. He goes extra carefully on the grazed parts, but even so, I still wince slightly. He's methodical, slow, his fingers warm. I realize he's stopped, and hasn't moved for at least fifteen seconds. Maybe he's done? I glance over my shoulder.

"All done!" he says, quickly, getting up. "I'll get you that tea." And he disappears out of the door again.

I fish my other T-shirt out of my bag and pull it on, then sit back into the sofa and close my eyes. The painkillers are kicking in now, and although I'm sore as hell, I don't feel so bad.

"Here you go, mate!" Danny says, returning with a mug of steaming tea. "I put sugar in too; warm, sweet tea is good for shock. Or so my grandma says, but she also says bread crusts make your hair curl, and that's bullshit, right?"

I smile. "I take sugar anyway."

He raises his eyebrows. "Oh. Well. *Good.*" He studies me for a moment. "How are you feeling?"

"A bit better. I think I'm fine. Honestly, you can go. Thanks for . . . sorting me out."

He nods. "OK. Call me if you start feeling bad. Or, better still, call an ambulance. I can see myself out." He grabs his rucksack. "See you then."

I nod. "See you, Danny."

He walks out into the hall, then comes back again. "Barney? I've been thinking. And I think this is the right thing to do. I'm quitting, OK? I'm gonna quit."

I stare at him.

He swallows, nods, and walks out.

32

I don't tell the others about Danny's resignation right away. I respond to their messages, saying I'm OK, but I lay awake that night trying not to think about my aching body: trying not to be resentful that I should still be basking in the warm glow of getting with Kyle, rather than dealing with all sorts of shitty feelings instead, and trying to work out what happens now, whether it's *actually* true that the VP would automatically be instated as president, and how much of a fight Bronte would put up.

At this point, I'm not sure the club could survive any more fights.

In the end, I reach the conclusion that the right thing to do would be to work out which of us came second in the original vote. First thing in the morning I message the rest of the committee with the resignation news and my proposal, and I'm pleasantly surprised that even Bronte agrees that it's the best way forward; she must really think she had the votes.

Of course, that's going to entail a trip to see Mr Hubbard with the rest of the committee, and begging Mrs Buchanan to let us see him.

But as it turns out, we don't need to beg, because Mr Hubbard asks to see us. Or rather, he demands it, slightly dramatically, by sending random year sevens to each of our classrooms during the first lesson to fetch us "immediately", leaving all of our peers in little doubt that, for some reason, we're all in epic amounts of trouble.

Mrs Buchanan looks up and raises her eyebrows as we all file in to the office. "Right," she says, picking up the phone on her desk and dialling an internal number. "Mr Hubbard? *They're* here." She glances up at us, looking really unimpressed. "Yes, very well. OK, then."

She replaces the phone. "Go on through." She waves in the direction of Mr Hubbard's door.

George, Maya, Bronte, Paxton and I shuffle in. We're not invited to sit.

"Where's Danny?"

Brontes smirks. "It turns out he wasn't up for the job after all."

Mr Hubbard sighs, leans back in his ergonomic office chair and looks us at all over steepled fingers. "I see. Well. That's a matter for another time. I've called you in here because a member of staff has alerted me to a proposed segment in your video about the provision of inclusive sex education at the school," he says.

"That's right," I say.

Mr Hubbard nods. "And what angle will you be taking with that?"

"Well, we're showing how the needs of LGBT students are badly catered for, like in a lot of schools, and sometimes completely ignored."

"I see." Mr Hubbard grimaces. "I'm not very happy about that, to be honest with you. The staff here do their best to provide a rounded PSHE curriculum. But there are certain limits. We have to be sensitive to the sensibilities of some parents, for example."

"You mean homophobes who still think you can turn kids gay by discussing it?" George says.

Mr Hubbard stares at George for a moment or two, then releases a breath. "People have different views on what's appropriate in these classes."

I stare at him. I can't believe I'm hearing this. I always thought Mr Hubbard was one of the good ones.

"That's bullshit!" Maya blurts out.

"Maya, that sort of language is—"

"I don't care!" she shouts. "It's bullshit! Our sexuality, or how we identify, isn't an 'opinion'. An inclusive education, knowing the facts, being given information that will keep us safe, isn't an 'opinion'; it's just a basic right that every student in this school should have!"

"Maya—"

"Stop pandering to bigoted parents!" she continues.

"It's pathetic!"

"Some parents have religious views that—"

"*Religious views?* We're real. We're standing right here. How about we deal with that rather than fairy tales?"

"Damn right!" Bronte adds. "Or what about queer kids from religious families who are themselves religious? Don't they deserve support when they might not get it at home?"

"And all this because Mrs Cavendish stuck her oar in?" George interjects. "She's as bad as these parents. Have you heard her PSHE lessons? There is so much barely disguised bigotry!"

"Be very careful," Mr Hubbard warns. "You can't go around slandering people."

George shakes his head. "It has to be *untrue* for it to be slander, sir."

"You want to see us in court?" Maya asks.

"Oh, we'll see you in court!" Bronte adds. "Good luck trying to win *that* case."

Mr Hubbard's eyes widen. He's seconds from losing it with us, and, despite the fact he's lost the argument, he's going to pull rank. "In submitting that video, you will be representing this school. If you want to campaign outside of that, that's up to you. But I'm not going to allow you to drag our good name and the good work this school does through the mud as part of the Rainbow Youth application. So take it out, or we'll withdraw the club from the competition. Now, go back to your lessons."

We start to file out. I know everyone else is as angry as I am, but we're powerless here.

"Wait!" Mr Hubbard says, suddenly brightening up. "I forgot, a load of swag turned up from Rainbow Youth; they send it to all the schools who are submitting applications." He heaves two large boxes on to his desk and starts to rummage through. "There's pens, badges, some T-shirts, baseball caps—" Mr Hubbard opens the flaps on the other box. "And these branded teddy bears. Here." He starts throwing them at us to catch. "Enough for you to have one each. Give the spare to Mrs Buchanan on your way out, with my regards." He looks at us. "*Smile*. It's not that bad." He frowns at me. "Is that a black eye, Barney?"

I stare at him. "It's nothing."

Whatever. I'm not going to be placated by a teddy bear or some T-shirt, I'm not interested in him now adopting his usual matey tone after he's just bollocked us for trying to tell the truth, and I'm not going to tell him what happened when he clearly doesn't give a crap.

We walk past Mrs Buchanan, who has an "oh dear, I told you so" sort of expression on her face. She's certainly not an ally either. I have an overwhelming urge to snog Pax all over her desk, just to rub her face in all the gay, but instead, I just plonk the gay teddy bear on it, who's wearing a vest top and waving a little Pride flag. "Love from Mr Hubbard," I tell her.

Mrs Buchanan, for the first time ever, *smiles*.

Seriously? Before it would only have taken a teddy bear to butter her up?

We don't go back to our classes. Instead, we round the corner, go through the double doors, and form a huddle under the stairwell.

"Are you OK, Barney?" Bronte asks. "That eye looks bad."

"I'm ... fine." My ankle throbs from having been standing on it too long. I subtly try to shift most of my weight to the other.

Pax kicks at the wall. "I don't know, everything that's happened, me and Barney in the changing rooms, him being attacked, Mr Hubbard just now – why are we even bothering? Whole school gay club? This brilliant, inclusive place? It's bollocks! If we do anything, we should expose them all."

I sigh. I have to admit, my heart's not really in this any more either.

"Or. . ." Maya says. "We gloss over it. We do what we originally planned. We shine the spotlight right on to every single one of them."

A smile spreads over Bronte's face. "We do a great video, make the school out to be perfect, we get through, and all the attention will be on the school. Then they *have* to play ball. They have to make it true. It keeps us visible and the school accountable. Maybe then we get real change." She looks at Maya. "Well, well. Someone's read the manipulation playbook!"

"I found it in your bag," Maya replies.

"Impressive. I mean it."

Maya shrugs, but looks kind of pleased.

I blow out a breath. "Will it keep them accountable, though? Won't they just take the glory, shout about this stamp of approval we've given them – *'Yay, we're so supportive of the LGBT kids – they even say so themselves!'* – and that just makes it easier for them to do sweet FA?"

"It's a gamble," Maya replies. "But what is life, if not full of risk?"

"She's right," Bronte agrees.

More to the point, I don't have a better idea. "OK. So we press on? We shoot the rest of the video, we big the school up, even though we know it's not true, and then they have to live up to the picture we've painted?"

George nods. "It's sneaky, and I quite like it. Nice one, Maya. Pax? You in?"

"If you lot are in, I'm in!" he slaps me on the back and I wince and gasp. "Oh, shit! Oh shit! Sorry! You OK?"

"Argh. It just stings still. And kind of sends a shooting pain right up my shoulder, but I'm good. I'll be fine."

"Barns, do you not think you should at least see the school nurse?" Maya says.

"What for? Wet paper towels? Nah, I'm good." I mean, I'm *sort of* good. I'm hurting, inside and out, but

I'm trying to be strong, because presidents are strong, and I want them to see me that way – especially after the blubbing wreck I was yesterday. "Hey, how about we have food at mine? Tomorrow? We can run through the last of the footage, upload it, then I can do the final bit of editing?"

"I'll do Persian Love Cake!" Bronte announces.

Maya's eyes widen. "That sounds like a *challenge*."

"It *could be* a challenge."

"Challenge *accepted*!" Maya says. "I shall do ... *Persian Love Cake*."

"Well, may the best woman win," Bronte says.

"Oh, *she will*," Maya replies.

I clap my hands, mainly just to remind them the rest of us are still here. "Cool. I'll check in with Mum and WhatsApp a time." I look at them all, feeling vaguely presidential for the first time ever, even though that really hasn't been agreed yet. "I guess with all the drama, and since we have some big fish to fry in the next twenty-four hours, we're putting the leadership question on ice for now?" I glance at Bronte, and she nods. "Cool," I say. "It'll be OK. We can still do this, team."

George and Pax arrive first, and have brought stuffed peppers (George) and roasted Mediterranean tartlets (Pax) – clearly giving me a run for my money. Bronte arrives with her Persian Love Cake, followed by Maya, with hers.

"May the cake wars commence," Maya says. "I hope

you used rose water, Bronte, although I know how hard it can be to find."

"But of course!" Bronte beams. "It's essential. Like using edible rose petals, which are quite a niche product."

"Mmm. But fine if you pre-empt that and get an Amazon Prime delivery."

"Mmm!" Bronte says, smiling.

There's another ring at the door. "Are we going to have to score your cakes?" I ask, as I hobble out of the kitchen. "Because I'm not sure we can stomach any more voting drama!" I twist the Yale lock and throw the door open.

"Hey," Danny Orlando says, grinning, and holding two stacked plastic tubs.

"What are you doing here?"

"Meeting, obviously." He steps past me. "I got your WhatsApp. And this time, I brought food. *Food* food!"

Danny strolls towards the kitchen. I shut the door, and unsteadily follow after him, utterly confused.

"Evening, all!" Danny says, ignoring everyone's bewildered expressions. "So, I made *coq*, that's c-o-q not c-o-c-k, *au vin*. How about that, then?! It'll need reheating." He looks at everyone. "Yeah?"

"Danny . . . you *resigned*," George says.

"Yeah, I know."

"So . . . what are you doing here?"

"We're having a meeting, aren't we?"

"Yeah, but you resigned!" George says again. "So, that

means you don't come to the meetings any more."

Danny screws up his face. "Not from gay club! I didn't resign from gay club! Oh my god, is that what you thought? I resigned from the football team!" He looks at me. "*Barney*! Duh!"

"That . . . really wasn't clear," I reply. "Also, *really*? The football team? But you love that team."

"Yeah, well, *I did* love it. He pulls out a chair and flops down. "But then our filming happened, didn't it? I heard what they did to you in the changing rooms. One of the lads told me at the start of the kick-about. And it's obvious what Nico did, especially with what he said to you, Barney." He sighs and looks down at the floor. "Nobody comes for my queer friends." He looks back up. "I'm not all bad, you know? I know right from wrong. And I know it's right to stand with you lot. So, screw the football team." He smiles. "Besides, they can't cook for shit, and you folk. . ."

The part of me that is massively disappointed and annoyed that I'm not, now, going to be president (I mean, seriously, how many times can this position be taken from my clutches at the last moment?) is completely neutralized by the part of me that is genuinely touched that Danny has just said all this, and that he's prepared to jack in the football team to be with us.

Maybe there's more to it. Maybe Danny still *is* a player, like George says, and maybe he's just decided that president of the club is better for his uni applications than football captain?

Who knows, but as we settle down to eat, and after Bronte has reiterated that Danny needs to call it the 'LGBTQ+ Society' and not 'Gay Club', we talk through the final bits of the video, and for the first time ever it feels like we're all on the same page, united, and ready to win this thing. Even Bronte seems to have buried the hatchet – for the moment, at least.

As I'm stacking plates into the sink at the end of the evening, and while Pax is busy doing the video uploads to my laptop, and the others are watching *A Christmas Prince 2: The Royal Wedding* (George's choice, natch) in the lounge, I feel a hand on the small of my back. It's Danny.

"How's the ankle, mister?"

"OK, I think. Better than it was, anyway."

"Good," he says. "I'm glad."

Our eyes meet, then he smiles, gives my back a little rub, and walks back through to the lounge. "Bronte? I give your cake nine out of ten. Maya? I give your cake ... *also* nine out of ten. We have a draw!"

I hear howls of outrage from Bronte and Maya, both demanding to know why they missed a point, to which Danny replies something about giving something to work towards, and how maybe we should have a "Big Gay Bake Off".

It's weird, everyone getting on like this.

It's weird, having Danny on our side, and how that somehow makes me feel like we're more powerful.

Maybe allies are just as important as anyone else.
Maybe an ally *can* be president of an LGBT society.

My phone vibrates.

Kyle: Hey.

Me: Hey.

Kyle: I just wanted to say. . .

Kyle: Even though I am editing our video and it's
V V V important. . .

Kyle: That I can't stop thinking about you and
can't concentrate and just really want to see you.

"What are you grinning at?" George has walked in, and is standing in the doorway, watching me.

I slide my phone back into my pocket. "Nothing. A message, that's all."

George locks eyes with me.

"I'm allowed some privacy, right?" I add.

He's still staring, then he takes breath. "'Course."

I nod.

He looks like he's going to say something, but thinks better of it and instead grabs his glass, turns, and walks back through to the lounge and the sound of Danny loudly

315

complaining that he hasn't seen *A Christmas Prince 1* and can anyone bring him up to speed?

I feel bad about keeping things from George. I know he's just trying to manage our public image. But also, I don't owe my whole self to this process. I'm allowed my own life. I'm not even president, I'm VP, and if I want ... whatever this is with Kyle, I can have it.

And I do want it.

I really like him.

33

Pax drags the final imported clip into the editing window. It's one that Bronte filmed, about how, as a school, Pride is a year-round celebration (even though it really isn't), and it's quite good, actually. She's an amazingly good liar. "Cool. So you're all good to go, I think." Pax turns to look at me. "Are you sure you don't need me to stay and help?"

It's a big night. Applications close in just a few hours, so this is going down to the wire. The idea that we all sit and do this together after dinner was mooted, but too many cooks, and all that. "I think I've just got to get my head down and do it," I say. "But, thanks."

Pax nods and reaches into his rucksack. "Have these, since I guess it'll be a long night." He hands me a big bag of Haribo and a Snickers.

I laugh. "You're a star, thanks."

"Cool, good luck, message if you need anything!" He

stands and moves to my bedroom door. "Um ... thanks, by the way."

"What for?"

"For everything." He gives me a light, easy smile. "Laters."

I've no idea what that's about, and I've no time to dwell on it. I'm up against it here. I start watching various clips back, deleting the totally useless ones and trimming the best ones, gradually building them up in sequence, before I start the fine adjustments between the cuts. It's painstaking, and it takes me ages, but slowly, frame by frame, I'm starting to see it take shape, and, you know what? With music and narration, and some nice start and end title cards, I think this is going to look quite good.

By eleven p.m. I'm nearly done. I found some great royalty-free music, and I've added that to the audio section, and the narration is finished, I've just got to line it up correctly so everything is in sync, and then adjust the volume levels so the background music dips when the narration happens. Fifteen more minutes' work – twenty, tops – then I can upload it. It calls for a celebration Haribo, or ten.

I savour the sugar hit for a minute then turn back to my laptop. I run my fingers over the trackpad, but, annoyingly, the screen's frozen. I try tapping a few random keys, not that pressing random keys is ever going to help, but sometimes I feel like software just needs a bit of a prod, and any kind of prod might help.

It doesn't, though. Ugh. It's entirely unresponsive, so I'm left with no option but to force quit iMovie and restart it.

I sit back and wait.

There's nothing to do but eat more Haribo.

iMovie has reloaded. It normally brings up the project you were working on, but, for some reason, it hasn't. I click through to Saved Projects. . .

The video isn't there.

I click back and forth, looking around, trying the "Open recents" option, but still . . . nothing.

OK, OK, no need to panic, because I'll be able to locate the project in the Finder. . .

Except I can't.

I'm holding my breath. My blood's running cold. But it's OK, it's OK, because this stuff backs up to iCloud automatically, so there will be a saved version of the video, maybe not quite as recent as I'd like, but the bulk of it should be. . .

Except it isn't.

I go into blind panic mode. I'm clicking around everywhere, frantic, urgent, because it's got to be here and I'm not prepared to accept that it isn't . . . because this has to be submitted tonight, in, like, forty minutes, and even if I got all the raw footage from everyone's phones again, there's not enough time now for me to edit it all together and make it look good, so this *has* to be here, and, you know, maybe I should have saved extra copies of this as I went along, maybe

I should have created extra folders in different locations, and made sure there were multiple backups, but this sort of thing doesn't happen. . . Why would it happen. . .? I mean, either way, it doesn't matter, because this is my fuck-up and I think I've just ruined the club's chances of getting through. We're not going to have an entry. And it's all my fault. Me.

I've screwed up big time.

I stare at the screen.

I stare because I can't believe it. Won't believe it.

I spend yet more time fruitlessly looking for the file. I shut everything down and restart the computer. But still. . .

Nothing.

I can't tell the others. It's too humiliating. They'll be nice about it, but their disappointment – the fact it's *me* who's let them down – I can't do it.

Minutes pass. Shock. I'm paralyzed.

I. . .

No.

Stop thinking, start doing!

I can't let this slip away from us, not now, not yet.

Submitting something has got to be better than nothing.

Could I cobble something together from some of the raw footage? I start to skim through it, all our corny introductions . . . the football section . . . the boys interrupting our filming by shouting "You're so gay!" at us. . .

You're so gay!

That's so gay!

Nico's poisoned words echoing around my head.

And still gnawing at my stomach.

Why bother pretending?

There's no time for a perfect finish. No time for gloss now.

Just tell it like it is.

I turn my camera on.

It's just me on the screen. No frills. No bells and whistles. There won't be time to enhance this with music or special effects. . . It's just me.

I hit record.

34

I know I should start this by being all upbeat and excited, but the fact is, *we've failed*. We've failed to upload the video we had planned, *don't ask*, but that probably doesn't matter because, the truth is, we've failed to be the school we wanted to be anyway.

We wanted our school to be seen as a role model. We wanted to show everyone what a wonderful, inclusive place it was. We wanted to inspire people, I guess. But that isn't the truth. And the last few weeks while we've been trying to make this video have really shown that. I don't know, maybe it never *was* the truth. Maybe it was just wishful thinking.

Here's the reality, anyway: me and the rest of the LGBT students put up with all the usual homophobic and transphobic slurs in the corridors. "That's so gay!" "You're so gay!" – all the usual. Somehow, it's never challenged by staff. Somehow it's always "banter" or even, would you believe, "Not meant as homophobic *in the context it was used*" – which has to be the biggest load of crap I've ever heard. Sorry for swearing. What else? We've endured full-on homophobic taunting in the changing rooms, culminating with me being physically attacked because I'm gay and because I'm trying to make things better for kids like me – here, look! Bruises. Sorry you had to see my chest there – I'm just giving you more reasons to not vote for us, I guess. We've had our school shut down any discussion of their sex ed programme, and how it's particularly lacking when it comes to LGBT students – it's like, sure we'll "support" our queer students, it's fine to be gay, as long as we're not *too* gay, as long as we're not talking actual gay sex, because *eww!* That's too icky for them. They don't want to engage, they don't care about us, they just want some tick-box diversity points and a quiet life. And probably the biggest joke of all: the students at our school voted a straight boy in as president of the LGBT society. We were trying to make the best of that – *look how inclusive we are!* – and don't get me wrong, he's a nice enough guy, but actually, that tells you all you need to know about the students at our school and the staff that ended up supporting the whole prank. And it tells you all you need to know about the messages LGBT kids at our school get sent, every single day. We're not important. We don't matter. We're a joke. Come and laugh at us because that's what we are – freaks in a sideshow.

So, if you're looking for a perfect example of a school where it's great to be LGBT, where it's a positive, happy experience, then that's not us. It's not Greenacre Academy.

But . . . we do pick ourselves up and we go back to school

every day. We do try. And we do understand what a lot of students face everywhere, the struggles they go through, for just wanting to be themselves. So, maybe that's what would make us good ambassadors for Rainbow Youth. We're not from a perfect school, but we get it, and so maybe we can be role models in that way? We're the kids who get knocked back at almost every turn, but we stagger back up again, we're fighting, and we're not giving up.

We're never giving up.

Except, maybe, on our chances of winning this.

Thanks for listening.

35

The upload completes at one minute to midnight. I've never submitted anything this close to the wire before and my nerves are shredded. All it would have taken was for the wifi to drop out and it would have been game over.

Although, what does it matter, it's game over anyway. Apart from the fact I've just had to submit a really basic, crappy video filmed on my laptop camera, where the likes of Kyle's team have basically staged a full-on Hollywood-style heist movie, I've made the fatal mistake of telling the truth – something no one ever wants to hear. You're either brave, stupid or too young to know any better to be the kid who shouts about the emperor not wearing any clothes. You have to play the game. People want positivity. *Everything's great. We're moving in the right direction. Don't you dare say any different.*

I come clean to the others the next day. There's no point trying to hide it, and I want to prep them for rejection.

Everyone's very nice about it, and they even say nice things about my attempt at a new video (even Danny, despite what I say about him in it), but it's very clear: I screwed up, and I'm definitely not presidential material. It's in my mind to resign as VP once the results are known – it'll be my fault we don't make the finals, after all.

Days pass. There's an LGBTQ+ Society meeting that I don't turn up to. Apparently the number of students who attended had fallen back a bit, after the initial flurry of interest, but it was still a good showing. They discussed some Pride festivities during the last weeks of term, so it was a good job I wasn't there. I'm in no mood to celebrate. Maya assured me no one was blaming me, but, hello? Who was editing the video at the very last minute? Who didn't back it up properly? Who owned the laptop that was probably too old and couldn't cope with all the big files, so crashed?

I've never messed up like this before. I'm so organized. I'm together. I'm reliable. That's who I am, and if I'm not any of those things, then who am I? I'm embarrassed I let everyone down, but I'm furious at myself. If I'd properly planned ahead, I could have foreseen this sort of thing happening. It's not like it's unheard of. Computers crash all the time. People are always losing their work. *What the hell is wrong with me?*

Part of me wonders if I'd taken my eye off the ball too much. Kyle has been renting an awful lot of space in my head recently. Thinking about him when I should have been thinking about the video. *Stupid*. It's why I don't message him, which is mean of me, since this isn't his fault. Of course, because he's the bigger person, and because he's actually nice and cares, *he* messages *me* on Wednesday evening:

Kyle: Would have messaged you sooner, but only just stopped swearing. An hour before the deadline, my CRAP LAPTOP crashed – lost the video! I did have it backed up, but not the latest version, so had to cobble together as best I could – no music, rushed voiceover, none of the special effects I'd put in. GUTTED. Everyone is blaming me, and sure, I guess it is my fault, but none of the other fuckers offered to edit it, did they? So, like, sure, blame me, but you were all too busy (a) chasing blowjobs (b) having a threesome (c) setting up fake Grindr profiles so you could get with some guy in his twenties even though you are practically jailbait. Delete as fucking appropriate. Motherfuckers. Sorry for venting. Feel better for getting this off my chest. How are you? X

His computer crashed too? I stare at the message. Swallow. But that's just a coincidence, right? How could it be anything else? Yet it feels . . . like a big coincidence. I don't know, I just cannot shake a feeling that something isn't right here.

Me: My laptop crashed too. Lost everything.
Back-up corrupted. Complete disaster, think we
can safely assume Greenacre Academy will not
be among the finalists.

Kyle: Wait. WHAT?! Yours crashed too?
That's . . . weird?

Me: A bit, yeah.

Kyle: I'm not one for conspiracy theories, but. . .

Me: I know, I know, me neither, but maybe it's just
bad luck.

Kyle: Did you manage to salvage anything?

Me: Nope! Had to rush record me talking to
camera for a few minutes. Utter drivel.

Kyle: I'm sorry, Barney. That sucks. I'm sure you
were great though.

Kyle: Barney?

Me: Sorry, couldn't type, laughing too hard.

I think about my next message. You know, now this is basically over, and let's face it, it is, maybe I can stop creeping about with Kyle, and maybe I don't have to overthink being with him so much, and maybe we could . . . screw it, I've no idea how this will end, and I'm not sure I care any more.

Me: Fancy meeting up? ;)

(Yes, I do add a winky face because apparently now, as well as being useless, I'm also shameless and thirsty.)

Kyle: Yes, but really busy right now. Essay deadlines coz of all the work I haven't done. But soon! OK?

My heart sinks. The one time I proactively ask a boy to meet up so we can probably do winky face stuff, and I get rejected for an essay deadline.

Me: Of course! No worries! Let me know!

Ugh. Way too many exclamation marks. I really need to learn to treat boys more like chess pieces: with a cool detachment, and an eye on the ultimate prize. I'm like a ten-year-old playing for the first time, excitedly zipping my queen in all directions and then inevitably losing.

> Kyle: Can I ask you something personal? About
> Paxton? I've seen the posts about you and him
> on your socials – I just wondered what the deal
> was?

My breath catches. Oh god. He's seen, of course he's seen,
why wouldn't he? We've been looking at the other clubs'
social accounts too. But what do I say? I don't want to lie
to him, but I also don't want to look like an arsehole. And,
more than anything, I don't want to hurt him.

> Kyle: OK, from the length of time it's taking you to
> reply, I'm guessing ... it's complicated?

> Me: Complicated, yes. But

And then I type, delete, type, delete, about five times.

> Kyle: Look, I get it, I do. And it's fine if you need
> to work out those complicated things. But I like
> you, Barney, OK? And I've never liked anyone
> before, like this, if you get me? Sorry. I'm trying
> to say I LIKE you.

> Me: I like you too.

Kyle: 🖤

Me: I wish I could see you. Explain more.

Kyle: I trust you. And, um. . . We could always meet ;) on the phone ;)

My heart skips a beat. He wants to winky face ... on the phone?

Kyle: But I mean on the phone, NOT on FaceTime or video call. (I don't trust you THAT much yet, hahaha!)

Kyle: Assuming you're home alone?

Me: OK, I think Mum's back in an hour.

Kyle: Very optimistic if you think this is gonna take an hour, haha! Also, do you have to mention your mum?

Me: Sorry. I'm not very good at winky face phone stuff.

Kyle: Go to your bedroom. Draw curtains. Relax. I'll call in five. ;)

OMFG. OMFG. OMFG.

I can't keep the stupid smile off my face as I remove the towel from over Lesley-the-guinea-pig's cage, turn my branded Rainbow Youth teddy bear back around on my shelf, and the Tom Daley calendar on my noticeboard. I couldn't have had any sort of eyes watching me while THAT TOTALLY EPIC thing happened. It's not the sort of thing Lesley, Teddy or Tom should have to see. Who knew it would be *that* good?

I'd be happy basking in some kind of post-orgasmic glow, but the doorbell goes, followed by some heavy and very insistent hammering. Either someone is dead, I'm being arrested, or it's a delivery driver who is double parked. I drop the white PE sock in my laundry basket, clatter down the stairs, wincing at my injured foot, and open the door.

"HOLY SHITBALLS WE GOT THROUGH!" Danny screams in my face.

"Huh?"

"WE GOT THROUGH, BB! We're one of *five* shortlisted schools to be RAINBOW YOUTH GLOBAL AMBASSADORS!"

I stare at him, because my brain cannot compute this information, although the thing I really can't get over is the fact he just called me "BB". "Say it again."

"WE GOT THROUGH!"

"Without shouting."

Danny puts his hands on my shoulders, leans in, and fixes me with his deep blue eyes. "The Greenacre Academy LGBTQ+ Society . . ." His voice is low, quiet, and somehow has the right frequency to send shivers up my spine, ". . . has been selected as one of the shortlisted schools who will attend the conference in London where we'll give a presentation and everyone will vote and we now have a very real chance of being Rainbow Youth's global ambassadors." His eyes drift to my lips, which makes me shiver, then back up.

"Really?" I murmur. My voice is all hoarse.

He nods. "You did it, Barney."

"*We* did it."

"No. *You* did it. Your piece to camera."

I little laugh escapes, and a wide smile spreads across my face. Danny smiles too, his hands still resting on my shoulders. "Can I come in, then?"

"Sorry, yes!"

He smiles again, playfully tickles the back of my neck and drops his hands away. I usher him inside. "Do the others know yet?"

"I have summoned them!" Danny grins. "Haven't told them what for."

"Umm, OK! My mum will be home soon, but it should be fine!"

"Well, the rest better hurry, then, because I've brought champagne. Well, stolen a bottle from my parent's stash. It's already chilled, so let's get popping." He pulls it out of his rucksack and hands it to me. "Barney?"

"Yeah?"

I'm distracted, putting the champagne bottle down, and only realize he hasn't spoken when I turn back around and look at him. He's just . . . standing there, lost for words, it seems.

He opens his mouth, but nothing comes out. His eyes drift to my lips again for a moment. He takes an unsteady breath. "Um. . ."

And the doorbell goes.

"That'll be the others," he says. He almost looks relieved.

I hold his gaze for a second. He's acting super weird, and I don't quite trust it. He's hiding something. "I'll let them in," I say.

He nods. Swallows. "You can tell them."

"*You* tell them. You're president."

"But it was *your* video."

The doorbell goes again. Followed by knocking.

"I think you should do it," I say. "You got the email, presumably?"

Danny nods. "Mr Hubbard forwarded it. OK. How about we both do it? Like, split it up, so you could say, 'We have news: Greenacre's LGBTQ+ Society. . .' and then I'll finish with, 'Is through to the finals of Rainbow Youth!' and then I can pop the champagne and you help me pour the glasses?"

334

The doorbell goes again, followed by George's voice. "BARNEY?!"

Danny grins. "I'll hide in the kitchen. Bring them through and we'll do our thing!" he hisses.

"Sure," I say.

There's a beat. And then he . . . bear hugs me.

"Oh. . . wow," I manage to mumble, as I feel my bones starting to be crushed.

"You're just. . . the best, BB."

"OK. Thanks."

He releases me, gives me a little wink, and hurries through to the back of the house.

I watch him go. There's something about how he's so pleased and excited that makes me smile. However hard I always try, I just can't dislike the guy.

I walk to the door. "George! Maya! Bronte! Paxton! Everyone's here, then, excellent. Come on in," I beam. "We have a teeny-tiny piece of breaking news!"

36

I'm in hell.

Or, more specifically, I'm in the clapped-out school minibus (zero suspension, smells of fish, emits so many diesel fumes we've sped up catastrophic climate change by about ten years already) with the rest of the LGBT club committee, including a massively overexcited Danny (who howled the obligatory "ROOOOOOAAAAAD TRIIIIIP!" before we left, and hasn't calmed down since), being driven by Mr Hubbard, with Mrs Buchanan navigating (using a *paper map*, I kid you not, like it's 1993, because 'You can't rely on technology!' and 'maps have never let me down!' – and I can't tell if she's trolling me – despite the fact we've already been in the wrong lane multiple times, and very nearly ended up heading north to York, rather than south to London, due to them having the audacity to change the road layout at some point in the last few decades). The Rainbow Youth conference is during the week, so no actual teaching staff were able to accompany us, hence why we've been saddled with these two jokers. Mr Hubbard wanted to see the winning entry, of course. Let's just say, I . . . recorded one especially for him, because otherwise I think he'd have pulled the plug on the whole thing, and after his sucky attitude towards us, we're still determined to shine a light on the school.

Maya and Bronte have made each of us an individual road-trip picnic. They did this, wait for it, *together*, last night. We've each got a sandwich, home-made vegan sausage roll, rocky road, and slice of spiced apple cake. Each picnic is wrapped up in gingham cloth and tied with string. It's very nice. I'm not quite sure what this means in a wider sense – Maya just muttered something non-committal about it being 'time to put our differences aside for the good of the club', in response to my raised eyebrow – and I'm just glad they managed to do this without killing each other. Maybe my words to Bronte when we were doing the filming helped. My god, if politics fails, I could be a relationship counsellor.

Meanwhile, George is trying to tweak the PowerPoint presentation while balancing a laptop on his knees, and swearing every time Mr Hubbard drives over a pothole (which is *frequently),* and Pax has just told Mr Hubbard that he "needs the toilet" and, after the usual discussion about how "he should have gone before we left" and "I did, but that was nearly three hours ago, and I've drunk a bottle of

Sprite since then!", Pax has now taken the nuclear option and threatened to piss his pants: "If that's really what you want me to do!" So now Mrs Buchanan is trying to establish the location of the nearest services with toilet facilities, using a map that is approximately thirty years out of date.

I stare out of the window and try to zone out of all *this*, and *in* to what these next few days in London might be like. Branscombe Boys got through too, so that means Kyle is going to be there. All the schools are staying at the same hotel that's been booked out by Rainbow Youth, and we're all in double rooms. Everyone knows what that means. It's hopelessly inevitable that by midnight tonight all the students will be wankered and the room-swapping will start. I mean, they're putting over fifty queer kids together in the heart of London, what are they expecting to happen? On the other hand, will I have to miss this incredible opportunity with Kyle ... because of the ongoing charade with Pax? That presentation can't come soon enough, because as soon as it's finished, Pax and I are officially over. I'll still go to prom with him. As friends. People do that. It's a thing.

We've been all over the social accounts of the other schools, checking out the competition. Unfortunately, so have Family Alliance, and some of the students have taken to having full-blown rows with them online after they tried to claim the conference was a full-on assault on decency and family values and is tantamount to "child abuse". They're clearly idiots, and impossible to argue with; it's like they operate in their own alternative reality. But we're not letting them get to us. This is our weekend, and we're going to make it epic.

The voting happens live, with three hundred students invited to watch the presentation, which is simultaneously live-streamed across the country to all other schools, who are able to vote online in real time for the club they think should be the global ambassadors. Although it's meant to all hinge on the content of the presentations, there's no doubt everyone's already forming opinions based on what we're posting. And to be fair to George, there's been quite a lot of interest in me and Pax, with comments about how "cute" we are together and how it's "so great to see a queer couple be so visible". Which I guess is all good.

Branscombe Boys seem very polished, if a little lacking in diversity in terms of the rainbow, since they all appear to be gay boys – something George reckons will play against them in the final vote.

There's a school from Islington, who haven't posted much, but just give off this very self-assured vibe, slightly like they're above it all, which will either speak to the "cool" kids or totally put most people off – hard to tell.

There's also a school from Newcastle, whose president is a girl who looks like they're the CEO of a major company – all power dressed in a suit, standing with crossed arms and a cold expression – and a school from Exeter, whose president is a non-binary person called KJ, and who, out of all the candidate schools, seem really *on it* in terms of LGBT issues.

I'm not denying we're up against it. But we didn't think we'd get this far. Rainbow Youth must have seen some potential in us. George reckons the laptop disaster was actually the best thing that could have happened. It meant I delivered a speech from the heart, so that's the strategy we're using again for our presentation. We're talking about how our school has failed us. Even if Mr Hubbard thinks we're doing something on pronouns.

"Mrs Buchanan!" Danny says, leaving forwards with his phone. "Turn on the Bluetooth, we need some *tuuuuunes*, and I've done a Big Gay Spotify Playlist, baby!"

"As long as it doesn't include that *dreadful* Katy Perry song!" Bronte shouts.

"Finally!" Maya says. "I never believed you liked it!"

"Of course I didn't," Bronte replies, turning to her. "I mean, I'll dance to it if drunk and—"

"You know all the words?"

Bronte shrugs and turns back to the front. "Bring on the tunes!"

Mrs Buchanan is very clearly against this idea, but it's Danny, Golden Boy, so she fiddles around with the controls on the dashboard, and, after about a million years with Danny talking her through what to press, the music starts and we continue down the motorway singing along to "It's

Raining Men", "Go West", "Dancing Queen" (naturally), some Madonna classics, "YMCA", and "True Colours" by Cyndi Lauper. I've got to say, it's an impressive effort from Danny.

"I'm about to urinate in my pants!" Pax shouts from the back. "If anyone cares? Is this a safeguarding issue, I'm not sure!"

"Mr Hubbard!" Maya chimes in. "Seriously! Paxton needs the toilet!"

It's obvious from their body language that Mr Hubbard and Mrs Buchanan are deeply regretting being on this trip – which is absolutely no more than what they both deserve.

We hit some slow-moving traffic, and by the time we finally pull into the services, Pax's eyes are bulging out and he's sweating. He leaps out of the minibus as soon as Mr Hubbard slides the door open, disappearing at speed towards the entrance.

"Careful of . . . traffic!' Mr Hubbard shouts after him, pointlessly, since he's just shot across half the car park and narrowly avoided being flattened by a reversing SUV.

"There's a picnic area round the side," Mrs Buchanan tells us. "Or there's food inside. Please, everyone, use the toilet facilities; we won't be stopping again before we get to London."

"Remember you're representing the school," Mr Hubbard says.

Bronte rolls her eyes. "Does that mean I *can't* solicit for sex work among the lonely HGV drivers, or that I should proudly tell clients that I'm from Greenacre Academy?"

"Ha, ha," Mr Hubbard replies, as he and Mrs Buchanan head off inside, in search of tea, fruit cake and exclusively adult company.

We're just debating the merits of maybe supplementing Bronte and Maya's picnic offerings with some portions of fries, and some nice cold drinks, when everyone's phones bleep, pretty much simultaneously.

Now, I've always assumed that those thrillers set in American high schools where some mysterious fiend sends threatening messages around revealing certain students' deepest secrets are nothing more than fiction.

At no point did I think I would be in the middle of it. And yet...

There on my phone, I'm tagged in to a post from an account called "Rainbow Truth".

Greenacre Academy's self-styled election advisor, George Piper, has been secretly dating Paxton Lee, who many of you will know as VP Barney Brown's boyfriend. Do you trust them to be YOUR ambassadors when they clearly can't trust each other?

I'm staring down at my screen. Not because I'm re-reading

342

it, but because I'm trying to work out how to play this, and I can't look up without deciding that because my facial expression needs to be completely constant with how I'm meant to be feeling. On the one hand, this is a surprise, since Pax likes George, and it's super cute, if this is true, that they've got together – yay and rainbows – but also, I'm a bit sad that George didn't mention it to me – but not my business, so OK – but then, I *am* meant to be dating Pax – that's what everyone thinks, and that's what George specifically has asked me to continue making people believe, so, in fact, *what the hell is this*? And where's it come from? And why?

Whatever the answer, it's already doing the numbers, racking up likes and retweets at an alarming rate. *Fuck*.

When I do look up, everyone's looking at George, so I look at him too. Poor George. But George will know how to play this. He'll have exactly the right response.

"Oh god," he says.

And it seems that's it. So now everyone looks at me, the scorned wife, as it were.

I blow out a breath and play it safe. "I mean . . . what's going on?"

"Yeah," Bronte says, "what *is* going on? George? *Have* you been seeing Pax behind Barney's back?"

"That is not cool, man," Danny adds. "See, this is exactly what I was talking about when I asked about skeletons in closets. And now look! Splashed all over social media for everyone voting to see!"

"George?" Bronte says again.

"Like, to me, this is potentially a resignation matter," Danny continues.

George doesn't even look at me. I wish he would. Just so I could get some sense of how we're planning to deal with this, but instead, he just nods. "You're right. I should resign. And that's what I'll do."

"Oh my god, so it *is* true?" Bronte howls.

"George—" I say.

"We can put an announcement out now; I'll catch a train back home as soon as we get to London."

"No!" I shout.

Everyone turns to look at me again.

"George, let's just tell them," I mutter.

Danny and Bronte both cross their arms and stare, really hard, at me.

I swallow. "Me and Pax aren't a thing. We were never a thing. We . . . faked it. We were fake dating. To . . ." I try to laugh, but it comes out like a strangled cry. "Capture the attention of the voters!" I sigh. "Stupid. Probably. Well, *clearly.* Point is, George has done nothing wrong." *Other than suggest this whole scheme, but that's a side issue right now.*

Bronte turns to Maya. "Did *you* know about this?"

Maya swallows.

"Oh. My. *God!*" Bronte screams. "So you've all been

344

lying!" Which, considering her fake Twitter comments during the election, is a bit rich.

"This is bad," Danny agrees, shaking his head. "This is really disappointing."

Bronte's red with rage. "Disappointing? It's a downright appalling way to treat the people who you're meant to be campaigning alongside! How long did you think you'd be able to keep this up before the truth got out?" She turns back to George. "And why the hell did you think to make it even more difficult by actually having a real relationship running alongside the fake one?"

"It just happened," George mutters, looking down at the ground. For the first time ever in this whole campaign, he doesn't have the answers, he doesn't have any spin, and I hate it.

I need to take back some control here. We've come too far. "Look, it happened, like George says. And we owe you an apology—"

Bronte laughs, mockingly.

"But we're finalists. And we have to give this our best shot. So how about we pick over the rights and wrongs of all this later?"

"It's not like *you* didn't fake anything during the campaign," Maya adds.

"Oh, come off it!" Bronte replies. "I may have created a situation to make a more general point—"

"Aka, *lie*," Maya says.

"And that was way before any of *this* was at stake. I should have known you couldn't be trusted. What was I even thinking getting back involved with you all?" She glares at Maya. "*Pathetic.*"

"Well, what you were *thinking*," Maya says, "is that you would make Danny's life hell, force him out, and take on the presidency yourself." She smiles at Bronte. "Just a guess."

"Is that true?" Danny says, eyes wide and hurt.

"No!" Bronte replies.

"OK!" I say, trying to dampen the flames before they take hold, and crucially avoid me being implicated in Danny's planned downfall too. "The wider issue here is how this anonymous Tweeter found out."

I glance at Danny, but he's just staring back at me with cold eyes, like he can't even get to grips with how disappointed he is in me.

"Well, who knew about your pathetic lies?" Bronte asks.

I shrug. "Me, George, Maya . . . and Pax."

"But no one knew specifically about George and Pax except George and Pax?" She turns to George. "Anyone ever see anything? See you and Pax together?" Bronte asks George.

George shakes his head. "Impossible. We've only ever met up at my house. Absolutely nothing in public."

Bronte nods. "Well, *obviously*, that doesn't leave many

options for where the leak came from. And the Tweeter is possibly one of you, too."

An ice chill sweeps over us all. So weird: I can actually feel it. I actually *shiver*. Me, George and Maya have been friends for ages. We're a tight trio, and I trust them more than I trust myself. It seems unfair that Pax should be the one under suspicion here, but what if he isn't everything he seems? But then, why wouldn't he be? What do I imagine is going on here? What possible reason would Pax have for sabotaging our chances?

George is almost certainly having similar thoughts. His face has gone pale, eyes darting around the ground, searching for answers, breathing shallow.

"He wouldn't. . ." I mutter to him.

"Pax?" Bronte says. "You mean, Pax?"

"Yeah."

"But what if he did?" Bronte says.

We stand in silence for a moment until Pax comes bouncing up to us. "Jeez, sorry about that!" he says. "I bought some Haribo if anyone fancies some?" He looks at us all. "What?"

"Did you get tagged in the tweet?" Bronte asks.

"Left my phone in the minibus," he says. "What tweet?"

"Paxton . . . everyone knows," George says.

He raises his eyebrows. "Knows. . .?"

"About you and me."

His mouth drops open.

"Someone tweeted about it," George adds.

Pax just stares at George. He's trying to take it all in.

George takes a deep breath. "Did you . . . tell anyone? About us?"

"What? No! Of course not!" Pax says.

"'Cause, if you did, that's fine, we just need to know—"

"I'm not sure I would say it's 'fine', George," Bronte interrupts. "None of this sordid little situation is remotely 'fine', is it?"

Pax snaps. "Fuck you, Bronte!"

"Fuck you, Paxton!" Bronte snaps back. "What's really going on here? Hard to tell what's real or what's fake with you lot at the moment. How do we know whom to trust?!"

"That's really unfair," I tell her.

"No!" she replies. "What's unfair is you lot weaving this . . . this web of deceit and treachery, it all backfiring, and getting us all implicated in your mess."

"Oh, here we go!" Maya chimes in. "Perfect Bronte, life's always so easy when you have everything on a plate already!"

"How dare—"

"*You* created this mess by insisting the whole school votes for president, meaning the actual issues became irrelevant and the whole thing became a circus!" Maya tells her. "*You* did that, because you knew there was no way you would win if it was just the club that voted because everyone hates your 'I'm so privileged but I still always manage to play the victim' guts and because a fair vote would have been too much of a fight for you, and you don't fight, do you? You'd never lower yourself to fight for anything or anyone!"

Three minutes later, when Mr Hubbard and Mrs Buchanan return, having impressed upon us the importance of remembering we're representing the school, they find a small crowd watching us all screaming obscenities at each other in front of the minibus, which is emblazoned with "Greenacre Academy" on the side.

37

Mr Hubbard gives us a massive bollocking and says he doesn't want to hear another word out of us until we reach London. But that isn't hard. No one wants to talk anyway. This amazing opportunity that we've all worked so hard for is now going to be the biggest disaster. And worse, it looks like it's split us all apart. It's destroyed the LGBT club. Even Danny, who can normally be relied on to cheer everyone up, is silent and moody. He doesn't sit next to me for the remainder of the journey, taking a seat behind me instead, curling up against the window and staring out.

He and I are, however, sharing a room at the hotel – which turns out to be a massive four-star place, right in the centre of London, near the BT Tower. I guess I expected something basic, like we get on field trips, but, of course, Virgin are bankrolling this, and they've splashed out – there's doormen, plush carpet, and the rooms have a "pillow menu". Shame none of us feel like we can enjoy any of it now.

It's weird. From actively hating Danny, I now find myself wanting his over-exuberant, unfiltered self in my life – at least from time to time – and the thought he might now think less of me is upsetting.

"Which bed do you want?" I ask tentatively.

He shrugs. "Either. This one's fine." He slings his bag on to the one on the right.

"Are you OK?" I ask.

"Yep."

And that's it. He throws himself on his bed, puts in his AirPods, closes his eyes, and starts listening to some music.

I mean, OK, *fine*. I have a quick shower in the en suite and change into a fresh set of clothes, ready for the welcome event downstairs in the conference suite. George messages me to say he and Pax are going to keep a low profile and stay in their room, and despite my protestations that we should just own it, he insists it'll draw attention away from us and our policies, and we don't need stoke the fires of the gossip any further.

I can't stop thinking about the anonymous message because it doesn't make any sense. Only George and Pax knew. I might not know Pax well, but I know him enough to feel sure he wouldn't have told anyone about him and George, if that's what they'd decided to do. And there's no outcome I can work out in which George would have a reason to leak that information himself.

So that means someone else knew. I wonder if someone

saw something, or heard something, maybe a little moment between Pax and George at one of our meetings and put two and two together?

And then I think, out of all of us, there is one person who has shown, time and again, the lengths she'll go to get what she wants, even if that means destroying the club in the process. *Bronte*.

But I've no proof.

I nudge Danny awake an hour later. He opens one eye and removes his AirPods. "Hey," he says.

"Hey. Time to go."

Danny groans.

"Get up, *Mr President*."

He yawns and rubs his hands all over his hair, making it stick up at random angles. His hand casually finds his crotch, and he readjusts the bulge in his joggers, before locking eyes with me, sending me into a panic that he caught me looking. "I just need a piss," he says, rolling off the bed.

I nod. "Um, you're gonna change, aren't you?" *I mean, he can't wear joggers to our first meet-and-greet event.*

"Yeah, whatever," he shouts through from the bathroom.

Getting Danny ready feels very similar to how I felt getting my five-year-old cousin ready for his parents' wedding. It's all reluctance, distraction techniques, and moody pouting.

"This was a mistake. I look like an accountant," Danny complains.

He doesn't, he's just looks preppy and clean-cut in chinos and a nice shirt. "You look great. Borderline handsome."

He almost smiles. "They should have held this thing at the Orlando Park Lane – our place has mini-bars."

"I suspect this place does too, when they don't have a bunch of teenagers staying over."

Danny nods. "I guess." His eyes meet mine. "I wish you hadn't lied."

"I wish I hadn't either." I sigh. "I'm sorry."

He doesn't respond to that, he just walks to the door. "Let's do this thing, then."

We meet Bronte and Maya (also sharing a room, thanks to Mr Hubbard insisting on gender segregation even in the face of an inevitable extinction event) on our way down. They are slouching against opposite walls, not even able to look at each other again (damn it – we got so close so reconciliation!), but at least they're here. Safety in numbers, as none of us are relishing walking into the conference room with all the other clubs. Meeting new people makes me anxious enough anyway. Meeting new people, all of whom will have seen a tweet about your relationship shenanigans, is vomit-inducing.

"Let's just act like nothing's happened," Bronte suggests. "We hold our heads high. At the end of the day, romantic entanglements and drama are part-and-parcel of the teenage experience. It's actually completely normal.

Let's just tell people that, if they ask. And who knows, maybe this Gossip Girl wannabe will leak stuff on the other clubs too?"

I give her a tight smile, but I'm uneasy. She's acting like she's nothing to do with the leak – *but it has to be her*.

We walk through some double doors and stop dead as the grey and serious occupants of the room all turn and stare at us.

"Are you here for the waterless urinal presentation?" asks a woman in a suit.

"Rainbow Youth?" I reply.

She smiles, sympathetically. "Next door. My nephew's a gay too."

I give her a thumbs up, while we all back out of the room, and head round the corner, where the next room is adorned with rainbow bunting and a glitter curtain over the entrance, which I suppose was a pretty big clue.

"Let's do this," I mutter, sweeping the curtain aside and making my entrance.

This time, no one looks. Honestly, it's a bit disappointing that we had more impact at the waterless urinal presentation. Here, it's immediately obvious we're the poor relations at the big, posh party. The room is laid out with rows of chairs either side of an aisle, all of which have goody bags on them. At the front is a projector screen, with some very fashionable adults standing around chatting, who I assume are the Rainbow Youth team. Meanwhile, around the outsides, very much sticking to their own clubs, are all our rivals.

"I need the toilet." Danny suddenly turns and darts back through the curtain.

"You just—" But he's already gone.

I'm desperate to catch Kyle's eye, so I home in on Branscombe Boys first, who are pretty easy to spot since they're all wearing their pristine school uniform – grey trousers and royal blue blazers, with white shirts and smart ties in a royal blue-and-white stripe. The boys are all identikit gay teen lads, with indistinguishable hair styles and faces. I mean, they're all very pretty. And they're all wearing the slimmest fit trousers they can get away with within their uniform regulations, revealing great legs and . . . more besides. But, I dunno, have you ever seen *Village of the Damned*, with all those kids who all look the same, move the same, and really freak you out? Well. . .

I don't realize it's Kyle at first. He's had a haircut. Gone are the cute curls, and now he's got some sort of Caesar haircut that takes him look really tough and hard. I don't think I like it, but maybe I just need to get used to it? He'll still be Kyle, after all. Cute and funny and awkward. He doesn't see me. He seems very busy holding court with the group of boys surrounding him, but he looks adorable in his school uniform and I get butterflies in my stomach, just seeing him here, and knowing our little secret.

The Islington school (it's got to be them, I'm pretty

sure I recognize them from their social media photos, but also they're so self-consciously couldn't-give-a-shit cool), are lounging about on the floor in the corner, a mix of people wearing baggy tops, baggy trousers, high-waisted jeans, some tie-dye stuff, and looking like they really want to be smoking roll-ups, drinking tea made with mushrooms and generally hanging around Camden or Shoreditch.

A tall girl, hair scraped back into a ponytail, wearing a light grey suit, shirt and tie, strides up to us, hand outstretched. "Christina, call me Chris," she says.

"Hello, I'm—"

"Bronte," Bronte says, literally stepping in front of me.

Christina, "Call Me Chris", takes her in, a slightly amused look playing on her face. "You must be Greenacre Academy, right?"

Bronte raises her eyebrows. "We might be."

"Well, you *are*, because I've already been round everyone else."

Bronte forces the merest hint of a smile.

"And you are. . .?" Call Me Chris smiles at Maya.

Maya clears her throat. "Ma-ya." It comes out somewhere between the noise a strangled horse would make and a horn on a train. She clears her throat again. "Maya."

"Nice to meet you, Maya."

Maya nods and swallows.

"So which of you is Danny? He's president, right?"

"He's in the bathroom," I say.

Call Me Chris sniffs, dismissively. "Well, maybe I'll meet him at the buffet afterwards. Hopefully see you there too, Maya?"

"Mmmm!" Maya giggles. *She giggles.* I'm going to give her so much grief about this.

Chris gives Maya a wink, blanks a fuming Bronte, and heads off back to the rest of her club.

I turn to Maya, and all I have to do is smile, because *she knows.*

"Let's make a start, folks!" one of the guys from Rainbow Youth shouts from the front. "Come and find a seat, and we'll get cracking!"

Mr Hubbard walks in behind us. "Ah, there you are. Mrs Buchanan is having to lie down with a migraine, and I've got some emails to attend to from school, so I'll leave you lot to it. Everyone OK? Good. Grab those seats at the front, they're free. It'll make you look enthusiastic."

Obviously we'd all rather die than sit in the front row. Events for "young people" invariably end up having a "Who's going to volunteer for this deeply humiliating thing?" element, and you stand more risk of being picked if you're at the front. We sit halfway back. Close enough to be keen, but not close enough to be singled out. The Branscombe Boys sit in the row in front of us, emitting wafts of Lynx and sex hormones. They are, no doubt about it, *hot*. And they know it. They're also completely aloof. It's like the rest of the people here don't even exist. Kyle hasn't even acknowledged me yet, but then, I guess if either of us is too obvious, people will start to ask questions. Maybe our hands will "accidentally" brush over the vol au vents at the buffet, or something else achingly romantic? I hope so. I hope they actually have vol au vents too. Retro camp buffet? Yes, please.

"Ooh, condoms!" Maya says, pulling a couple out of her goody bag and back to being all perky and fun after meeting Chris. "One of them's strawberry flavour." She passes it to me. "Your need may be greater than mine, now that you're publicly single again."

"All the bags are the same, I have my own."

"What if you get *really* lucky though?"

"Pfft."

"Seriously, Barns, if you can't get laid at an LGBT youth conference, I'm not sure there's a whole lot of hope."

In the seat to my right, Bronte shifts uncomfortably, huffs, and pretends not to be listening to us.

Anyway, there may be more hope than Maya realizes, of course, although the hope in question is sitting just in front of us, facing forward, very composed, very professional. But I'm sure he'll loosen up when I finally manage to get him alone. How could I engineer that?

Maya's still fishing around in her goody bag. "Keyring . . . pin badges . . . bottled water. . ."

"*Gay* bottled water, I hope?"

"Stop saying *gay* when you mean LGBTQ+," Bronte mutters, under her breath.

"I mean, it must be *GAY*," Maya replies. "Ooh, a book on GAY sex and relationships. . ."

"Better late than never."

"It very clearly says 'LGBTQ+ sex and relationships' on the cover," Bronte says.

"And lube. Wow."

"What? Really?"

Maya shows me the little bottle.

I actually blush.

"I like these people," she says.

"I know, they almost seem . . . like they haven't got their heads in the sand."

It suddenly occurs to me that Danny hasn't come back, but just as I twist around to check, "Patrick" (he/him, short, blond hair, and preppy) and "Amber" (they/them, younger than Patrick, probably more fun, bouncing around in black jeans and a baggy shirt with penguin prints on it) introduce themselves and welcome us all to the Rainbow Youth Global Ambassadors Conference.

"I'd like to start with a big round of applause for our corporate sponsor, Virgin Atlantic!" Patrick says.

Big whoops and cheers for that and the prospect of those upper-class flights to NYC!

"And I'm delighted to confirm that we'll be joined at the presentations tomorrow by one of our new LGBT celebrity patrons!" Amber announces. "They're being kept heavily under wraps until the big reveal, but we think you're all going to be very excited to meet them!"

"Oh my god," I whisper to Maya. "Elton's gonna be here, for real!"

"Or maybe Harry Styles?"

"Is he LGBT?"

"Who cares, it's Harry Styles."

She squirts me with some of the lube.

"Stop that! What are you doing?!" I hiss.

"Getting you ready, baby."

Bronte clears her throat and gives us both a death stare.

"Tonight, folks, is an opportunity to relax and get to know each other," Patrick continues. "Sure, we're looking for one overall winner, one school LGBTQ+ society to be our global ambassadors, but ultimately, we're all one, big family. We've got food for you all tonight, followed by a board games evening – with an LGBT twist!"

I perk up at this: I mean, I dread to think what the LGBT twist is going to be, but board games sounds good! It won't be chess, of course . . . or *could* it be???

"We hope all this will give you the opportunity to facilitate some synergies. . ."

Maya sprinkles me with another squirt of lube. I breathe heavily and give her side eye.

"You are just gonna *slide* into facilitating those synergies, baby," she purrs. "*Frictionless!*"

"Tomorrow morning, you'll have time for any

last-minute prep for your presentations; then, after lunch, you'll meet our VIP celeb and our sponsors. . ."

There's an "Oooooh!" from everyone here.

"And then the moment we're all waiting and here for: the presentations. Each club will have their allotted five minutes onstage when you'll tell us, and all the other LGBT societies watching online, whatever you want to tell us. Voting happens live – none of that old-fashioned counting-ballots business here! – thanks to our online and on mobile voting app, which will collate the votes from authenticated accounts in real time."

Amber steps forward. "Your goody bags have plenty of things you might need, including pens, a notepad, lots of Rainbow Youth merch, and even our very own branded condoms. . ."

"Think of us while you're getting it on!" Maya whispers.

"If any of you need more, just come and find me, Patrick, or any of the other Rainbow Youth team. No questions asked."

"How much sex are they expecting will happen?" I whisper.

"Loads," Maya says. "And, great news, you're ready to hit the ground running." She squirts me with more lube.

"Stop it!" I hiss.

"So, that's us," Patrick says, smiling. "Congratulations to all of you for making it this far, and—oh, one last thing: I should mention we're aware of a tweet that's been circulating concerning . . ." *He actually looks at us, I mean, could you possibly try to make it more obvious?* ". . . one of the candidate clubs, and I just want to say, *folks*, let's keep it decent, shall we? We are all so much better than that. And at the end of the day, stuff like that will not necessarily be a measure of how good a club might be as our global ambassadors."

Necessarily?! How about just *not?* It's *not* a measure. Jeez.

"Let's do dinner!" Patrick announces, clapping his hands together.

As if by some kind of queer magic, the wooden partition wall down the right-hand side of the room concertinas back to reveal an adjoining space which has been set up with tables we can sit around, as well as a set of long tables along the far wall, with food and drinks piled on them. It's impressive; although, in what must rank as one of my all-time most disappointing life moments, I do hear a hotel supervisor tell a member of staff, "No, the vol au vents are for the waterless urinal people next door!" and have to witness a platter of what I think are chicken and mushroom ones in a white wine sauce be taken away, when they were so very nearly within my reach. It's OK, we have pizza and lots of it, presumably because of the assumption that teenagers love pizza – which I do, I just love kitsch buffet food more. I would kill for pineapple and cheese on a cocktail stick, but a stuffed-crust Meat Feast is fine.

The Branscombe Boys are right over there, heaping slices on paper plates even as Amber is telling people that the vegetarian and vegan pizzas are on the far right. There's also garlic bread, and the obligatory accompanying joke about "if you're not planning on snogging anyone tonight!" as well as barbecue chicken wings, some salad (which we all know will go completely uneaten), litres and litres and litres of fizzy drinks, and a load of apple pies, ice cream and chocolate brownies that they've also put out at the same time as the savoury food. No judgement – but that's not really the way to do it – but OK.

Bronte comes up behind me. "Go and eat. I'm going to speak to Patrick and Amber. Fuck their 'necessarily' shit, they need to say it can't be a factor in the vote!"

"I mean, yes, totally agree with you," I say. "Although, I'm not sure what they can do? You can tell people not to factor it in, but you can't control what's running through people's minds when they hit the vote button."

"You sound like George."

I click my fingers. "They're missing this, up in their room. I should grab some pizza and bring it up to them."

"I'll do it when I'm done with Patrick and Amber," Bronte says. "Go and schmooze, since you're VP and *where the hell is Danny anyway?*"

Maya's on her phone. "I'm calling him." She nods at me, cocking her head towards the crowd around the pizza table. "Go and schmooze." She glances at Call Me Chris and gives a flirty little wave, which Bronte clocks and makes a very visible effort to ignore.

I shuffle towards the pizza, simultaneously deep in thought about Bronte (what's she playing at? Is this the plan? Cause a problem and be seen to be the one who solves it? But why? Makes no sense!) while also desperately hating every second of being all by myself around loads of people I don't know. At least the food can be a distraction. I grab a paper plate and help myself to a slice of the Hawaiian.

"Pineapple on pizza? Brave choice." It's the guy from the Islington school. I glance at his plate. He has a big heap of salad and a slice of something without cheese. "Milo," he says. He's dressed in a suit, with a bold red-and-black diamond pattern, complete with a white cravat thing. He looks like a playing card.

"Hey. Barney." I shake his hand.

And we're both immediately aware of how sticky I am, and he doesn't even try to hide the flicker of disgust on his face.

"Sorry, I'm covered in lube," I tell him, with a laugh. Good to make a joke out of this, plus mentioning lube is sure to break the ice.

It doesn't. He gives me a weak smile. "Nice meeting you." And he stalks off, doubtless in search of less sticky company.

I turn around the other way, desperate to find someone to talk to because everyone else is talking to someone and it's just me in this awkward hell, and come face-to-face with Kyle. I breathe a sigh of relief. "Heeeey!"

Kyle looks at me with an expressionless face. "Hey. Kyle." He offers his hand.

Ohh, OK. We're playing this completely like we've never met before, which is probably wise, and kind of makes me slightly horny in a weird way.

"I'm Barney," I say. "Sorry, I'm sticky. *Lube.*"

Kyle nods. "I'm looking forward to your presentation."

"And . . . same! Me too! Can't wait to see what you guys have come up with!"

"Might see you for the board games later, then."

"You got it. Maybe they'll have chess?"

He flinches. "God, I hope not. Can you imagine? That would suck."

That comment catches me off guard, and I feel a pang of panic, before I realize he's just playing the game, and I'm probably being just a bit too familiar by mentioning chess, *our* game. I watch as he walks back to the rest of the Branscombe boys and I hear him say, "Meeting in my room in twenty minutes, OK? I want us to run over everything for tomorrow before this stupid gay board games evening."

Weird, hearing him talk so confidently, and like he's in charge. He was so nervous and gentle with me. Awkward, even. I think I prefer awkward Kyle to confident Kyle, but maybe this is his thing more than going on a date, and, honestly, I get it, because I feel the same.

Hopefully I'll get him on his own later, and we can talk properly, without the risk of someone overhearing us and putting two and two together.

I glance over to Maya, who is now standing at the edge of the room, a finger stuck in one ear to drown out the noise, waiting for Danny to pick up. Bronte's chatting to Amber and Patrick. I feel like a spare wheel. I slink off to an empty chair at an empty table, sit down to concentrate on my pizza and hope one or both of them will join me before I finish the slice and have to go and get another one.

"OK to join you?"

I look up and see one of the kids from the Exeter school.

"KJ," they say. They've got black, bed-head style hair, and they're dressed in baggy jeans and a hoodie, which immediately puts me at ease.

"Barney, and sure."

KJ sits down with their plate of pizza. "So, do you find these forced 'getting to know each other' things as awkward as I do?"

I laugh. "*Oh god.* Yes. Yes, I do."

KJ laughs too. "So far, I've been totally judged by that Milo guy from Islington. I mean, OK, fashion isn't my thing, but I'm not sure it's his either!"

We both glance over to where Milo and Call Me Chris are standing in a small group, both vying for dominance in a conversation that seems to only include them, as the others just watch, exasperated. We turn back to each other, simultaneously roll our eyes, and laugh.

"No, but seriously, we only entered this for a bit of fun. We didn't realize loads of the schools would be taking it *quite* so seriously." They take a bite of pizza. "I mean, is it just the New York trip everyone's interested in? Is that what it is?"

I shrug. "They *have* showered us with swag, to be fair."

"Do you mean free condoms and lube? And some . . . badges?"

"Well, yeah. Don't forget those T-shirts and branded teddies they sent when we entered."

KJ frowns. "What teddies? Did you get teddies? Where were our teddies?"

"You didn't get any? We got one each."

"No! I feel robbed! Well, then it does make sense. *Teddies.*"

Bronte strides up to me, grabs a chair and sits down. "Sorry, excuse me," she says to KJ. She leans into my ear. "I've just been chatting with Patrick and Amber. I was buttering them up, being grateful for everything they're doing, thanking them for the freebies. Barney: *they didn't send out branded teddy bears.* They know nothing about them!"

I meet her eyes and a cold chill prickles through me. "OK, so . . . that's odd. Is that . . . odd?"

I don't know what this means.

It feels like it means something, though.

367

And then both our phones chime and there's an all-caps message from George on the group WhatsApp:

George: MY ROOM NOW. MAJOR
EMERGENCY.

38

Maya and Bronte head straight to George and Pax's room, while I go and see if Danny's in ours, since no one can get hold of him still.

"Danny?!" I say, pushing the door open and flicking on the lights.

I walk in to find Danny cocooned under the duvet. "No, go away," he mumbles.

"What are you doing?"

"I have a headache," he says. "Why are you here?"

"Looking for you! You need to come to George's, like *now*. Is your phone off or something?"

"It's on silent, *I have a headache*."

"So you keep saying."

He emerges from under the covers and blinks at me in the light.

"I'll be waiting outside." I don't want to risk him

disappearing again, and he's behaving really weirdly. "This is urgent."

"Fine, whatever."

A few minutes later and Danny emerges, all bed-head hair, grey joggers, white T-shirt and white socks. No shoes. "Just along the corridor, right?" he mutters, giving his hair a vigorous rub, making it stick up even more.

"Right."

An impatient-looking George is standing in the middle of his room when Pax lets us in. Bronte and Maya are already there.

"Sit," George tells us. "We have a major problem." He holds up some sort of plastic rectangle thing with two wires coming out the end. "We've been bugged."

"What is that?" I say.

"It's a bug, Barney!" George says. "A listening device."

"Really? Isn't that something only MI5 can do?"

George shakes his head. "You can pick up these things for thirty quid on Amazon. They're battery powered, they work over the mobile phone network, and you just have to dial in to listen. I was trying to figure out how the truth about me and Pax got out. No one knew. We never mentioned anything about *us* in any of our messages or calls. We only ever got together in my bedroom at home. At first, I thought maybe one of the apps on our phones might have been some kind of Trojan-horse listening app. But I went through everything, and it seemed fine."

"Which meant our anonymous troll used another method," Paxton adds. "A hidden listening device."

I feel the blood drain from my face as I realize. "In the branded teddy—"

"Branded teddy bear!" George confirms, holding one up, its back opened up and stuffing pulled out.

I stare at it in disbelief. "But who—"

"Never mind *who* for now!" George shouts. "We have to assume each bear was bugged, and since each of us took one home, I need to know *exactly* what might have been overheard so we can establish some kind of damage limitation strategy."

My heart starts pounding. . .

"Everyone, now is the time for total honesty," George continues. "Whatever it is, however humiliating, awkward or upsetting, just get it out in the open. *What could these bugs have heard?*"

"For me, literally just a lot of rows with my mum about why I'm not revising," Pax says.

My ears, ringing. . .

"I do a lot of singing along to Britney," Maya confesses. "Some of the notes may be a bit off, but I'm not sure that's anything that will lose us this vote."

Breathe. Breathe. Breathe. . .

Maya looks sheepish. "And also . . . I may have. . . I may have got my guitar out and written a . . . not particularly accomplished ballad about . . . what it's like to like someone who means loads to you but you don't seem to mean much to them . . . featuring a love interest who might share a name with someone in this room." She looks down at the floor, while Bronte stares at her, open-mouthed.

"Bronte?" George asks.

She takes a deep breath. "Piggles isn't dead."

That news makes even me look up and forget about everything for a second. Everyone's mouths have dropped open.

Bronte shrugs. "Sure, I faked it for sympathy. You must have suspected that." She looks at our outraged faces. "You can't hate me, we're all in this together now. Total truth. So there it is." She glances at Maya again, who quickly looks away again.

"Barney?"

I look up at George and swallow. "Um. . ."

"*Barney*?"

I swallow again. "I mean, I put the bear in my bedroom so . . . you *know*, I guess . . . bedroom stuff?" I look at him, pleadingly.

George screws up his face. "If you mean what I think you mean, how much actual noise are you making doing that?" George blows out a breath. "Never had you down as a screamer, Barney."

"I make zero noise when I ejaculate," Danny pipes up.

"Ugh, Danny, *seriously*?" Bronte complains. "Do we have to discuss this?"

"Just saying. Not only that, my face stays completely expressionless. I could be having an orgasm right now, and you wouldn't know." He nods and looks at each of us, face completely still. "See? That little bug would have picked up *nada* from me."

"I had phone sex with a boy I met online," I say, as quickly as I can. I bury my face in my hands. "Oh my god."

I hear Maya chuckle. "OK, well on the list of things I never thought I'd hear come from Barney Brown's lips, that's up there in the top five!"

"*Who?*" George says.

I look back up at him. "Does it matter? Besides, they have to dial in to listen, right? So I'd have to be pretty unlucky if they just so happened to dial in during the exact . . . minute, *or period of time*, whatever," I clear my throat, "that it took."

"Minute? Ah, *bless*," Bronte says.

Danny tuts. "You need to work on that, dude."

I glare at Bronte and Danny, breathing heavily through my nose. "Anyway, so what are the chances?"

"I'm not asking about the chances, I'm asking *who* this guy is?" George says.

I take an unsteady breath. "I'm allowed some privacy, right? You and Paxton wanted privacy, and I get that, this stuff is hard, sometimes, you don't want to live it all out in the open with people watching and commenting and throwing in their opinions and views. You know, since we started this campaign, I feel like everything I've done has been monitored and dissected, and I just wanted something for me, and me alone, OK? Is that so wrong? Something which no one else knew about or was part of. Just me. My thing. This ... *he* was, *is*, my thing. So ... just let me have it, *him*, OK? Let me."

George fixes me with a stare. *"Barney."*

"He doesn't go to our school, OK? OK, so now you know."

"Barney."

"His name's Kyle. OK? So, I've told you his name, and now you know."

"Barney."

"OK, so, this is why I didn't want to say, but it's all fine, trust me, but he goes to Branscombe Boys." I nod.

George's eyes widen. Alarm, I think.

"He's really nice. Really good guy." I swallow. "He's ... um ... he's here, actually, at this conference..."

Everyone's just staring at me, mouths open.

I swallow again. "Because ... because he's in their LGBT society." I nod. "So."

There's silence for what feels like a year before George quietly says, "You. Fucking. Idiot."

"No, George, *no!"* I say. "No, he's cool, honestly, he is. And, and here's the thing: we both explicitly agreed that we wouldn't share any details of our competing entries, that was our big condition, so there's no conflict of interest here. Just ... two boys ... who like each other."

"How did you meet?"

"On ChessNation. He likes chess too."

"And then what? How do we get from 'rook takes queen' to whacking off over the phone?"

"We chatted online, we sent a few emails, bit of banter, decided to meet up in person, we got on. . . I mean, just the usual ways people meet, I guess?"

"Why were you sending emails?" Pax asks. "Why not just message?"

"Oh my god, he . . . as a joke, right, and this doesn't affect anything, but he wanted to send me the manifesto of one of the guys who was running to be their president. OK? We were sharing *very vague and non-specific* stories of . . . election woe, I guess you would call it, and, *as a joke*, he sent me this wild manifesto this Ben guy made to illustrate how he was dealing with the same sort of thing too. Harmless."

"Just a manifesto?" Maya says.

"Yeah." I nod. "Oh, and a cutesy little gif thing."

Maya stares at me.

"What?" I say.

"Did you have to click on the gif?"

I blow out a breath. "I mean, sometimes you have to click on attachments to open them! I mean, yeah, I think I clicked it, it opened, and it was a cute gif of. . ." I stop, as a horrible, horrible realization hits me, but maybe . . . no, because it's just a coincidence. Right?

"A gif of what, Barney?" George asks.

"A . . . teddy bear," I say, in a small voice.

"*FUCK*!" George shouts, head in his hands.

"But, hang on!" I say. "Why? What's the motive here? There isn't one! Sure, Branscombe Boys want to win this thing, but they've been up against hundreds of schools across the UK – there would have been no point in singling us out. Even at this stage, they're still up against three other schools, other than us. So why do it?"

Maya nods. "He's kind of right. I agree this teddy thing is weird, but why would that have anything to do with this Kyle guy?"

"Hold up," Bronte says. "Something's ringing a bell here." She taps a finger on her phone, thinking, then dials a contact, putting it on speaker.

Big Mandy picks up. "What do you want, you utter psy—"

"OK!" Bronte says. "Let's park that thought there! You're on speakerphone – I'm calling with an LGBTQ+ club emergency. Didn't you once mention there had been some sort of drama, a few years back, with Branscombe Boys?"

We hear Mandy breathing down the phone. "Yeah," she says, eventually. "You guys were all in year 10 at the time, so we never discussed it all with you – it's kinda grim and the key party wanted to keep it all hush hush, 'cause everyone looked up to him so much. It was when Ed Lester was president. He was dating this guy called Xander who was president of the Branscombe Boys club – always going off to Berlin, or Amsterdam, or Barcelona on little breaks. Very nice. Except that was all being paid for by Xander, who was embezzling the money from the Branscombe Boys' LGBT club, which had been given school money, PTA money, some private sponsorship, and even some grants. . ."

"What happened?" Bronte asks.

"Of course it ended badly. Ed found out Xander had been cheating on him. He was understandably upset. He got revenge by shopping Xander to the school *and* the police. Xander got expelled, and the LGBT club had its funding removed. Banned from applying for any grants for six years. Branscombe Boys have hated us ever since – it was Ed who did it, but they've been looking to get us back ever since. It runs deep. To this day, their club suffers because of that."

"Gotcha," Bronte says. She looks at me. I can't believe this. Any of this. Ed and Xander? The golden couple? Not so golden after all? Am I going to have anything left after this conference, or will all my hopes and dreams be totally crushed?

"So it all boils down to Ed Lester?" Bronte says.

"Yeah," Mandy replies. "Teddy was wild."

"Wait, what?"

The atmosphere in the room turns ice cold.

"Teddy – oh, I mean Ed. We – well, his closest mates – always called him Teddy."

There's this weird buzzing in my ears.

377

However much I want to fight against it, the coincidences are too much. And the unlikeliest thing of all: the idea of Kyle actually fancying me. Too good to be true. I should have known.

"OK," George says, calmly. "If Branscombe have infected your laptop there's a high chance they'll know exactly what our presentation will be tomorrow, and they'll either steal it, adapt it, or make sure their presentation trashes whatever we're talking about. So. Maya? Will you sweep it for viruses?"

Maya nods.

"Get your laptop," George mutters.

I stand, but just as I do so, our phones all bleep.

"Hold on, breaking news," George says, reading the notification. "'SOUNDS like Barney Brown, the VP of Greenacre Academy's LGBT club is having his own little affair too! Maybe these folk are just too busy with their messy relationships to be global ambassadors?'" George looks back up at me. "And, oh joy, there's an audio file."

39

"Ohh . . . oh yeah . . . yeah, I am . . . uh . . . oh god . . . oh yeah . . . uh, I'm harder than maths . . . oh, that's it, there you go. You wanna grab my pawn? Is that what you want? Rub it gently, right there, rub the top of my pawn. . . Oh? Is that right? Well, I've got an English Opening right here for you. [giggle] . . . You'll do that with your big, strong knight, huh? That sexy beast! OK, you sweaty stallion, give it to me. Yeah, that's it— Oh? What's that? Now you want to mate me? Yeah, is that what you want? Go on then, mate me. Mate me hard with your big king! Check! Mate! Oh! Oh yeah . . . I think I'm gonna . . . uh, uh . . . aaaaaAAAHHHH FAT SAM'S GRAND SLAM!"

George quietly slides his phone back in his pocket.

No one is looking at me.

"'I'm harder than maths'?" Bronte says, after a bit.

Danny blows out a breath. "I dunno, maths *is* pretty hard."

"I honestly don't know what bit of this is worse," George says. "The sexy chess talk or the fact you apparently scream out musical theatre song titles when you come."

I shake my head. "I don't . . . that's not something that normally. . ." I look down at the floor. I've never been this humiliated. This whole campaign has hollowed me out, taken every last bit of respect I had for myself, and left me with nothing. Now, I'm just a laughing-stock.

"Look," I say. "I'm going back to my room. I'm not coming to the games night. I can't. I don't want to ever show my face in public again. "

"Barns, wait!" Maya says.

"It's OK. I just want to be alone. I'm sorry, everyone. OK? I'm sorry for everything."

I shuffle out, walk unsteadily down the corridor, fumble for my key card and let myself back in to my bedroom. The moment the door closes behind me, I burst into tears. It's so much. The embarrassment, the hurt, being tricked into a sexual act by Kyle, the fact this audio exists now and probably will for ever, and that's any career in politics ruined, the people I've let down, the shame crawling over my skin. . .

It has to be Kyle. Aside from the massive coincidence that the troll knew when to dial in to the bug, he specifically told me we had to do this on the phone. A video call wouldn't have worked – you could identify the other party – but a bug recording only one half of the conversation ensures no one knows who the other person is. When he spoke to me on the phone that time, he said, "Go to your bedroom". How did he know I wasn't already in there? *Because the bug wasn't picking any audio up.* I'm such an idiot. *Such an idiot.*

I curl into a ball on the bed, shaking from the sobs, never having felt so alone.

Everyone's going to hear that audio. Everyone here. Everyone at school. Teachers. My mum. . .

I don't hear the door click open so I jump when I hear the voice.

"Barney?"

Danny's voice is soft. He gently sits down on the bed next to me, his hand on my back.

I can't even form words I'm so choked up.

"It's OK, Barney. It's OK."

But it's not OK. I'm a disappointment. A failure.

I'm disgusting.

But Danny doesn't go. He just sits, his hand gently rubbing my back. I don't know why he's bothering being nice to me. I don't deserve it. "You don't have to stay with me," I manage to mutter. "Just go back to the others. Go to the games night. You shouldn't have this ruined just because of me."

"Right," he mutters. He gets up, flicks the kettle on and starts poking about at the complimentary drinks tray. "I'm not going anywhere, BB." He comes back over, hauls me up so I'm leaning back on some pillows, hands me a tissue, then returns to the kettle and a few moments later, hands me a mug of hot chocolate. "We actually have much better complimentary drinks trays in our hotels, but

381

apparently this is 'a hug in a mug'," he tells me.

"I think I'd rather have an actual hug," I mutter, before remembering I'm talking to Danny.

"Oh, well, that can happen too," he says.

He takes the mug back off me, puts it down on the little bedside table, sits on the edge of my bed and wraps his arms around me. It's a really nice feeling. Just for a moment, everything feels OK again. I feel safe. He's warm, and strong, he smells lovely, and he holds me tight.

I eventually extract myself from him. "Danny, go to the games night, seriously."

"I'm not leaving you."

"Honestly, I'll be OK. I think I just want to be alone."

Danny looks at me and sighs. *"No."*

"It'll be fun."

"I don't like board games."

"OK, well, there'll be food."

"I . . . don't like food."

I meet his eyes, sigh, and smile. After all this, he's a genuinely good guy. I pick the mug of hot chocolate back up and put it to my lips.

"I need to tell you something," he says. "Since all our secrets seem to be coming out."

I glance at him, still sipping the drink.

"I had a thing with that guy, Milo, from the Islington Academy. At summer camp."

I try to swallow my mouthful without choking.

"Thing? What . . . what do you—"

"Oh, come on, you know what I mean!"

I stare at him.

"It just happened once," he says. "One night. There was alcohol involved. It. . . We. . . I dunno." He looks at me and chews his lip for a moment. "I've never told anyone. Only you."

"OK," I say. "So . . . did you know he was going to be here, or—"

"Of course I didn't! Do you think I'd be here if I knew some guy I once . . . you know, once . . . would be here too?"

I nod. "Guess not."

"Right. I walked in to that meet and greet earlier, and there he was! Nightmare."

We're both just looking at each other in silence. I should know what to say, he's just opened up and told me something really personal, I should be better than this, but honestly, this has blindsided me.

"Was it fun?" I venture, a smile playing on my lips.

He folds his arms. *"Barney."*

"Just wondered."

"Yeah, well."

I raise my eyebrows.

"Yeah," he relents.

A smile spreads across my face.

"Shut up," he says. "This isn't a smiling matter."

"Sorry."

"It only happened once."

"I know."

He sighs, rubs his hair, and comes to sit down next to me again.

"Why did you tell me?" I ask.

"'Cause it's just another secret, isn't it? And one that has a high chance of coming out before the end of this hellish conference, 'cause Milo's the type of guy who isn't discreet – in case you couldn't tell by the way he dresses."

I blow out a breath. "So, all this time . . . we thought we had a straight boy as our president, and actually, maybe you're—"

"Stop right there," he says. "I *don't know* what I am, OK? I don't know. I'm not looking for a label right now. You seem to love them, and maybe, if you're sure, maybe they're a good thing. Maybe they help. But from where I'm sitting, they seem scary. They seem final."

"They don't have to be final," I say. "They can change. People change, and labels can change."

"Hmm," he says. "But as long as you've *got* a label, right?"

I frown. "What do you mean?"

"I mean, you can be part of the club, you're welcome, as long as you've got a label. As long as you're deemed gay, or queer, or whatever, *enough*. But I've never really got that, because what counts?"

"Danny—"

384

"No, tell me! I'd love to know. What would have been enough for you guys? How *gay* would I need to be, Barney? What's the pass grade here? Would I have to come out? Would being bi be enough? What if I'm bi but dating a girl, is that *gay* enough for everyone? I mean, 'questioning' is part of the acronym, so how does that work? Is that only, what? Twenty per cent? Is that a fail? Do you have to have sex with someone of the same sex? Does it have to be penetrative? Or is a handjob OK? *Is that gay enough*? Or could that be dismissed just as experimentation, and not count? *Are you gay enough*, Barney? How many guys do you need to have phone sex with to be able to advocate for guys who get off with other guys? And if you are, then what about lesbians? How can you be lesbian enough to represent them?"

I take a deep breath. I've . . . never heard Danny talk like this before. He's never taken anything seriously, he's . . . a joker. "I agree with you. But you stood on stage and literally told everyone you were straight."

"Yeah? Well maybe I am. Maybe I'm not. I dunno, do I?"

"OK, I get it," I say. "But the point is, that's all fine, we're open to everything at the club."

"Really? 'Cause that's not the impression I got! All bitching about me behind my back. Pretty sure you wanted to force me out as much as Bronte did. George gave me the bad fork that time at dinner! Don't think I didn't notice – that was deliberate. That's a *micro-aggression*."

"Danny, you came in as *president*. What does that say to LGBT kids at our school?"

He nods. "I know. And I'm sorry. I don't know how to resolve that – if you want to be part of it, but you don't want to say you're LGBT, or you can't say, for whatever reason. So you have to say you're straight, else there might be trouble. So what do you do? It's why I kind of liked your take, Barney, when you talked about everyone just being in the club? That felt nice. That felt like it didn't really matter, you could take your time, no pressure, no expectations . . . as long as your heart's in the right place. My heart *is* in the right place, Barney. It's just. . . *I'm* not."

I sigh and nod, bowing my head, realizing what a long, arduous journey he's had to get to this place, and how I haven't helped that one bit, when I could have. I could have made things easier for him. Danny was never the enemy. He was one of us all along. "I'm sorry." It doesn't seem enough, but it's all I've got.

"I looked at websites. I tried to research LGBT stuff. I tried my best to be what you wanted. Do you know how confusing it is? On Twitter, no one agrees on anything. From what I can see, literally *everything* is problematic in some way."

I look back up at him, straight into his eyes. "I'm sorry, Danny."

He nods. "It's OK. It's OK. And for what it's worth, I'm sorry too. For letting Nico be part of it – hijacking it, being openly homophobic. For hurting you. I won't ever forgive myself for that."

"OK, but can I ask one thing, though? 'Cause I'm confused. You getting elected as president? You must have known what was happening? People planning and plotting behind our backs? So . . . was that all a joke? Did you run on the quiet as a joke?"

He breathes unsteadily for a moment, dropping his eyes away from me, before giving an almost imperceptible nod. "It was Nico's great idea. I never thought it would take off, or work. But it got out of hand. Everyone thought it was hilarious. I get why, now. Because, despite our school supposedly being such a great place to be gay, the reality is very different, isn't it? There's this facade of tolerance, but really, lots of people are sick of LGBT issues and students being so visible. They resent it, because they don't understand what it's like, and they don't understand that being cishet is so goddam *easy*. They think it's about LGBT people getting special privileges, when they're not, even though their special privilege is being able to sail through their lives, liking and loving who they like or love, being who they are, and never getting a single piece of grief for it. So, for them, fucking up the election was their way of saying, 'we've had enough of your LGBT shit', I guess. That was the vibe I was getting, anyway."

He glances at me, to check my reaction, I think. Thing is, I know he's right about that. I sense it too. All of the time.

"But why did you go along with it?" I ask.

He laughs. "I should say, first, those lads aren't all bad. We have fun. The footy team are great, most of the time. The camaraderie, the high of the games, I even quite like the banter. But there's also another side to it all, where showing the wrong sort of emotion, or kindness, is seen as weakness; how you've got to 'be a man'. You can't be soft. You can't *feel*. Especially not for other people and especially not for other boys. I could have refused to go along with it. If I was a better person, I probably would have. But . . . I'm not, and I'm scared, and I wasn't ready for people to be talking about me like that, saying things . . . saying I might be. . ."

I nod.

"I wasn't ready for that. And that's what would have happened. 'What you care about the homos so much for?'; 'Why do you give a shit about them, Danny?'; 'Are you one of them, is that it?'; 'Oh my god, Danny Orlando is a fucking gay boy! A fucking queer!' If you're not doing the hunting, you become the hunted. That's how it works. So, there I was, swept away with it all, but then . . . then I met you all, got to know you all properly, and I thought . . . *know what? Maybe I can make this work. Maybe this'll be fun. Maybe this is what I need to help . . . work myself out.* And, in that sense, it was a good cover, because the lads all thought I was there as a joke, but I knew I was there . . . because actually, I wanted . . . *needed* . . . to be. Except . . . I didn't find what I thought I would. I thought I might find understanding, kindness or something. But mostly, all I got was hostility." He looks at me. "Don't tell anyone."

"I won't."

"I can't control what Milo does, but please, I beg you, I'm not ready to—"

"*I won't.*"

"I don't even know if I am."

"I know. And *I won't.*"

He nods, stands again, paces to the window, then turns back to the room. "I realized something else too. Being . . . in the club." He swallows, and looks at me, lips slightly apart. "I mean, maybe you guessed, but . . . I really like you."

My eyes widen.

He just means as a friend.

"I don't just mean as a friend," he clarifies.

He does not mean just as a friend.

I mean . . . *what?* The idea of . . . me? Danny Orlando? Polar opposites, and then some! The handsome sports jock, and me . . . King Dork? What is he talking about? How long has this been a thing? Why does he think I might have guessed? Have I missed something obvious? Is this another elaborate trick? Like Kyle tricked me? Is he laughing at me, really? Because of course this couldn't be real – *who do I think I am?* – or . . . all this time, has he . . . it's so ridiculous, so much to take in, compute, understand, it makes no sense, it's plainly *stupid*, I can't help it, I laugh.

He looks unbelievably hurt.

"I'm sorry," I say, "I—"

"No, I'm sorry. I've said too much. I'm being stupid. Forget it."

"Dan—"

"Forget it, OK?! Just forget it. I'm, um . . . I'm going to let the others know you're OK, I'll take your laptop so Maya can check it over, and then get some air, and—" He grabs my MacBook and strides to the door, throwing it open as he hurries out, letting it slam behind him.

40

I'm woken up by a hammering at the door and I realize at some point last night, I just fell asleep, still wearing my clothes. My eyes are crusty, neck aches, I feel like shit. Also, Danny's not here. I did head out the door after him last night, but he'd vanished sharpish, and I really didn't fancy chasing after him and inevitably bumping into people in all my shame and humiliation. I wanted to shut myself away, phone off, duvet over my head, and pretend none of this was happening – so that's exactly what I did. I waited up for hours. As it got later and later, I tried his mobile. He eventually text me back:

Danny: Don't worry about me. I'm OK. Get some rest.

Danny didn't come back before I drifted off, so I've no idea if he came back, got up earlier, left me sleeping and crept out for breakfast, or . . . I shake the idea off. Of course he came back. Where else would he be?

I remember laughing at him telling me he liked me.

I remember everything he told me...

I still can't get my head around it all.

There's hammering at the door again, so I roll myself off the bed, stagger to the door (I feel wrecked from a horrid mixture of all the crying and staying up late fretting about Danny), and open it.

"Thank god!" George says, barging through.

He walks straight in, turning to face me once he's in the centre of the room. He looks me up and down. "OK, (a) you look like crap, (b) you stink and (c) you have really obvious morning wood, can you please ... I dunno, do something about it?"

I slump down on the edge of the bed, leaning forwards, elbows on my knees, head in my hands. "Good morning to you too."

"Where's Danny?"

I shrug. "At breakfast, isn't he?"

"Breakfast ended an hour ago, and no, he wasn't." He pulls a tragic, dry-looking croissant from his satchel. "I brought you this. In case you were hungry. Sorry, I forgot to get any jam or butter and they're really stale and horrible. Shall I just bin it?"

"Yeah," I mutter. "But thanks for the thought."

George lobs it in the bin where it lands with a heavy thud. "So? Where is he, then?"

My throat tightens, the panic rising. "Out jogging, or something equally ridiculous?"

"Last I saw him, he told us you were fine last night, gave Maya your laptop, and then he said he was heading out to get some air." George runs his hands through his hair. "He seemed . . . *off*. What happened up here?"

"Nothing," I say, looking down at the floor.

I only get silence in response to that, so I look up at George, and he's staring at me, like he knows that's a lie. "In other less-than-ideal news," he says, "Bronte is currently being interviewed by the police after she got into a small fight with Chris from the Newcastle school last night."

"*What*?! What happened?"

"She punched her, Barney. She punched her in the face. Chris is pressing charges. The police would have come last night, but this is London, so they have more urgent crimes to be dealing with – terrorism and stabbings and so on – rather than teen drama."

"Why did she punch her?"

"Because she kissed Maya. In the foyer. Which sent Bronte into a tailspin of rage, because she has always, and I quote, 'loved Maya', 'just wants her back', only dated Big Mandy because 'there was a gaping void in my life but that void was *you*, Maya', and assorted other melodramatic things." George gives me a tight smile. "Maya's delighted. She thinks it's terribly romantic, having two girls actually fight over you. Which, I guess, it is. Not that we condone violence."

"God, no."

"But a suitor punching a love rival is something you'll find in several Christmas rom-coms, so we'll overlook it."

"Uh-huh."

"Although it's unclear if that's a defence in law."

I nod. "So, we're starting our big day with our president missing and Bronte potentially being arrested?"

"You forgot 'and our presentation almost certainly being at risk, because a boy flirted with you'. But yes, that's the summary. Your laptop was infected, by the way. It would have given someone remote access. Maya found the bug. In the emails Kyle sent. So. Now you know for sure."

I groan.

"Don't feel too bad," George continues. "*The boys spent all of last night flirting and charming anyone else here who likes boys – they weren't remotely fussy. It was tragic to watch. Someone who I believed is colloquially known as 'BJ Ben' was all over Milo from Islington Academy, and they went to his room together, and the others all hooked up with people from the other schools. Meanwhile, the light was on in Kyle's room all night, with other Branscombe Boys scurrying in and out, like bees delivering pollen to the queen. I mean, they have quite the operation going. They'll know exactly what everyone else is going to say, and they'll make sure they trump it. You know what? Don't ever play by the rules*. That's what I'm taking away from all this. You think you're playing the game, but you're not. There are people out there who haven't just rigged it, they're not

394

even playing – they're just making you think they are. They're playing their own game – that's how they get what they want."

"Um . . . do we need to tell someone Danny's missing?" I say.

"Probably. If he is. Is he?"

I groan again. "Maybe we should speak to Mr Hubbard."

"Yeah," George says. "He's kinda got his own problems right now." His eyebrows raise. "Oh, of course! You don't know! So, one of the bugged teddy bears went to Mrs Buchanan, right?"

I nod.

"She took it home. And it turns out *she's having an affair with Mr Hubbard!*"

I feel my eyes nearly pop out. "*What*? I mean WHAT?!"

"Plenty of gruesome details, including some awful *panting* and . . . *words*, sexual *words* that no student ever wants to hear their head teacher saying, all captured, and released as an audio file late last night." He blows out a breath and screws his face up. "OK, so, you are *not* going to want to know this, because once I say it, you won't be able to un-know it, as it were, so I'll keep it brief – one word – and it's not something everyone's into, so I guess they served a certain *need* in one another, but . . . *bondage*."

I feel a weird mix of hysteria and sick.

395

"Those boys really have done a number on our school. They've certainly got us back for what Ed Lester did to them. Hubbard and Buchanan are both married – I don't know if you knew that – but spouses are upset, and, you know, *scandal*."

"Oh my god," I mutter.

"Still," George chirps. "I guess we still have to tell Mr Hubbard one of us is AWOL. He needs to know, right? It'll tip him over the edge, but he needs to know."

"Hey," I say, "I haven't had you alone since we got here, but I just wanted to say I'm happy for you and Pax."

George smiles, relaxes a bit, and sits down next to me. "Thanks. Thanks for telling me how he felt. I'm sorry I didn't—"

"Don't be. It's no one's business but yours."

"But I'm sorry for not being more understanding when you said last night about wanting some privacy and just not wanting other people getting involved. Because I get that. You know, for so long, I've shut myself off from any possibility of romance, and it's because I was scared. I get . . . so much grief. I know you know that. *So much*. And, I've learned to deal with it, because I have to – I *shouldn't* have to, but I want to get on with my life, so what do you do? And that's fine, but introducing someone else to that? That scared me. Will they get grief too? How will that make them feel? Will it scare them off? Will it hurt them? I didn't want anyone hurt." He shakes his head. "When I told my folks I was a boy, they were . . . well, they weren't totally surprised, I don't think. I guess there had been clues, but they were OK with it. I couldn't ask for better parents. It was only ever other people who were the issue."

George gives me a small smile. "Me and you aren't so different, though, are we? 'Cause you're scared too."

"You think?"

George chuckles. "Oh, Barney, c'mon. Yes. *I do think*. You're scared of anything where you haven't planned the ending."

"Yeah, well . . . I like to be prepared."

"Same," George agrees. "But it turns out, some of the *best* stuff hits you right out of the blue."

We both sit in silence for a moment, while I let that one sink in.

"It was Pax who asked *me* out in the end," George says. "Asked me if I'd seen Dolly Parton's *Christmas on the Square*, and, if not, would I like to?"

I smile.

"I mean, of course I'd seen it, but I told him it would be lovely to see it again."

"You love Dolly."

"Love her!" George laughs. "Come on," he says. "Come and meet the LGBT celeb downstairs."

I shake my head. "I can't face people, George. I can't do it."

"*You* don't have to. Not on your own. Maya and Pax are

397

waiting in my room, and *we'll* face everyone *together*. Like always. And you've done nothing wrong. *Nothing*. It's that little Kyle shit who should be ashamed, not you." George cocks his head towards the en suite. "Go and sort yourself out and meet us outside your door in twenty minutes. I'll go and see if I can track down Danny, and um . . . get Bronte released on bail, or whatever." He shakes his head. "*Wow*."

When I emerge downstairs in the hotel foyer, I'm expecting a silence to fall, maybe some gasps, and certainly some appalled glances. But no one even bats an eyelid. I guess our own dramas always feel like the main event, but by the sound of what George was telling me, there's been a whole load more drama since yesterday evening.

The LGBT celeb isn't Elton. Nor is it Stephen Fry, or Laverne Cox, or Ben Whishaw, or Elliot Page, or Tituss Burgess. I'm standing here, in my best shirt, and some freakin' *cologne*, and it isn't any of those people.

It's some guy who's a celebrity chef, I think from morning television, who I've never heard of. He's signing copies of his new cookbook, so I go up to say hello anyway – you never know, maybe he *knows* Elton and friends, six degrees of separation, and all that.

"Would you like a signed book?" he asks.

"Um, thanks."

He uncaps his Sharpie. "What's your name?"

"Barney."

He writes it carefully, signs with a flourish and hands it to me. "Fifteen pounds."

"Huh?"

"Discount price!" He smiles, like he's done me a favour. "RRP is fifteen *ninety-nine!*"

I'm so embarrassed about thinking they would be free (like everything else has been here – I mean, totally reasonable of me!) that I just pull my wallet out and hand him the twenty I have in there.

Maya and Pax are by my side the moment I've wandered away. "Did you actually buy one?" Maya asks.

"By mistake. Is this guy the LGBT celeb?"

Maya nods. "Yeah, and more bad news: Virgin Atlantic are sponsoring this event, but it's just funding the hotel hire, freebies and the online voting tech. There's no actual trip to the US in the offing."

My heart sinks. No Tom Daley, and no trip to New York? Was any of this worth it? "Are you absolutely sure?"

"I asked Patrick. Just after I gave my statement to the police about Bronte. *Barney.* Two girls – fighting over *me!* It was so exciting and beautiful." She gets lost in a moment of apparent ecstasy. "I mean, obviously it's awful as well – there's never any call for a sharp punch to the face. Well, hardly ever. Hmm, well, sometimes, I guess."

"Are you two back together, then?" I ask.

"You know, the one impression I always got from Bronte was that I didn't mean that much to her. I wasn't perfect enough. I felt like I was nothing to her, and sometimes, worse, that I was an actual irritation. She never needed me, Barney, she seemed to have it all. And now she's *literally* fighting for me."

"Except now she might end up in prison," Pax adds.

"Like *Orange Is the New Black*?" Maya has a look on her face that, although it's worrying, there's part of her that finds that idea quite sexy. "Shut up, Paxton, she won't," Maya continues. "Will she?"

"Looks like you're in luck," I say, glancing over to the door, where George is walking in with Bronte, who is dressed in sunglasses and a headscarf, *a la* avoiding the paparazzi. "Our resident lawyer and general saviour has pulled it out of the bag again."

"She's back," George says, as they walk up to us.

"Welcome back, Bronte," I say.

"Sssh!" she replies. "I've brought shame on the society. Shame on myself. Shame on lesbians everywhere. Don't draw any attention to me," she says, adjusting the sunglasses that everyone is already wondering why she's wearing indoors, "I'll just go to my room and lie low – and maybe leave by the rear entrance later?" She grasps George's arm. "Can you arrange that, George-y?"

George winces. "Not if you pointlessly add a cutesy 'y' to the end of my name, no."

"Sorry," I say, "can I just check, have the charges been dropped, or what?"

Bronte nods, gravely. "As chance would have it, the alleged incident took place in a CCTV blindspot, meaning it's her word against mine, and the facial swelling and bruising could have been caused by any number of things – she might have tripped and fallen, for example." She runs her tongue over her lips. "Plus my dad knows the Chief Constable, so."

I roll my eyes and remember George's new realization: *Don't play by the rules, because no one else is.* I smile as Maya takes Bronte's hand in hers, and gives her a kiss on the lips.

"Violence is never acceptable," Maya says.

Bronte nods. "I know. And I'm ashamed. I've already arranged for Interflora to deliver a same-day bouquet and box of truffles to Chris so we can start afresh."

Maya's eyes widen.

"Don't worry," Bronte chuckles. "You're getting some flowers too!"

"I didn't say a word!"

"You didn't need to. I can read you like a book, Maya Phillips."

Maya smiles and they kiss again.

It's nice to see Maya happy and it's surprisingly nice to see them back together. Maybe that's why they say opposites attract; maybe that's what you need. Maybe it's what I need. Maybe that's what Danny is to me, and I am to him, and maybe I shouldn't worry about what the ending of that might be. Suddenly, I miss him, and want him back here.

He was brave, he went out on a limb and opened himself up to me. And I just laughed at him. I mean, I didn't, I was laughing out of nerves and disbelief, but that's not what it would have looked like to him.

"Any news about Danny?" I ask, quietly.

George shakes his head. "He's got two hours before the presentations start. I've let Mr Hubbard know. In between his calls to his divorce lawyer. Otherwise. . ."

I swallow. "I have to do it?"

George nods.

"It's your time to shine, Barney," Bronte says. "And, I, for one, believe in you."

"Ditto," Maya says.

"Same," says Pax.

"You're all just saying that because none of you want to do it."

"Correct," Bronte replies. "But Danny did make you VP, so it definitely goes with the territory." She gives me a sarcastic smile.

I'm really pleased for her and Maya, but Bronte's still a total bitch.

Two hours later, and Danny is nowhere to be seen. I'm worried about him. I ask Mr Hubbard about going out to look for him, but he reminds me we're in London, there's literally over one thousand five hundred square kilometres of city, it would be like looking for a needle in a haystack, and his wife wants the house, so, like, he really needs to call his lawyer back. He has alerted the police, and Danny's parents, but since he hasn't been gone twenty-four hours, and he's seventeen, no one, including his folks, is apparently that bothered. "He probably snuck into a club and pulled an all-nighter!" his dad told Mr Hubbard down the phone. "The kid can look after himself. He's planning to go backpacking next year, so I dread to think what he'll get up to."

I've read and re-read the presentation notes a load of times, and I've flicked through the PowerPoint slides, but, the truth is, I'm just not feeling it. Even leaving aside the fact I think Branscombe Boys will have stolen all our best points, I'm just not feeling any of it any more.

I grab my pile of notes and head out of the room and downstairs, because it's time to get this over with.

That's when I see him.

Lurking by the lifts in the foyer. *Kyle.*

He looks up and locks eyes with me. A flicker of *something* on his face. Amusement? Panic? I can't tell.

The hurt hits me like a double decker bus. And then the anger.

Fuck it. I stride over. "You fucking little shit."

Kyle frowns. "I'm sorry? What have I done? What *exactly* have I done?"

"Kyle, I have your emails. I have messages from you! If you think—"

He puts his hand up to stop me. "Whoa. Have you?

Are you sure about that? I don't recall emailing you from *my* email address or calling you from *my* mobile. I mean, if you're so sure, try now, by all means. Call me. Go ahead." He slides his phone out of his pocket, ready for the screen to light up when I ring.

Of course. Probably in a bin, or a field somewhere, there's a burner phone with the evidence already wiped. Somewhere in the ether there's an email account, ostensibly belonging to Kyle, but which could actually belong to anyone, because it's untraceable, at least it is to me, just a kid, who's been well and truly screwed over by some boy who he thought liked him. His laptop never crashed at all. He just told me that to throw me off the scent. What a dick.

Kyle smiles smugly and slides his phone back in his pocket. "OK?" he says.

He steps past me and heads towards the conference suite.

"I liked you!" I blurt out.

He freezes.

Kyle doesn't turn back. "Seriously, Barney, don't be so fucking desperate, it's really unattractive. Besides, I've got a boyfriend – been together a year now. He's called *Ben*?"

He pulls the door open and walks through.

I try to steady my breathing. But I've done enough crying. I've done enough feeling sorry for myself. I've done nothing wrong here. And I'm not going to play this game, because that's letting *them* win.

The conference hall is rammed. As well as the core club members, who are all sitting down at the front, they've bussed in another three hundred students from other schools, especially for the occasion. Along with them, of course, are hundreds of other schools watching live, online, and all of them get to vote via the special app on their phones, paid for courtesy of Virgin Atlantic, who won't also be flying any of us to New York. There's a real buzz in here, the energy is electric, but it's washing over me. I'm lost in thought. Confused thoughts, about me, Danny, this whole competition, everything that's happened, everything I've done, everything I've ever believed. They've juggled the running order and put us on last, in the hope Danny might show, but I'm pretty sure he won't. Whether it's Milo being here, or how he's been treated as president, or whether it's me, he's decided he's out. I'm not sure I blame him.

Milo from Islington Academy kicks things off, with a surprisingly unoriginal presentation about doing more to tackle homophobic bullying in schools, with a series of slides that's mainly statistics, and not much in the way of solutions or ideas. It's uninspiring, and, to be totally honest, he looks completely shagged out. But then, he is, isn't he? Up with BJ Ben most of the night.

Next up, it's KJ from Exeter, and they do a really good piece on queer history, and how teaching it in school might give some context to those students who privately (and sometimes, not so privately) wonder why so much time is devoted to LGBT issues when most people are straight, or why Pride is necessary. KJ is persuasive, and a charismatic presenter – I like them.

Kyle and Ben from Branscombe Boys take the stage. They're a polished double act. Kyle is VP – something he failed to tell me – and, just like yesterday, he's now full of confidence, having dropped the "adorkable" act he put on with me. It's nauseating. Both what he did, and how badly I fell for it. Complete with slides (so it doesn't seem like they just copied other presentations on the fly), Kyle and Ben talk about the importance of queer history and how a lack of knowledge about this feeds into so much homophobic bullying, which they claim a lot of is down to cishet students being ignorant of the realities of the past, not understanding the "legacy of hatred" and thinking LGBT students are still fundamentally different and wrong. They go on to discuss the impact this has on LGBT student's mental health, before adding a very familiar section on LGBT inclusive sex ed, as one way of normalizing the queer experience for everyone. Just when I think they've royally screwed everyone over though, they really twist the knife.

Kyle takes centre stage, confident, owning the space, speaking into his head mic. "We really hoped to be able to stand up here today and tell you are that Branscombe Boys was a model school. That we were perfect role models, both in terms of support from school authorities, and allyship from all our students. But I'm afraid the reality is very different – and I cannot, in all good conscience – stand on this stage and lie to you. There is still homophobia at our school. There are teachers who do not get it. Do not understand. And there's often a limit to how far the school, and students, will go to show their support. And in a private school like we are, that limit is usually reached when some parent gets stroppy and threatens to pull their kid out of the school – taking their fees with them. So, no, we're not perfect role models. . ."

Kyle glances at me, just briefly, just enough so that I know this is *very* deliberate and he's enjoying every second of it. "But we get up, and we go into school every day, and we *try*. We work to make things better. And we understand. So, if you want perfect, that's not us. But if you want real – vote Branscombe Boys!"

There is a crazy amount of applause. Kyle tries to stay humble-looking, but I can tell he's lapping it up, enjoying it, and thinking it's in the bag now.

Call Me Chris from the Newcastle school is up next. Her speech lacks confidence and originality and it feels like we've heard it before . . . because we have – it's about mental health and it's weirdly similar to what Kyle and Ben just talked about. I barely listen anyway. I put the notes for my speech down on the floor. I won't need them. I won't need the PowerPoint either. If we've got any hope now, it's down to me. It's down to me, and it's down to doing what I should have always done: speak from the heart.

41

Look, we got into the finals because we made a video in which we were going to say Greenacre Academy is one big gay club! I know. Bold idea. But we thought people might go for it. The idea that we were so inclusive and everything was great at our school. But then the video got deleted, and I made a new video in which I admitted that Greenacre actually isn't a model of inclusivity. Far from it. We have real problems: queer kids are treated as a joke at best, our sex ed is abysmal, and we even have homophobic violence – I literally have the scars to show for it. I won't show you. None of you need to see my non-existent abs. Anyway, our argument had been that we should be the global ambassadors because despite our school's crappy culture, we're role models who understand what other kids go through and do our best to change things.

But you know what? That's not true either! We're not role models. And in the last few weeks, in some ways we've been our worst selves. We've lied to the voters about the sort of people we are, we've fake dated, we've had fake break-ups to try to get sympathy, we've made up stories about bigoted parents complaining about LGBT books, we've pretended our pet guinea pigs have died to deflect attention from the stuff we've done wrong, but worst of all: we've constantly lied to each other. We've backstabbed and fought, and we've torn each other apart. Pretty much all of us in the committee have lied to each other, and none of us can be proud of ourselves for that.

I LOVE our gay club: it was the one place I felt free and honest – but somehow, these past few weeks, we've just tied ourselves up with our own lies.

I recently learned something, though. I learned something really important about SHAME. Someone leaked an audio file of me having phone sex. A disgusting invasion of my privacy, and probably criminal, true. But why am *I* the one who feels shame over it? Why am *I* the one who couldn't leave my hotel room last night? Why do *I* feel shame after someone beats me up and calls me a poof? Because all kids – but queer kids especially – are taught *shame*. It is what the homophobes want for us, to keep us down, to make us suffer. To keep our true selves hidden. And it works. Because those feelings of shame eat away at your pride and your courage, and make you frightened. Frightened to come out. Frightened to even question who you might be. Frightened that people will turn against you, because who you are is so despicable to them.

We lost sight of that during this process too. Especially me. We're an LGBTQ+ society. We're supposed to make it easier for people, not harder. People who might not quite be sure. People who just needed some time and some space and some understanding. No judgements. But for those people . . . *that person* . . . we made it much harder.

So yeah, I guess we were supposed to come out here and say we know what other kids go through, and that certainly *is* true. We know that shame pretty well. And you know what? We're each a work in progress, trying to work out how to beat it. And I think we will. Someday. I know we will. Because we'll fight. And we need to fight together.

But it's *not* true that we're role models, so you should all vote for Exeter, they seem pretty great.

Or Newcastle. Or even the school from Islington.

Not Branscombe, though, they're total shits.

42

Everyone's applauding. I guess that made some kind of sense then? I can't actually remember much of what I did say – I just talked. That is not like me. Like George said, I normally need to know the end before I can even make a start. But, perhaps, that's not always the best way to do things. Living in the moment isn't a great strategy for chess . . . but I think it might be for *life*.

My attention's drawn to movement in the front row, as George, Maya, Bronte and Pax get to their feet as they clap. Other students take that as their cue, and get to their feet as well. I take it with a pinch of salt (people give standing ovations these days for barely anything) but I nevertheless soak it up for a moment more. Then I look towards one of the exits at the back of the auditorium, and there's Danny, standing, also clapping, in between wiping his eyes. I lock eyes with him, smile, and give him a little

411

salute – because he's a fighter, like me, and we're on the same side.

He laughs and salutes me back.

There's a short interval while everyone gets a chance to make their choices via the app and the votes are counted and verified. The last point is particularly important – I wouldn't put it past Branscombe Boys to have hired a Russian bot farm to swing things in their favour.

"Hey," I say, as I walk up to Danny in the foyer.

He smiles, his eyes still a bit red and puffy. "Hey."

"I'm sorry – about last night. You ... took me by surprise."

"Didn't see *that* move coming, huh?"

I laugh. "Not in a million years. Did you ... mean it?"

"Yeah," he says, his voice hoarse.

I go in for a hug and we wrap our arms around each other. "You were brilliant up there just now," he murmurs in my ear. "Truly, Barney, completely *epic*."

"Thanks, Danny." I'm conscious the others will be here any second, and I know he probably won't want to talk about this in front of them. "Talk properly later, yeah?"

He pulls back from me, nods, and I give him a smile. I can't believe this is even happening. Not the speech, or this conference. Me and him. I can't get my head around it.

George strides up to join us, Maya, Bronte and Pax in tow. "So, what happened to you?"

"Oh, um..." Danny looks shifty. "I needed to get away, like . . . I guess I freaked out. I'm sorry. I'm sorry for letting everyone down and messing it up." He glances at me. "On the plus side . . . would that amazing speech have happened if I had been here?"

George almost smiles. "I guess not."

"I went into Soho," Danny says. "So, it's amazing, I went to this place that serves coffee and stuff, *all night*, stayed there for ages, then found this other cafe, also open all night, never closes, and I ate eggs benedict at three in the morning!"

It figures why he looks so utterly wrecked. The boy's not been to bed.

"Had a few propositions, actually," Danny continues. "I politely declined. Met these old ladies who were pulling an all-nighter, and they bought me cocktails! You know, I want to live here. As soon as I can. London's great. We need to be here. Let's all rent an apartment together! Oh my god – how brilliantly gay would that be?!"

He seems genuinely excited about this, which is sweet. Also, fair play, it does sound like fun, and we would surely always have the best food *ever*, although I can already imagine Bronte making a rota for chores, Maya annoying her by leaving her washing up in the sink, and George being driven mad by incorrect stock rotation in the fridge. But also, *fun!*

They're serving refreshments to keep us entertained

while we wait, but it's clear everyone is on tenterhooks, as no one's really bothering with them. I get a lot of compliments from students at other schools, but then there's also lots of overheard chatter about people "finding it hard to choose" and even some online stuff in the discussion forums Rainbow Youth have set up, about whether they agree with everything I said or not.

Eventually, after what seems like *way* longer than it should be, Patrick's voice comes over the PA system: "Folks! The votes have been counted and verified – we have our winners. Please return to the auditorium for the results!"

It takes another age for everyone to file back in and settle down. It's killing me. This time, we can sit where we like, and we choose to sit right at the back, which seems the easiest way to make a swift getaway, if needed, e.g., if we do so badly we come last, and/or get no votes at all. I mean, if there's one thing this process has taught me, it's to take nothing for granted.

Danny's on the edge of the row. Me next to him. George on my other side, with Maya, Bronte (who are holding hands) and Pax sitting behind us. Danny nudges my leg with his. "It'll be OK," he whispers. "Whatever happens."

He smiles at me, my stomach flips, and I realize, yeah, it will, actually. Everything we'd lost, we've now got back. And one thing especially: being there for each other, whoever we are, and wherever we're at.

"What a conference!" Patrick booms through a mic on the stage. "Everyone at Rainbow Youth has been really impressed with the amount of thought and effort that has gone into all your presentations. When it comes to selecting global ambassadors, we really do have an embarrassment of riches."

He continues to talk about being proud of ourselves, how there can only be one winner, and so on, and so on, all the usual shit, before thanking the sponsors again, and the LGBT celeb.

"Please, put us out of this misery," George hisses.

"Over four thousand votes were counted via the app this afternoon, which have all been verified. The winning LGBT society, and our global ambassadors for the next twelve months is. . ."

43

The first time, I just don't hear it.

Sheer disbelief, I guess.

Then Patrick repeats it. "GREENACRE ACADEMY!"

I'm staring at the stage, while the entire room explodes in cheers and whoops around us.

"Really?" I whimper.

Danny clutches my hand. "You did it, dude." And then he turns to the others, shouting. "WE DID IT!"

And that's it, we leap out of our seats, hugging, laughing, shouting, crying. Patrick is calling for us to come to the stage, so we all start making our way down the aisle, receiving handshakes, back slaps, and applause as we go. On the huge projection screens on the stage, they're streaming live footage from the schools that weren't able to be here in person, and they're all cheering and clapping too. I can't. . . It's epic, it doesn't seem real, but it is, and we're here, and we won, but this is also a win for love and kindness and decency and respect and a win for a better future; of that, we'll make sure.

We make it to the stage and Patrick hands Danny the mic. As president, it's his job to make the acceptance speech, and I hope he'll at least be able to do that, because I sure as hell don't have any more words to say right now.

"Hey, everyone," Danny says, smiling. "Thank you so much!"

Everyone quietens down.

"Hi. So, I'd like to say, on behalf of Greenacre Academy's LGBTQQIAAP plus Society, that we're thrilled, we're deeply honoured, *thank you* for voting for us, thank you for putting your trust in us, and thank you for giving us this chance. As Barney said, we're all works in progress, but we will do everything in our power not to let you down, to fly the flag for queer teenagers *globally*," he laughs. "Globally! How cool is that?!"

There's laughter from the audience too. His easy, sweet charm is impossible not to like.

". . .And to make a difference. To . . . affect change." He takes a breath. "You know, I went into this whole thing as a bit of a joke. I admit it. But being part of things has given me chance to learn. And be better. And I think that's part of what Barney was saying earlier. I can't wait to get stuck into everything we're going to do this year, I really can't. But . . . I'm not the person who should be leading things. I may have started as a joke candidate, but people like Barney Brown never saw this as a joke. Barney cares, he genuinely cares, he's not in this for himself, he wants to make the world a better place, and I know he'll work hard to try to do that. So, I'm going to take up my place on the committee, but I want to hand the reigns over to Barney. Barney's your president. He was always your president. Charlie Brown may be a 'good' man, but Barney Brown is a *great* one."

He turns to look at me.

I'm crying.

I'm crying because no one has ever said anything like that about me ever, and I didn't think anyone ever would. I've always assumed people see me as the geeky kid, who does his homework on time, goes the extra mile, gets the grades, the kid who everyone thinks is just a dork. I've always played the game, and I thought I'd established that playing the game gets you nowhere? Boys like me don't ever really succeed. We just get taken advantage of and shat on. I know how it works. I thought I did.

"Oh," Danny says, turning back to the audience again. "Sorry, that was meant to be my big finish but I never even introduced myself to you all." He clears his throat, and puts on his smile. *"I'm Danny Orlando."*

Danny turns back to me, puts his left hand on my waist, hands me the mic with his right, leans in to me and whispers, "Also, I fancy you so freakin' much, you little stud muffin!"

Stud muffin?! Well, that makes me burst out

laughing – so ridiculous – but it puts a wide smile on my face anyway. I hope Rainbow Youth don't mind that we're playing out so much political drama, live on stage. Patrick's smiling, so I guess he's fine with it. I look out at the sea of expectant faces. My people. I don't know most of them, but we're all the same and we're all on this journey together, and that fills me with so much pride, and so much awe, that I don't quite know what to say. What would be enough? How can I sum up what I really feel for everyone here, and everyone watching, and everyone else, all of us, out there?

In the end, I just speak from my heart: "This isn't about who's president, this is a team effort. So let me introduce you to the gang. I love this little squad, and I hope you'll love them too. Danny, Maya, Bronte, Paxton and George. Yes, we're a bunch of backstabbing, venomous, lying, cheating snakes, but these peeps are also the best, most loyal, passionate, funny and brilliant people you could ever hope to be best friends with. And they can all cook great food – what more do you want?! I love them. And I love you. And at the end of the day, that's what all this is about. It's about love."

Danny and I are back in the bedroom. It's an oasis of calm, and a chance to get changed before the big party Rainbow Youth are throwing tonight, at a big event space on Park Lane. (*Thanks, Virgin Atlantic!*) After my little speech, there were photos and interviews, and there was even a TV crew from an online LGBT station, plus a queer radio station and various podcasts.

The other candidates were full of joy for us – well, except Branscombe Boys, who disappeared sharpish and haven't been seen since. Tomorrow, it's the first official day of our office, and there is so much to think about, organize and plan. But that's tomorrow. Today, *tonight*, it's about us. And right now, it's about me and Danny.

He closes the door behind him.

And we're both just looking at each other.

"Hey," he says.

I smile. "Hey."

We both take an uneasy step towards each other, both of us walking like we've never actually put one foot in front of the other before, and then Danny says, "Screw it," and bounds over to me, wrapping me in his arms, while I wrap mine around him.

I burrow my face into his shoulder, still not quite believing I'm doing this, and he's letting me, and this is happening, it's real, me and Danny, Danny and me – really? And while I can't get my head around it, it also doesn't feel wrong. It feels right. *Very* right.

"Barney," he murmurs. "We literally have half an hour to get ready, but the thing is . . . uh . . . huh. The thing is, I have really struggled to keep my hands off you since I got back, and we're about to go out for god knows how many hours, and I think I might explode if we don't . . . um. . ."

"We haven't even been out on a date!" I mutter into his

shoulder. I'm smiling, but he doesn't know that.

He pushes me back a little, looking straight into my eyes. "You've been in my Audi! I told you that you looked like Noah Schnapp!" He grins. "That's called flirting, dude! And what did you think that hot tub and barbecue at mine was?"

"Um . . . a meeting?"

He screws his face up. "I *knew* you didn't get it. Well, that was a date, OK? It was to me. Even though I thought you were dating Paxton at the time, and I was basically trying my luck, I really enjoyed it. You said you did too." He smiles, eyes searching my face, then prods my nose with his finger. "*Boop!*"

"What the hell was that?"

"I 'booped' you. It's cute. Girls love it. I guess . . . boys might too?"

I let myself smile. But this is all too quick. He'll get bored of me. I'll let myself go there, and he'll get bored of me. That's how this really ends. Dammit. I need to stop thinking about endings.

He must read my mind, or else my face is giving everything away. "I know." He sighs, and sits down on the edge of one of the single beds. "Look, I know you've been through some stuff, and I know that might make you extra cautious of people messing you about, or not meaning what they say. And I know. . ." He bites his lip a bit. "I know . . . what my reputation is. Around school. Ladies' man,

421

whatever. Date 'em and dump 'em. No strings. *Whatever.* But, I want you to know . . . that's not me. It's 95 per cent exaggeration that I didn't correct. And, I think, in the past, it's true I haven't wanted to commit, but that's maybe out of knowing that it would be wrong to, 'cause my heart's not in it. It's not really what I want, even if I was trying desperately hard to prove to myself, and the world, that it was. You. . . Barney. . ." He swallows. "I know I feel differently about you. For the first time in my life, I've met someone who I can't stop thinking about, who I care about, who makes me laugh, who I just need to be near to feel instantly better about life, who . . . makes me feel alive somehow, and that person isn't any one of the obvious people at school that even I thought it would be. It's you, and I'm so, so glad I found you, and I'm so, so happy. And I want you to know, I'd never hurt you. God, the idea of *anyone* hurting you kills me, I just couldn't live with myself. And if not doing anything is best for you, because you don't want to, or it's not right for you, I totally respect that, and I hope we can be mates. But if you *do* . . . if that was something you might like. . ."

"Oh, Jesus, Danny, just kiss me already."

I slide on to his lap, straddling him, and he wraps his arms around my waist, pulling me into a long, deep, slow kiss, before he leans backwards on the bed, me on top, his hands on the back of my head, as we kiss some more, and some more, and more and—

"Barney," he murmurs, "I know there's a serious lack

422

of LGBT inclusive sex ed, and that's a major issue, but—"

"I don't think we need sex ed," I murmur back. "I mean, we do, in the wider sense, but, right now, I think we can work this out."

"You're late," George tells me, as Danny and I step out of the lift. "I've sent you numerous messages."

"Sorry," I say. "There was a delay."

George nods, crosses his arms, and waits.

"A button fell off my shirt," I add.

A smile plays on his lips. "You're both very flushed."

"Man, it is *so* hot in our room!" Danny says, fanning his face.

"Yes!" I add. "The air con is broken. I think. So hot. *Boiling.*"

"Come on," George says, "We're the guests of honour, we don't want to be late."

It's a short walk to the Tube and then a few stops to Hyde Park Corner, so it shouldn't take us too long. George leads the way round to reception, while Maya scoots up alongside me. "Mmmm!" she purrs. "What's that scent?"

"Oh, um . . . it's Danny's actually. Hugo Boss, I think."

Maya nods, knowingly. "No, it's not that I can smell. I think it's more like . . . frantic sexual relations? Are you familiar with that one?"

"Only very fleetingly," I tell her, keeping a poker face.

It's going to be a great night. I can feel it. Everyone's dressed up, Rainbow Youth have arranged entertainment (oh, I *hope* it's Elton this time!) and food and drinks, and then there's a DJ. Everyone's invited, a true celebration of who we are, but also who we're going to be. There's talk of an unofficial afterparty. A couple of people from the Islington Academy know someone who might be able to get us in somewhere, even though we're not quite old enough.

"I hope they get us into a gay club," Bronte muses, as we walk.

"A *what* club?" I say, flashing her a smile.

She gives me a light punch on the arm. "Obviously I mean an LGBTQQIAAP plus club."

"The only 'erasure' we want in the club is the eighties band!" I quip.

Bronte rolls her eyes. "*That* is one hell of a niche joke that no one's gonna get, Barney!"

But our laughter stops when we round the corner and walk into the main foyer, and a scene of commotion. Kyle is sitting on one of the sofas – it looks like he's been punched, blood dripping from his nose, and he dabs it with a tissue. Patrick is on his mobile, and students from the conference are crowding around the entrance doors.

I walk over to Kyle and Patrick. "What's happened?"

Kyle sighs and flicks his eyes to mine. "There's a protest outside. Those stupid Family Alliance people who think this conference is 'promoting' lifestyle choices they don't agree with. I walked up to them and told them what I thought of them. There was a bit of a fight. Hey, guess I deserved it, right? Karma's a bitch, huh?"

I glance towards the entrance, aware now of the chanting outside, and catching a glimpse of some people holding placards. I look back at Kyle. "Of course you don't deserve it. Are you OK?"

Kyle stares at me in disbelief. "Jesus, Barney, after everything, how can you be so—"

"Yeah, I know, you're a total bellend, and that's the polite version, but you don't deserve to be punched just for being who you are and standing up for that."

Kyle shrugs. "I'll live."

"Right," Patrick says, coming off his mobile. "The police are on their way. Meanwhile, there's a back entrance out of the hotel we can use, so I suggest we get everyone together and hopefully—"

"No," I say.

Patrick stops, and I'm aware everyone is looking at me.

"We don't hide," I continue.

"Barney," Patrick says, "It might not be safe – there's fifty or sixty of them, they—"

"We don't hide," I repeat. "And there might be fifty or sixty of them, but there's hundreds of us. So what are they gonna do? We're gonna go and celebrate. And we're not going to hide. Everyone's going to see us. *Fuck them.*"

Patrick nods. "All right. OK. And, yeah, you're right. I'll get as many staff here as I can, plus your teachers, I don't want anyone getting hurt."

"Thanks," I say. I turn to face the assembled crowd of students. "Everyone? We're gonna do this. We walk out of here, and know what? Do it hand-in-hand. Whether you like that person, fancy them, they're your mate, or you're just making a new friend, every single one of us walks out of this building hand-in-hand with someone else. Because we're together, we're united, we're family, and no one is ever going to destroy that."

There's applause and shouts of "Yes!"

And that's what we do.

Bronte and Maya.

George and Paxton.

Then Danny takes my hand, squeezing it, gently, his finger tickling my palm, as we walk out into the barmy evening air.

Students hand-in-hand in front of us.

And behind us.

Like those who came before us.

And those who will come after.

We won't ever stop.

We just want to live.

We just want to be who we are.

We won't play by your outdated rules or live by your outdated ideals.

It starts, and ends, with love, that's all.

We're heroes.

We're legion.

And we're going to change the world.

Join us.

AUTHOR'S NOTE

There was no such thing as a "gay club" when I was at school. Section 28 made sure of that. So one of the best things about doing author visits in schools today is seeing how much has changed, and how there are now loads of LGBTQ+ societies, full of the most fabulous, kind, wonderful teenagers you could ever hope to meet. In a world of social media outrage, vile opinion pieces in national newspapers, and with so many people out there who wish the LGBTQ+ community harm, these kids are a beacon of hope. They understand the importance of community. They get why we need to stand united. This book is a love letter to them.

If you're a young person reading this, maybe your school has its own LGBTQ+ society – and maybe you could join? I imagine it'll be amazing. But, if your school doesn't have one, maybe you could set one up? Grab some friends. Unite. Do something for Pride. Go full-Barney and run for president! Get some LGBT books in the school library. You've got some already? Get more!

Ask your school to organize an LGBT author visit – maybe with me! Haha! And, remember, there are many awesome people out there who offer help and support to LGBTQ+ youth; check out the list of organizations below.

To me, this all boils down to people just wanting to live their lives; to be who they are, and love who they love. Remember, we're stronger together; so, whatever you do, whatever way this works for you – in, out, straight, gay, loud and proud, or quiet and questioning – it doesn't matter, there's no one way to do this, there's no right way to do this. All that matters, like Barney says, is that you join us. Let's build a future that is open, accepting and kind. And have fun doing it.

Simon x

ONLINE RESOURCES

https://www.stonewall.org.uk

https://www.theproudtrust.org

https://www.thekitetrust.org.uk

https://www.allsortsyouth.org.uk

https://www.mermaidsuk.org.uk

https://switchboard.lgbt

ACKNOWLEDGEMENTS

I've always wanted to write a school election story, but the initial idea for *Gay Club!* was actually that of my brilliant editor, Linas Alsenas. It combined two things I will always enjoy writing about – backstabbing elections *and* LGBT kids – and so here we are!

Gay Club! was originally the working title. I loved it, but I didn't in a million years think we'd end up with the book actually being called that. I owe a huge amount of thanks to the whole team at Scholastic UK for putting their trust in me, and not only letting me go super gay on this book, but fully embracing that, and making it even *more* gay with that fabulous cover. I'm so grateful to everyone at Scholastic, not just for this book, but for the last six years' worth of books – they've backed me and supported me all the way. Folks, you could not ask for more wonderful, generous people to surround you. So ... Liam Drane for that stunning cover; my publicist, Harriet Dunlea; Ella Probert and the marketing team; Sarah Dutton; Lauren Fortune; Catherine Bell; Antonia Pelari; the Rights team;

the Sales team; and Linas Alsenas (again!) – *thank you* – and I hope we have many more adventures together.

Some other key folk who helped with this book: my fab agent, Joanna Moult at Skylark Literary; copyeditor Pete Matthews; and proofreader Jenna Mackintosh – thank you! And huge thanks also to Jay Hulme and Charlie Morris who both read an early draft and provided me with valuable feedback that I'm really grateful for.

I've been genuinely touched by the support and love of other authors and media folk, especially this lovely lot, all of whom I really admire and who provided such lovely quotes: William Hussey, George Lester, Ciara Smyth, Becky Albertalli, Wibke Brueggemann, Dean Atta, Lev Rosen, Julian Winters, Phil Stamper, Calum McSwiggan, Rebecca Root, Adiba Jaigirdar, Matt Cain, Rob Gillett and Matthew Todd.

There are so many wonderful and supportive booksellers and bookshops out there, but I wanted to mention and thank Jim, Uli, Erica and the team at Gay's the Word; Matt and the team from Queer Lit; Gay Pride Shop UK; Bear Hunt Books; and Through the Wardrobe Books. Thanks too, as always, to the brilliant sales reps from Bounce.

Thank you to the school librarians and teachers who continue to support my books and get them into the hands of students who need them (I love you all!), and thank you to the bloggers, Instagrammers, TikTok-ers, reviewers, and journalists for helping get this book out there – we couldn't do any of this without you.

Love to Sarah, Mum, Jonathan, Liz, Alfie, Tricia, Sue and Peter, and, of course to Beau and Dolly, who didn't really help, but are, at least, cute.

Finally, thanks to all my very loyal and lovely readers. Every time you get in touch, it makes my day better. I really hope you all enjoy *Gay Club!*

ABOUT SIMON

Simon James Green is the world's leading authority on awkward teenage boys*, mainly because he was one. He has written a number of desperately awkward young adult novels, including *Noah Can't Even* (longlisted for the Branford Boase Award); *Noah Could Never* (longlisted for nothing, despite it being a work of comic genius*); *Alex in Wonderland* (nominated for the Carnegie Medal); *Heartbreak Boys* (picked by *Attitude* magazine and Gay's the Word bookshop as one of the best LGBT novels of the year); and *You're the One That I Want* (winner of the Bristol Teen Book Award). Simon is also the author of two picture books, *Llama Glamarama* and *Fabulous Frankie*, both illustrated by Garry Parsons, and two middle-grade books, *Life of Riley: Beginner's Luck* (finalist for the Blue Peter Book Award) and *Sleepover Takeover* (also great, of course).

www.simonjamesgreen.com

Twitter & Instagram @simonjamesgreen

* probably

MORE BOOKS BY SIMON JAMES GREEN

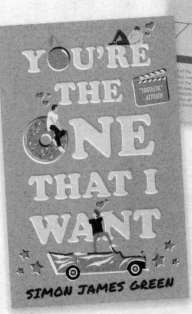